LITTLE LAMB LOST

LITTLE LAMB LOST

A NOVEL

MARGARET FENTON

IPSWICH, MASSACHUSETTS

For my father
Peter C. Herring, LCSW
with love from your lamb chop

ACKNOWLEDGMENTS

So many people have helped make this book possible. Thanks to Pat, Maryglenn, Susan, and the many talented folks at Oceanview Publishing for giving me such a warm welcome. Without a doubt, this project never would have happened without input from the members of my writers group throughout the years: Joan, Heidi, Sonny, Coco, Linda, Cindy, Pam, Karen, Jack, and Fred. To the members of the Birmingham Chapter of Sisters in Crime, thanks for the eight years of mystery-related fun so far. To the Top of the Hill Social Club, thanks for giving me your invaluable feedback and friendship. Very special thanks to Brian R. Overstreet, lifelong friend and attorney at law, for answering some vital legal questions, and to Christina L. Brown, CRNA for her help. Thanks to Jan and Tim and the Children's Services division of JBS Mental Health Authority for a great first career. To child welfare social workers in Jefferson County, Alabama, and elsewhere, thank you for all the very important and difficult work that you do. As always, thanks and love to my family for their encouragement. Last but not least, my love and thanks to my wonderful husband, Bill, for supporting my pursuit of this crazy dream.

LITTLE LAMB LOST

CHAPTER ONE

I believed I could make a difference in the world until the day Michael Hennessy died. Maybe I inherited this crazy conviction from my father. Decades ago, he defied my grandfather, a White Citizens Council member, and became a Freedom Rider. Or maybe it came from my mother, who, before I was even the proverbial twinkle in her eye, marched with Dr. King from Selma to Montgomery. Their passion for social justice guided me, inevitably, to my career in social work. *Make the earth a better place, Claire,* they'd said. That was their legacy.

It wasn't an easy legacy. It took fifty-hour work weeks, endless paperwork, and a lot of difficult choices. I'd worried myself out of many a good night's sleep, questioning whether I'd made the right decision to leave young victims in a certain home, with certain people. Wondering whether or not mommy and daddy had squandered the food money on booze, cigarettes, and drugs. Hoping the kids would go to bed without fear, hunger, or bruises.

Over the years I'd developed a sense for recognizing the families that weren't going to make it, the parents who couldn't hold it together. Usually I was able to get the kids out before the situation totally derailed and anyone got hurt. I was good at reading people. And I'd never lost one. No child under my care had ever died.

Until that Tuesday in June.

My cubicle mate, Russell, and I were taking calls while the secretary for our unit went to an early dentist appointment. The phone, as usual, was ringing nonstop.

"When did Jessica say she was going to be in?" I asked over my shoulder. Russell and I worked a foot apart, back-to-back, every day. We were close — not only in proximity.

"I think she said nine thirty."

"One more hour. What a morning."

The phone rang again, and Russell let out a noise of frustration. "Damn, I'm never going to get this form done."

"I'll get it." I punched the appropriate button on my phone and answered, "Jefferson County Department of Human Services, Child Welfare Division."

All I heard was breathing. Hard, deep breaths that turned into wracking sobs. Then, "Cl…Claire…He…he…I don't…I didn't…"

"Hello?" I didn't recognize the woman's voice. "Hello? Who is this?"

The sobs grew fainter as a man came on the line. An authoritative voice. "Claire Conover?"

"Yes?"

"This is Detective Ed Brighton. Birmingham Police Department. You're the caseworker for Ashley Hennessy and her son, Michael?"

"Yes." A tingle of fear radiated through me, starting in my stomach.

"I'm sorry. Michael's dead."

"Dead?" The tingle exploded into full-blown panic.

Behind me, I heard Russell stop writing and turn in his chair.

"How?"

"We don't know yet. I'll need to speak with you as soon as you are available. If —"

"You're at her apartment?"

"Yes, but —"

"I'm on my way." I hung up, numb.

Russell asked, "What is it?"

"Michael Hennessy's dead. That was the police. I have to go."

I tried to think about what I needed to take with me.

I grabbed my satchel full of forms, my purse and keys, and for no apparent reason, three pens. Michael. Michael was dead. I couldn't think for all the curly blond, blue-eyed images rushing together in my mind.

"Sit down a sec. You look like you're about to pass out." Russell placed a delicate hand on my shoulder and gently pushed me into my chair.

"No," I said, rising again. "I'm going. I have to go see Mac." Mac McAlister was the supervisor of the unit. "And Dr. Pope." Teresa Pope was the county director.

"I'll get Mac. You sit."

Moments later he was back, our heavyset boss frowning behind him. Bushy white hair ringed Mac's head like a crown. At times he was my mentor, at times my worst enemy. I had a feeling this was going to be one of those worst-enemy days.

"Tell me what's going on."

"The police just called. Michael Hennessy is dead. That's all I know. I have to go. I told the detective I'd be there."

"Okay, okay. Just calm down for a second. Then we'll go. Remind me about this case."

With twelve social workers in his unit, all of us with twenty-five cases or more, there was no way he could remember them all. Not without my chart. I pulled the thick, russet case file out of the cabinet and handed it over. He flipped through it while I propped myself up on the edge of my well-worn desk.

"I got the case a little over two years ago. The first part of April. We got a report from Michael's pediatrician. He suspected the mother, Ashley, was using drugs. I went to the house where she was staying. It was a filthy crack den, really." I took a deep breath, remembering the stench of urine and the people passed out on tattered couches in the living room. "She was living with some guy. She was high as hell when I arrived, no food or milk or anything in the house. I came back to the office, filed a request for a pick-up order, went out there with the police, and got Michael that same day."

I took another deep breath, recalling Ashley's hysterics as I drove away with her baby. "We had the IM two days later." The IM was the intervention meeting, the plan for the family and the agency to work together toward reunification. "Ashley was supposed to do all the standard stuff: go into treatment, get a job, pass her drug tests, and take parenting classes. I got her into St. Monica's Home the day after the IM for drug and alcohol treatment. According to the staff there, she really worked the program. Was going to her aftercare meetings and everything. She was clean."

"And Michael?"

"He went to foster care. Ashley took about a year and a half to complete everything, and Judge Myer gave her custody again about two months ago. I really thought..." My throat closed a little and I cleared it. "I really thought she was going to make it."

One of the few who would make it. Most of the families I worked with were angry, resentful, and unremorseful. They hated DHS and that rancor spread to me, the representative of the State, the member of the evil government that refused to stay out of their lives and let them raise their children the way they saw fit. Never mind the abuse, neglect, alcohol, or drugs.

But Ashley was different. She'd accepted my interference as the opportunity it was, hung onto the programs I'd offered like a life buoy. She'd embraced the Twelve Steps like it was her personal contract with God, sobered up, and made things right. She was one of the few clients that made me feel like I could really change things for the better, like my parents said.

"She ever beat Michael?" Russell asked.

"No! Well, I don't think so. I wouldn't say she was the greatest parent in the world, she lost her temper sometimes, but it was more yelling than anything else. She was really trying to practice the stuff she learned from the parenting classes. Time out and all that. I never saw any marks on him. She knew she wasn't supposed to spank him. I made that very, very clear. She was scared to death I'd take him away again."

Mac asked, "What about Michael's father?"

"Never been in the picture. She told me she wasn't even sure who he was."

"Other relatives? What about her parents?"

"Ashley ran away when she was fifteen. She said her stepfather physically abused her. He's dead now, but I tracked her mother down when I first got the case. From what I could gather, she was definitely not a good placement for Michael. She's on abusive husband number three. There's no other family that I know of."

Mac thumbed through the chart for a few more moments. "Let's go talk to the police. Let me do the talking. We'll have to bring Legal in eventually, but I want to get a good handle on what happened first."

That struck a nerve. A little boy was dead, and Mac was already talking about lawyers. He was worried about what this was going to do to the department and its reputation. I hadn't even had time to absorb what happened, for God's sake. I slung my purse over my shoulder and again picked up my briefcase.

Mac said, "And I'm driving. You're in no shape."

I protested while following him to his office so he could get his keys. The glass-fronted supervisors' offices surrounded the maze of cubicles where the caseworkers sat. The cubicles had started to buzz with activity. Word of Michael's death would spread like wildfire, and I could feel the stares of my colleagues beginning already.

Ten minutes later, I watched the warehouses and small businesses of the east side of Birmingham fly by. Sweat trickled down my temples as the air conditioning in Mac's car struggled to overcome the suffocating heat. More images of Michael Alexander Hennessy, aged two years and ten months, played through my mind. He was dead. And it didn't really matter how. Fingers of blame would be pointing my way. Because I was the one who was supposed to have kept him safe.

CHAPTER TWO

Most of Birmingham's neighborhoods were once mining or mill towns, little communities where everything was owned by a company. Avondale was no exception, the neighborhood's name the only remnant of the long-gone Avondale Mills. Many of the houses built by the textile mill in the early part of the twentieth century still stood, although many sagged underneath rotting wood and peeling paint. Interspersed among them were newer apartment complexes that had popped up in the sixties and seventies. Ashley and Michael lived in one of these. Cheaply constructed, with vertical siding on the outside painted a deep forest green.

Ashley's apartment was on the first floor of building one. A narrow passageway led to the front door and smelled like rotting garbage. Someone had painted a gang sign in white spray paint next to her neighbor's window. Ashley's doorknob hung loosely. It had been like that ever since I could remember. Her worthless landlord was supposed to have replaced it. It locked, but she pushed a chair in front of the doorknob at night just in case.

Still, it was a home. Maybe not in the safest neighborhood, but a roof over their heads. I'd brought Ashley here the day she'd signed the lease. She'd been so proud to get a place of her own. Today it was unusually quiet. I wondered if the neighbors knew what had happened or if the presence of the cops had everyone hiding inside.

The man who answered Ashley's door was tall and tan, his muscular body topped off with a gray crew cut. He had a distinct ex-military air to him, and I half expected him to bark an order.

"I'm Mac McAlister, and this is Claire Conover. From DHS."

"Detective Brighton." He shook both our hands with a firm grip and stepped aside to let us in. The room was much as I remembered, with dingy white walls and a pervasive fog of cigarette smoke. The furniture was stuff Ashley had acquired gradually from places like the Salvation Army and the Alabama Thrift Store. An oak table with a water stain on one end. Four mismatched, scratched wooden chairs. The couch, a beige and brown plaid circa 1980, had a small tear on the arm.

Ashley slumped on the couch, her unwashed brown hair hanging past her shoulders. Her hazel eyes were swollen and red. I reminded myself, as I did every time I saw her, that she was only twenty-three. Six years my junior. Her history of hard-core drugs and booze made her look much older. Her skin was roughened, and she was missing two teeth on the right side of her mouth. In one hand she held a cigarette, in the other a wad of wet tissue. She saw me and stubbed out the smoke in an ashtray on the chipped glass coffee table.

"Cl...Claire. I, I..." It seemed my arrival was going to trigger a fresh wave of sobs. I put my arms around her and patted her back. She pulled it together, sniffling, and reached for more Kleenex.

"This is my supervisor, Mac McAlister."

She nodded. "I remember. He was at my first meetin' with you."

I looked at Detective Brighton. "I hope we aren't disturbing you."

"No, Miss Hennessy and I were just winding up. I've asked everything I need to for now. I'll leave you alone. We'll need to talk again when we get the results of the autopsy." The detective placed his hand on Ashley's shoulder. "Get some rest." Genuine kindness was there, but it clashed with the sharpness of his personality. I wondered if the solicitousness would last once we knew what happened to Michael. "Miss Conover, and Mr. McAlister, can I talk to you outside?"

I answered him, "I'm afraid before I talk to you, I'll need Ashley's permission."

"Go ahead, I ain't got nothin' to hide."

I pulled a release form out of my bag. I hated to. Paperwork at this moment seemed heartless, but if there was ever a time to cross my *t*'s and dot my *i*'s, it was now. Mac was right to be concerned about the legal consequences of Michael's death. Especially if this case wound up getting us sued. And chances were good that it would. I fished out a pen and filled in the form. Ashley signed without even looking at it, then started to cry again.

"Okay."

We stepped outside to the passageway where the detective lit his own cigarette. "Tell me about DHS's involvement."

I deferred to Mac, who told essentially the same story I had related back at the office.

After he finished, Brighton looked at me. "When was her last drug screen?"

"Last week. I got the results yesterday. It was negative."

"She gets them regularly?"

"She's on the color system." He nodded, signaling that he knew what it was. All my clients with drug issues got tested randomly. Ashley phoned a number every day and a recording announced the day's color. Hers was aqua. If her color was named, she had to leave a urine sample at the lab. No exceptions, no excuses. In any given week, one person's color might not come up at all, or it could be called up to seven times. DHS liked to think it kept them honest.

"She hasn't had a dirty screen in a year and a half, and I haven't seen any evidence of backsliding," I said. "No suspicious behaviors, no running around with her old crowd. She hasn't been avoiding me. No new neglect or abuse reports from anyone. She never missed work and —"

Brighton held up a hand. "Okay, okay. We don't know if she's done anything wrong, so you don't have to defend her. There was no immediate evidence of physical abuse on the body, and no obvious head injury, so we'll just have to wait and see what's going on."

"What could've killed him? Did he choke on something?"

"The paramedics that responded to the nine-one-one call said he was deceased when they arrived. They didn't see anything in his mouth or throat. My guess is that he ate something that caused his death. We'll see what the coroner has to say after the autopsy."

"When will that be?"

"Probably tomorrow."

Mac and I both gave Brighton business cards, and he promised to keep in touch. We went back into the apartment where a devastated Ashley was still sitting on the sofa. I sat beside her and rubbed the back of her worn green robe. Mac perched in one of the dining chairs placed across from us.

I asked, "Ashley, can you tell me what happened? I know you just told the police, but I need to know."

There was a faraway look in her eyes. I dreaded bringing her back and making her go through it again.

"I worked last night." Her janitorial job was from five to ten. "I went to Dazzle's to pick Mikey up." Dazzle was Michael's babysitter. "I got there about ten fifteen or so. He was asleep, like he usually is, on the couch. Dazzle was in her nightgown, ready for bed, just like every night. She gave me a picture he colored for me, and we woke him so I could take him home. He slept all the way here in his car seat. I woke him up again so I could put on his pj's and help him brush his teeth. I poured him some orange juice in a sippy cup, but he was too tired to drink it. He left it on the coffee table. Then he fell asleep right here next to me," she touched a place on the couch, "with his blanky." I knew she meant the fleece blanket printed with lambs that Michael dragged everywhere. "I watched some TV. Then I carried him to bed about eleven thirty."

Her eyes filled with tears again. "And that's it. I swear. It was just like every single other night."

Now the hard part. "Then what?"

"I woke up at six, like always. Some mornings I get me and Mikey dressed and go to the nine o'clock AA meetin' at St. Monica's. Sometimes I just stay here. But by ten thirty he has to be at Dazzle's so I can get to work." Ashley's day job was as a waitress, from eleven to four. "I didn't go to a meetin' yesterday 'cause I needed to go do laundry. I went into Mikey's room to get him up and sort his dirty clothes, and he wasn't in bed."

She inhaled through her rising emotion. "So I came out here, and he wasn't on the couch, so I looked in the kitchen." She glanced toward the galley-style room behind us. "He was on the floor. He was blue. Oh, Claire, he was so blue. I tried shaking him, but he wouldn't wake up."

I could feel my own heart racing and my throat was tightening again. I swallowed back tears and glanced at Mac, whose face was unnaturally still.

"I called nine-one-one. There wasn't nothin' they could do. The police came. Lots of them, lookin' at everything. Taking pictures and videos. Then the guy from the coroner came."

"Did Michael eat anything? Maybe he had a reaction to something. Like an allergy."

"He didn't have no allergies, and I don't think he ate nothin'."

"He couldn't have gotten into anything?"

"I babyproofed this house just like you showed me."

That was true. All the sockets were covered, and the last time I'd looked, all the cabinets were fitted with those little plastic gadgets that kept the doors from being pulled open. The cleaning supplies and chemicals were as hidden as possible. Medications, even the over-the-counter ones, were put away in Ashley's bedroom.

"Well, I guess the police will give us more answers." I deliberately avoided the word autopsy. "Why don't you go get dressed? Mac and I can wait for you, and then I want to take you to Nona. I don't want you to be alone today. Or tonight."

I looked at Mac for confirmation. "That seems like a good plan."

Nona Richardson was the director of St. Monica's Home for Recovery where Ashley had lived for her first three hellish months of rehab. She and Nona shared a special bond. Nona would make sure Ashley didn't run off and get high again. I'd hate for Ashley to blow her sobriety, and if she were ever going to, it would be today. And I couldn't say I'd blame her.

Mac and I waited while the shower ran. I began to wander around the apartment, still shaky and restless. Except for a quick peek, I didn't go into the kitchen. It didn't look any different than usual. The avocado counters were wiped down and clean dishes drained in the sink. I don't know what I expected to see. A chalk outline. Michael's ghost, maybe. Some sign he had died there.

I paced over to the hallway, pausing by the door to Michael's room. It was closed, and I left it that way. I walked the length of the living room again. On the wall above a metal cart that supported a small TV were two collage-style picture frames for photos, the kind sold at Wal-Mart for about seven bucks. One was dedicated to Michael. His first picture was there, the one they'd taken at the hospital just after birth. Another was at his first birthday party, taken by his foster mother as he blew out a candle on a cupcake. She'd sent me a copy too. The rest were more recent snapshots of him playing in a small plastic pool. Ashley had been absent for so much of his young life, these were probably all the memories she'd been able to capture of him. And now he was gone forever.

In the second collage were some people I recognized. One picture was of Dee, Ashley's mom, sitting in a white resin chair underneath a tree. Another was of Ashley's best friend. In the third, two girls I'd never seen before leaned on the hood of a car. A fourth showed three guys about Ashley's age sitting on her couch, laughing. The reminders of how happy Ashley had been before last night made me uncomfortable, and I started pacing again.

Mac said, "Sit down, you're making me nervous."

"Shouldn't we be nervous?"

"Right now, it looks like a very unfortunate accident. Nothing anyone could have prevented. What's your schedule look like today?"

I pulled my day planner out of my satchel. "I have an intervention meeting at two, then I have to write a court report. I was planning to catch up on other paperwork this morning."

"Reschedule the IM. This is going to take up the rest of the day."

"To say the least."

Ashley rejoined us, dressed in faded jeans and a T-shirt, her still-wet hair tight in a ponytail. "I have to call work." I knew she meant the restaurant.

"Want me to do it?"

"No, it's okay." She uncradled the cordless phone and went into her bedroom, closing the door. A few minutes later, with evidence of fresh tears on her face, she emerged. "I'm ready."

She had packed a small overnight case, which she carried in one hand. In the other was Michael's blanky. My throat did that thing again.

Mac's expression still revealed little emotion, but now I had the feeling it was taking more effort. "I need to head back to the office," he said. "Are you okay to drive once we get there?"

I nodded. "I'm fine. Really."

As we made our way to Mac's Cadillac, I couldn't help but notice a car parked alongside the curb across the street. An old Dodge Charger, painted a garish lime green, with chrome twenty-four-inch rims. Ashley glanced at it, once, then twice, quickly. The driver slouched, a sideways baseball cap low over his forehead. He cranked the engine and roared away as we buckled up.

It was a mostly silent ride from Avondale to downtown. Mac dropped us off in the parking lot of our four-story office building, a former department store. "You coming in?"

"No, I think we'll just go to St. Monica's."

The heat was stifling in my seven-year-old Honda Civic. I cranked the AC up all the way, but felt myself beginning to perspire again under my thin blue shirt. Birmingham, trapped in a valley between two mountain ridges, was hazy from the constant smog that hovered from June through September. A cool breeze would've been nice.

Ashley leaned her head against the passenger window. She looked worn out. I turned onto Fourteenth Street and drove to the south side of the city. St. Monica's Home for Recovery sat halfway up Red Mountain, overlooking downtown. A boardinghouse built for steel workers in the 1800s, it was a mammoth place with an old-fashioned front porch, columns and all. The surrounding area had morphed from middle class to slum to upper class. The Catholic Church had been lucky to purchase the house during its slum phase and could make serious money on the property if they wanted to move the home. Nona, however, wasn't about to let that happen. She was there for life.

I parked in the small alley that bordered the house. One of the residents was sweeping the steps. Ashley and I entered through the leaded glass door into the living area. Four or five women relaxed on couches, engrossed in a courtroom show on a console television. A woman at a small secretary said Nona was in her office. Ashley and I made our way down the hall to a small enclosed area in the back that had once been a screened porch. Nona was behind her massive, cluttered desk. She lifted her over-two-hundred-pound frame out of the chair and immediately put her arms around Ashley, who started to cry again. "There, baby, hush now."

Nona was proud of her African heritage and wore flowing mud-cloth dashikis and headwraps. I watched as Ashley's face sank into the soft folds of Nona's earthy tunic. Nona knew how to handle tragedy. She was no stranger to it herself. Raised in segregated Birmingham, she dropped out of Parker High School when she was seventeen. Kicked out by her tyrannical father, she began drinking and lived from flophouse to flophouse until a priest found her and straightened her out. Father Clark ran St. Monica's until Nona took it over upon his death several years ago. Although there were a number of good treatment facilities around, St. Monica's was my first choice because of Nona.

After several more minutes of "Hush, baby," Ashley's tears ceased, and she dried her face on the tissue Nona handed her from the box on her desk. "You and I are going to stay together tonight," Nona said to Ashley. "Why don't you take them things up to my apartment?" The third floor of the boardinghouse had been converted to a two-bedroom apartment when Father Clark founded the home, and now Nona lived there. "Here," she flipped through a chunky ring of keys until she found the right one. "I'll be up in just a minute and make us something to eat, okay?" We watched Ashley retreat to the staircase off the hall.

"How'd you find out?" I asked.

"Dazzle called me. Poor woman." Michael's babysitter and Nona had known each other for years through the A.M.E. Zion church. "She's in a right state. The police are at her house."

"I'm going over there now."

"I wonder what in the world could've happened to the poor child?"

"The coroner will do an autopsy, probably tomorrow."

"You think it was an accident?"

"God, I hope so."

Nona walked me out to my car. On the way, another one of my clients, Cheyenne, spotted me.

"Oh, shit. We didn't have an appointment today, did we?"

"No, I'm here on another matter."

"Good."

As Cheyenne stormed into the house, I asked Nona how she was doing. "She's angry. Arguing with the staff. Doesn't want to do her chores. Doesn't want to be here."

"She's not going to make it, is she?"

"No, I wouldn't think so. Not this time."

I sighed. It was sad for Cheyenne's three kids, who would go up for adoption.

I was halfway to Dazzle's house when Mac called my cell phone. He summoned me back to the office, stating that Dr. Pope had cleared her schedule for the afternoon.

This was the meeting I was dreading. Dr. Pope was relatively new in the position of director. She was the best one we'd had in my five years with the agency and I had a lot of respect for her. Despite the chaos that happened on a daily basis, she was always calm and well-spoken. I'd never seen her get angry, and I hoped I wouldn't now.

CHAPTER THREE

On my way back to the office I called poor frantic Dazzle to tell her I wouldn't be over.

"Oh, Claire, what a mess. The police are here, going over everything. Taking pictures and videos. What in God's great world could've happened to him?"

"I don't know. Listen, I want to come see you, but I've got to go meet with my supervisors. Can I stop by tomorrow?" Probably best not to get in the cops' way, either, I thought.

"You know you can. Lord have mercy, you're not in trouble over this, are you?"

"Too early to tell." My stomach tensed at the thought.

She wailed a long cry. "Oh Lord, what a mess."

I tuned through all my favorite radio stations on the way to the office and in the end just shut it off. After finally finding a parking space, I dumped my stuff in my cubicle where I ran into Russell.

"Hey, I'm going out to get lunch," he said. "You want something?"

I didn't, but I knew he'd harass me about not eating if I didn't order something. "Sure. Whatever." I handed Russell a ten out of my wallet and spent the next twenty minutes distractedly canceling meetings and checking my voice mail. I picked at the sandwich Russell delivered to my desk, then retrieved the Hennessy's chart and went to find Mac.

He was in his office, on the phone, with an empty Tupperware container at his elbow. He finished his call and asked, "You ready?"

We made our way up to Dr. Pope's fourth-floor corner office, decorated in a serene fashion that suited her personality. Soft taupe carpet and a large, cherry-finished desk and table. Peaceful landscapes on the walls. Through the windows I could see the towering glass and masonry buildings of the financial district.

Mac and I joined Dr. Pope and three men at the round conference table. One of them, Brian Shoffner, I already knew. Nice guy, and a competent lawyer. He'd been the attorney for the agency on the Hennessy case. Dr. Pope introduced the other two suits, an attorney and a representative from the state office in Montgomery.

Let the "cover your ass" begin, I thought. As if Michael's death alone wasn't tragic enough, there was the fallout at DHS. Right now, Michael's death appeared to be an accident. But just in case it wasn't, my superiors were going to make damn sure I'd done everything I was supposed to, from the moment I'd received the initial report two years ago to the moment last night when Michael took his final breath. I'd gone over the case in my head a million times already today, and I thought I'd done everything right. Still, my palms were sweating. I wiped them subtly on my pants.

For the next three and half hours the team dissected the case. I felt like I was being interrogated; the only thing missing was a bright spotlight shining in my eyes. Both attorneys took notes as I answered question after question. They scrutinized every form, every narrative, every court report, and every court order. We discussed the timeline of the case, Michael's birth and health history, and Ashley's past. I'd missed only two objectives during the years I'd worked with the family and everyone agreed they were minor oversights. The representative from the state office requested a copy of the entire chart.

When the meeting was over, Dr. Pope concluded with, "I'll be making a statement to the press that we don't comment on investigations. We'll try to keep names out of it if we can. I can't promise that though. Claire, I don't have to remind you that you're not to comment on this, either, right? No matter how ugly it gets."

"I know."

I had a pounding headache. It was four thirty. Russell was out on a home visit. I picked up the phone, hung it up, and called it a day.

Outside hunkered satellite vans from both the FOX and ABC affiliates. Any death of a child would be picked up by the press on the police scanners. From there it only took a phone call to a source or one of the victim's family members to find out whether DHS was involved. Our cases were supposed to be kept confidential, but it didn't always work that way. If Michael's death was an accident, we'd be the feature story tonight and the whole thing would blow over. If my brewing fears were true and Ashley had a role in Michael's death, then this was only the beginning. If the slightest hint existed that DHS could have prevented this, every news outlet was going to play that angle. The public would demand that someone take the fall, and the blame game was the media's favorite sport. Too much bad press and I'd be gone faster than a losing Alabama football coach. And maybe Mac too. Maybe even Dr. Pope. I'd seen it happen before. DHS had been in the spotlight before for some poorly handled cases, and it seemed like reporters were always waiting for us to screw things up.

A familiar-looking reporter from FOX bounced on the balls of his feet and swung his arms in impatience, waiting to broadcast live for the five o'clock news. As I sneaked to my car, he spotted me. I sped up, racing to my Honda and slamming the door in his face just as he cried, "Hey!" I threw the car in reverse and backed up recklessly, speeding to the exit of the lot.

My headache intensified. In crawling traffic I made my way to the on-ramp of I-65, and for the next forty minutes did what the locals called the sixty-five shuffle: the long, slow drive to the suburban communities south of downtown.

I exited the interstate at the summit of Shades Mountain and wound through serpentine streets to my neighborhood. I'd bought a small house in Bluff Park only four months earlier, after years of saving and months of searching for the right place. Built in 1953, it needed a lot of updating. I spent every spare hour away from work fixing it up myself. So far I'd peeled acres of stubborn wallpaper and polished the hardwood. Tonight I planned to work on the small bedroom I was converting into an office, painting it a soft yellow. Normally I relished the thought of changing into my paint-splattered T-shirt and shorts and loading up the roller, but right now it just seemed like work.

I pulled into my carport and sat there, trying to force myself to go inside and watch the news. I didn't want to hear what they had to say. After a couple of minutes with my throbbing forehead on the steering wheel, I backed out and drove toward Shades Crest Road. Within five minutes I parked in the driveway of the sprawling red-brick, ranch-style house where I'd grown up. This nut hadn't fallen far from the tree.

My father's Toyota hybrid was there, covered in political bumper stickers and telling me he was home. A blast of cool air greeted me as I opened the door. "Dad?"

"In here."

I walked through the foyer to the living room. Virtually nothing in the house had changed since I was a kid. An oil portrait of my late grandfather hung above the fireplace. His Dutch features, including his square jaw, fair skin, and summer sky blue eyes, had been bequeathed to my father. And to me. And to my younger brother, Chris.

On this same green carpet I'd taken my first steps and held slumber parties in junior high school. In this room lived the memories of my mother before she died of breast cancer when I was thirteen. Memories of me and my brother joking and roughhousing. It was a home built on laughter and love. What all my clients should have had, but didn't.

The furniture was still the same, too, except now the tweed sofa and chair were shoved against a cream-colored wall so my father could practice Tae Kwon Do. Dad was dressed in his *gi*, with a yellow belt tied around his waist. His milk-blond ponytail was longer than mine and touched with gray. He was flushed from the exercise, making the crescent-shaped scar on his left cheekbone stand out white on his face. The story behind the scar was one I'd heard frequently growing up, about how he and the other Freedom Riders had been beaten and arrested in May of 1961, trying to get to New Orleans to support the desegregation of the interstate bus system. He'd been twenty years old and spent two months in jail.

Dad completed a front snap kick and a couple of punches. He was in better shape than me.

"Hi. What's up?" he asked.

"One of my clients died today."

Dad stood up out of his stance. "Shit."

"You're not kidding. Do you have any aspirin?"

"Sure. Hang on." He walked down the hall toward the bedrooms. I waited, massaging my temples, until he returned with two Tylenol.

"Thanks." I headed for the kitchen and swallowed them with a sip of water.

Dad followed and asked, "What happened?"

"I don't know yet. His mother found him dead this morning on the kitchen floor. She just got him back two months ago."

"You think she killed him?"

"There weren't any immediate signs of abuse. They'll do an autopsy, then we'll know more."

"What'd Mac say?"

"We spent the whole afternoon going over everything. All the policies were followed correctly."

"So you didn't do anything wrong?"

"I don't think so. I need to watch the news. They were already camped out at the office when I left."

The den was a sunken room three steps down from the kitchen, paneled in dark wood. A sliding glass door led to a patio with a view of Oxmoor Valley and the Robert Trent Jones golf course below. I sank into one of two enormous recliners and reached for the remote.

"Do you want a drink?" Dad asked as he walked to the built-in bar in the corner.

"No, thanks. It'd probably make my headache worse."

He poured himself a shot of Gentleman Jack over ice and joined me. We watched the last ten minutes of the national news, the usual stuff about the economy and foreign policy, then I switched to FOX for the six o'clock newscast.

We were the second story, right after a homicide in north Birmingham. My jaw clenched as the pretty anchorwoman began with, "Police were called to an apartment in Avondale today to investigate the death of a two-year-old boy. Fox Six has learned that the child may have been involved with the Department of Human Services. We go to Jeffrey Vale for the story."

The picture changed. In the background was our office building, the windows reflecting the late afternoon sun. The camera focused on the impatient young man I had escaped from earlier. In one hand he held a microphone, in the other his notes. "Thank you, Kathleen. Fox Six has indeed learned that Jefferson County DHS may have been involved with this child's family. However, County Director Dr. Teresa Pope issued a statement earlier that they are unable to confirm or deny their role in this case, or to comment on an ongoing police investigation." He consulted his notes. "Furthermore, a Birmingham Police Department spokesperson said that a cause of death has yet to be determined and is still under investigation. An autopsy scheduled for tomorrow will give the police more information about what could have led to this terrible tragedy. Back to you, Kathleen."

I muted the sound as Kathleen went to a story about the City Council. My jaw relaxed. Okay, so far so good. My name wasn't mentioned, and they weren't verbally crucifying Ashley. Yet.

Dad interrupted my thoughts. "Did I ever tell you about the time one of my clients committed suicide?"

I looked at him, surprised. Dad was a psychologist, semiretired. His practice, founded when I was about Michael's age, had thrived for years, but now he kept only a few clients in his caseload. "When?"

"Oh, about twenty years ago. You were about ten or so. Your mother was still living. The thing was, I knew this guy was going to do it. I got him committed to a psychiatric hospital and he stayed three days. The day after he left, he wrote a note to say good-bye to his family and shot himself in the head."

"God."

"I was terrified I could've done more to prevent it. Terrified his family was going to sue me. They never did, but I stayed up nights going over everything, making sure I'd done everything I was supposed to."

"Yeah, but my kid didn't kill himself. He was only two."

"I know, but my point is that sometimes you do everything right and things still go horribly wrong. Things you don't have control over."

"Tell me about it."

Dad got up and lifted me with two hands out of the chair. He wrapped his arms around me in a reassuring hug. "So don't beat yourself up about this too bad, okay?"

"I'll try. I'm going home. I'm sensing a bubble bath in my near future."

"You don't want something to eat? I've got some veggie burgers in the freezer or some tofu." Dad was a part-time vegetarian. Vegetarian until someone mentioned the words "bacon cheeseburger." Either way, his cooking was atrocious.

"No, thanks, I've got stuff at home." I did feel better. Dad's talk helped. That and the Tylenol.

At home I sank into a peony-scented tub for an hour. I tried to read, to distract myself from thoughts of Michael and Ashley and what could have caused this tragedy. It didn't work. Visions of Michael's body, lying on the cold linoleum, crept into my mind between every paragraph. I gave it up and went to bed, tossing and turning myself into a nightmare world where I was in a sailboat with drowning children all around me. And I didn't have a single life preserver.

I snapped awake at five thirty, and despite the sleep my eyes felt gritty and tired, like I hadn't rested at all.

I went to work and as my fellow caseworkers trickled in, managed to focus on my court reports and filing. As soon as it was nine o'clock I called Nona. She said Ashley had a rough night, but she was trying to find things to keep her busy. Then I left and went to Dazzle's.

Dazzle Martin's house was within walking distance of East Lake Park, named after the large body of water in the center, and I remembered as I drove past how Michael had loved to feed the ducks. I could feel my eyes start to sting. Falling apart now would do no good. I buried my feelings about his death as I turned onto Dazzle's street and shut the car off in front of her house.

Technically, I suppose Dazzle's little enterprise could have qualified as a day care. During the morning she watched four preschool-aged children, and a couple of older kids joined them in the afternoon. Getting her day care license, however, would have meant renovating her nearly one-hundred-year-old house to meet the building and fire codes, not to mention all the inspections to keep her license. It would have been too expensive. Since most of my clients couldn't afford commercial day care centers, without sitters like Dazzle — who got her toys donated and charged just above what was necessary to feed the children — they certainly wouldn't be able to get jobs and do all the things DHS asked. So we turned a blind eye. I was more than a little worried that if whatever killed Michael had come from her home, they were going to shut her down.

Dazzle was a slightly stooped woman in her mid-sixties. Her skin was a smooth, dark black and she had the most perfect, polished white teeth I'd ever seen. When she smiled, those teeth were framed by deep dimples and it was easy to see how she'd gotten her nickname as a teenager.

Today, however, there was no smile, just Dazzle standing at the door, dabbing at the corners of her eyes with a paper napkin. "Come in," she said. "I just got done sittin' down with the chil'ren, tellin' 'em about Michael. I tol' them that he died and wen' to heaven, and now he's an angel. We prayed for him. Do you think I did right?"

"Exactly right."

"Some o' their mammas was asking about the funeral. Asking if they should take 'em. What do you think?"

I followed her into the family room. "I wouldn't. Kids that age don't understand the service, and the burial, if there is one, would just terrify them. I'd have a separate ceremony for them and their parents. Maybe at the park. I've heard of one ritual where the kids release balloons with good-bye messages tied to them. That I think they'd understand."

"That's a good idea."

Three children entertained themselves in the colorful family room, which looked as though someone had dumped a giant toy box into the middle of it. Clustered on the walls were a half century of photographs of Dazzle's family, including her deceased husband, her three kids, and seven grandkids. One of her grandchildren sat on the couch, mesmerized by Big Bird on the television. Another girl about the same age was deeply engrossed in the play kitchen set. A younger, Hispanic-looking toddler made quite a racket with a singing keyboard. "Let's go in the kitchen," Dazzle said.

An enormous wooden table dominated the kitchen that served as both dining area and craft headquarters. A naked Barbie lay face down on the paint-stained surface. Dazzle positioned herself where she could see the kids through the door.

"Did the police say anything yesterday?"

"Nothin', just took a lot of pictures and asked me what he done yesterday. And what he ate."

"What did he eat?"

"Bless his heart, he was goin' through a peanut butter phase. Wanted it on everythin'. So for lunch he had peanut butter crackers an' an apple, and for dinner a peanut butter sandwich with jelly and some string cheese."

"I was thinking he might have had an allergy. How was he after he ate? Any complaints about not feeling well or anything?"

"No, not at all. He was jus' normal."

"Was he more tired than usual?"

"No. He went down on the couch about nine, and his mamma picked him up a little after ten, like always."

"He didn't hit his head yesterday, that you know of?"

"No, he never said nothin' about that. I watch 'em close, and I didn't see no accident or fall or nothin'."

This wasn't allaying my fears. Michael's death seemed less and less like an accident. The small girl who had been play cooking wandered over and patted me on the leg. She couldn't have been older than four. She was a beautiful girl of mixed race, with soft, curly black hair and caramel-colored skin.

"Michael died. He's in heaven."

"I know."

"He's an angel. He has wings. I want my Barbie." I handed her the doll, and she skipped away.

I said good-bye to Dazzle and left for my ten o'clock home visit. As I descended the concrete steps in front of the house, I noticed something was wrong with my Civic.

She was sitting lower than she should have been. I crept forward, scanning the street left and right. No one around. A dog barked in the distance, but that was the only sound from the wide, tree-lined street.

I crouched to look at each of the tires. All four of them bore a two-inch wide slit, near the rim.

"Damn it," I swore out loud. "Son of a —"

"You awright?" Dazzle called from the stoop.

"Somebody slashed my tires."

"Oh Lawd, Lawd. What next?"

No kidding. What had I done to deserve this? I had trouble believing it was a random thing. In my experience, these types of attacks were deliberate. I'd been the victim of vandalism before, three years ago, when one of my clients spray painted "bitch" in orange on the side of my car. At the time, I'd had a pretty good idea who'd sent the message. Not this time. The thought scared me.

"You want to call the police?"

I debated. Whoever had done this was long gone, and it was doubtful that anyone would be caught. Dazzle's neighbors were mostly widows and retirees, and it was unlikely any of them saw anything. Still, I'd probably need the police report to file the insurance.

I pulled out my cell. "Yeah, I'll do it."

Dazzle went in to watch the kids, and I waited until an officer arrived. I gave a quick statement to a young policeman who said I could pick up a copy tomorrow at his precinct. I called my client to cancel our meeting. Then I called a tow truck, and a chatty old guy transported me and my vehicle to the Tire Warehouse. An hour, and two hundred and twelve painful dollars later, I was on my way.

I picked up a late lunch on the go, went to Family Court for a hearing that was continued, then on two more home visits. By four o' clock the stress and the lack of sleep were catching up to me.

I was back at my desk, yawning and writing case notes, when my cell phone sang its little tune. Nona, from St. Monica's. She spoke low. "That detective just called looking for Ashley. I think he's on his way over. I got a bad feeling about this."

"I'm on my way." I slapped the phone shut, snatched my stuff, and bolted for the car. Traffic creeped and the stoplights seemed in some giant electronic conspiracy against me. By the time I got to St. Monica's, a white Ford Taurus and a Birmingham police car were in the alley beside the house. The lime green Charger was parked across the street.

I left the Civic behind the patrol car and was halfway up the steps to the porch when Detective Brighton came through the door, followed by a uniformed officer and Ashley, in handcuffs. Nona was behind Ashley, wringing her hands.

"Miss Conover." Detective Brighton nodded once to me and shot Nona a look. "Imagine finding you here."

Ashley's head was down, her long, straight hair hiding her face like a curtain.

"What's she under arrest for?"

"Right now she's charged with negligent homicide, child endangerment, and possession of a controlled substance. That's to start with."

Then he said the words I'd been dreading for almost two days. "Michael died of a drug overdose." He paused to consult the small spiral notebook in his pocket. "Gama hydroxybutyrate."

CHAPTER FOUR

As we stood on the steps of St. Monica's, Brighton continued reading from his notebook. "GHB was found in significant quantities in the victim, in a sippy cup, and in a pitcher of frozen concentrate orange juice taken from the refrigerator at the residence of Ashley Hennessy." He closed the notebook with a triumphant look. It pissed me off.

"Ashley?" I said. Her head bent lower and she wouldn't look at me. "Ashley?" I turned to Brighton. "I can visit her in jail, right?"

"Tomorrow. Now, you gonna move that car or am I gonna radio to have it towed?"

I moved my car into the street and watched as the police officer led Ashley by the arm and placed her in the backseat behind the cage-like divider. Brighton's Taurus sped off after them. The green Dodge was gone.

I pulled back into the alley and joined Nona on the porch, sinking slowly onto one of the blue-painted steps. I could hear the women inside the house gossiping like crazy about Ashley's arrest. Nona lowered her large frame beside me and patted my back as I pressed my fists to my eyes. Ashley had killed her son. She was on drugs again, and had fooled me totally. How could I have misjudged her so completely?

"Damn," I said.

"I know."

"I really thought she was clean."

"Me too."

"GHB. Damn. How could I have missed it?"

"We both did."

"It doesn't make sense."

"How?"

"Ashley did crack mostly, right? Some pot. And booze. She never told me she did GHB."

Nona's comforting strokes continued. "Girl, you know what addicts will do to get high if they really want to. If they're desperate enough, they'll snort, shoot, or smoke just about anything. What they did before don't much matter."

"But GHB? Why now?"

"I don't know. She certainly didn't tell me she was using again. Maybe we'll never know what triggered this."

"Do you suppose she's back with Smash or Trash or whatever his stupid street name was? The guy she was living with when we took Michael away?"

"Flash. I don't know."

"That was it." Flash, real name Gregory Bowman, was Ashley's boyfriend at the time I'd first met her. And her pimp. And her dealer. Although as dealers went, he was pretty small-time. I remembered him as a skinny, pale guy with platinum-dyed spiky hair. He was big into rap, a gangster wannabe, usually dressed in baggy basketball jerseys and matching shorts. With lots of jewelry. I couldn't stand him. He'd stalked Ashley when she first came to St. Monica's to the point where Nona eventually had to get a restraining order. Now that I thought about it, he was the type of guy who would drive a lime green Charger with chrome rims. He was also the kind to slash someone's tires.

"Now," Nona said, pushing herself up off the step and helping me stand, "you go home and get some rest. I got some things I gotta do. We're taking up money for Mikey's funeral, and I got some calls to make."

"That's sweet." I retrieved my purse from my car and gave her a twenty, the last of my cash. "Here. For Michael." She took it and put her arms around me as I inhaled her sweet, musky scent.

"You take care."

"You too."

Thirty minutes later I parked the Honda in my carport. Before changing clothes, I went into my half-painted home office. My computer was there, on a cart in the middle of the room, under clear plastic. It was a twenty-first century contrast to the rolltop desk I'd inherited from my maternal grandmother that sat next to it, also under plastic. But what I wanted was in the closet.

As a licensed social worker, I was required to get thirty hours of continuing education credit every two years. Last year I'd gone to a workshop put on by a local police officer in the Youth Services Division in conjunction with a program designed to intervene with kids at high risk for substance abuse. It was informative, mostly because the officer had spent nearly all of his time going over what drugs were popular these days.

Since I was cursed with an obsessive need for organization, it was easy to find the crate file where I had put the handout and my notes from the conference. I pulled it from the folder marked "CEUs," sat on the floor, and refreshed my memory about gama hydroxybutyrate.

Commonly know as GHB, G, Liquid X, or the date rape drug, it was popular with high school kids and clubbers. A lot of kids used it after doing Ecstasy at raves, because GHB brought them down after the manic effects of Ecstasy. When taken, it gave the user sensations similar to being drunk, with decreased motor function, slurred speech, numbness, blackouts, and in the case of overdose, coma and death. It was especially deadly when paired with alcohol, and it wasn't uncommon for people on GHB to smother if they passed out face down, or to drown in their own vomit. Ugh.

Only a small amount of GHB, like a capful, was enough to get high. GHB and its analogs, or similar drugs, were made of common chemicals and could be concocted in any kitchen. It exited the system rapidly and was hard to detect in a drug screen. Maybe that's why Ashley had always tested negative.

The worst feature of GHB, according to the police officer, was that it was colorless. It had become so rampant in some local high schools that it had prompted administrators to ban students from bringing bottled drinks to school. That didn't stop them though. GHB could be kept in almost any container, like a fingernail polish bottle. It had a salty taste, and was most often used by placing it into a sweet cocktail, soda, or juice to disguise it.

My guess was that Michael had woken up sometime early Tuesday morning, thirsty. He drank his juice, which had enough GHB in it to put him in a coma before he stopped breathing. He'd just gone to sleep. A painless death. I wished that was some comfort.

I refiled the packet of information and, sore from sitting on the floor, stretched and went to change clothes. I pulled on a pair of pink and white flannel boxer shorts and an old "Race for the Cure" T-shirt and went back into the office. I uncovered the computer and plugged it in, intent on further researching GHB and its effects.

When I hit the blue button on the computer case, the machine made a horrible noise. Sort of a metallic clanking. Nothing at all came on the screen. I turned it off, quickly, then tried again. Same awful noise.

"Damn," I muttered, then let loose a few more expletives. I couldn't live without my computer, and now I had to find time to go get it fixed. And money. Home improvements were sucking every extra cent out of my meager paycheck. Not to mention the new tires. I couldn't afford any more major expenses right now.

Back in the bedroom, I changed again, this time to a paint-splattered "Ski Copper Mountain" T-shirt and a pair of cutoffs. As I rolled a small section of sunny yellow paint onto the wall, I felt my stress level ease. Then my cell phone rang.

"Girl, your agency is in a world of shit, no?"

Royanne Fayard. We'd been best friends since the fifth grade. Was it six o'clock already? "You watching the news?" I ran into the living room and grabbed the remote.

"Yeah, channel twelve."

I flipped it to the ABC station and both Royanne and I listened.

The male reporter was standing in front of the brown brick edifice of the Criminal Justice Center, otherwise known as the jail.

"Thanks, Dan. A Birmingham Police Department spokesperson today confirmed that Ashley Louise Hennessy has been arrested in conjunction with the death of her two-year-old son, Michael Alexander Hennessy. The autopsy report showed that the youngster died of an overdose of the drug GHB. Sources tell us that Ms. Hennessy has a history of drug addiction for which she was in treatment. As we reported last evening, it is believed she was under the supervision of the Department of Human Services. Dr. Teresa Pope, DHS's county director, stated again today they are unwilling to comment on an ongoing investigation, but assured me that should any blame lie with any social worker in her department, harshest disciplinary action would be taken. Tonight, the question remains why this child was left in such a dangerous situation. Back to you, Dan."

I sank down onto the sofa, sick. The reporter's voice played again in my head. Such a dangerous situation. Harshest disciplinary action.

Royanne said, "Wow, I feel sorry for whoever had that case. You think they'll get fired?"

"I can't talk about it." My voice was hollow.

"What's that supposed to mean?"

"It means I can't talk about it."

"It wasn't your case, was it?"

Royanne knew me well enough to interpret my silence.

"Oh shit. Oh Claire, I'm so sorry."

"I really can't talk about it."

"I know. Oh, man."

"I guess we'll have to see what happens."

"Are you okay?"

"I will be."

"Do you still want to do lunch tomorrow?"

Royanne and I had a standing lunch date every Thursday unless some emergency of mine prevented it. I visualized my schedule in my head. No court appearances, just a couple of meetings. And I had to get by the jail to see Ashley. "Sure."

"Then I'll see you tomorrow. You sure you're okay?"

"I'm okay."

Through the phone I heard the long wail of a child's cry. It had to be Olivia, Royanne's two-year-old daughter. Only she could scream like that. Royanne and her husband, Toby, had two other children, Richard, aged four, and Alicia, aged six. All of them were close to my heart. "Uh-oh. Trouble brewing. Gotta go."

"See ya." I closed my phone. So the witch hunt had begun. I knew it would, but knowing it was coming wasn't going to lessen the impact. I spent the rest of the evening finishing the office, letting the repetitive motion of the paint roller ease my mind like the physical version of a soothing mantra. I finally collapsed into bed late, exhausted.

The next morning I went in early to finish case notes and write a quick e-mail to Mac about my slashed tires. Russell moped in at eight, complete with to-go coffee from O'Henry's Coffee House, his highlighted blond hair still wet from the shower. "You read this?" he asked, holding out a copy of the paper.

"No. Bad?"

"Not good."

I took the folded paper and found the headline on page one. CHILD WELFARE AGENCY LETS CHILD DOWN.

The article, written by some idiot named Kirk Mahoney, recounted everything that had happened so far in Ashley's case, including the fact that Michael had died from a GHB overdose and cited "sources" that confirmed Michael and Ashley were working with DHS. My favorite quote was, "The Department of Human Services has long faced scrutiny for the way that it handles its cases. Years of mismanagement and incompetence may have resulted in another tragic, needless death."

I fumed, cursing, and resisted the urge to throw the paper against the wall. "Incompetence? Really! What the hell does that son of a bitch know about anything!"

"I know." Russell agreed. "And DHS will insist on your maintaining confidentiality, effectively making it impossible for you to defend yourself. At least in public."

"Thanks. You're really cheering me up."

"Sorry. Can I have my paper back? I want to read the rest of the news." I gave Russell his paper and gathered my stuff.

I went to a meeting with a therapist about a client, and by ten was parking next to a meter a block away from the Criminal Justice Center. It was a fifteen-story building with high, horizontal windows, designed to let in minimal light and deny anyone a view of the outside world.

Security was tight. My purse and briefcase were X-rayed, then I had to leave them, along with my phone and keys, in a locker. The Sheriff's Department officer who checked me through pointed to the elevator and directed me to the second floor.

It seemed like everything in the building was dirty. The elevator walls were marked with smudges and fingerprints, and the whole place had a smell of unwashed bodies, like a gym.

I stepped off the elevator directly into the visiting room. A row of scratched, wooden cubicles with tall glass windows separated visitors from the inmates. The booths had narrow stools barely large enough to perch on, cemented into the floor. Telephone handsets hung on the side of each cubicle so the visitors and the inmates could talk. A uniformed guard stood at the door that led to the rest of the jail.

I expected to have to wait for Ashley, but as I stepped off the elevator, I saw her. She was sitting in the last cubicle, wearing a baggy suit of orange stripes, talking on the off-white handset with a guy. I could see his profile as they spoke. He was fortyish, with untamed wiry, dark brown hair and an untrimmed beard. He had on dark blue rugged pants — the ones favored by auto mechanics and other manual laborers — with a short-sleeved burgundy polo shirt over a potbelly.

I stopped, wondering who he was, not wanting to interrupt their discussion. As I watched, he placed his free hand on the glass. Ashley did the same, in a gesture that was as close as they could get at the moment to an intimate touch. Her expression was one of tenderness I'd seen before, when she looked at Michael. A look of love.

Her expression changed abruptly when she noticed me. She said something urgently to her visitor and they hung up. He rose off the stool. I tried to read the blue logo on his shirt as he jammed his hands in his pockets and rushed past me to the stairs. I started to say something, but only got as far as "Hey" before he was gone. The heavy metal door boomed as it shut.

Ashley looked upset. I took the man's place on the stool and picked up the handset that was still warm. "Hi," I said.

"Hello."

"How are you holding up? Do you need anything?"

"A one-way ticket to Mexico."

"Anything else?"

"No. Wish I could smoke." I remembered it'd been about eighteen hours since her last cigarette. Maybe that accounted for the attitude.

"Who was that? That just left?"

I watched her compose the lie, eyes darting back and forth as she hesitated. "Nobody. Just some guy from some church."

"Try again."

"Look, he said he wanted to pray with me, so we prayed. What was I supposed to do, tell him to go to hell?"

"What's his name?"

"I don't know."

"C'mon, Ashley. That wasn't some stranger. You know him. Who is he?"

"I'm done here." She started to hang up the phone.

"Wait, wait! Okay, it's none of my business."

"You got that right."

"What about Flash? Somebody slashed my tires yesterday. That sounds like something he'd do, doesn't it? Is he back in the picture?"

She wouldn't make eye contact with me.

I asked, quietly, "Were you using again?"

She didn't say anything. "Ashley, you were always honest with me. I still believe in you. You were doing so well. But I can't help you if I don't know what's going on."

Her gaze finally met mine, and in her eyes was the deepest sadness I'd ever seen. "You can't help me. No one can." She hung up the handset and, head down, approached the guard who buzzed her through to the other side.

CHAPTER FIVE

Pondering Ashley's secretive behavior, I checked out at the security station, retrieved my bags, and walked into the bright summer sun. Cicero's words were etched above the door of the building: "We are in bondage to the law so that we might be free." Seeing them reminded me of another of his quotes: "The first duty of a man is the seeking after and the investigation of truth." What was Ashley's truth? Was she using again? Or protecting someone? The guy at the jail, maybe? Or Flash, if she was back with him?

I made a quick pit stop at the ATM and went back to the office to wait for Royanne and our standing lunch date. She and I both work downtown. She's a loan officer at Birmingham Financial Bank. On Thursdays, we take turns driving to our usual restaurant, and this was her week. I dropped my briefcase in my office and went down to meet her in the lobby.

I was resting an arm on the tall central desk where our two receptionists, Nancy and Beth, sat. Nancy was telling me about her family's recent vacation to Disney World when a man walked in. He stopped in front of Beth, who was taking a call, and waited for her to finish. Average height, with spiky black hair, and eyes two shades darker than the light blue dress shirt he was wearing. The shirtsleeves were rolled up, revealing strong forearms. He had a round face and ruddy cheeks. There was something very Irish — and very cute — about him.

He caught sight of me and smiled. A nice smile. "Hi," he said with a nod.

"Hi," I said.

"You work here?" He squinted at the ID badge hung around my neck on a breast cancer awareness lanyard. "Claire?"

"Yep."

"Must be a difficult job."

"Some days are better than others."

He broke out that charming smile again just as Beth routed her call and hung up. He turned to her and said, "I'm Kirk Mahoney. I've got an eleven thirty appointment with Teresa Pope."

Mahoney. Shit. My hand went up automatically and covered my ID. Kirk turned to say something to me as Beth called upstairs. He saw the look of fury on my face before I could mask it.

"What?" he asked.

It was too late to hide the contempt. "Read your article this morning."

"Oh, I see. Care to make a comment?"

"I can't do that."

"Then I'll see what Dr. Pope has to say." We stood there in awkward silence, with me shooting him dirty looks, until the silver elevator doors opened and Dr. Pope walked out. She was well put together in a suit that complemented her brownish-gray bob. She greeted Kirk with a handshake and all the friendliness in the world. She saw me, and the angry expression on my face, and asked, "Claire, you okay?"

"Sure."

She threw me a skeptical glance and cordially invited Kirk up to her office. She pressed the up button and moments later Russell exited the elevator as they entered. I got one last dagger look in before the doors closed.

"Wow. Who's the hottie?" Russell asked.

"Bite your tongue. He's the guy who wrote the article in the newspaper this morning."

"What are you doing down here?"

"Waiting for Royanne."

"That's right, it's Thursday."

"Want to join us?"

"Thanks, but I don't have time." He glanced at the clock above the front desk. "I've got a lunch meeting with one of my clients. See you."

Russell walked out through the glass front door, the seal of the State of Alabama painted on it. Five minutes later, Royanne bounced in the same door. With big breasts, wide hips, and blonde hair teased out to the stratosphere, she bounced everywhere. "You ready?"

"Yeah, let's go."

Her minivan, still running, was parked in the fire lane. We settled in and she pulled onto Third Avenue North. A couple of miles later she asked, "You okay?"

I realized that I hadn't said a word since we left. A little ember of anger toward the reporter was still burning in my chest. And Ashley's eyes, laden with such intense misery, haunted me. "It's that case."

"Right. The one you can't talk about."

"You see the paper this morning?"

"Not yet. Why?"

"Some jerk named Kirk is already calling me incompetent. Except he doesn't know it's me."

"Of course you're not."

"I know."

"Claire, it's not like you killed him. His mother did."

My ember burned a little hotter, and I jumped to Ashley's defense. "That's just it, I don't think so."

"Well, maybe not intentionally."

"She was doing really well. I don't think she would have done anything to hurt her kid. Any more than you'd do something to endanger one of yours."

"So, accidents happen."

"Maybe."

"I feel sorry for the rest of the family. What about his poor grandparents? Can you imagine, having your grandchild die and your daughter locked up for homicide?"

DHS's policy was to try to place a child with relatives first, not foster parents. Two years ago, I'd met with Ashley's mother, Dee, to ask if she could care for ten-month-old Michael while Ashley got straight. At the time, Dee was in tough shape financially, and I had some concerns as to whether or not she could afford a baby. Dee was hardly the cookie-baking, story-reading type. But it did make me wonder if anyone had called her and her husband. Had Ashley, before she went to jail? I should go out there, I thought, this afternoon, just to see how they were doing.

"Claire?" Royanne said, bringing me back to the present. "You gonna be okay?"

"Sure. This will pass, eventually. Her trial and all will be hell, but I'll be all right."

"You think you'll get fired?"

"I don't think so. Not unless something comes up that I didn't know about."

"What would you do if you did? Get fired, I mean?"

Good question. For the first time, I thought about it. I'd held other social work positions before this one. I'd done interventions with the homeless, often under bridges and in alleyways, getting substance-abusing vets into treatment centers. Then I'd gone to grad school, gotten my M.S.W., and worked for a short while at a community mental health center before coming to DHS. This job was by far the most stressful. The hours were long and the decisions life-and-death. At times it could be dangerous. Still, I enjoyed the investigative side of it. Did I really want to give it up?

"I don't know." I wasn't ready to reevaluate my career choice. The idea was depressing. Too depressing.

Los Compadres Mexican restaurant was located in a strip mall on a busy corner. It was a popular lunch spot, and groups of diners were already filing in to be seated.

"Can you go get us a table?" I asked. "I need to make a quick call."

"Sure."

I stood outside the car in the heat and, fanning myself with one hand, dialed a number with the other.

"Brighton," he answered. He sounded like his mouth was full.

"Detective, it's Claire Conover. I'm sorry to disturb you, but I was wondering if I could ask you a question."

"Sure." He swallowed whatever he was eating.

"I saw Ashley this morning, and I'm worried about her. Is she on suicide watch?"

"She is."

"Oh, good. Do you know if her court date has been set?"

"Tomorrow afternoon at two. It's going to be a short trip to sentencing."

I was suddenly on a carnival ride, the earth tilting sideways. "She's going to plead guilty?"

"She's not even electing to bond herself out of jail. She's claiming she's responsible for her son's death."

"I can't believe that."

"Maybe she was tired of being a mommy."

No, no way. I'd seen them together, her and Michael. Seen them play together. Seen her read to him. Seen the way she looked at him. No way. I was so stunned I couldn't say any of it out loud. Instead I croaked, "No —"

"There was enough GHB in that orange juice to kill them both, easily."

"There was?"

"There was. Who knows? Maybe it was a murder-suicide thing and she chickened out."

My voice wasn't working. "No. No, not —"

"We'll see what she has to say in court. But, yes, she is on suicide watch."

"Thanks."

I clapped my phone shut and steadied myself before going in. Ashley, a deliberate child killer? Murder-suicide? That was crazy. Ashley had never shown a hint of regret about having Michael. I'd have noticed. Wouldn't I?

The restaurant was crowded and loud, with the mariachi music playing from speakers overhead adding to the din of conversation. Sombreros and bright-patterned Mexican blankets decorated the walls. I found Royanne at a table for two in the back.

"I ordered your usual, okay?"

I was still shocked at Brighton's revelation and wasn't hungry. "Fine." Royanne studied my face and decided not to pursue it. She changed the subject.

"You remember Bo?" She had to talk loudly over the music.

"Who?"

"Bo, the friend of Toby's who helped move your stuff."

Oh, yes. Toby had sweetly volunteered his pickup truck, and he and his friend had lugged my furniture from my Southside apartment to my new house four months ago. Nice of them, but I had no illusions that it had been anything less than another step in Royanne's continuing conspiracy to get me married.

"What about him?"

"He wants your number."

I tried to remember what he looked like. I knew he was a deliveryman for the bottling plant, like Toby. Red hair and freckles came to mind. And he had massive muscles. Like Howdy Doody on steroids.

"Oh, Howdy Doody," I muttered.

"What?"

"I said, oh, hallelujah."

"No need to get sarcastic. If you don't want to go out with him, just say so."

"I don't want to go out with him."

"Why?"

"Because."

"That's not an answer."

"Yes, it is. I've seen you use it with your kids."

"That's different."

"Why?"

"Because it's what I say when I don't feel like explaining."

"There you have it."

"He's a nice guy."

"I'm sure he is. I just don't want to go out with him. My life is hell right now, and it's only going to get worse. The last thing I need is a blind date." Or any date. Not that I didn't want to get married. Someday. And have kids. But my history with men lately consisted of one disaster after another. None of them were capable of understanding my work schedule, accusing me of neglecting our relationship when a crisis situation kept me out all night. As if I wouldn't rather be spending time with them instead of rearranging some child's life forever.

Royanne said, "Okay, okay. I'll figure out something to tell Bo."

Our usual waiter, Pablo, brought our lunches, and I managed to work up enough of an appetite to finish a chicken taco. Royanne entertained me with stories about her six-year-old, Alicia, who was always doing something funny. By the time lunch was over, I felt better.

I had thirty-seven phone messages to return that afternoon. The first three were routine work stuff. The fourth got my attention.

"Ashley's in jail because of you, bitch. What happened to your tires is gonna happen to you." The message ended. It was a man's voice, low and rough. Not one I recognized. This wasn't the first time I'd been threatened, nor would it be the last, assuming after all this was over I got to keep my job. Usually my clients said what they had to say, and that was the end of it.

But this message was a little different. Maybe because my tires had already been cut. That showed he, whoever he was, was serious. I was mad, but I also felt a little prickle of fear in my gut. I buzzed Mac and he came over to our cubicle to listen to the message. He'd document it, but beyond that there wasn't much he could do. The State of Alabama had yet to spring for caller ID, so there was no way to know where the call had come from.

I had a sneaking suspicion it was Flash. I remembered his harassing phone calls to Ashley during the first days of her stay at St. Monica's. This was definitely his MO. While it was possible the message could have come from anyone angry about Michael's death, that kind of anger was usually directed at the agency, not at me personally. After all, only a few people knew I was Michael's social worker. Flash was one of them.

After Mac left, I went back to the rest of my messages. Three of them were from Michael's former foster parents, devastated about what happened and wanting to know if there was anything they could do. I told them to contact Nona, then picked up the phone to call her myself.

The secretary connected me immediately. "Nona Richardson."

"It's Claire. How're you holding up?"

"That's the question I was going to ask you."

"I'm okay."

"I was gonna call you this afternoon. Cheyenne left this morning."

Not that I was surprised, but I was still disappointed. "When?"

"She took off right before lunch."

"Okay, thanks." Her kids, who had been in foster care for years, would have to go up for adoption. I scribbled a note on my to-do list to call Legal and start the termination of her parental rights.

Nona went on. "Nice article in the paper this morning, huh?"

"Tell me about it. Have you seen Ashley?"

"I went by there about an hour ago. She's so sad."

"I know. I made sure she's on suicide watch. What's got me puzzled is that, according to Detective Brighton, she's going to plead guilty. Has she said anything to you about that? Or anything about what happened?"

"She wouldn't talk to me at all, which is unusual. She always confided in me, even during the worst part of her recovery. I was there for her detox. I've seen her at rock bottom. She's never clammed up like this. I'm worried."

"Same here. Listen, Michael's former foster parents want to donate money for his funeral. I told them to call you."

"Thanks. We're trying to set the service for next Tuesday. I'll be in touch."

I was grateful to Nona for planning Michael's service. But what could you say about an existence that was so short and filled with so much trauma? There wasn't an apology big enough to cover what the grown-ups in his life had put him through. As I gathered my things to go see Dee, Michael's grandmother, I wondered if she would want to eulogize him in any way. Or, considering her rocky history with her daughter, if she would even show up at his memorial.

CHAPTER SIX

It was just past three thirty when I left DHS for Ashley's mom's place. She lived in the northwest corner of the county in a tiny coal mining community called Adger. To get there I navigated to Allison-Bonnet Memorial Drive, named for Neil Bonnet and Davey Allison, two deceased NASCAR drivers. With the Talladega track only about an hour away, this town was crazy about racing.

As I drove northwest, suburbs turned into towns and soon became hamlets. When the street names changed to county road numbers, I knew I was getting close and had to consult the directions I'd copied from the case file.

I hoped Dee was home. She worked at an auto plant in the next county, on the assembly line. Truth be told, she probably made really good money. Maybe even more than I did. But a string of bad marriages had left her living paycheck to paycheck. From what Ashley told me, her previous husbands stuck her with mounds of debt she was still trying to pay off. She managed every month to scrape together enough for the bills. Her third husband, Al, drank or gambled away what was left.

I made a final turn onto the gravel driveway in front of the Mackey's house, a double-wide prefab on a wooded acre. Some of the cream vinyl siding was mildew stained, and parts of the bottom skirting were missing, showing the pipes underneath. A fire pit in the side yard was used to burn trash since no pick up was available out here. Around the blackened area lay a few plastic cups and cardboard beer boxes that hadn't made it into the inferno. I walked up a narrow dirt footpath, past an algae-covered birdbath, and up four steps to the front door. An air conditioner jutted out of the window next to the door, so I knocked loudly to be heard over its whirring.

Dee opened the door. Some of her features were similar to her daughter's, especially the long, straight brown hair. She was shorter and heavier than Ashley, but the resemblance was there. I guessed she was about to leave for work, since she wore a navy jumpsuit with the car company's logo on the left side of her chest. She greeted me and invited me in.

Al was there too. No surprise, since he didn't have a job. He had thin brown hair and two days of stubble on his face. He wore shorts, and over his large belly a T-shirt sported the slogan of a New Orleans oyster house. "Eat Me Raw" was emblazoned on the front. He was focused on a baseball game on TV, the Braves versus someone I couldn't make out. The Blue Jays, maybe. He lounged in an enormous green recliner and didn't bother to get up when I entered. The ends of the armrests of his chair were black with dirt. One had a built-in cup holder that cradled a condensation-covered can of Bud Light. It was twenty past four. Oh, well. It's always five o'clock somewhere, right?

Dee offered me a seat on the couch. Al swiveled around to face me but didn't mute the television.

I cleared my throat. "Have you heard about Michael? And Ashley?"

Dee answered, after a glance at Al. "Ashley called us Tuesday mornin', when the police was still there."

"Oh. I just wanted to come out and say how sorry I am about what's happened. Is there anything I can do?"

"I'm gonna try to go see her tomorrow. Me and her need to talk about what to do about the funeral."

"One of Ashley's friends has gotten together a fund for the burial and is planning a memorial. She's trying to set it for next Tuesday. Did you have something particular in mind that you wanted to do?"

Dee looked relieved, and at the word "fund," Al's gaze snapped to attention. "No, I don't think so. Whatever her friend wants to do is okay with me."

"How are you holding up?"

Al decided to stick in his two valuable cents. "We're all right. Cain't say I'm surprised at what happened. That's what you get when you mess with drugs. That kid's prob'ly better off dead than havin' some crack whore for a momma."

There was no use in defending Ashley; it would be pointless. But I felt sorry for Dee, stone-faced, next to me. I continued as if Al hadn't opened his fat mouth. "I'll have her friend Nona call you when the arrangements are finalized. I'm sure if you wanted to say a few words, she could arrange it."

The thought of speaking to a crowd of people clearly made Dee nervous. "Nah, that's okay. I wouldn't know what to say, no how. I got to be at work at five, so I gotta go." I rose along with her as Al's concentration returned to the game. I wondered which team he had bet on.

Dee picked up her purse and keys from the messy counter separating the kitchen from the long, narrow living room. "Bye, baby," she said to Al.

"Bye." He took a swig of the beer.

Dee walked me to my car. I said once again how sorry I was about Michael's death.

"Thanks. I'm gonna miss that kid. I don't know if Ashley told you, but she'd been bringing him up here on the weekends some. They was up here just last weekend. I got me one of them inflatable pools and we put it out here in the yard with the sprinkler an' all. He had so much fun splashing around." For the first time since I'd arrived, I saw her eyes darken with grief. "And Ashley, she was doing so good. She was thinking about going back to school. Getting her GED, and maybe taking some classes someplace. She always did do good in school, before she ran off."

I nodded. "I bet she'd do well."

Tears began, leaking slowly out of the hazel eyes that were so like Ashley's. She wiped them away with her fingers. "I gave her some money. It wasn't a lot, jus' two hundred dollars. Something she could use to help pay for school someday. Al found out and got so pissed. He said she's an adult now and needs to stand on her own two feet."

The thought of Al Mackey as anyone's life coach almost made me laugh out loud. I held my face somber as Dee continued. "I guess I can see his point, but I just wanted to do something to help her."

"If she were my daughter, I'd have done the same thing."

"Really?"

"Sure."

"Now I gotta get me some money together for the lawyer."

"Do you know who Ashley's lawyer is?"

"I found her one Tuesday. His name's Samuel Hamilton. He's supposed to be real good."

I knew "Sam the Ham" by reputation. He was fond of high-profile defense cases and courtroom theatrics. And she was right, he was good. I had one more question to ask her. "Dee, do you think that Ashley could've spent the two hundred dollars you gave her on drugs? Do you think she was using again?"

"I guess she coulda. I ain't seen her high lately, and believe me, I know when she is. I was kinda shocked when I heard how Michael died, 'cause it didn't seem like she was into drugs again. I know the signs." Dee sniffled and wiped her face one last time. "I gotta go, I'm gonna be late."

"I'll call you soon."

I backed my car out of the driveway. Following her fifteen-year-old Chevy Cavalier all the way to the interstate, I reflected that Ashley's mother knew her pretty well. And that made two of us who didn't think she was on the junk again.

GHB was done in capfuls, a fact I bet Ashley knew. She was no rookie when it came to drug use. If she put the GHB in the orange juice, she must have known that the amount could have killed her. And Michael. Why would she put a ton of it in a pitcher? Then pour

Michael a sippy cup full of what was essentially poison? She'd worked so hard in rehab and afterward to build a life for them both. By my reckoning, someone else had put the GHB there and Ashley didn't know about it.

If she'd been partying the night before and one of her buddies made the juice, why not say so? Why not point the finger at the person who did it? Ashley's silence was troubling. Was she protecting a friend? Someone who had been there that night? Maybe. The only alternative was that she didn't know who put the G in the pitcher, either. Which meant it was an attempt on their lives.

I didn't think anyone would knowingly murder a small child. Who would want to OD a toddler on purpose? Was the overdose meant for Ashley? Probably. So who would want to kill her? That seemed to be the question. Flash? He fit the profile of an abuser to a T. He had a history of being violent and dangerous.

Or Ashley's stepfather, maybe? To keep his wife from sneaking her money? Would he go that far? The thought stayed in the back of my mind throughout the evening.

Friday morning storms were imminent. After calling our secretary to tell her I'd be in a little late, I searched through the phone book and found a place that fixed computers. The shop was in Hoover, not far from my house. I unplugged the computer and lugged it out to the car, tossed in an umbrella, and headed down the mountain.

The sky opened up while I was driving, thick raindrops slamming into the windshield. The repair place was in a small shopping center near the Galleria, the large mall that was the hub of this upper-middle class, soccer-mom city. I parked my car next to a minivan. On its door was a graphic of a computer with an arrow on the monitor pointing upward and the words HIGH TECH underneath the picture. Fearing water would further damage the machine, I struggled to carry it under one arm while attempting to keep it — and me — under the shelter of the umbrella. By the time I shoved my way through the glass door, I was soaked from head to toe.

Two men were in the shop. A Middle-eastern guy who looked to be in his early twenties was restocking boxes of software onto metal racks that filled most of the space. The other, a man about my age, was working behind a counter. He was hunched over a tableful of electronic thingamajigs, an open computer case in front of him, a small screwdriver in his hand. A bank of computers purred on more tables behind him. He heard me banging through the door and jumped up so fast he whacked his knee painfully on the table. "Let me help you with that."

He reminded me of a tree. He was easily over six three, dressed in dark khaki pants and a loose, green polo shirt tucked in over a flat stomach. He rushed over and relieved me of the computer, placing it on the long red counter where the cash register sat.

"Thanks," I said, shaking the water off my hands and wiping it off my face. My hair was drenched, and my short-sleeved sweater was sticking to me like cling wrap. He was looking at me expectantly, a few chestnut-colored curls of hair loosely draped across his forehead. Bright green eyes stood out behind a pair of geeky tortoise-shell glasses.

"How can we help you?"

"Um, my computer's broken." Well said, Claire.

"What's the problem?" He went behind the counter and retrieved a pad of work-order forms and a pen.

"When I turn it on it makes a clanking noise, and nothing comes on the screen." I was dripping all over the floor. The young man who'd been stocking the shelves disappeared into a back room and brought me some brown recycled paper towels. I thanked him.

"It won't boot?"

"Nope." I tried to dry myself off a bit with the towels.

He wrote something on the pad. "Sounds like your hard drive."

"That's what I was afraid of. Are they expensive?"

"About a hundred bucks for the drive, and another fifty for the labor. Plus a diagnostic fee."

Damn. That was almost two hundred bucks I was hoping to put

toward new countertops for the kitchen. Not to mention the bill I'd paid for the tires. Oh, well. "Okay." I agreed, biting my lip.

Seeing the look on my face, he gave me a small smile. "Tell you what. I'll waive the diagnostic fee and labor costs, and only charge you for the hard drive."

"You don't have to do that."

"I know, but I'm a nice guy." His smile widened, but he looked away abruptly when I smiled back.

"Thanks."

He went back to writing on the work order. "I'll need some info. Your name and address?"

I gave them to him. He had small, neat handwriting. "Work number?"

"The Department of Human Services." I fished out a business card and handed it over.

His eyebrows went up. "You've been in the news a lot lately."

"Tell me about it."

He wrote my work and cell numbers on the form. Not looking up from his writing, he asked, "Is there a Mr. Conover?"

"No." I tucked a wet wisp of blonde hair behind my ear. Dragged a finger underneath my eye, and sure enough, it came away black. My mascara was running.

He asked, "Did you bring your discs?"

"Discs?"

"Your software, to reload the machine."

"I didn't think about it. Do you need them today?" I glanced at my watch. "I've got to get to work."

"We're open tomorrow from ten to five. I should have your drive installed by then, if you want to bring them by."

"Okay, I'll do that."

We shook hands as he thanked me for coming in. Mine was wet and cold, his was warm and strong. "Let me give you a card." He took a business card from a black metal holder near the cash register. Printed on it was the same logo I'd seen on the van outside, along with the name GRANT SUMMERVILLE and the shop's numbers and address.

I put the card in my purse and said, "See you tomorrow, Grant."

"I'll be here."

A Starbucks was next door to the shop, and I decided a tall latte was in order. I bought a paper from a coin-operated box outside the coffee house, ordered my drink, and settled down at a table for a minute to wait on it. I scanned the first page, full of stories about the latest terrorist plot and the president's recent trip to Asia. The only local news was about a drug bust on I-459. I read the list of obituaries. Michael's wasn't there.

As the college-age girl from behind the counter delivered my latte, I flipped to the editorial section. Three missives about DHS helped make up the letters to the editor section. All three railed on my agency, using words like "shame" and "tragedy" and the ever-present "incompetent." One ignoramus even called for Dr. Pope's resignation.

Granted, over the years I'd known some incompetent social workers. And it seemed that some mishandled case was always dominating the national news. But some of us were quite able to do our jobs, thank you very much, and do them well. I was one of them, or so I thought before Tuesday. The letters stung and reinforced my fear that I'd missed something.

Then it got worse. I flipped to the next section. As I expected, Kirk Mahoney was present in full force. The oversized headline asked: WHAT'S WRONG AT DHS? I took a sip of the hot house blend, feeling the heat slide over my tongue and down to the pit of my stomach.

CHAPTER SEVEN

The headline of Kirk's article filled me with dread. Reluctantly, I read on:

> For several years, the Department of Human Services has been haunted by deaths of children under its care. Six years ago, infant Annabelle Litton was shaken to death by her father, just days after DHS opened her case. Then LaDarren Baker, a foster child, died from a suspicious skull fracture. Now little Michael Hennessy can be added to this list.

I remembered those cases. The first happened just before I was hired. Our director had been asked to resign, along with the caseworker and her supervisor, since the case wasn't investigated when — or how — it should have been. In the second one, the foster parent was never prosecuted but the worker in the foster care unit was reprimanded. Unfairly, I thought. She was a friend of mine. I kept reading:

> DHS's new director, Dr. Teresa Pope, vowed when she was appointed to increase the level of supervision over the caseworkers and to reduce caseload sizes. She has stated repeatedly that worker incompetence will not be tolerated. But can Dr. Pope guide this agency into greater accountability and ensure the safety of the county's smallest citizens?

Mahoney went on to outline Dr. Pope's background, from her Ph.D. in social work from Columbia University to her previous job as the head of a local mental health center. Most of it I already knew. Mahoney was a genius at leaving just a trace of doubt as to whether or not she was qualified to do the job. Then,

> While Dr. Pope states that she cannot comment on Michael Hennessy's death, she would like to reassure the public that many of the reforms needed have been put into place. "Caseloads have been reduced to a more manageable level, and a new licensing requirement has been added for all employees. We still need more funding to increase salaries and recruit more foster parents."

Good for you, Dr. Pope. You go, girl. I read Mahoney's last paragraph.

> These improvements, however, are too late to help two-year-old Michael. The question remains why this child was placed in danger, with a parent unable, or perhaps unwilling, to keep him out of harm's way. Dr. Pope asserts that an investigation is underway at the State level, and should the agency be found culpable, disciplinary action will be swift and exhaustive.

I reread the last paragraph again. I had to hand it to Mahoney. The article was good. It made DHS sound competent, but defensive. And it laid out just enough blame to be good reading. Damn him.

I folded the paper and threw what was left of my latte in the trash. I fumed all the way to the eastern precinct to pick up a copy of my police report. Then to the office, where numerous phone messages waited for me. One was from Nona, confirming Michael's memorial for Tuesday at eleven a.m. at Harris and Sons. I wrote it on my calendar. I returned a few calls to clients, then worked on my case notes from yesterday, including documenting my meeting with Dee and Al. As I was filing the paperwork in the Hennessy chart, I realized something was missing.

I'd never run a background check on Al.

I combed through the chart again, making sure I hadn't missed it. Ashley's was there, so was Dee's. All clear. Why hadn't I done one on Al? I tried to remember back to when I got the case. Was Al married to Dee then? I couldn't remember. If he hadn't been her husband or boyfriend at the time, I wouldn't have done one.

After writing down some information and putting the chart away, I took the elevator up to the fourth floor. Along with the director's office, the Adult Services Department was here, and I walked through their area. Over the last four days I'd noticed more inquisitive looks coming my way. Some people were discreet about it, shooting me furtive glances as they passed my cubicle. Some were more overt, and many had stopped me to express their condolences. The Adult Services folks were the same. After what happened to the workers in the cases Mahoney mentioned in his article, I couldn't blame them for their curiosity about what was going to happen to me. I wondered myself.

I came to what was once the customer service desk of the former Barwick's Department Store. Behind the glass sat Michele, who ran our records department. She was a few years older than me, with short brown hair and an air of organized efficiency. A computer and high-speed printer stood ready on a built-in workstation behind her. Stacks of paper in black plastic trays covered the rest of the surface.

"Hey," she said to me, sliding open the small window. "I've been worried about you. How're you doing?"

"I'm okay I guess."

"You heard anything about what the State's going to do?"

"Nothing yet."

"By the way, I've got some bad news for you."

Like I needed that. "What?"

"My cousin found a girlfriend."

So that was it. Michele was another active member of the

"Conspiracy to Get Claire Married." She'd been trying to fix me up with her forty-something-year-old cousin for months. She swore up and down he looked just like Rob Lowe. Inwardly, I was happy to hear someone had snatched him up.

"Oh, that's too bad."

"She's real nice, and they seem pretty serious."

"My tough luck, I guess."

"Y'all would have made a cute couple. What can I do for you?"

"I need a Registry check."

She handed me an 8-1941 form. The Registry was the State's record of who had been accused of child abuse, and whether the case was founded or unfounded. I filled in the little biographical data I had on Al, mostly just his name, address, and age, and handed it back to her. "Give me a sec and I'll do it now."

I waited, leaning on the desk and watching her type all the fields into the computer. She hit enter and turned back to me. "So, my cousin has this friend—"

I held up a hand. "Stop. I don't do blind dates."

"Why?"

"Because they are always a disaster." My mind drifted back to the last blind date I'd agreed to, after graduate school. He didn't want a date, he wanted sex. It had taken me over an hour to extricate myself from his wandering hands and call a cab home.

"Not always."

"For me, always."

The printer behind her made a little click and a whirring noise. A second later it spewed out pages.

"Uh-oh," Michele said, "It looks like your boy's had a few number ones on the Hit Parade."

I closed my eyes as my stomach sank. Damn, damn, damn. Michele paper clipped the sheets from the printer and handed them to me. "Here you go."

"Thanks."

I stood at the desk and studied the pages. At the top in all caps was listed the name of the alleged perpetrator. Allen Pierce Mackey. He was forty-one. The last known address listed was different from his current one. Hair: brown. Eyes: brown. Height: 5' 11". Weight: 280. That was him all right.

Below that was the alleged victim. Heather Lynn Mackey. Parents: Tina Lynn Mackey and Allen Pierce Mackey. Heather's date of birth was listed too, and after a quick calculation I worked out that she was now twenty. I checked the date of the first allegation. She'd been three years old.

Listed below were two columns, the codes for what we had investigated in Al's case and the findings. There were three entries. The first said PHYSABCH UNFSUS. Physical Abuse of Child, and the agency had ruled it unfounded but suspicious. Meaning that a child in Al's care showed suspicious injuries he denied causing, but the circumstances seemed to be more than a mere accident.

Next was PHYSABCH FOUN. Physical Abuse of Child, Founded. Meaning that the caseworker had solid evidence that Al had abused this girl. That case was when Heather was seven. Another PHYS-ABCH FOUN was the same year, when she was almost eight. What our system couldn't tell me was whether or not Al was prosecuted. Those records were kept by the justice system, not DHS. There might be a footnote in the record, or there might not.

So, Al Mackey was a child abuser. And I hadn't known a thing about it.

Michele interrupted my reading. "Are you going to want to see the chart?"

"Yeah."

Michele filled out a blue 8-1705 form, Request for Record. I signed it after she handed it to me. "You let me know if you change your mind about my cousin's friend."

"Okay. I wouldn't hold your breath though."

I took my blue form down to the basement. The cavernous area that once stored additional inventory of clothes, shoes, ties, and handbags in the 1930s was now filled to the ceiling with electric racks of case files. Social workers weren't allowed in, but instead rang a buzzer at a door once we stepped off the elevator into the small hallway. I hit the button and waited.

Dolly opened the door, as usual. She'd been with DHS since God was a boy. Her hairstyle was a gray sixties bouffant that never moved, and her clothes were from the same decade, dowdy dresses with over-sized collars. Her skin was paper thin and just as pale. She was sweet, though, and I was fond of her.

"Hello, Claire," she said. "What do you need?"

I handed her my blue form and we made small talk. She didn't mention Michael. I wondered how much she knew about what went on upstairs, since she spent most of her day in this dungeon, purging old charts.

She went to find the chart I wanted and returned with it several minutes later. I thanked her and took it to my office. Behind my desk, I opened the faded brown folder and began to read.

It took me forty-five minutes to go through it all. The investigating social worker on the first case, seventeen years ago, was someone whose name I didn't recognize. She was long gone. Her case notes revealed she'd been contacted by a babysitter who'd reported that three-year-old Heather had several bruises on her bottom and the back of her legs. Interviews with both parents were conducted. Tina denied ever spanking Heather. Al admitted to spanking her after she ran into the street, but stated he hadn't left the bruises. He claimed those were from her falling off the end of the slide in the backyard. Her parents were referred to parenting classes at the agency and the case was closed.

The next social worker was someone whose name I did recognize. Danessa Brown, now a supervisor in the foster care unit, one floor above me. She'd been an investigator thirteen years ago. I read her meticulous notes. When Heather was in second grade, Danessa was called out to the school by the guidance counselor who'd noticed several bruises on Heather's legs. Heather revealed how she got them from her daddy spanking her, and the case was sent to court on a dependency charge. That was so the court could supervise the family and place Heather out of the home if needed. Al was required to go to parenting classes, ordered not to spank the child under any circumstances, and to attend AA meetings. The case was left open for oversight by DHS.

Danessa made regular contact with Heather, as required, and noted that two months after the court appearance, Al moved out. I got the feeling from reading between the lines that sobriety was too much of a strain on his marriage. He visited regularly with his daughter, though, and just before she turned eight, more bruises appeared. Once again, brave little Heather told exactly where she got them, the case went back to court, and Al was ordered to have no contact with his daughter whatsoever. The case was closed a year and a half later after no further incidents.

I closed the chart and put my face in my hands. All this time, Al Mackey's record was two floors below me and I didn't know. How was the state office going to react to that one? Why in the hell hadn't I run his background check two years ago?

Time to go see Danessa. I took the chart with me up the stairs to the third floor and made my way to the perimeter of the foster care unit's area. She, too, had a window office with a plate glass front that overlooked cubicles in the middle, just like Mac's. Hers was more cheerfully decorated, with plants and jazz concert posters.

Danessa sat behind the large desk. She was in her late forties, and I speculated she was getting close to the magic twenty-years-of-service mark. A lot of our long-timers left at that point, since they could draw full retirement from the State. She had soft black hair that rested on her shoulders, a few gray threads visible. Crows' feet and laugh lines stood out like wood grain in mahogany. A pair of half-moon reading glasses balanced on her nose. She had a boisterous personality and a lot of spirit. I wouldn't have minded being in her unit, come to think of it.

She was writing something, but stopped when she saw me in the doorway. "Claire! What you up to, girl?"

"Can I interrupt for a sec?"

"Sure, come on in."

I stepped in and closed the door, then took a seat in the burgundy metal-framed chair in front of her desk.

She asked, "How have you been? I heard about that case of yours." Funny how no one used the word "death." Like it was bad luck or something. Like saying Macbeth in a theater.

"Yeah. Michael."

"You afraid they're gonna make you a scapegoat?"

She didn't mince words, so neither did I. "Yep."

"Fight for it, girl, you hear? If you don't want to leave, don't let them make you."

"I'll try."

"Not good enough. You're too good to go someplace else. If you want this job, make sure you keep it."

The pep talk cheered me a bit. "Thanks."

"What can I do for you?"

"I wanted to pick your brain about a case from thirteen years ago."

She hooted. "Girl, you know I can't remember what happened last week, but I'll try."

"The Mackey case. The little girl was seven. You did two abuse investigations in the same year. Bruises. Dad was the perp. He wound up moving out and the court ordered him to have no contact. Ring a bell?"

She thought back, her faraway gaze on a framed Wynton Marsalis poster. "Oh, yeah," she said slowly. "Al. Little girl was Heather. Smart kid. Pretty, too. Lots of wispy black hair, just like her momma. Only child, thank God. He was a drunk."

"That's him. I don't suppose he was ever prosecuted?"

" 'Course not. The mother didn't want Heather to testify against her own father, and he probably wouldn't have done much time anyway. Wasn't worth it to the D.A. Why? What's his sorry ass done now?"

"My kid that died? He was his stepgrandfather."

"Oh, crap. You think he had something to do with it?"

"I don't know."

"Your kid OD'd, right? On mamma's drugs?"

"He OD'd. I'm not sure the drugs were mamma's."

"Al's MO was more smacking them around. If your boy —"

"Michael."

"If Michael had been beaten to death, then I'd be suspicious for sure. Is Al doing drugs?"

"I don't think so. He's still a drunk, and a gambler."

"Nice."

"No kidding. Thanks for the info."

"Hang in there, kid. And remember what I said."

"I will."

I returned the file to Dolly in the basement and went back to my cubicle to get my things, where I literally ran into Michele.

"There you are. I was looking for you. You want to go to lunch?"

"Thanks, I'd love to, but I've already got plans."

I headed north a few blocks to the Top of the Hill Grill. The restaurant squatted on a small rise of ground near the Convention Center, and was walking distance from the courthouses and towering financial institutions downtown. It was a popular lunch spot for those who wanted something hot and fast. The fare was typical diner stuff, hamburgers and club sandwiches and a daily special. It was also where Ashley had worked every weekday from eleven to four.

I circled the block and parked at a meter. Hoofed it back to the restaurant, made my way around the chalkboard sign announcing the specials, and went in. A long green Formica counter ran the length of the space, and a few small tables sat in front of the windows. The place was half full but buzzed with loud conversation. The special today was fried catfish, and the oily rich smell pervaded the place. The bells on the door jangled and I froze.

Sitting at the counter, in front of a crumb-covered plate, was Kirk Mahoney.

CHAPTER EIGHT

Today's dress shirt was pink, sleeves again rolled to just below the elbows. The pink emphasized the ruddiness of his skin and made his blue eyes a shade lighter than I remembered. He was chatting up a waitress with purple-streaked hair and ketchup stains on her apron. The bells on the door announced my entrance and caught their attention. Kirk the Jerk's eyebrows went up.

"Well, hello, Claire from DHS. What brings you here?"

"I'm here to eat lunch."

"Not fond of good food then?'

The unamused waitress snorted a "huh" and cleared his plate away.

"I wouldn't come here again," I said. "She'll probably spit in your food."

"Why do I have a sneaking suspicion you'd be fine with that?"

I bit back a smile, took a seat at the counter several stools down from him, and pointedly stared at the menu. In my peripheral vision I saw him look at his check, lay down a ten out of his wallet, and stand up. He swaggered over and hovered at my shoulder. His cologne mixed with the smell of frying oil and fish.

"Come take a walk with me."

"No."

"Why not?"

"I don't have anything to say to you."

"Yeah, yeah, yeah." He lifted the laminated menu out of my hands and laid it down on the counter. "Five minutes," he said, executing a gentle grip on my upper left arm. "I won't bite."

He led me out the door. The heat of the day was peaking and, after the rain, it was muggy. Steam rose off the sidewalk. Kirk put a toothpick in his mouth, which bobbed up and down as he talked. "Walk with me to my car."

"What is it you want?" I asked.

"I want to know why you hate me."

"I don't hate you. I don't hate anybody. I hate what you are doing to — my agency." I almost said "to me" but caught myself in time.

He stopped and faced me. "What? What am I doing to your agency? The article I wrote about Dr. Pope was very fair."

I lost it. "Hah!" I sputtered, "Are you kidding? You've done nothing but point out all of our failures. Bringing up all those old cases. Using words like incompetent and mismanaged, and making us sound like a bunch of unfeeling idiots."

I was really getting mad now. I could tell because my eyes were filling with tears. I always cry when I'm really angry, but I didn't want Kirk to see that. Trying in vain to calm myself, I went on. "Why the hell don't you ever write about all the good stuff DHS does? About all the kids we save from sexual abuse. Or about all the crack babies we've found homes for? About the kids we've taken out of dangerous meth labs? We save lives, damn it! Lots of them. But nobody ever hears about that." My voice was cracking and my eyes were welling up again. I brushed the tears away quickly with my hand.

Kirk took the toothpick out of his mouth. His head cocked and his eyes squinted as he studied me. Then he finally put two and two together.

"It was your case, wasn't it?"

Through clenched teeth I said, "I can't talk about it." I whirled around and walked quickly back to the diner. Thankfully he didn't follow me. In the distance, I heard a car door shut, then the engine roar as he drove away.

I took a second outside to compose myself. I pulled a mirror from my purse to make sure what was left of my mascara wasn't streaking down my cheeks. It wasn't, but my face was red and I was sweating. I put the mirror away, went back in, and sat down.

The purple-haired waitress approached me. "You okay?"

"Hi, Brandi. I'm fine. Don't I look fine?"

"You look rattled. Don't worry, he asked a lot of questions about Ashley, but I didn't answer them. She don't need all of her business up in the paper."

Brandi was Ashley's best friend. They were the same age, twenty-three. Brandi didn't have any children yet, and she didn't have the same history of addiction. But Brandi had enough violence and pain in her past to be able to relate to Ashley. It was the cement that held their friendship together. I'd met her twice, once here at work and once at Ashley's apartment when I'd done a spot-check on Michael. That day, Ashley and Brandi had been sitting on the sofa, barefoot, talking and giggling. A different time. A different Ashley.

"Have you seen Ashley?" I asked.

"I haven't been able to get off work during visiting hours. I'm going tomorrow."

"She looks miserable."

"I'm sure."

A portly gray-haired man in a navy suit sitting at the other end of the counter said, "Excuse me —"

"Be right there," Brandi said to him. "Are you going to want anything to eat?" she asked me.

I scanned the menu. "Sure, um, the hamburger, I guess. With chips."

She scribbled my order on her pad, tore off the sheet and placed it in the window that led to the kitchen. I continued, "Can I ask you something?"

The elderly man said again, "Excuse me —"

She rolled her eyes. "Hold on." She walked the length of the counter, slapped his ticket down in front of him, and whisked his plate away just as he shoveled in the last bite. He left without leaving a tip. Brandi put his plate in the window and came back to me. "Sorry. What were you saying?"

"Do you know if Ashley was seeing anyone?"

She looked uncomfortable. "Why?"

No immediate denial. I decided to tell her. "I keep seeing this green Dodge Charger around. Looks like something Flash might drive, and someone slashed my tires and left a threatening message on my voice mail at work. Sounds like something he might do. Do you know if she was hanging out with him again?"

"She wasn't. I know that for sure. She hates him."

"Then I went by the jail to see her. There was a guy there. They looked like they knew each other pretty well. He had kinda wild hair, brown, and a scraggy beard. Short and heavyset. Ring a bell?"

She didn't say anything for a moment. "I don't know —"

"You heard about the autopsy, right?"

Her eyes went wide. "No."

"Michael died of a GHB overdose. It was in the orange juice in the fridge and in his sippy cup. The detective on the case told me there was enough to kill both of them in the pitcher. Do you think Ashley would pour Michael a cup of juice she knew was laced with drugs?"

Now she looked horrified. "No!"

"Then something else is going on. Rumor has it Ashley's going to plead guilty. For some reason she won't tell anyone what's up. If this guy, whoever he is, knows something about what happened that night, someone needs to talk to him."

A small bell rang behind her. She turned and grabbed three plates off the window, and, balancing one effortlessly on her forearm, delivered them to one of the tables. Then she came back.

"Well?" I asked.

Her voice lowered almost to a whisper. "His name's Jimmy. Jimmy Shelton. He's a maintenance worker in some building around here. He came in for lunch right after Christmas. He and Ashley started talking, then he came in more and more often till it was, like, every day. They'd flirt, you know, and I was picking on her about it a few months ago. I asked her if she was going to go out with Jimmy and she was like, nah, and I said how come, if you like him and all, and she said but he's so much older. And I said that didn't matter. And then she said that she could never go out with anybody that didn't want kids."

Uh-oh. "She said that? That he didn't want kids?"

"That's what she said. So anyways, lately she's been acting weird. Like she's always in a good mood. So I asked her what was going on and she was like, nothing. But I got the feeling that maybe she had a boyfriend. But she wouldn't tell me nothing about it for some reason. Maybe it was Jimmy. I don't know. I know it wasn't Flash. Maybe he was giving her a hard time, but she wouldn't hook up with him again."

From the way Ashley'd looked at Jimmy from behind the glass at the jail, I'd bet money he was the mysterious boyfriend. Could Ashley have killed Michael because the man she loved didn't want him? It had happened before. A famous case about a woman who'd drowned her kids in a lake drifted into my mind.

The bell rang again and Brandi took my hamburger and chips from the window and set the plate in front of me. "Enjoy," she said, and went to take an order at a table. It dawned on me that she was very busy, working alone in Ashley's absence. I wondered how long the manager would let that go on before hiring a replacement for Ashley. Not long, I would imagine. Too bad, because Ashley had really enjoyed this job.

My hamburger was tasty in that greasy-junk-food kind of way, but I ate less than half and only a few chips before asking Brandi for a box. She brought me one and watched as I loaded what was left into it, then clasped the lid closed. Wiping my hands on a napkin, I asked, "Will you call me if Ashley says anything about what happened the night Michael died?"

"Sure. I'll see if I can get her to talk to me."

"And if Jimmy Shelton shows up here call me, okay? And give him one of these?" I fetched two business cards from the holder in my purse and handed them to her. One for her and one for Jimmy. My cell number was handwritten over my name.

"Anything else?"

"I'm going to go by and see her next week. Monday, I hope. I want to see if she'll let me look around her apartment. Maybe I can get some idea of what might have happened."

"Monday's a holiday. I wonder if they'll have visiting hours? And I have a key to Ashley's place."

She was right. Today was Friday, July first, which meant Monday was the Fourth. I had a long weekend.

"Do you want the key now?" Brandi asked. She pulled a dense cluster of keys from her apron pocket and began to unring one.

"No, that's okay."

"Okay." The keys went back in her apron.

"Michael's funeral is Tuesday at Harris and Sons. It's at eleven."

"Dang, I have to work. There's nobody to cover. Do you think they'll let Ashley go to it?"

"I don't know."

Brandi reached again into her pouch and tore off my check. "Here. I'll call you if anything comes up."

"Thanks."

"You really think she'll go to prison?"

"I'm sure of it, unless someone finds a way to prove she didn't do it."

I paid the cashier with a twenty and left Brandi a generous tip. I decided to leave my car where it was and walk to the Criminal Courthouse. It was just a few short blocks away and driving would be more trouble than walking. I put my leftovers in the car and fed the greedy meter fifty cents for another two hours.

The familiar logo-covered television station vans were clustered outside the courthouse. I took off my ID, ducked around them, and walked as quickly as I could through the door. I had my bag X-rayed at security and, after asking the guard to check the docket, made my way to the Honorable Charles Rollingwood's courtroom. I appeared often at family court, and on rare occasions at civil court in custody battles, but this was my first trip to a criminal court. I had no idea what the rules were. At family court everything was pretty casual, with social workers, probation officers, and attorneys coming and going in and out of the courtroom as they pleased, so long as a trial wasn't going on. Here, I figured I'd go in and sit down and if I wasn't supposed to be there, someone would let me know.

I opened the heavy wooden door to the courtroom and saw the judge's tall bench was empty. Four pew-like rows of oak seats were to the left, and I immediately spotted Dee and Nona, sitting together. Dee had on a blue-gray tweed jacket over a brownish-black dress. The jacket and dress didn't quite match. Her long hair was rolled at the ends into soft curls that she fidgeted with, twirling them around her fingers. Nona was in one of her usual African-inspired prints, a somber black and olive green outfit with a matching turban over her hair. She smiled a greeting when she saw me and I sat down next to her.

"Hi," she said. "How are you?"

"Hi, Dee. Hi, Nona. I'm hanging in there. How about you?"

"Staying busy," Nona answered. "You got my message about Michael's memorial?"

"Yeah, thanks again for doing all that."

"Reverend Croft is doing the ceremony. He's good."

A man in a trendy suit sat down on the bench in front of us. I vaguely recognized him from the TV news. Lawyers began to trickle in and out, conversing, and Samuel Hamilton came in and took a seat at one of the two tables that faced the bench. The D.A. entered and sat at the other.

A uniformed guard brought Ashley in, handcuffed. She was dressed as I'd seen her before, in the orange stripes that hung off her small frame and made her look so tiny and vulnerable. The handcuffs were removed and she sat by her lawyer, only turning once to see the three of us sitting there and giving us a small nod. She was poised on the edge of the chair, rigid, as though by holding herself tight she could keep it together.

I turned, hearing the door open again, and saw Jimmy Shelton ease in and quietly sit two rows behind us. He had tamed his wild hair a bit, and wore a striped tie. As Ashley turned around and spotted him, the corners of her mouth curved up in a small smile as if to say she was okay.

I was on the verge of getting up to go sit with Jimmy and introduce myself when the door opened yet again and in walked — surprise, surprise — Kirk the Jerk. He saw me, slid down the bench, and nudged my arm playfully with his elbow. "Long time no see."

My instinctive reply was to tell him to go straight to hell, but I didn't. Instead I ignored him.

"Aren't you going to introduce me to your friends?"

"Sure." I turned to Dee and Nona. "Ladies, this is Kirk Mahoney. He's the man who's been writing all the lovely articles in the paper lately about Michael's case."

Nona looked at Kirk like he was something dead that had washed up onshore. Dee didn't know what to do, and muttered "Hi."

"Gee, thanks," Kirk said to me. "I'm sorry I upset you earlier."

There was no point in responding to that, so I opted for stony silence again. He said, "I don't understand why you're so upset. I'm just trying to tell the truth."

I faced him and said in a fierce whisper, "Really, Kirk? Is it really about the truth? Or is it about finding the most convenient person to blame? Making everyone believe that it's the government's fault instead of focusing on what really killed Michael. The drugs. And all the horrible things that people do to each other. The cycle of abuse that makes people want to get high." I glanced at Dee, making sure she couldn't hear me. "Ashley's problems started long before DHS got involved. They started the day she was born. But you never hear about that, because there's no easy solution."

His eyes narrowed at me as he grinned. "You know, you're kinda cute when you rant."

"Oh, shut up."

"All rise." The bailiff's sonorous voice echoed throughout the room. We dutifully stood as Judge Rollingwood took his place behind the bench. He had an air of being in a hurry. The whole court staff, come to think of it, looked a little rushed. All of them were trying to finish work and start their long holiday weekend.

"Be seated," the judge said. After everyone complied, he studied a sheaf of papers for several minutes. "Mr. Hamilton."

Ashley's attorney stood behind his table. He had full, salt-and-pepper movie-star hair, and a beautifully tailored suit. All ready for the cameras.

"Yes, Your Honor."

"I understand you have a plea agreement for me."

"We do, Your Honor."

I held my breath, unable to do a damn thing as Ashley's fate unfolded.

CHAPTER NINE

The courtroom was dead quiet as everyone waited for the judge to speak. "Very well," he said. He flipped back through the papers again until he came to the first page. "Ashley Louise Hennessy, you are charged with one count of negligent homicide and one count of possession of a controlled substance. How do you plead?" The D.A. had dropped the other charge of child endangerment, I noted.

Ashley stood, ramrod straight, and in a clear, high voice announced, "Guilty." She said it like she owned it.

I was the only one not surprised. Kirk's eyebrows lifted as he scribbled furiously in a pocket-sized notebook. Dee sucked in a sudden short breath and covered her mouth with her hand. Nona's head bent quickly as if to pray.

On second thought, maybe I wasn't the only one who wasn't shocked. I caught a glimpse of Jimmy in the back row, head nodding in support. What did he know about it?

The judge answered Ashley. "You have entered a plea of guilty and are hereby sentenced to a term of five years, serving not less than one year in custody, with the remaining four years to be served on probation. Do you understand the terms of this sentence?"

"Yes."

"Do you have anything to say?"

"No." Her tone was confident.

Judge addressed the D.A. "Anything to add?"

"No, sir."

"Mr. Hamilton? Anything else?"

"Yes, sir. We would like to request that Miss Hennessy be allowed to attend the memorial service for her son. It's Tuesday at eleven at Harris and Sons in Southside."

Judge nodded. "I'll send the order to the jail."

"Thank you."

His Honor wished Ashley good luck before rising. We all stood again as he ducked into chambers. Ashley nodded to all of us before the bailiff led her out through a door at the back of the courtroom. Dee was crying, Nona was comforting her. The attorneys and the D.A. milled around together, talking. I turned to the back pew quickly, intent on asking Jimmy to wait a minute, but he'd vanished.

With a touch on my arm and a flirtatious smile, Kirk said, "See you around," before he left. Nona got Dee calmed down and we walked outside together. I told them I'd see them Tuesday, then went back to the office.

The place was starting to empty out early just like the court. I waved good-bye to Russell, who was driving out of the parking lot as I pulled in. I scanned the parking lot for a lime green Charger. Nothing. I took the stairs to the second floor and anxiously checked my voice mail.

Nothing from the tire slasher. The first message was from Mac asking me to come to his office when I got in. The next two were from clients needing various items and information. I wrote them down on my list of things to do, which was growing longer by the second. The fourth message was from Royanne, and in typical Royanne fashion was one rambling sentence: "Hi Toby and I wanted to know if you want to come over Monday for a cookout and we are going to grill some hot dogs and ribs and Mamma and Daddy are coming and she's making cole slaw and you can just bring whatever so call me."

Really wanting to avoid Mac altogether, I picked up the phone and dialed Royanne's cell. I confirmed I'd be at her house Monday at noon, and said I'd bring dessert.

It was time to bite the bullet so I walked around to Mac's office.

He was taking advantage of the fact that most of his unit had departed early and was hard at work signing off on charts. I knocked softly on the glass and he motioned me in.

"Sit down." His office was so much more utilitarian than Danessa's. Just two single brown chairs and a row of filing cabinets along one wall. A place to work, not relax. "How are you holding up?"

I shrugged. "Okay, I guess. Ashley pled guilty and got a one-four split."

"How do you know?"

"I went to her hearing."

"Why?"

"Because I wanted to see what was going to happen."

"But it's not your case anymore. Michael's dead."

"I know. But I still care what happens to Ashley. If she is responsible for Michael's death, then she needs all the support she can get."

"What do you mean, if? She just pled guilty."

"I know, but it seems weird to me that she would have been so careless. Stupid enough to have so much GHB in the apartment, and then give it to her son."

"That doesn't change things."

"I know."

"We'll be closing the case as soon as the State is finished with it, and Ashley isn't your problem now."

His get-over-it attitude was ticking me off. I was getting the feeling Michael was just another number to him. A name to be crossed off so a slot on my roster could be filled. "I'm going to Michael's memorial on Tuesday. It's at eleven."

"Remember not to talk to anyone from the press."

Christ, what was this? Did the man think I was in the third grade? I fleetingly wondered if he'd lost confidence in me. It hurt.

"I know," I snapped. "I won't." No way was I going to tell him about my run-ins with Kirk the Jerk.

He sensed I'd had enough and dropped the subject. "What's going on with your other clients?"

We spent the next hour and a half talking about the rest of my caseload. Mac appeared satisfied I hadn't been neglecting my job in the midst of the Michael tragedy and seemed reassured. Until I said, "Um…"

"Oh, no. I hate that. I hate it when you lead with 'um.' It's always bad news."

"Yeah, well, sort of."

"What?"

I came clean. "I realized as I was doing some filing in the Hennessy chart that I never ran a background check on Michael's step-grandfather."

"And?"

"So I did one this morning, and he had three hits."

Mac gave a long, frustrated, count-to-ten sigh. "Why wasn't it done before?"

"I don't know. I can't remember when Al and Dee got married. Maybe they weren't together yet. Most likely, when we had the first intervention meeting and it became clear that Dee wasn't a good placement for Michael, I just stopped the process and never went back and finished it after Michael was returned to Ashley. I don't know."

"But Al had contact with Michael?"

"Recently Ashley had been bringing Michael out to the Mackey's to visit. I didn't know anything about it. I knew she got along okay — barely okay — with her mom, and she didn't like Al, so she hadn't seen them in a while. I didn't know she was working on repairing the relationship with her mom."

"What was the allegation against Al?"

"Physical abuse of his daughter. When she was three and seven. One unfounded and two founded. He was ordered no contact."

"You have the Registry report?"

"It's in the chart."

"Make me a copy and put it in my box. I'll have to forward it to the State with a letter of explanation."

"Sorry." I really was.

"Michael didn't have any bruises on him, did he?"

"No, not according to the detective. And I never saw anything on him."

"It may be nothing. I don't know what the State's going to say about this, though. Does Al have a drug problem?"

"Just booze. Beer, mostly. And gambling. Dee gave some money to Ashley recently and he got mad about it."

"Mad enough to kill her kid? That's a stretch, don't you think?" I started to answer, but he opened a file on his desk, my cue to leave. "We'll see what the State says."

I went back to my cubicle and photocopied the Registry report as Mac had asked, slipping it into the plastic box mounted outside his door with a sticky note of explanation. Doing so reminded me of something else I had to do.

I went to the fourth floor. The Adult Services section was as empty as my own. I wound my way through the maze of cubicles to Michele's desk at Records.

She was putting things away when she saw me coming. "Oh, no. I was just leaving."

"Come on, one quick check. Please?"

She tapped her watch. "Time to go. Long weekend. The kids are waiting on me." Michele had two sweet, smart teenagers, a boy and a girl. "We're going to the beach."

"Please?"

"Oh, all right." She rebooted the computer and we talked about her weekend plans while it warmed up. She handed me the Request for Registry Check form and I wrote Jimmy Shelton's name down, aka James and Jim Shelton.

She took it from me. "That's all you got, just a name?"

"That's it."

She quickly entered the fields and we waited while the computer searched the files. Michele's feet tapped on the linoleum tiles. The machine beeped and a blue message box flashed on the screen, "No Record Found."

"Nothing." Michele said. She printed it for me and powered down the computer.

We walked to the elevators together as she told me more about the condo her family had rented for the holiday. At the second floor we said good-bye and wished each other a good weekend.

I spent an hour clearing my desk and attacking my to-do list, and by the time I packed up my briefcase and shut down my computer, I felt like I'd gotten enough done to be able to relax some over the Fourth. Traffic was horrid going home, the interstate crammed with families going three hundred miles south to sun worship at Gulf Shores or Orange Beach. It was almost six thirty when I pulled into my driveway.

My little house was a welcome sight, its white paint and black shutters giving it a neat appearance. The black iron scrollwork columns that supported the carport and portico were my favorite features. I gathered the mail and inspected the small, sloped yard as I walked the concrete path that led from the driveway to the front steps. The grass needed cutting, which my father usually did for me, and the boxwood shrubs against the house were a bit brown. The purple and gold impatiens I'd planted by the stoop this spring were on their last legs. The plants looked tired, worn down from the summer heat.

I unlocked the front door and dumped the mail on the table in the small dining area. The house was cold, chilled by the air conditioner. I shivered and turned the temperature up. After changing into shorts and a T-shirt, I poured myself a glass of Riesling, then another, as I channel surfed in the living room. Nothing good on. My mind wandered to the barbeque at Royanne's this weekend, and I took a few cookbooks down from the cabinet in the kitchen and resettled on the couch. I'm not much of a chef, lacking both interest and skill. I was browsing through a *Southern Living* cookbook and was about to break into my leftover cheeseburger when the door to the carport opened and Dad entered, calling hello. He was in shorts and a Cozumel T-shirt, his ponytail wet from a trip to the pool.

I called hi and put the book on the coffee table. He spotted it and asked, "Are you cooking? 'Cause I brought stuff from the diner." He held up a white plastic bag with two Styrofoam boxes in it.

"No, no. Royanne's having a cookout Monday. I'm supposed to bring a dessert. I can't decide between apple or cherry pie."

He walked back to my small kitchen and put the bag down. "Both are good. And patriotic."

I set the table with paper napkins and plastic knives and forks and poured a glass of the Riesling for Dad as he unloaded the boxes. The Bluff Park Diner was our local meat-and-three, just minutes down the road from Dad's house. He'd brought me the meatloaf, which I loved. It was thickly sliced, heavy on the garlic and onions, and covered with ketchup. Dad had the vegetable plate. Once we'd tucked in, he asked, "How're you holding up?"

"Okay I guess," I answered, talking around a mouthful of mashed potatoes. I swallowed. I told him about my tires.

"Who do you think did it?"

"It wasn't random. Whoever did it left me a message about it at work. I think it was someone involved with this case, probably Mom's ex-boyfriend."

"You be careful."

"I will. I haven't heard anything from him lately. I think he's the type who'll blow off steam and let it go. All mouth, no muscle. Oh, and Michael's mother pled guilty and got one to five years."

"Yeah, I saw that on the news."

"Was it bad?"

"They didn't mention you or DHS. Just that she'd been sentenced."

"Michael's memorial is Tuesday. That's going to be tough." I stabbed a few bacon-laced green beans with my fork. "It still doesn't make any sense."

"Why?"

"First, Ashley's not the GHB type. Second, if she was using again and partying the night before, she would have known the juice had drugs in it. She wouldn't have given it to Michael. Third, if she didn't do it, why take the fall?"

"Was she partying the night before?"

"She says not. She says she was working."

"Did they do a drug screen when she went to jail? That would give you some idea if she was lying."

I made a mental note to call Brighton on Tuesday. "I'll check on that. Although I don't know if it would show GHB. That stuff gets out of your system pretty quickly."

I wondered for the hundredth time who had sold Ashley the drugs, if they were hers. Flash? More and more questions about his role in Michael's death were nagging me. Was he the man in the green car? Did he slash my tires? Why would he blame me for Ashley's arrest? And was he hanging out with Ashley again? Maybe it was time to find out what he knew. I might be teasing a tiger, but I decided to track him down.

Dad reached over and sliced off a hunk of my meatloaf.

"I thought you were a vegetarian," I said.

"This doesn't count."

I wasn't about to argue with that.

CHAPTER TEN

Dad stayed to watch a documentary on PBS with me. He left around eleven, and before dragging myself off to bed I hunted down the software discs that the guy at the computer store needed. After retrieving them from some storage boxes in the office closet, I slept a heavy sleep, thanks to the wine.

By Saturday morning the air had cooled to a more comfortable eighty-something degrees and the day promised to be beautiful. I scurried down the driveway in my bathrobe to get the paper, the plastic bag warm from the sun. I unrolled it like a bomb technician handling explosives: very carefully and with a serious feeling of dread.

First I checked the obituaries. Michael's was there, short and sweet:

HENNESSY, MICHAEL ALEXANDER. Beloved son, aged two, passed away Tuesday, June 28. Services to be held Tuesday, July 5, at Harris and Sons on University Boulevard at eleven a.m. In lieu of flowers, the family requests donations to St. Monica's Home for Recovery.

St. Monica's address was listed, but no mention of surviving family. I skimmed the front page. The main stories were about the heavy rain yesterday, which had caused some flooding, and the governor's trip to Washington D.C. Nothing about the case. I turned to the local section. There was a short piece by Kirk, just a couple of paragraphs about the sentencing and Ashley's reaction. A small picture of her leaving the courthouse, handcuffed. Nothing else. Then I flipped to the letters to the editor. Nothing about DHS. Hopefully the public had vented all they were going to. It appeared the media storm was abating, at least. I exhaled a sigh of relief worthy of a bomb technician, cut the short article and obit out, and put them in my purse to file in the Hennessys' chart at the office. Then I read the rest of the paper and took a shower.

I put on my scruffiest jeans and a faded vintage T-shirt, wore my hair in a ponytail and no makeup. After dropping off the discs, I was going to try to track down Flash and didn't need to stick out like a social worker in the process.

High Tech had an electronic door chime that sounded as I entered. Grant came out of the back room, a travel cup of coffee in hand. He greeted me with a small grin as I handed him the discs. Looking them over, he said, "This should do it. The problem was your hard drive, just like I thought. I should have these loaded by the end of the day. We're closed tomorrow and Monday."

"Thanks. I can swing by Tuesday and get it."

"Uh, actually I was going to ask you — I don't know what your situation is —" He stopped and started over. "I was wondering if you were doing anything for the Fourth."

Oh Christ. He was asking me out. The last thing in the world I wanted to do was to go out with anyone, much less some geek. But he was looking at me with such a pained expression. Poor guy. He was so shy. Not bad looking, either. Maybe his luck with women had been as bad as mine with men. What the hell, I thought. "Not in the evening."

"Then do you want to go see the fireworks with me?" His face was turning bright red.

"I'd love to," I lied.

The grin returned. "Great. Tell you what, if you want me to pick you up at your house, I can deliver the computer and hook it up for you. Is that okay?"

"Perfect." I gave my address to him again along with directions.

"About eight?"

"Sounds good."

It was nearly noon when I hit Malfunction Junction, the tricky inter-section of three interstates in the heart of downtown, then exited off I-20/59 into Ensley. I wound my way through one economically de-prived area and into another called Wylam. It was one of many poor, predominantly black areas on the west side of town. Martin Luther King Jr. once called Birmingham "the most thoroughly segregated city in the United States," and sadly not much has changed. Few busi-nesses were still open in the heart of this neighborhood, and many of the buildings were boarded up and covered in gang graffiti. I thought about all the wealthier — and whiter — areas south of town and felt sad. Our fine city, considering its history of church bombings and poignant letters from jail, should set a better example.

After a bit of driving around, I found the house where I'd first laid eyes on Ashley and Michael. It looked much the same, a shabby yellow two-bedroom bungalow with a weedy yard. The street bor-dered a factory that made some kind of asphalt product, and a chem-ical smell permanently hung in the air.

I was taking a risk coming here. It was the first of the month, time for the disbursement of paychecks and government benefits, and that meant a lot of drug dealing going on. Several teens in red clothing stood on a corner close to the house, watching me drive slowly down the street. Two young men on pimped-out bicycles rode in small cir-cles in front of them. Neighbors sat in old metal chairs on their front porches, staring intently at my car with no sign of welcome.

I'd put my purse in the trunk before I left the computer store. Now I locked my car and, trying not to look conspicuous or afraid, walked to the door. I knocked softly, surreptitiously glancing over my shoulder now and then. I wished I had the police with me like the last time I was here. One of the bicycle riding guys looked over my Honda, inside and out.

No answer. I knocked again, harder.

The door was opened by a skeletal black man in his early twenties, in torn red sweatpants and no shirt. I could see his ribs. I could also see I'd woken him up and hoped it wouldn't get me shot. He rubbed his eyes and didn't say anything, just waited for me to state my business. I did, quickly.

"Flash here?"

His wiry Afro stuck up in different directions. "Nah, man, he don' stay here no more." His voice was husky from sleep.

"You know where I can find him?"

"He moved back in his mamma's."

"You know where she stays?"

"Someplace in Fultondale."

"Thanks." He shut the door, hard. I scampered back to my car, nodding to the boys on the bikes and getting surly looks in return. I got out of there, fast, and didn't breathe normally again until I was back on the interstate, heading east. I looped through the junction onto I-65 North, and after a few exits pulled off the highway into a gas station in Fultondale. This particular suburb was more racially diverse, but solidly blue-collar. Home to truck drivers and steel workers.

I filled up and asked the old man behind the counter if I could look at his phone book. I scanned the list of Bowmans in the area. A Gina Bowman was listed in Fultondale, her house on a street near the high school. Deciding it couldn't hurt to try, I went to the address.

Gina Bowman's house was on a hill. A square box, sided in white aluminum, with green awnings over almost every window. It looked remarkably like all the other houses on the street. No lime green car visible from the front, but a narrow drive led to the back of the house. I parked at the curb, climbed the steps that led to the door, and rang the small round bell.

The woman who answered was in her late forties, her dirty blonde hair fixed in a mullet that had gone out of style twenty years ago. She had a face that was all fine cracks and creases, radiating outward from a puckered mouth. The eyes were bloodshot to a bright red, and at first I thought I'd woken her too, until the pot smell wafted out of the door.

"Hi," I began. "I'm Claire Conover, and I'm from DHS. Are you Gregory's mom by any chance?"

"Yeah."

"Is he here?"

"Yeah."

"Can I talk to him for a sec?"

"He in trouble?"

"No, not at all. I just want to ask him about a woman he used to know."

"Come in."

I followed her into the house. The marijuana smell was overwhelming. The living room was dim and tiny, stuffed with mismatched 1950's furniture and a ridiculously huge big-screen TV. It was blaring QVC, which competed with the staccato beat of rap music from another room. A plastic ashtray on the coffee table held a tiny scrap of joint and a roach clip. The shag-carpeted floor flexed when I walked.

"Sit down." Gina gestured toward a chair by the window.

"Thanks." She went down a short hallway and I could hear her banging on a door, shouting over the music, telling Flash he had company. I recognized the rap song as one by Ludacris.

Gina returned, reached for a pack of Basic cigarettes lying on the coffee table, and lit up. "What's this about?"

"Gregory used to hang out with a woman named Ashley Hennessy. Her child died this week. You might have heard about it."

She nodded, taking a drag. "Yeah. The kid that overdosed."

"That's him. Michael."

She studied me long and hard for a minute, and in her stoned brown eyes I could see the question she was afraid to ask. I waited.

She asked, "Was — was Gregory his father?"

"I don't think so. Ashley told me she was already pregnant when she met Gregory."

"Oh." A bit of disappointment, and relief, in her voice. "I wondered, 'cause that's Gregory's middle name."

"What is?"

"Michael. Gregory Michael Bowman."

"Ah, I see." Well, well. Had Ashley named Michael after Flash because she loved him? The thought made me sick. Or maybe because he was his dad? I guess she could have lied to me about when they met. Very interesting. It made me wonder if there was anything else Ashley had lied about.

"Does Gregory have a green Charger, by any chance?"

"Nuh-uh. It ain't his."

"What do you mean?"

"It's his friend's. Ray-Ray's. He borrows it some."

Flash walked in, wearing a red Chicago Bulls jersey and saggy long red shorts. He looked paler and skinnier than he had two years ago. His hair was still platinum blond, but styled differently than I remembered. Now it was short on the sides and stuck up in a ridge straight down the middle of his scalp. He was smothered in the silver jewelry that had given him his nickname. He sure wasn't called Flash because he was quick.

"Hey, Flash."

"Christ. What the fuck you want?"

I tried, in an instant, to match his voice to the phone message. I couldn't be sure.

I glanced at his mother, who was staring blankly through the filmy curtains to the world outside. A lifetime of regret in her expression.

"How about two hundred dollars for new tires?"

He scoffed. "I don't know what the hell you talkin' about."

"You heard about Ashley? And Michael?"

"Yeah. What about it?"

"You seen her lately?"

"What's it to you, bitch?"

"Was she using again?"

"Fuck if I know. We'd still be together if you hadn't put her in that place, and that bitch hadn't gotten the fuckin' restrainin' order."

He picked up the pack of cigarettes and lit up, just as his mother had.

"You give her any drugs lately?"

"Why?" He exhaled a cloud of brown smoke.

"I want to help her."

"By lockin' her up? You were a great fuckin' help before. Why don't you just get the fuck outta here and leave me alone? Or you'll be real fuckin' sorry."

Stupid little creep. I checked my anger and tried a different tactic.

"C'mon, Flash. Was she using again? Maybe we can help her. Get her out of jail."

"I didn't give her shit."

"Michael died of a GHB overdose. You ever do G?"

He laughed, short and loud. "Ha! G? I ain't no fuckin' kaleidoscope kid. Neither was Ashley."

"Kaleidoscope kid?"

"Kaleidoscope. That bar down near Lakeview. That's where all them ravin' X-heads hang."

I had one last question. "Were you Michael's father?"

"Shit, man, I better not be. I told that bitch if she got knocked up it was her problem. I ain't fixin' to pay no fuckin' child support."

Nice. Gina had been listening to all this in silence. I realized where her earlier reaction had come from. On the one hand, maybe she thought a grandchild would have given her the opportunity to do things right. A do-over, so to speak. Then again, what if he had turned out like Flash?

After Flash stormed back to his room with one final curse, I said good-bye to Gina and drove carefully home. If I'd gotten pulled over, there was no way any police officer would have believed that I hadn't been smoking weed. I reeked.

Dad had cut the grass while I was gone. I took another shower as soon as I got in, trading my stinky outfit for a pair of comfortable shorts and a different T-shirt. I spent the rest of Saturday afternoon running errands, to the grocery store and the bakery. I gave up on the idea of making anything for Royanne's barbeque, instead going to Edgar's Bakery and getting an apple pie. Heck, they made a better one than I could any day.

Then, on Sunday, all hell broke loose.

CHAPTER ELEVEN

Sunday morning I awoke in a good mood and made my way down the driveway as usual in my robe. I lugged the two-pound paper into the dining area and made myself comfortable with a cup of Sumatran coffee. The front-page news was about a pharmaceutical firm. They'd gotten permission to start drug trials in conjunction with the university on a new medicine for a sleep disorder. Another article discussed the search for Birmingham Southern College's new basketball coach. The sports section was already predicting how the University of Alabama's football team was going to perform, even though the start of the season was well over a month away. I always loved fall, when Birmingham went Crimson Tide crazy. Except for the Auburn fans, of course. There was no in-between, either.

It wasn't until I'd looked through the stack of ads and had gone on to the Comments and Editorials section that I choked on my coffee. On the front page was the headline MOTHERS AND ADDICTS. By Kirk Mahoney.

> Last week brought the overdose death of little Michael Hennessy, two-year-old son of Ashley Hennessy, now serving up to five years in jail for negligent homicide. Ms. Hennessy is only one of hundreds of drug and alcohol users whose addiction impacts the lives of children. Claire Conover, a caseworker at the Department of Human Services familiar with the Hennessy case, points to the cycle of

domestic violence, emotional abuse, and drugs as the real culprit that destroys the lives of our city's youth.

Oh, shit.

> Birmingham's shelters are full of women whose own biographies mirror that of Ashley Hennessy's. April Schulz, a resident of The Harbor, a homeless shelter for women and children, is one of those victims. "I started drinking when I was thirteen," she states. "My father used to beat me and my sister. I drank to escape." Ms. Schultz's children have been in and out of foster care for the past eight years. "It's tough on them. They want to come home."

April Schultz wasn't my client. But the next one was.

> Cheyenne Phillips, another resident of The Harbor, has lost custody of her children for the last time. "They're going up for adoption. I'm not getting another chance."

So that was where Cheyenne had landed after St. Monica's. I'd wondered. Kirk went on to interview a sociologist from the university in Montevallo, who correlated the histories of drug use and foster care in the United States. The last section of the article discussed new and novel approaches to dealing with the problem, including in-home parenting services and one local OB/GYN who offered addiction counseling and recovery along with prenatal care. The article concluded with:

> Programs like these, not government agencies, may be the best hope for children of addicts.

I was in so much trouble. God only knew what Mac and Dr. Pope were going to say. I was considering placing a preemptive call to Mac when my cell phone rang in the bedroom. I unplugged it from its charge cord and checked the caller ID. The office. Not good.

"Hello?"

"I need you to come down here." Mac.

"Sure."

I didn't need a college degree to tell how pissed he was. I threw on jeans, a polo, and my Birkenstocks. Hell, if I was going to be fired, at least I was going to wear comfortable shoes.

I flew downtown at a speed that would have made a Talladega NASCAR driver proud, jogged through the empty lot behind the building, and went to the front door. Mac was there, dressed for church and waiting with a key. He let me in and locked the door again.

He didn't say anything other than to nod a greeting. When Mac goes quiet, it's very bad. We entered the elevator together, and the higher it rose the more nauseous with dread I got. The silver doors slid open and we marched our way to Dr. Pope's office.

She was dressed out of the L.L. Bean catalog. Chic and sporty, in a golf shirt and long walking shorts. She pointed to the conference table and I sat down. She and Mac sat across from me, stern looks on their faces. I stiffened and readied myself for the words they were about to say: You're fired. I was financially, emotionally, and professionally screwed.

Today's paper was sitting on the table. Dr. Pope began with, "You've seen this?"

"Yes."

"You were specifically instructed not to talk to the press."

"I know. I didn't."

"Then how do you explain this?"

"I ran into Kirk Mahoney a couple of times. Once here, the day he interviewed you. In the lobby."

"I remember."

"Then, after the article about you came out, I ran into him at a restaurant. He asked me to comment on the case, and I didn't. But I was mad about the article he'd written about you. So I said something to the effect of why didn't he write about all the good stuff we do here. About all the kids we rescue out of bad situations instead of making DHS sound bad. He's taken what I said and turned it around to something I didn't say." My words were coming out haphazardly.

Mac said, his tone sarcastic, "You just ran into him at a restaurant, and somehow he figured out that you were the worker on the case? You didn't say anything at all to him about it?"

I squirmed. "Um, the restaurant was the Top of the Hill Grill."

Mac, now even madder, said, "I see."

I said, by way of explanation to Dr. Pope, "The Top of the Hill Grill is where Ashley Hennessy worked."

Mac asked, "What were you doing there?"

"I went by to check on Brandi. She's Ashley's best friend. And to tell her about the memorial on Tuesday."

Dr. Pope said, "And that's the last time you saw Kirk?"

"I saw him again at Ashley's sentencing. But I didn't say anything to him, I swear. Well, not much, anyway."

Dr. Pope sighed, fingering the corner of the newspaper on the table. "See, Claire, the problem is now the agency looks bad. Because of Mr. Mahoney's article, it appears as if we are trying to shift the blame away from us. I've been doing damage control all morning with the press and the state office. I think I have it under control. I appreciate your trying to defend me and your client and the agency, but you really shouldn't have said anything at all."

Mac barked, "When we said don't say anything to anyone, we meant it. This also violated the confidentiality of our clients."

"I know."

"You didn't mention Cheyenne at all?"

"No! I would never do that. I think he just went down to The Harbor and met her. It's just a coincidence that she's also mine."

Dr. Pope strode once across the room. "Here's where we are, Claire. Your involvement with this case is over. Period. We have no reason to keep the case open, and you have no reason to have any-

thing to do with anyone involved in it. The state office hasn't said anything about letting you go, but if your name comes up again they may
not give me a choice. Understood?"

"What about the memorial on Tuesday? I'm going." That last
statement came out a little more forcefully than I had intended. Now
was not the time to argue.

"I know you want to pay your respects." Dr. Pope said. "You may
even feel there was something you could have done to prevent Michael's
death. Even if there was, it's over. Whatever prompted Ashley to use
drugs again, we may never know. She's pled guilty, and DHS is out of
it. Understood? I strongly suggest you stay away from the memorial."

"What does that mean? I want to go."

She glanced at Mac. "I can't forbid you to go, but I really don't
think you should."

Mac stood and placed his hands flat on the table and leaned toward me. "You are on thin ice. Get it?"

I got it.

I apologized repeatedly for everything, including bringing them
down to the office on a Sunday. Mac warned me once more to keep
my nose clean, and I left, able to breathe again and with the relieved
sensation that I'd dodged the bullet. For now.

At home, I read the article again and fumed. I changed to old clothes
and went out to weed the pitiful-looking beds near the house. With
every stem I plucked, I pretended it was Kirk Mahoney's neck I was
snapping. Very therapeutic. I watered the plants, cleaned up the small
concrete patio in the backyard, and washed the outdoor furniture.
After that I cleaned out the storeroom in the carport and washed my
car. By the time I finished I was sore, and it felt like I'd been beaten.

I turned my attention to my answering machine. Its message light
was blinking like a red-alert button. The first one was from my
father, who saw the article in the paper this morning and wanted to
know if he needed to change the sign at his office. Changing the sign
from Conover & Associates to Conover, Conover, & Associates was

something he'd wanted to do forever, to the point where it was now a joke between us. I called him back and told him about my morning.

The second call was from my brother, Chris, a nurse in Orlando. I talked to him for an hour. The third call was from Royanne, confirming the cookout for tomorrow. The last three messages were hang-ups. I wondered briefly if Flash had gotten his hands on my home number.

Late Monday morning I dressed in light shorts and a tank top and, with apple pie in hand, went to Royanne and Toby's. Royanne lived in a 1970's split-level in the suburb of Pelham. The house was crammed with furniture and toys, and always loud with the cries and shrieks of their three kids. Royanne thrived on all the chaos, but I have to admit sometimes it drove me nuts. Her parents' Buick was already there when I arrived, along with another truck I didn't recognize.

Royanne greeted me with a hug at the door and took the dessert. Roy and Anne, her parents, were on the deck already, ice-cold Miller Lites in hand. The strange truck turned out to be Bo's, the friend of Toby's my alleged best friend was trying to fix me up with. He muttered a hi as I shot Royanne a look. Today Bo looked like a goldfish, with bright orange hair and a vacant, surprised look on his face. I spent most of the afternoon playing with the kids, talking to Royanne's parents, and avoiding him.

After we'd all stuffed ourselves on ribs, chicken, potato salad, cole slaw, and apple pie, I helped Royanne with the dishes. "How's work?" I asked.

"Fine. We just had a big account come in, so I'm working a lot on that. What about you? What'd Mac say about the article?"

"Nothing good." I summarized yesterday's events for her.

"Jesus."

"Yeah, I gotta watch it."

"So are you going tomorrow? To the memorial?"

"Yeah."

"Why?"

"Because. Lots of reasons. I want to see who shows up, first of all. See their reactions. I'm still not buying that Ashley knew the drug was in the juice. And," I swallowed hard, "I just want to go, that's all." To say good-bye.

Royanne's kids ran screaming into the kitchen. The eldest, Alicia, squirted the youngest with a water pistol. Richard, the four-year-old, retaliated on behalf of his younger sister by hitting Alicia in the back with a foam ball. Alicia giggled. Olivia wailed. Royanne bellowed, "Outside! Now!"

That's what childhood was. Laughing, giggling, pretending, playing. Not lying dead in a tiny coffin. I stared out the café-curtained window above Royanne's sink and started to shake. My eyes welled. Damn it. I'd been doing so well, not letting myself go there. Not picturing Michael like that. Or Olivia. Or Alicia. Or Richard. Or any of my other clients. I brushed the tears away quickly and struggled for control as Royanne finished shooing her brood out of the sliding glass door. She caught the look on my face and said, "You okay?"

"Sure." My voice was hoarse.

"Bullshit."

"Let it go."

"Fine."

We washed dishes for a few more minutes, and then Royanne said, "I thought after a while we could send the kids upstairs to play and we could watch a new movie I got it's a new DVD that action one with Bruce Willis —"

"I can't. I've got to go soon. I've got a date."

Her eyes went wide. "Really? You? With who?"

"A guy named Grant Summerville. I met him at the computer store."

"A computer geek, huh? What's he look like?" Her tone was skeptical.

"He has nice green eyes."

"Well, have fun. You deserve it."

I didn't think I did, but I could try.

CHAPTER TWELVE

Neither Grant nor I were going to have much fun on this date if I didn't haul myself out of the dumps, so when I got home I loaded the CD player with my favorite old-school tunes. A little Van Halen and some Def Leppard did the trick. I styled my hair and put on makeup. Chose a distressed denim skirt and a red cap-sleeved top to wear. Maybe the red and blue was a little bit too patriotic. To hell with it, I thought, as I slid on my shoes. 'Tis the season.

Grant arrived at seven-fifty. He looked cute, in a gooberish way, in a short-sleeved button-down, shorts, and sandals. At least he wasn't wearing socks. He put the computer and my discs down on the stoop long enough to give me a quick hug hello. He had to bend way down to do it. He smelled good. Like shaving cream.

He carried the computer into the house and stopped for a second to take in the sage-colored walls and the beige furniture. "Nice place. You been here long?"

"About four months. It still needs a little work."

"Where do you want this?"

"In here." I walked him to the office, where the computer cart and desk were back in place minus the plastic drop cloth. He put the computer in its spot and ran the cables to the monitor and printer, then plugged it all in and hooked up the mouse and keyboard. He booted it up and typed in a few things, checking to make sure it all worked. I watched his long fingers move rapidly across the keys.

"Done." He powered down the machine. "You ready?"

I wrote him a check for the repairs, got my purse, and locked the door behind us. The sun was setting and the air was cooler. Someone on the street had been doing yard work and the scent of new-mown grass lingered. I caught the blinking glow of fireflies rising in the trees, and the raspy hum of crickets. The neighborhood was gearing up for celebration, bottle rockets popped and a Roman candle whistled. Grant had come in the company van and held its door open for me as I climbed inside. No seats were in the back, but instead the walls were lined with metal racks with bungee cords stretched across the front of them. For transporting computer parts, I reasoned. The floor at the back of the van was empty except for a quilt and a picnic basket.

"Where're we going?" I asked.

"It's a surprise. You like surprises?"

"Yeah, sure. Well, sometimes. It depends." He laughed.

The cockpit was tricked out with gadgets. I noted a GPS system, a DVD screen, and an MP3 player. The MP3 player softly played a Taylor Hicks song. Grant hummed along, drumming his fingers on the steering wheel in time to the music. I started to relax.

"So, how long have you worked at High Tech?"

"I opened it about two years ago."

"You own it?"

"Yep. I did some time after college as a corporate programmer, then worked for a bank, then an insurance company. I decided I was tired of busting my ass for someone else when I could open up my own place. That way I could make more money and have more control over what I did."

"That must be nice. To work for yourself, I mean."

"It is. It's hard work, though. Long hours. I've got three employees now, and I'm looking for a fourth. So we're growing, and that's good."

We talked about his background as he drove toward downtown. About where he went to college and where he had worked before. He knew his way around well, which prompted me to ask if he grew up here. He told me about growing up on Air Force bases around the world until he and his parents and sisters landed at Maxwell in Montgomery. His parents still lived near there.

"What about you?" he asked. "Are you from here?"

"Oh, yeah. My family's been in Birmingham for six generations now. My great-great-great grandfather came over from Holland when the city was brand new, in the 1870s. He was a builder. My family owned a construction company for years before my grandfather sold it when he retired."

"Is he still alive? Your grandfather?"

"No, he died when I was eight, five years before my mother. I never knew him. My father, well, he was — is — kind of a radical. He and my mom were real active in the civil rights movement. They went to protests, worked with CORE, Dr. King, did the march on Washington, and all that."

"That's cool."

"Yeah, it is. I guess it's where I get my do-good mentality. But my dad and grandfather didn't get along so well because of my dad's beliefs. My grandfather liked the old status quo, and my father couldn't stand that. So I never got to know my grandparents. Not that I agree with my grandfather's racism, of course, but sometimes I wonder why my father couldn't find some sort of middle ground with him, you know?"

"There is such a thing as being too radical."

"Or too dedicated to a cause."

Grant headed for Southside, toward the University of Alabama-Birmingham campus. He found a place to park, then took the basket and quilt from the back. We had to walk a couple of blocks before reaching a quarter-acre patch of grass outside one of the dorms.

From here we could see the top of Red Mountain, home to the giant statue of Vulcan. The Roman god of fire and metalworking symbolized Birmingham, celebrating our iron and steel industry. In one hand, Vulcan held a completed spear to the sky, and in his other a hammer. The fireworks would be launched from the ten-acre park around the huge statue. We would have a great view.

Grant spread the quilt on the ground. "This okay?" he asked.

"Perfect." The quad wasn't too crowded since most of UAB was on summer break. Only a few other student-age groups sat on blankets nearby, their outlines just visible in the streetlights. Grant unlatched the picnic basket. "I brought wine. I hope that's okay."

"Sure."

He took out a small corkscrew and opened the Chardonnay, pulling the cork out with a pop. The basket held two wine glasses snapped securely to the lid. He poured a glass for each of us, then went back to rummaging in the basket. "I didn't know if you'd be hungry, so I brought some cheese and crackers. And some fruit." He laid the fare out on an oval plate on top of the basket. I checked my watch. The fireworks wouldn't start for a few minutes.

"So," Grant asked, after munching on a cracker, "How long have you worked at DHS?"

I didn't want to spoil the evening by thinking about work, but I answered him anyway. "Five years."

"You like it?"

"Yeah." I sipped the wine. It was crisp and sweet.

The silence was awkward for a second, and I realized that I was making him uncomfortable. "I'm sorry." I checked around us to make sure we wouldn't be overheard. "I've had a really rough week at work."

"I saw your name in the article in the paper yesterday. The kid that died, he was your case?"

"Yeah. And my bosses were furious about the article. I almost got fired."

"Why? I didn't think it was that bad. I thought it raised some good points."

"My bosses didn't see it that way. They said it made us look like we were shifting the blame."

"Were you?"

"No!" I snagged a slice of apple from the platter and played with it a minute, then voiced what I'd been thinking deep down for nearly a week. "Maybe Michael's death was my fault." I ate the apple.

Grant pushed his glasses higher on his nose. "How do you figure that?"

"I should have been more attentive. I should have been there more. I should have been able to see what could happen."

"Well, when you learn how to predict the future, be sure and teach me how. I could make a killing."

I gave him as much as of a smile as I could muster, took another sip of wine, and voiced the other thought that had been nagging me, day and night: "What if it happens again?"

With a sympathetic look, Grant reached over and gave my hand a squeeze. The first of the fireworks exploded with a pop, lighting the mountain in a starburst of red, white, and finally blue. The people around us oohed and aahed. Grant stretched his long legs out, leaning on one hand, his wine in the other. I followed suit, throwing my head back to see the sky explode again and again into streams of color. Reds, golds, greens, blues. Grant and I reclined shoulder to shoulder, taking in the beauty.

The finale, twenty minutes later, was an amazing frenzy of sound and color. After the last report echoed over the valley, Grant packed the picnic basket and folded the quilt. When we reached the van he asked, "Do you want to go get a drink somewhere?"

"Sure." We discussed the fireworks as he drove down University Boulevard. After University changed to Clairmont, he took a left into the Lakeview District. The bars and restaurants there were crowded. The patrons tended to be a bit older than the ones who frequented Southside and the UAB area. More yuppies than college students.

Grant parked next to a place called Fuel. The name was a tongue-in-cheek homage to the fact that the lot was a gas station in the thirties. Where pumps once stood, a patio was filled with wrought-iron tables. Inside the rock-faced building, dim lighting and dark wood gave the small place a pub-like feel. Posters of vintage cars decorated the walls. I'd been here several times before, hanging out with coworkers after a long day.

"This okay?" Grant asked.

"Oh yeah, I love this place." We walked to the terrace where I said, "Why don't you grab us a table out here and I'll get us some drinks."

"Okay. A beer for me, I think. Something dark."

"No problem."

I opened the heavy wooden door and went inside. Most of the tables were occupied, tops laden with empty bottles and glasses. Someone laughed loudly. I elbowed my way to the bar and held out a ten, trying to get the bartender's attention. He eventually made his way over to me and I ordered a Michelob Ultra and a Negra Modela. I was tipping him when it dawned on me where I was. Lakeview.

"Hey," I called to the bartender, "You know a place called Kaleidoscope?"

He nodded to the door, his hands busy mixing a gin and tonic. "Two blocks north, one block west." He topped the G&T with a lime wedge and passed it to a woman in a black halter.

"Thanks." I grabbed the beers and went to where Grant had found us a table near the railing. I sipped the Michelob, the ice-cold liquid chilling me through, then rested the cool top of the bottle on my bottom lip.

"What?" Grant asked.

"What?"

"You have a look on your face. Like you're planning something."

I laughed. "What if I was?"

"I'd like to know what. And if I'm involved."

"You want to be?"

"Depends on what it is."

"You mind if we take a little detour?"

"Where to?"

"There's a place around here called Kaleidoscope."

"I've heard of it. You want to go dancing?" He looked horrified at the thought.

"No, no, no. I don't dance. In public. Anyway, I just want to check the place out."

"Why?"

"I just do."

"Okay." We took a few minutes to finish our beers and decided to walk the ten minutes or so to Kaleidoscope. "You sure you don't want to tell me why we're going here? I mean, if we're not going to dance —"

I was tempted. "Just bear with me for a while, okay?"

"If you say so."

The nightclub was a curvy, two-storey structure made of glass and steel. The front windows were painted with bright neon colors in geometric patterns, with Kaleidoscope in small white letters on the glass door. A bouncer dressed in all black stood sentry, checking IDs. Another man, smaller in stature but dressed the same, took everyone's money. The cover charge was ten bucks. I paid a twenty for me and Grant — over his protests — and went in.

Crowded and loud was my first impression. And the girls outnumbered the guys nearly two to one. Most of the girls were dressed in tight, sexy clothes. Some had thongs peeping out above their pants and skirts. At nearly thirty, I was at least five years beyond the average age. The dance floor, in the middle of the space, was jammed with bodies grinding together to a song by Pink. Lights in every color of the rainbow flashed with the beat of the song. I glanced at Grant. His eyes were fixed on the massive wall of television screens at the back of the room that surrounded the deejay's window. Each TV was playing an ever-changing pattern of colors and lines that swayed with the tempo. All the movement made me dizzy.

The bar was to the left, a metal staircase to the right. As we walked past the bar, I asked Grant if he wanted a drink. He declined. The bartender was frantically busy, hands flying as he mixed cocktails and popped open bottles. His head was shaved and on his neck was a large tattoo. It took me a while to discern that it was some sort of bird with flames around its feet. A phoenix.

The staircase led to a balcony that overlooked the dance floor. I nudged Grant and pointed to it. He nodded. We eased our way up the crowded stairs slowly and found a spot to lean on the rail and watch the action. On benches along the wall behind us a few couples were making out.

"Here we are," Grant shouted. "What are we looking for?"

"We're just looking." Truth was, I had no idea what I was looking for. Someone dealing drugs, I guess. Although I had no idea whether they'd do it openly in such a public place. Or someone I could talk to about it, maybe. Come to think of it, this was really a bad idea. I was just about to suggest that we go when someone behind me yanked my arm.

"I thought that was you, but I couldn't believe it." Russell. My cubicle-mate was dressed in a vintage, flowered button-down and tight jeans. Behind him was Heinrich, his current boyfriend. Heinrich was a big blond from Germany, a graduate student in chemistry at the university. Heinrich kissed me on both cheeks in the European fashion. "Hey, Russ. Hey, Heinrich."

"'Allo, Claire." Heinrich said in his thick accent.

"What are you doing here?" Russell asked.

"Just hanging out. This is Grant." I gestured toward him. He nodded to the guys and went back to studying the wall of electronics. Russell leaned in so he could talk with me without being overheard. Not that you could overhear much with the music blaring. "He's your date?"

"Yes," I said in his ear.

"He's kinda cute in a really nerdy sorta way."

"Thanks so much."

"Really, what are you doing here?"

"I told you, hanging out." The music switched to a song by the Black Eyed Peas. The lights strobed faster, like colored lightning.

"Bullshit. This isn't your scene." He scoffed, "Or his."

Russell knew me too well. "It's about the case."

"Saw the article. You talked to Mac yet?"

"Yesterday. He and Pope brought me in."

"Ugh. On Sunday? And?"

"They almost fired me." I summarized the meeting for him.

"Thank God they didn't."

"Yeah. Anyway, remember the guy Ashley was with when we got Michael? Flash?"

"Yeah, sorta."

"He said this is where a lot of people get GHB."

He laughed. "So you thought you'd come down here and see if you could score some?"

I was annoyed at him for laughing at me. More annoyed that he was right. "Oh, shut up. I don't know what else to do. Something funny is going on and I'm grasping at straws."

"Stay out of it, like they said."

"No." I sounded like a petulant child. Marilyn Manson's version of "Personal Jesus" began to thunder in my ears.

He put his arms around my waist and said, "Okay, okay. In fact, a lot of people here are into the alphabet drugs. X, G, Special K. You might want to talk to Lucas, the bartender. His brother Donovan owns this joint. Not tonight, though. He's busy."

"Thanks."

"Just don't get fired. I'd miss you."

We said good-byes all around and Grant and I left. He was yawning on the way back to the van. "Sorry," he said.

That got me started. After I yawned, I said, "No, it's okay. It's late. Thanks for indulging my whim." He really had been remarkably easygoing on this little adventure.

The crowd at Fuel had grown even bigger. Grant opened the van's door for me, as he had before. The atomic clock on his dashboard said ten-fifteen. He cranked the engine and we started back to my house.

"Are you going to tell me why we went to Kaleidoscope?"

So I did. All of it. About my history with Ashley and Flash, how my tires were knifed, and how Ashley'd gone to treatment with Nona and done so well, and about the GHB in the juice and her pleading guilty and the mysterious Jimmy. And Dee and Al and his founded allegations and gambling and drinking. I had to leave most of the names out, but it felt good to lay it all out there, even if it was a bit jumbled.

He was a good listener. Giving the case some thought, he said, "You're right. Something doesn't seem logical. Not if she was really doing well."

"That's what I think."

Grant pulled into my driveway and killed the engine. "You know what I think?"

"What?"

"I think I'd like to kiss you." He reached a hand to the side of my face and gently brought mine to his. His kiss was soft, tentative. An invitation.

And to my surprise, the geek was a good kisser. Something inside me melted, and just as I was going to ask him to come in, he stopped.

"What?" I asked.

"There's a man sitting on your — porch."

CHAPTER THIRTEEN

Sure enough, I could see the silhouette of a man sitting on the top step, backlit by the porch light, a small, flat package beside him. He had short, spiky hair.

"Son of a bitch," I said into Grant's clean-smelling neck.

"Boyfriend?" His tone was concerned.

"No."

"Ex-boyfriend?" His tone more hopeful.

I laughed. "No. That's the damn reporter who's been writing all the articles about me."

"Want me to take care of him?"

That also made me laugh. The vision of all-arms-and-legs Grant wildly taking swings at Kirk the Jerk. "No, thanks, I'll handle it."

"I should go. I gotta work early."

"Yeah, me too." I gave him one final peck on the cheek and eased out of the van. "Thanks for everything. I had a great time." I realized after I said it that it wasn't a lie.

"I'll call you."

I shut the door and watched as he backed out of the driveway, then turned to Kirk, who was now standing at the base of the steps in cargo shorts that showed off his muscular legs. A T-shirt with tight bands edging the sleeves did the same for his arms. A cellophane-wrapped mix of flowers was in his hand.

"Hi," he said, goofy grin in place.

"What are you doing here? How'd you find out where I live?"

"I'm an investigative reporter. I have sources."

I pulled my keys out and strode past him to the front door. "What do you want?"

"I wanted to know if you'd seen the article Sunday, so I thought I'd drop by."

"I saw it." I unlocked the door.

"I brought you flowers. Can I come in?"

A few neighbors were still outside, lighting fireworks and shooting bottle rockets in the street. I didn't want to get into it with him in public, but I didn't necessarily want him in the house, either. I deliberated.

"Come on," he said. "We need to put these in water."

I shrugged, and he followed me inside.

"Nice place."

"Thanks."

I stomped through the living room into the kitchen, opened the fridge and got a bottle of Ultra. Kirk followed, watching as I twisted the cap off and lobbed it into the trash can. I took a big swig.

"Sure, I'd love a beer, thanks for asking. You're welcome for the flowers, too. Got a vase?"

I nodded and fetched one out of the cabinet over the refrigerator. As I filled it with water, Kirk helped himself to a beer. I unwrapped the flowers and plunked them into the vase. Some of the petals fell off the daisies.

Kirk watched from across the kitchen, then asked, "What's with you?"

I slammed my beer down on the counter. "That fucking article of yours almost got me fired."

He stopped midsip, his eyes wide. "You're joking."

"I'm not."

"Why?"

"My bosses think your article made it look like we were shifting the blame. Trying to take the heat off of DHS."

"That's not what I meant. You made some good points at the courthouse. I was just bringing them out."

"And you had to put my name in the damn thing, didn't you? I'm not allowed to talk to you, but there's my goddamn name in the paper."

He looked confused. "I thought you'd be happy with it. You know, someone telling your side of the story."

"They sure as hell didn't see it that way."

"I'll fix it. I'll talk to Dr. Pope again."

"No! Christ, what part of *I am not allowed to talk to you* don't you understand!"

He set his beer down and was next to me in two strides. His cologne was musky and sweet. He grabbed me by the shoulders and pushed me against the stove. The knobs that controlled the burners pressed into my lower back. His kiss was rough. Grant's had been an invitation, Kirk's was a demand. My hands lingered on his chest a moment, then I pushed him away. "What the hell are you doing?"

"I've wanted to do that since I met you."

"Get out."

"Go out with me."

"Ha! Sure, that's going to happen. I thought I made myself clear."

"Come on."

"Kirk, you're going to cost me my job. My career. Just drop it, please."

He studied me for a moment, hurt blue eyes so intense I couldn't stand it, so I looked away. He picked up his bottle and toasted me. "Thanks for the beer." He took the drink with him, slamming the front door.

His five o'clock shadow had pinpricked my chin, leaving a stinging sensation. I rubbed it but it didn't go away. I turned off the lights, locked the doors, and went to bed, listening to the faint explosions from still-reveling patriots and feeling frustrated in more ways than one.

Tuesday. Michael had been dead one week, and today he'd be laid to rest. I wondered if there was ever going to be a Tuesday in my future when I wouldn't think about him. I searched through my closet to find something appropriate to wear. Settling on a navy pantsuit and a cream silk shell, I added some conservative jewelry and clipped my hair into a large barrette at the nape of my neck.

A storm front was closing in and high, gray clouds moved across the sky, pushed by waves of warm wind. I grabbed my umbrella and briefcase and inched to work in the traffic.

It had been a busy weekend for my voice mail. I spent a frantic two hours trying to arrange a placement in a mental health facility for a kid, updating Mac, filling out forms, and returning calls. I got as much done as possible, and at ten fifteen put it all aside and drove to Harris and Sons Memorial Chapel. I was early, but I wanted to make sure I had time to talk to Ashley before the Sheriff's deputies whisked her back to jail immediately after the service.

Harris and Sons was all about comfort. A young valet was waiting to park my car as soon as I made the turn into the drive. A long green canopy covered the L-shaped sidewalk all the way to the front door. The funeral director met me in the lobby, shook my hand solemnly, and showed me to a reception room where coffee and water service was set up. I poured myself a cup of the bitter java. A framed picture of Michael sat on a table, the familiar blue steps of St. Monica's in the background. Nona must have taken it.

Dee and Al arrived. She was in the same mismatched outfit I'd noticed in court, hair again rolled into curls at the ends. Al had traded his raunchy T-shirt for a more appropriate black shirt and black jeans. After greeting me, Al left us standing near the door and went for coffee.

"How're you doing?" I asked Dee.

"Okay, I guess."

"And Al?"

"All right."

"How long have you been married to Al?"

"Just about two years."

"Was he married before?"

"Yeah. Once. He has a daughter a little younger than Ashley. Him and her never see each other."

"How come?"

"Her momma, she done poisoned her mind against him. Told her a bunch of lies about her daddy, so now she don't want to see him."

Interesting. Al had out-and-out lied to Dee about why he couldn't see his daughter.

"How long did you and Al date before you got married?"

"About a year. Why?"

"I was just trying to remember when I first met him."

"It was after Michael went to the first foster parents. You arranged that visit for me."

That's right. Al and Dee had requested a visit, which I set up at the agency. She'd introduced him as her boyfriend. Michael was already in foster care, and the visit was supervised at the office, which might explain why I never did the background check. It wouldn't have affected Michael's safety. I made a mental note to tell Mac.

Al had been stopped by the funeral director, who was shaking his hand and expressing his condolences. I moved on to my next question.

"Was Al home the night Michael died?"

"I dunno. I was at work."

"Does he usually stay home while you're at work?"

"Sometimes he goes out to the dog track. Or to see his guy."

"His guy?"

"The guy he bets with."

Ah, his bookie. "Does he owe him a lot of money?" I already knew the answer, from Ashley. She'd told me a long time ago that Al had a problem and that he'd lost a lot.

"Not as much as before. He only owes him about thirteen now."

"Thirteen thousand?"

"Yeah. Really, he's doing better."

So who knows where Al was the night Michael died. For some

reason, that made me nervous. And what about this bookie? Was he the type to threaten someone's family? Like in the movies? It sounded outrageous. Didn't it?

Other people were starting to arrive. Nona walked in with Dazzle, both in pretty church clothes. All of Michael's former foster parents showed up, and I spent time chatting with them, one eye on the door. Nona greeted several women I didn't know. I assumed they were women Ashley had gone to treatment with, or who were in her after-care group. Finally, the elusive Jimmy walked in, soon followed by Ashley.

They'd allowed her to change out of her orange striped jumpsuit into a plain gray dress with a white collar. Her hands were cuffed in the front, her ankles chained together. Her gaze strayed to the picture of Michael but didn't stay there. Moments after she entered, the director announced, "Ladies and Gentlemen, we are ready to begin the service. Please follow me to the chapel."

We filed into the church-like room. I sat in the back row where I had a pretty good view of all the mourners. Al and Dee sat in the front row on Ashley's right. Jimmy was on her left, looking awkward in a white dress shirt that had seen better days. The rest were scattered here and there throughout the chapel. No sign of Flash. A lanky gray-haired black man in a clerical collar approached the podium.

"Good morning. Thank you all for coming today. Let's begin with a prayer." All heads bowed. Reverend Croft offered a short prayer for Michael, then thanked God for the support of everyone present and prayed for help for the family during this difficult time. His voice was a sing-song down comforter.

He finished with "Amen," and walked to the small casket in front of the lectern. It was draped with Michael's blanket, the fleece one printed with lambs that Ashley had taken with her when we left the apartment last week. The reverend stroked the soft cloth.

"When I first met Ashley last week and learned about Michael — when she showed me this blanket and talked about his favorite toys — I was reminded of the eighteenth-century poem by William Blake, 'The Lamb," from *Songs of Innocence*." He went back to the podium and read it, ending with "Little lamb, God bless thee!

"The apostle John called Jesus the Lamb of God. Lambs are often associated with sacrifice, just as God sacrificed his only son so that the sins of the world would be forgiven. Because of God's sacrifice, we shall all be welcomed into the kingdom of Heaven, no matter what our age, or sins."

He continued preaching as my mind wandered. I studied the people in the chapel to avoid looking at the small box that held Michael's body. Ashley's head was bent. Jimmy was close to her, his arm resting on the back of the pew and his hand patting her shoulder gently from time to time. Nona and Dazzle rocked and nodded to the cadence of the Reverend's voice, occasionally adding "Amen" to something he said. Dazzle was crying, streams of tears fell down her cheeks and were caught in a tissue. Al's gaze wandered the room, Dee sat rigid.

Reverend Croft concluded his eulogy and nodded once to a staff member in the wings, who turned to a control panel and hit a button. An instrumental recording of Eric Clapton's "Tears in Heaven" played through the barely hidden speakers in the ceiling. I felt emotion rising inside me and stuffed it down, quick. It was harder this time. Every time.

Sacrifice. The Reverend had nailed that one right on the head. That's what Michael's death was about. Ashley had sacrificed her son. And her freedom. For someone or something. What was I willing to sacrifice to find the truth? My career? Maybe so. To prove I wasn't wrong about Ashley. To protect the belief that my instincts were right. And to assuage my own guilt that I could have done something more.

The song ended, and Reverend Croft concluded the service with the Twenty-third Psalm and another prayer for Michael. He invited us all to accompany the family to the cemetery for the interment. As everyone filed out, I hurried to my car. In the warm vehicle I watched the funeral staff load the tiny coffin into a hearse and drive out. The sheriff's deputies placed Ashley in the backseat of their car and followed. Jimmy went to a battered black pickup with a silver truck box in the back. Dee and Al were in her Chevy, and Nona and Dazzle had come together in Nona's Kia. I turned my headlights on and joined the caravan, led by a Birmingham police officer on a motorcycle, blue lights flashing.

We paraded to Elmwood Cemetery, through the massive iron gates, and onto a narrow paved road that wound through acres and acres of headstones. At the southwest corner of the graveyard, another green canopy awaited us, a few chairs underneath on an outdoor carpet. The deputies walked Ashley to the front row, where she sat between her mother and Jimmy. She clutched the blue lamb blanket as the little casket hovered over the grave. Others filled in the rest of the seats, and the deputies and I stood respectfully in the back.

The burial was brief. Trees around us swayed as the reverend struggled to be heard over the rushing breezes. He prayed again, then quoted Genesis. "Dust thou art, and unto dust thou shalt return." The casket was lowered, and Ashley sprinkled a bit of earth on it. In my mind, I said good-bye and apologized to Michael. Reverend Croft thanked us again for coming, and it was over.

The mourners hugged Ashley, one by one, and walked to their cars. The reverend left. Dee and Al left. The deputies gave Ashley some space, standing twenty feet or so away. Jimmy went back to his truck, leaned against the door and waited. I walked toward him, looking back over my shoulder to see Ashley, alone, standing over the open grave and talking to her dead son.

I approached Jimmy, who was watching Ashley with his hands in his pockets. His hair and beard were whipping in the wind. "Mr. Shelton?"

"That's right."

I held out my hand and he shook it. "I'm Claire Conover. I was Michael's social worker."

He nodded. "Ashley told me about you."

"I saw you at the jail that day. You're Ashley's boyfriend."

"You could say that."

"Mr. Shelton —"

"Jimmy." His voice was deep.

"Jimmy, you know how Michael died?"

"Yes."

"I'm having a hard time believing that Ashley was using drugs again. Or that she would have them where Michael could get into them. Am I wrong? She seemed to be doing so well."

Both of us watched Ashley, still speaking in earnest to the wooden box in the grave.

"Leave it alone," he said.

"Leave what alone?"

"Ashley. Everything." His dark brown eyes focused on mine as he leaned close. "You'll get hurt. Understand?"

"But, um . . ." As I stammered, shaken by the threat, he edged around me and went to Ashley. When he placed a hand on her shoulder, she turned and his arms enfolded her. It looked as though she were crying.

The two deputies were still some distance away. As Jimmy and Ashley whispered together, I made my way over to the officers and pulled out my ID. "I'm Ashley's social worker. Can I have five minutes before you take her back?"

Cops and social workers are cousins. We're all part of the same family of folks whose job it is to care for the suffering and the endangered. I thought the ID would gain their support, and I was right. The younger of the two deferred to the older, and he nodded. "Five minutes." Ashley and Jimmy approached us, his hand gripping her elbow. He gave her one last hug and kissed her forehead, shot me another warning look, then went to his truck. The deputies walked to their marked car, chatting. The wind drowned out what they were saying.

I focused on Ashley. "I'm so sorry about everything. Do you need anything?"

Her head stayed down, eyes locked on the perfectly manicured grass. "No, I'm just ready to get back to jail."

"Ashley, what happened? Where'd the GHB come from?"

Her head snapped up. "Why won't you just let it go? It's over. Michael's dead. I don't even have to talk to you no more."

"I want to help you."

"Why? What the hell difference does it make?"

"It matters to me. A lot. I had faith in you. So I was wrong?"

"Yeah. Okay? Yeah, you were wrong. I'm exactly where I should be. My son's dead and it's all my fault."

"So you put the G in the juice?"

"Just drop it. Please. You don't know what you're getting into. These are dangerous people. They'll kill me. They'll kill you."

It took a second for that to sink in. "You know who killed Michael?"

"I mean it. Drop it."

"But — if you know who did it, who's responsible — they can re-verse your conviction. You can get out of —"

"No! I'm where I need to be."

"But if you didn't put —"

"My whole fucked-up life caused Mikey's death. My bad deci-sions, my addiction. It's God's way of punishing me."

"No —"

"Yes. And while I'm being punished, they can't get me. Stay out of it, Claire."

One of the deputies walked over and took Ashley's arm. "Time's up."

"If you'll just let me help —"

"No! It's too late."

"I'll come visit you."

She shrugged as the officer led her away. Once again, they helped her into the backseat. The sound of ankle chains tinkled over the wind.

I had zero business going anywhere but back to DHS. Enough work was piled on my desk to keep me busy until the end of the year.

Instead, I flew down Sixth Avenue to the north part of downtown. Found a place to park, fed the meter, and went into the Top of the Hill Grill.

The special today was roast beef, and the smell of the rich brown gravy jolted my stomach, reminding me it was time to eat. It was twelve after one and the lunch crowd was thinning out. Brandi was taking an order at a table as I sat at the green counter. She finished and came around to me. Noticing my dark suit, she asked, "Was it awful?"

"It was sad, yeah."

"How's Ashley?"

"Okay. Did you see her this weekend?"

"Yeah, I went up there Saturday. Brought her some money for her commissary account. She looks terrible."

"She say anything about Mikey?"

She shook her head. "All she said was that she deserved to be in jail. I asked her what that meant and she said she didn't have no life on the outside so she might as well be in prison. I tried to tell her that was just her grieving talking, but that's all she'd say. It's good she's in there, 'cause I'd be real worried about her killing herself if she wasn't."

"Jimmy been back in here?"

"Nope. You want some lunch?"

"Sure, something to go. A BLT." Brandi wrote the order and slipped the sheet into the window. While we waited, she cleared a few tables in between listening to my report on the funeral. My sandwich appeared in the window in a white paper sack with the ticket taped to it. Brandi set it in front of me, then pulled her keys out of her apron.

"You still want the key, right?"

"Sure. Did you tell Ashley I'd asked about it?"

"No."

I hadn't asked Ashley, either, but I knew what the answer would've been. I didn't care. I picked up the small silver key and my sandwich.

"Brandi, you ever been to a place called Kaleidoscope? In Lakeview?"

"Sure. The dance place. Sometimes."

"You ever go there with Ashley?"

"Two or three times." Seeing the surprised look on my face, she quickly added, "But Ashley didn't drink or nothing. I made sure. We just went for a girls' night out, like. Just to go dancing. She left Michael at the sitter's. I'd never let her touch nothing to drink."

"Okay."

"Why?"

I didn't feel up to a long explanation. "I was just wondering. It came up, that's all."

With a puzzled look, Brandi bid me good-bye. I paid at the register and wolfed down the sandwich, hardly tasting it, on my way to Avondale.

I parked in front of Ashley's apartment. Several other cars were there, including Ashley's beat-up old Saturn. Another was being worked on by a middle-aged black man. He was changing the oil. Ashley's doorknob still hung loosely on the cheap door, and the gang sign was still on the wall.

I readied the key to unlock the door but stopped when I heard voices. From inside the apartment. I pressed my ear to the door.

"Tom, you are only ten questions away from becoming a millionaire. We'll be right back." Music. A game show. Then a commercial. Why was Ashley's TV on?

Instead of using the key, I knocked, and a man opened the door.

CHAPTER FOURTEEN

I was expecting Jimmy, or maybe Dee or Al, but not the guy who opened the door. Sandy blond hair, curly, cut short. An Eddie Bauer logo, unobtrusive, on his tee pocket. Diesel jeans. Not a cheap dresser, this guy. His body hadn't yet broadened in the back and shoulders. A spray of freckles across his nose only added to his youthful appearance. And I knew him, from somewhere.

"Hello!" He greeted me cheerfully. "Are you a friend of Ashley's? 'Cause she's locked up." His eyes were greenish-blue. Something about his eyes nagged at me.

"I know. I was her social worker. Who are you?"

"Oh, you're Claire. C'mon in." He swept an arm wide in invitation. I entered the apartment, which was a mess. Definitely not the way Ashley left it. Empty beer cans, cigarette butts, and snack bags covered the coffee table. A dirty shirt lay wadded on the floor and a tangled blanket was on the couch. He threw himself onto the sofa, shoved the blanket aside and said, "Have a seat." He muted the game show.

"No, thanks." I examined the room. Dishes were piled up in the kitchen beyond. I spotted the collage of pictures hanging over the television, and realized where I'd seen him before. He was one of the three guys sitting on the couch in the picture. "Who are you?" I repeated.

"I'm Zander. I'm a friend of Ashley's."

"I would hope so, since you're in her apartment."

He laughed, loudly. "Yeah. I'm gonna house-sit for a while until she gets out."

"That may be a long time."

"Yeah, I know. A year. You got any cigarettes?"

"Don't smoke."

"Damn, I gotta go get some."

"Zander, huh? What's your last name?" I asked, facing him.

He licked his lips once, then again. "Why?"

"What's your last name?" I gave him my best I'm-not-playing tone. It usually worked on kids.

"Madison."

Zander Madison. Zander . . . Alex . . . Zander . . . Alexander Madison. Holy crap.

He'd been watching me while I put the name together. "You wouldn't be a junior, by any chance?"

He giggled. "Good guess."

"As in The Madison Group?" One of Birmingham's largest business conglomerates.

"Yep."

"And the Madison Center?" The newly renovated skyscraper downtown.

"Yep."

"And the Madison Sports Complex?" Brand-new acres of soccer, football, and baseball fields in a nearby suburb.

"Yep." He giggled again. "Do y'suppose if they named a street after my dad it'd be Madison Avenue?" He flopped around and guffawed like it was the most hilarious thing anyone had ever said. "Or maybe they'll give him a Square Garden. Ha!"

Life is too good when you laugh that hard at your own jokes. It dawned on me what had bothered me about his eyes. They were dilated. I looked around for whatever he'd been using, my gaze searching until it rested on the end of a small glass tube sticking out from underneath the couch. It was charred with residue. He was as high as a kite in a hurricane.

I nodded to it. "That your pipe?"

"Yeah, you wanna hit it?"

"No, that's okay."

He shrugged, still smiling. "More for me."

There was something else. The eyes. I sucked in a deep breath as it hit me. Those same eyes, in a picture I saw this morning. They were Michael's.

"You were Michael's father." Michael Alexander Hennessy. So Ashley had given him his daddy's name after all. And his grandfather's.

He sat up, suddenly serious. "What makes you say that?"

"He had your eyes." And hair color, come to think of it. And the curls, too.

The compulsive lip-licking started again. No doubt dry mouth, or a tic, from the drugs. "I'm going to miss that little guy."

"Wait a minute. You knew him?"

"Sure."

I looked at the pipe again, flabbergasted. He picked it up and stroked it like it was something precious. "Don't worry. Ashley had strict rules when it came to visiting Michael. She wouldn't let me near him if I was on anything. She could always tell. I wasn't allowed to go anywhere with him, and she watched me like a hawk when I was here. So he was safe."

Apparently not, because he was dead. "Were you here the night he died? Last Monday?"

"I came by for a bit, yeah. Right when they got home."

"You're aware of how he died, right?"

"Yeah. GHB. Totally blew me away."

"Was it your G?"

"No way! I told you, Ashley would never let me bring anything around here. She was real serious about staying clean. It just about killed her when you took Michael away the first time."

"You think the G was hers?"

"I don't know. Ashley and me, we were never into G much."

"So what do you think happened?"

"Ashley was a popular girl. She had lots of friends. Any one of them could have mixed the stuff and left it here."

"To kill them?"

"What do you mean?"

"The police have said that there was enough GHB in the pitcher to kill both of them."

"So some idiot mixed too much."

"What do you think happened, Zander?"

"I don't know."

I wasn't buying it. I wondered if he was the self-proclaimed idiot who brought the GHB here. Zander dug around for cigarettes, finally finding an open pack under a large bag of M&M's on the coffee table. He lit up.

"How did you and Ashley meet?" This romance between the son of one of Birmingham's richest and most well-known businessmen and an abused country girl from Adger didn't make sense.

"I was partying with this dude and we went to some house in Irondale. He said he knew this guy that had some really good rock. She was there, and we hooked up."

Hooked up in this case meant got high and had sex, I was sure. "And then she got pregnant?"

"Yeah, a few weeks later." He dragged on the cigarette.

"Where were you when Michael was taken away?"

"Around. I mean, it's not like me and Ashley were ever really a couple, you know. We just hooked up every now and then."

"You know Flash?"

"I know who he is, and that Ashley got drugs and shit from him." He tapped the end of his cigarette into the overflowing ashtray on the coffee table.

"You know how she did that?"

"I know she had sex with him, to get stuff. Ashley and I, we don't judge each other. That's what makes our relationship so special."

Ashley had sex with far more men than just Flash and Zander. Luckily her HIV test had been negative two years ago. I wondered if Zander's would be.

"Do your — did your parents know about Michael?"

He licked his lips again and sucked on the cigarette. "Oh, hell no. Well, I take that back. They know I got a girl pregnant. My father gave some money to," he made quotation marks with his fingers, ashes falling onto the sofa that Ashley had saved so carefully to buy, "have it taken care of."

"And?"

"And Ashley and I bought some really good shit with that money."

"So he has no idea his grandson just died?"

He shrugged and crushed out the smoke.

"Does he know about your drug habit?"

"Oh, yeah. He thinks —" He giggled again. "He thinks I'm in rehab right now. In Ar-i-zona." Whatever he was on — crack, I suspected — was taking full effect. His eyes were glazed and his words were starting to slur.

I was silent, taking it all in. Ashley lied to me about not knowing who Michael's father was. And she allowed him access to Michael. What else was she lying about?

I started toward the door. "I gotta head back to work. Take care of yourself, Zander."

He was sinking lower onto the couch. "Why don' ya stay 'while. Hang out."

"No, thanks. I have to go to work."

"Work sucks. My parents want me to work. Want me to go into finance. Crunchin' numbers. Can you 'magine? How fuckin' borin'."

"I'll see you around, Zander." I locked the door behind me as he unmuted the TV. The unlucky contestant had not won the million dollars.

It was starting to drizzle as I went back to the office. When I got there, Mac had left a case file on my desk, an emergency that had to be investigated immediately. Because of the level of injuries, I wound up having to take the boy and his brother into custody and spent the rest of the day and most of Tuesday night finding them a foster home. I didn't make it home until almost midnight. When I got there, a vase of gorgeous pink roses was sitting on my front stoop. The rain hadn't smeared Grant's handwritten note, thanking me for a great time and hoping to see me soon. I unlocked the door, put the roses on the coffee table, found his card, and called his cell phone.

"'ello?" His voice was throaty. I'd woken him up.

"Hey, it's Claire. Sorry. I woke you, didn't I?" I could hear a narrator's drone in the background on the TV.

"'s okay. I fell asleep on the couch." The TV went silent. "How're you?" he asked through a yawn.

"I'm fine, just got home from work. I was calling to thank you for the flowers. Pink roses are my favorite." Their aroma was filling my living room.

"Glad you like them. Long day, huh?"

"Yeah, I had an emergency to deal with."

"You free Saturday night?"

"Sure."

"How about a movie? And dinner?"

"Sounds good." We chatted a bit before saying goodnight.

Wednesday was another busy day, dealing with the remnants of yesterday's emergency, the shelter care hearing at court, and the rest of the stuff I'd left on my desk. It was Thursday before I had half a second to think about Ashley and Michael. And Zander Madison.

Royanne and I were meeting for our usual lunch date, although it was a little early to accommodate my twelve thirty intervention meeting. It was my turn to drive, and at ten fifty I pulled up to the front of the towering headquarters of Birmingham Financial Bank. BFB's building was all silver, the mirrored glass reflecting the other skyscrapers around it. Royanne was waiting in the expansive lobby and quickly jumped in the car.

"Gawd Almighty I'm so sick of summer already." She fastened the seat belt across her ample bosom and adjusted the vents to blow on her full blast. Her big blonde hair didn't move.

"Amen." I slid into the traffic and headed south. Our early arrival at Los Compadres meant we avoided the crowd, and we were seated immediately. Pablo brought our drinks without being asked. We ordered and when we were alone Royanne asked how I was doing.

"Okay. I went to Michael's funeral on Tuesday."

"Oh, God. How awful."

"Yeah, it was sad."

"I can't imagine. I don't want to imagine. If it were one of mine —"

"I know." I gave her a quick rundown of the memorial service, then moved on to other gossip. Royanne insisted on hearing every single detail about my evening with Grant. I admitted that I hadn't had a bad time with him, and actually found him kind of attractive. That confession invited merciless teasing until Pablo brought my chicken tacos and her burrito. Halfway through my first taco, I asked, "You know anything about The Madison Group?"

She swallowed a bite of refried beans. "Sure, why?"

"I was just wondering what they did."

"Lots of stuff. There's MAS, Madison Accounting Services. They do corporate accounting. That's the largest company in the group. Then there's Madison Investments. And Madison Realty, they do corporate real estate. And, of course, the Madison Foundation that does a lot of local charity work. They sponsor that huge golf tournament every year. Why?"

"Just wondering."

"Nuh-uh." Royanne met my gaze. "You never just wonder. What's up?"

"You know anything about the Madisons?"

"Alexander Madison is the owner and CEO of The Madison Group. He started thirty years ago as a corporate accountant at another firm, eventually working his way up the ladder to CEO, then left and started his own. It's grown from there. Why?"

I played with the straw in my Diet Coke. "You know anything about his family?"

"He's married. His wife's name is Karen. Two children, Alexander Junior, called Zander, and Kaylin. Why?"

"How come you know so much about them?"

Royanne took another bite, then scanned the room quickly to make sure no one was listening. "You remember on the Fourth when I said I'd just gotten this huge account?"

"Yeah."

"Madison Accounting Services is trying to buy another firm. They'd become the largest corporation of their kind in the southeast. I can't say anything more about it, but BFB is doing the loan for the buy. If everything checks out. That's not for public knowledge."

"Hmm."

"Now, why are you asking? And please God don't tell me that Alexander Madison is some raging pedophile child abuser."

I laughed. "Not that I know of."

"Seriously, then, why all the questions?"

"I was more curious about his kids than him."

"Kaylin is still in high school. She's seventeen and just finished her junior year at ASFA." ASFA was the Alabama School of Fine Arts, a by-application-only public school for talented kids. "Zander is twenty-two. He's a sophomore at Auburn, majoring in finance. He's doing summer term."

My eyebrows shot up in surprise at that last statement. "Oh?"

"What?"

"Nothing."

"Bullshit. C'mon. I just told you something in confidence. Now it's your turn."

"I can't really talk about it."

Royanne threw her fork down, hard. It rang sharply on the stoneware plate, startling me and the couple at the table next to us. They stared. Royanne turned red. Her voice climbed an octave as it got louder.

"Shit, Claire! What the hell? You know something that could make or break the biggest deal of my career and you sit back and give me the but-I-can't-tell-you bullshit? No way. I'm not putting up with this. You tell me what you know now or I'm walking out of here and I'm not talking to you ever again."

CHAPTER FIFTEEN

I made a stammering attempt to answer Royanne. "I don't . . . I can't . . ."

She snatched her purse from the back of the chair, got out a five and some ones, and threw them on the table. Then she stomped out.

Pablo, noticing the ruckus, hurried over. "Everything is okay?"

"Sure. I just need our checks." He tallied them for me as I gathered Royanne's money off the table. I took the checks to the register and paid, getting change to leave a tip for Pablo. He gave me a worried wave as I left.

Royanne was leaning against the passenger door of my car, the butt of her skirt against the dirty white paint. Her arms were crossed and her mouth was set in a tight line. She'd never been this mad at me, not even during all the petty crap of junior high school. I unlocked the doors. "Get in."

We fastened our seat belts, then she folded her arms again and stared out of the window. I pulled onto Green Springs Highway toward downtown.

"Come on, Roy. This is ridiculous."

She didn't answer. A mile or so down the road, I'd had enough. I pulled into a parking lot next to some softball fields and stopped, facing the fence, leaving the car running. A children's summer league was practicing T-ball. The sweaty kids couldn't have been older than six. I watched as one baseball-capped kid whacked the ball off the T and ran hell-bent for leather toward first base. The coach on the pitcher's mound took his time getting to the ball and lobbing it to the boy at first, who caught it. The runner was already safe. I thought about what to say to Royanne, carefully.

"Did you see Michael's obituary in the paper Saturday?"

She wouldn't look at me. "No."

"They printed his whole name. Michael Alexander Hennessy."

She whipped around to face me. "Alexander?"

"Yep."

"He was Zander's kid?"

I pursed my lips and didn't answer.

"Does Zander have a drug problem? Like Ashley?"

Again, I was silent.

She buried her face in her hands. "Oh God. Are you telling me that my client and the head of one of this city's most powerful companies had a grandson by a crack whore who murdered him?"

"Hey now—"

"That's what she was."

Yes, that's what Ashley was. She was also damaged. Abused. Starting at a very young age. There but for the Grace of God, as they say. Plus, her effort to straighten herself out was a journey harder than any I hoped I'd ever have to make. I didn't say any of this out loud.

We stared absently as a pigtailed girl hit the ball all of three feet and ran, arms pumping. Safe again. Royanne ran a hand across her mouth and said, "Well, we'll just have to deny the loan."

It was my turn to look quickly at her. "Why?"

"Are you kidding me? Alexander Senior's reputation *is* that company. If that's destroyed, there go the investors. If this gets out—"

"It's not going to get out. Nobody knows. Alexander Senior doesn't even know."

"What do you mean?"

"Senior thinks he paid for an abortion."

"Oh God."

"So nobody knows, except me and you and the two people in the room when Michael was conceived."

"It'll get out."

"Maybe not."

"Sure it will. You already said that reporter — what's his name, Mahoney — is on this story. Suppose he doesn't let it go? Suppose he finds out about the Madison's connection to the dead kid? And their son's drug problem?"

At the mention of Kirk's name, my fingers went to my chin, then my lips.

"He's done with the story, I think. And I don't know how he'd find out the connection."

"You did."

"Yeah, but that's different. Michael and Zander looked alike. I knew Michael and could put two and two together."

"And Mahoney can't? He's a bird dog. They all are."

That was true. One whiff of a newspaper-selling, circulation-building scandal and I had a feeling Kirk would sell his mother's soul to Satan to get it.

"Give me some time. Let me talk to Kirk, see what he knows. If he's done with it, then it'll all blow over."

"So he's 'Kirk' now?"

"Kirk the Jerk."

"I can give you a week. I can stretch out the audit of MAS's assets until then."

"Thanks. I'd hate for Alexander Senior's company to suffer because of a grandchild he didn't even know about."

"You don't know that."

"What?"

"How do you know that Alexander Senior didn't know about him?"

She was right. It was an assumption on my part that Zander had told the truth. What if Alexander Senior did know about Ashley and Michael? What would he do to protect his company from the possible scandal? Kill them both? Where would the head of a multimillion dollar company get his hands on enough GHB to kill two people?

From his drug-addict son, that's where. I chewed all this over in my head as the kids in the dugout took the field.

"Do you know him? Senior?" I asked.

"No, I haven't met him yet. I imagine I will when we do the final deal. Mostly I'm working with his CFO and a couple of VPs." She started to laugh. "Whaddya want me to do, ask him about Michael? So, Mr. Madison, your assets look good, you had a strong second quarter, and by the way, did you know your coke-snortin' son knocked up a crack whore?"

It was my turn to be pissed. "Knock it off."

"Why?"

"Ashley's a person. So was Michael."

She bit her lip. "You're right. I'm sorry."

I reached over and squeezed her arm, which morphed into a hug. "Me, too." We broke apart and after thinking a second I asked, "So what about Mrs. Madison Senior? What'd you say her name was?"

"Karen. She runs the Madison Foundation. Does a lot of charity work. The golf tournament is only part of that. She's also done some stuff with Children's Hospital, the homeless shelter downtown — what's it called — The Harbor. And," Royanne snapped her fingers and looked at me. "Our Mothers Have Wings."

Our Mothers Have Wings, or OMHW, was an organization I'd been very active in for several years. Founded fifteen years ago by a woman who also lost her mother to breast cancer, OMHW's mission was to raise awareness about multigenerational disease and the importance of regular screenings, mammograms, and genetic testing. I'd run their grief group for daughters of breast cancer victims until six months ago when I had to give it up as the business of buying my house interfered.

"Huh. I don't think I've met her." Not unusual. OMHW had at least fifty regular volunteers. "I'll call Kelsey this afternoon, maybe see if I can wrangle an introduction."

"Why?"

"To see if they knew about Michael. Ashley was doing so well. I just can't accept that she's responsible for Michael's death."

"Nothing is going to bring him back."

"I know. But I owe it to him to find out what happened. And why."

I put the car in reverse and backed out, then headed downtown. In front of the BFB building, Royanne gave me another hug before exiting the car. "Be careful," she said.

Back at work, my cubicle was quiet. Russell was out. I could tell I had messages waiting by the small orange light on the phone. No call from Flash. I called a client back, then phoned Kelsey, the volunteer coordinator for OMHW. She was a pretty, petite blonde whose super-bubbly, ex-sorority-girl personality made her perfect for recruiting and retaining volunteers.

"Hey Claire! I'm so glad to hear from you! How's the new house?"

"Coming along. How're you?"

"I'm great! I hope you're calling because you've got some time to volunteer. You know, we've had so many calls about the grief group, I really think we need to start it up again."

We talked about the logistics of that for a while, and I promised to think about it, then asked, "So, what's coming up?"

"We've got an Angels Aware lunch tomorrow at The Club. You want a ticket?"

"Who's the speaker?"

"A radiation oncologist. He's going to talk about new targeted radiation therapies."

Sounded like a blast. "How much are the tickets?"

"Eighty bucks."

Yow. That was a pretty hefty chunk out of my paycheck for a lunch. Interpreting my silence correctly, Kelsey said, "I'll tell you what, if you'll come early, say about ten thirty, and help Marlie set up and run the registration table, I'll give it to you for twenty."

"Sold." I made my next call, and Detective Brighton picked up after the second ring.

"She pled guilty," he said, after I identified myself.

"I know, I was there."

"What do you want? It's over."

"Just a quick question. Did Ashley have a drug screen when she was arrested?"

"No."

"Why not?"

"Because A, we don't have the facilities to do that at the jail. And B, because the surrender of bodily fluids is something we'd need a warrant for. Not many people will pee in a cup just because you ask them to. It would be too time consuming to get warrants for everyone we arrest. By the time we did, they'd be clean."

"Oh."

"Nice try, but it's over. There's no use in defending her now."

"Thanks, Detective."

"Take it easy."

So much for that. I might never know whether Ashley was high the night Michael died. I consulted the thick phone book in my desk, then punched in a new number.

Half of me prayed he wouldn't be there. Maybe I'd go straight to voice mail. But no, my typical luck held true, and he picked up after the first ring.

"Mahoney."

I froze.

"Hello?"

"Hi, Kirk, it's Claire Conover"

"Hello." Frosty, to say the least.

"I was calling to say I'm sorry about what happened the other night."

"No problem."

"I didn't mean to hurt —"

"Like I said, no big deal. Forget it."

This was followed by a few moments of awkward silence. I struggled for some way to bring up Ashley's case without being too obvious. "So, now that DHS is out of the spotlight, what are you working on?"

"What makes you think DHS is out of the spotlight? Your agency is never out of the spotlight."

"Well, I meant now that Ashley's case is over."

"I guess you'll have to buy a paper and find out. Later."

He hung up.

Damn.

I cursed at the phone, which didn't make me feel any better. Before I forgot, I filled out a form to turn into Mac so I could use comp time for the Angels Aware lunch the next day. As I slid it into his box, he motioned me into his office from behind the glass. I retrieved the form and brought it in with me.

"What's this?" he asked, reaching for it.

"A comp time request. OMHW is having a luncheon tomorrow and they need a volunteer. I'll be back by two." Mac knew I'd volunteered with them in the past.

"You should take the day off tomorrow. You've earned it with the week you've had. You've got plenty of comp time."

"Thanks. I'll think about it." I turned to leave.

"Wait, Claire. I need to tell you something else. Have a seat."

I did, and he said, "Dr. Pope heard from the state commissioner today."

"And?"

"And the attorney general's office wants the Hennessy record."

That cold, blood-rushing-to-my-feet sensation again. Just like the day Michael died. "Christ."

"Now, there's no need to panic yet. They just want to look at it. To look at our role, and the court's. They're worried the reunification might have been rushed."

The A.G.'s office would look at it, all right. Then decide whether or not to hand it over to the grand jury, who could pursue criminal charges of negligence against the agency. That could mean indictments: of me, Mac, Dr. Pope, the judge on the case. Hell, everybody.

"Jesus," I said, as if more blasphemy would help.

"Claire, we've got an awful lot of ground to cover before anything happens. If anything happens. I debated about even telling you, but I thought you had the right to know."

"Thanks."

"I mean it. Just do your job like you normally do. I'll let you know when it's time to worry."

"Okay."

With thoughts swimming in a sea of anxiety, I went back to my cubicle. I tried to focus on my other cases and put Mac's revelation about the A.G. out of my head, but it didn't work. A week ago I thought being fired would be the worst thing ever. Suddenly it seemed like the best-case scenario.

CHAPTER SIXTEEN

I worked late into the evening Thursday, seriously considering Mac's suggestion about taking a day off. After much deliberation, I left him a note saying I wouldn't be in Friday, then went home.

It was close to seven when I unlocked my door, dropped my brief-case to the floor, and immediately ditched my work clothes for denim shorts and a T-shirt. There was a message on my machine from Dad. I returned his call and caught him up on everything. Then I fetched the corkscrew and a half-decent bottle of Pinot Grigio. I parked my-self in one of the wrought-iron chairs on my patio and put my feet up on the other.

I stared absently at the whispering oak, hickory, and pines in my backyard. Birds pecked seeds at my feeder, a colorful parade of car-dinals, blue jays, and chickadees. The sun went down, turning the cloud-streaked sky pale gray, then pink, then orange. It wasn't until I finished the fourth glass of wine that the uneasy sensation started to subside. As Mac said, it wasn't time to freak out yet. I'd done my job to the best of my ability. Michael's return home hadn't been rushed. Ashley tested clean for eighteen months straight, a hell of a long time by DHS standards. The record was all in order, with the exception of some minor details. Details that wouldn't have caused Michael's death. No way they'd hold me accountable, right?

The problem was the political aspect of the thing. As long as the public focused on this case, the politicians would use it to make them-selves look good. The commissioner would, for sure. So would the attorney general. Maybe even Dr. Pope. Look at what we are doing to stop child deaths in our state, they'd proclaim. We are cleaning up DHS. And I'd get thrown under the bus. I hated feeling this way. I hated the constant anxiety. Not to mention the cynical way I was viewing the world.

Maybe I should just chuck it in. Resign, and join the ranks of child welfare workers who were victims of burnout. No more long hours, angry clients, hurt children. The idea was tempting. But what else would I do? I could do many things with the master's degree I had. I merely had to choose one and find a job. But I'd miss DHS. I'd miss Russell, and Mac, too, on some level. And I still believed I owed Michael answers. I deferred any career decisions, poured myself another glass of wine, and went in to watch some TV.

After flipping channels for a while, I gave it up and went to bed. I woke up Friday with a hangover. It took three cups of coffee and a bagel to make me feel better. I dressed in a light pink suit with white piping and fastened an inch-tall pin to the lapel, a gold angel with wings spread open over the letters OMHW.

My first stop was the jail. I left my purse at security as I had before and took the still-grungy elevator to the second floor. Several other inmates were visiting with loved ones. I parked myself on the last available concrete-footed stool and waited while the guard brought Ashley to me.

She looked like a washed-out version of herself. Her brown hair draped limply around her pale face. The neck of her faded uniform hung so that her shoulder was exposed. She adjusted it after she sat down. Whatever irritation I'd felt toward her dissolved.

She picked up the receiver on her side of the cubicle. "Hey," she said in a small voice.

"Hey. How are you?"

"Okay. You know. Like the Big Book says, one day at a time."

"I thought the service for Michael was nice."

"Me, too. Nona did a good job."

"Why didn't you tell me about Zander?"

Her eyes filled with tears, which she immediately wiped on her jumpsuit. "I hated not tellin' you about him. But I couldn't. You know who Zander's daddy is?"

"Yes."

"Zander's daddy didn't want me to have Michael. He gave us money to . . . anyway, I couldn't. I just couldn't. That was my baby." She wiped her eyes on her sleeve again. "I may not have had him for long, but at least I had him."

That got to me. I took a second to gather my emotions and put them in their box. Then I said, "Zander said he was at your house the night before Michael died."

"He came by."

"Did he bring the GHB?"

"No. He wasn't allowed in the house if he was high. I meant it, too. I wasn't about to get caught havin' nothin' to do with drugs again."

"So he wouldn't have hurt Michael? Or you?"

"No way. I know Zander's got problems, but he was a good dad."

I hated to think what rating scale we were using if Zander Madison qualified as a good father. Probably the same one that would rank Al Mackey as a good husband. I raised a skeptical eyebrow.

"No, really. He was. He's got problems. He's an addict. I been giving him stuff to read about the Twelve Steps. He tried to get straight before. He ain't there yet, but he'll get clean when he's ready. He was real good about bringing me and Mikey stuff. Sometimes he brought me money or diapers or toys for him. That's why we couldn't never tell Zander's dad about Mikey. If he found out, he'd take away Zander's money. And, well, we needed it."

Alexander Senior's best move would be to adopt a little tough love and cut Zander off altogether, but saying it wouldn't make any difference. It was also easier said than done. "Okay. If Zander didn't bring the GHB to your house, who did?"

"I don't know."

"But you have an idea. What's Flash got to do with all this?" I told her about my visit to his house. "Was he stalking you again?"

Her eyes teared up again. "Claire, really, just forget about it. I pled guilty. It's over."

"Not for me it's not." A hot stab of anger wedged itself into my gut and stayed there. "I'm in serious trouble. Not only have I been threatened, but I could lose my job. Or worse."

"Why?"

"The State of Alabama is investigating whether giving Michael back to you was a mistake. My mistake."

"No —"

"Yes. I could wind up taking a lot of the blame for this. If you know who killed Michael —"

"No! I —"

"Was it Jimmy Shelton?"

"Leave Jimmy out of this. He don't know nothin'. "

"How can I reach him?"

"You can't. Leave him alone." This time the tears spilled over, and she didn't bother wiping them away. They made dark speckled drops on one of the orange stripes. "Please. I'm sorry about your job. I am. But knowin' what happened ain't gonna make any difference. Not for me or Mikey."

"Why?"

"Just leave it be."

Nothing I said was making an impression. I gave up. "Do you need anything?"

"No."

"Really?"

"Well —"

"What?"

"Zander's supposed to be paying my bills for a while. There was a power bill due when I got locked up. And the cable one too. Could you run by the apartment and make sure Zander paid them? Make sure there ain't no mail in the box? Mamma said she could do it, but it's way outta her way to come into town."

"No problem."

"You sure? Please don't be mad at me. I promise, if I could tell you everythin', I would."

Her tear-streaked face was pitiful. "I'm not mad." I gave her a re-assuring smile. "I'll come back and visit after I check on your mail."

"Thanks."

"Take care of yourself, Ashley."

We hung up, and the guard, with one hand firmly gripped on Ashley's arm, led her through the door to the jail. I took the elevator down to the lobby and retrieved my bag, then drove south on 20th Street and over Red Mountain.

I passed the entrance to Vulcan Park, memories drifting back to the Fourth of July and my date with Grant. I turned onto a road that wound its way up the mountain, through the wrought-iron gates of The Club, to a broad, covered driveway where uniformed valets waited. The restaurant, with its carpeted lobby and gilded mirrors, was the polar opposite of my last destination.

The hostess checked a list and waved me through to the dining area. Marlie, a woman I'd volunteered with before, was spreading a pink damask tablecloth onto a long trestle table. Boxes of pink roses sat next to the table. Seeing them triggered thoughts of Grant, again, and that I needed to call him to confirm our date for tomorrow.

Marlie and I chatted easily as we set up the registration table, stacking piles of literature about Our Mothers Have Wings next to brochures about breast cancer and breast health. We placed the pink roses in bud vases on each of the round luncheon tables along with the printed program for today's talk. The entire back wall of the room was glass, with doors that opened to a large terrace offering a spec-tacular view of downtown Birmingham.

Back at the registration table, we organized the name tags and the registration list and waited for the attendees to arrive. I scanned the list of people coming, relieved to see Karen Madison was on the first page of the forty or so names listed. At ten to eleven the first of the women arrived, most of them dressed exquisitely in expensive suits. I greeted people, handed out name tags, pointed out the rest room. Kelsey came in, with the guest of honor in tow, and led him to the head table. At last, at eleven twenty, I overheard a woman say to Marlie, "Madison. Karen Madison."

I turned from the person I was checking in to see a tan woman in her late forties. Maybe early fifties. Her hair was dyed ash blonde and it looked like she had just stepped out of the salon. The white silk suit she was wearing wouldn't have fit me, even if I could have waved a magic wand and lost at least ten pounds on the spot.

Five people were waiting behind her to check in. Marlie thanked her for coming, marked her name off the list, and handed her a pink-framed name tag. As she walked into the dining room, I said to Marlie, "Be right back." I grabbed my purse from under the table and took off before Marlie had a chance to protest. I followed Karen to the table she chose, near the back, and as she settled herself I hung my purse on the chair next to hers. For good measure, I wadded up the delicately folded linen napkin and placed it on the chair. Then I scooted back to the registration table.

I checked in two people waiting as, over my shoulder, I heard Kelsey's "Good morning" echo over the sound system. We welcomed a few stragglers as Kelsey gave a short speech about the history of Our Mothers Have Wings. Lunch would be served first, with the doctor's speech over dessert.

When they started serving the food, Marlie and I left the three remaining name tags on the table and joined the others. Marlie headed for the head table to sit near Kelsey, while I went to the place I had reserved earlier. The five ladies at my table were already eating a first course of a mixed greens salad. Introductions went around the table as I poured vinaigrette and helped myself to one of The Club's famous orange rolls. I nodded a greeting to Karen when it was her turn to say her name. No one asked each other what they did for a living. It was assumed this kind of thing was it.

Small talk broke the ice as the women conversed with those next to them. Karen and the lady on her other side were discussing favorite vacation destinations as I munched my salad, sipped my iced tea, and used my best table manners. I waited until they had revisited St. Croix and Naples and there was a break in the conversation. Then, as etiquette dictated, Karen turned to me with a smile.

"Claire, isn't it?" She double-checked my name tag.

"Yes, that's right." I pretended to study hers. "Karen. Nice to meet you."

"Nice to meet you too. Have you been volunteering with OMHW long?"

"About five years. I lost my mother to breast cancer when I was thirteen."

"Oh, I'm so sorry."

"Thanks. What about you? Did your mother —"

"Yes, four years ago."

"Then I'm sorry too. I used to lead a group for grieving daughters."

"I've heard of it. Kelsey told me how great it was. Maybe I should have come."

"We're hoping to get it going again soon." I shot another obvious glance at the tag on her chest. "Madison. As in the Madison Foundation?"

"Yes, that's us."

She had Zander's eyes, I noticed. Michael's eyes. Green-blue, intently focused on mine. "That's a wonderful organization. You do so much for the community." Two of the other women at the table were listening to our conversation and concurred.

"Thank you. We try. There's a lot to do."

"Well, I know OMHW appreciates any help they can get." I cast my first line. "It's just so important to educate women about their risks, especially if they've lost a relative to breast cancer. I mean, it could save lives. The lives of your children. Or, grandchildren."

I studied her carefully, and it was there. The slight jerk in the eyebrows, the just-a-little-too-quickly way she tore her gaze from mine, the intense, sudden interest in her empty salad plate. I pressed it. "Do you have kids?"

Then relief. Convincing herself I'd just made an innocent remark. "Oh, yes. Two."

"Grandchildren?"

A nervous laugh. "No, no. Mine are still a bit young for that."

"Oh, I'm sorry. How old are they?"

"My youngest, Kaylin, she's seventeen. In high school. My son's in college."

"That's wonderful. What's he studying?"

She was growing more and more uncomfortable by the second, the carefully coiffed image starting to get tenuous. "Finance, like his father."

"That's great. Where?"

"Auburn."

"So he's home for the summer?"

"He's doing summer term."

"Oh, so he'll be graduating early."

"We hope so." She was desperate to change the subject now, as the white-jacketed waiter removed our salad plates and refilled our teas. "Lunch smells delicious," she said. But she wasn't going to get off that easily. Another woman at the table picked up the kid thread and shared that she had two daughters, both in college. That sparked more stories about offspring as the waiter brought our chicken, until it eventually came around to me again when one of the ladies asked if I had any children.

"No, not yet. Maybe someday. I'm not married." I flashed my bare left hand. "Of course, nowadays, a lot of people have them without getting married."

Karen Madison dropped her knife. It fell off the edge of the plate and left a sauce stain on the tablecloth. She picked it up and placed it back on her dish. The other women went on about out-of-wedlock births and teen pregnancy and how times had changed. I jumped back into the conversation with my second hook. "Speaking of kids, did you see the story last week about the toddler who died? Overdosed on drugs."

That did it. Karen Madison started to shake. A small tremor in her hands and only noticeable if you were looking for it. She picked up her napkin from her lap and wiped her mouth indelicately, smearing her lipstick. "Excuse me," she murmured, and walked quickly toward the bathroom.

Leaving the ladies discussing the shame and tragedy of Michael's death, I followed Karen.

CHAPTER SEVENTEEN

Karen Madison had locked herself in one of the stalls. I leaned on the marble vanity and waited, noting that the elegance of The Club permeated even to the ladies' room. I studied the intricately patterned wallpaper until the toilet flushed.

She saw me resting against one of the sinks, my arms folded. Whatever composure she'd managed to regain dissipated like a spray of perfume.

Voice shaking, she said, "I thought I recognized your name from OMHW, but that wasn't it. Your name was in the paper. You were the social worker on the case."

"What case?"

"You know damn well what case. Michael's case."

I paused. Then, "You have his eyes."

All the strength left her like the air out of an untied balloon. Her knees buckled, and I moved forward to catch her if she collapsed, but she held out a hand, stopping me. I retreated. She bent over, gulping breaths through her mouth for a minute, then stood up straight. The first signs of tears glistened in her eyes and she fanned them away. Outside, Kelsey was introducing the speaker.

"Why are you doing this to me?"

"I want to know what happened to Michael."

"His mother killed him."

"I don't think so."

"How did you find out he was my grandson?"

"I was going to ask you the same thing."

Another gulp. "My son, Zander, he has . . . a problem. With drugs."

I nodded. "Go on."

"His father and I are desperate. We've tried—we've done all we know how to do. We've sent him away. We've tried locking him in the house. I thought, one day, if I could just find out where he went. Where he got the drugs. Two weeks ago, Friday morning, I followed him. He went to Ashley's apartment. He took Michael to the park. I confronted him. Oh, God."

She was shaking again, on the verge of collapse. In the dining room, the doctor was talking about research results. Karen covered her eyes.

"Do you want to sit down?" I gestured to an upholstered bench near the door.

"You don't understand."

"Tell me."

"No one can know about this. Please."

"I'm not going to tell anyone. Does Alexander Senior know?"

She nodded, once. "You must think I'm a terrible person, but if this got out—"

"I understand. I swear, I won't tell anybody."

"Alexander could lose everything. I don't know what his board of directors would do if they found out about Zander. About his problems. They might lose confidence. Do you know what I mean?"

"I do." I stepped forward and gently touched her arm. "I promise. I didn't find out who Michael's father was until recently. There's no need to put it in the DHS record or to make it public. I just want to know what happened to Michael."

"Ashley killed him."

"Ashley's—" Another woman from the luncheon entered the rest room, smiling and nodding to us. Karen, more together now, greeted her back. We waited until the other woman finished, washed her hands, and left.

I picked up where I'd left off. "Ashley's screens were all clean. She was doing well."

"So she relapsed."

"Maybe not."

"What, you think it was Zander? That it was Zander's drugs?"

"What do you think?"

I could tell the thought wasn't a new one to cross her mind. She mumbled, "I don't know."

"If it was, then Ashley's protecting him."

Another luncheon guest entered the bathroom. Karen said, "We'd better get back."

We returned to the table. My chicken was gone, replaced by a slice of cheesecake topped with a mound of strawberries. I picked at it as I tried to look like I was paying attention to the doctor, who was reciting statistics about success rates of various cancer therapies. But my mind was on Karen. And her husband. Both of them had quite a motive for murder.

The doctor wound up his talk and Kelsey thanked us all for coming. Karen gave me a long, pleading look. I nodded and mouthed, "Don't worry," as the women at the table said good-bye and gathered purses. I stayed behind to help Kelsey and Marlie pack up, watching as Karen put on a confident smile and said a few friendly words to Kelsey before leaving, head held high, out the double doors to the valets' area.

I was home by two, glad to strip out of the confines of the skirt and into shorts and a tee. I meandered into the kitchen, opening the refrigerator for lack of anything else to do. Three ice-cold Michelobs sat on the top shelf and on impulse I grabbed one. Careful, I told myself, you'll wind up like Al Mackey. Big potbelly and a dirty recliner, drunk at four in the afternoon.

I didn't have to worry. I fell asleep on the couch before I hit the bottom of the bottle. I woke with a start from a strange, colorful dream, hearing the familiar sound of the mail carrier's Jeep as it started, stopped, and started again. I heaved my lazy ass off the couch to go get the bills.

Mail. Damn. I was supposed to go by Ashley's and make sure Zander had paid the bills. I'd forgotten. I was tempted to blow it off until Monday, but then I remembered she'd said some of the bills were late. Two more days could matter. After a quick visit to the bathroom, I pointed my car to Ashley's.

The interstate was jammed with cars. It was just after four o'clock and the beginning of rush hour. I turned onto back roads and wound my way to Southside, through UAB's campus and eastward. The route was taking me straight past Lakeview. On a whim, I hung a left, then left again until I was in the parking lot next to Kaleidoscope, the dance place. There were three other cars in the lot.

What had appeared a cool, contemporary structure last Monday now merely looked like the former-medical-office-turned-bar that it was. The neon-painted windows didn't look nearly as hip in the glaring sunlight. No bouncers stationed outside to monitor access. No faint reverberations of music.

Why was I here? I studied the glass-and-steel building, chin on the steering wheel. Whatever way this investigation turned, this place always seemed to come up. Now I knew Ashley had been here too. And Brandi. What were the odds Zander was a patron? Pretty good, I'd say. He loved to party, and this was a good place to do it.

Staring at the building was getting me nowhere. I thought for a few minutes, devising a plan to find out what I needed to know. When had Ashley been here, and with whom?

Snapping my fingers, I reached for my purse. Dug around in its belly until I found what I was looking for. Shut the purse in the trunk, and went to see if Kaleidoscope was open.

It was. Three men were inside. One was in the deejay's little room, behind the Plexiglas window among all the TV screens. The sets were off, their square faces dull black. Another man stood in the middle of the dance floor, watching the third who was working on an enormous speaker pulled out from the wall next to the bar.

The space was vastly different in the daytime. It looked stripped, all its magic gone, like being in the Tunnel of Love when the lights go up. A sour smell of old beer mingled with stale cigarette smoke and a spirituous hint of booze.

The man in the deejay booth manipulated some controls. He spoke into a microphone as he looked at the man on the dance floor, and his voice filled the room. "Okay, try it now."

I flinched as the rapid beat of a Narcotic Thrust song shook the air. The music halted and the deejay announced, "Donovan, you have a visitor."

Donovan was evidently the guy on the dance floor, in the black suit. He turned around, saw me, and held up one finger. I nodded. He said something to the man working on the speaker and then walked over to me.

"Sorry, we're having some trouble with the sound system. Can I help you?"

"Hi. I'm Claire Conover."

"Donovan Grayson."

"I was wondering if I could ask you a few questions?"

He studied me, starting at my bare legs and working his way up to my face, with just a slight layover at my breasts. I took the moment to assess him, too. The suit was well cut. A silver tie and black shirt. Trendy. Brown hair, receding, and dark brown eyes.

I was too underdressed to be a salesperson and his curiosity was getting the better of him. "Of course. May I ask what this is about?"

"I'm trying to find out what happened to a client of mine."

"Let's go up to my office."

He led me to a stairway behind a door in the far corner. The deejay's little room was at the top of the stairs, and an office across the hall from that. It was large and well decorated with modern furniture and a bright abstract-patterned rug on the tile floor. On the far wall was a cluster of framed newspaper articles and pictures. Donovan's glass-topped desk was laden with papers and stacks of CD cases with names like Junkie XL and Electric Indigo. He closed the door and gestured to a chair. "Please. Now, what's this about?"

I pulled out the newspaper article I'd dug from my purse, the one about Ashley's sentencing that I'd meant to file in the chart, and showed it to him. "I'm trying to find out if this woman has been here recently, and, if so, who she was with."

He scanned it. "That's the woman whose kid died of the overdose. She pled guilty."

"That's right. She used to come here with a friend."

He handed the article back to me. "Who's she to you?"

"I used to work with her." I left it vague. If it somehow got back to DHS that I was here, I was in big trouble. Okay, bigger trouble.

"Where?"

He wasn't going to let it go. "I was her son's social worker. I'm trying to piece together what might have happened the night the boy died. I heard she hung out here sometimes."

"I see. The person you want to speak with is my brother, Lucas. He's the bartender most nights."

"Oh."

"Hang on." He reached into his inside jacket pocket and pulled out a phone. He scrolled through his phonebook, hit dial, and said, "Where are you?" Then, "So you're on you're way here?" A second pause, then, "Come to my office when you get here." No greeting, no good-bye. He snapped the razor-thin phone shut and relayed to me, "He'll be here in just a few minutes if you care to wait."

"Thanks."

I wandered over to the large wall of framed memorabilia. One photo was of Donovan standing with a group of men on a golf course. Another was Donovan cutting a ribbon to open a club, a crowd of supporters behind him. I recognized the building as a country-western bar I was dragged to once for a bachelorette party. Fiddles. Three of the frames contained articles from the entertainment section of the paper about club openings. Kaleidoscope was the subject of one, Fiddles another. Another I didn't recognize, Flow.

Behind me Donovan said, "Can I get you something to drink?"

"No, thanks. How many clubs do you own?"

"Three, as of now. Another one opens this fall in Inverness." Inverness was a suburb southeast of town. He rose, picked up a gray business card out of a glass holder and offered it to me. ECLIPSE ENTERTAINMENT. DONOVAN GRAYSON, OWNER. Two circles, a black overlapping a white one. Professionally printed.

"And Lucas is your brother? Is he an owner, too?"

"No, just me."

"Who's older?"

"We're twins," he said. "But you'd never know it from looking at us. We're fraternal."

"Oh." To kill time I kept asking questions. "And how long have you been doing this?"

"I opened my first club when I was twenty-two. Three years ago."

He was twenty-five, four years younger than me. He looked older. I said, "Wow, and now you own three?"

"Four, when Goal opens in October. It's a sports bar and restaurant. I'll be breaking into the restaurant business for the first time."

"That's impressive."

"Thanks." He accepted the compliment easily. A person used to praise.

The door opened and Lucas walked in. He saw me and stopped short, surprised. "Oh, sorry. I didn't know there was someone here."

He looked much as I remembered. Shaved head, tattoo reaching up the left side of his neck. What I thought was a phoenix the first time was actually a man with wings. The flames below the figure were not flames, but the sun. Icarus.

"This is Claire Conover," Donovan said. "She's a social worker. She wanted to ask you about someone who may have visited the club."

The mood in the room had suddenly altered. Lucas and Donovan hadn't said more than two sentences to each other, but I could sense a current of emotion between them. Something dark. Mac's wisdom floated to the top of my pool of thoughts. Something he'd taught me years ago. Pay attention to what you are feeling when you are with your clients. Your own emotions are a mirror of theirs. If you feel defensive or angry or afraid, so do they. So what was I feeling now? I searched deep, and realized it was fear. I wanted out of that room.

Lucas was looking at me expectantly. I held out the newspaper clipping. "Do you know this woman?"

"Sure, that's Ashley. Her kid just died."

"She came in here sometimes?"

"Yeah, with her friend Brandi."

"When was the last time you saw her here?"

He thought back, blue eyes on the ceiling. "Oh, let's see. About three weeks ago, I think. About the middle of June. It was a Saturday, the day we were running the rum drink specials."

"The eighteenth," Donovan supplied.

"But Ashley didn't drink. She'd gotten sober," Lucas said.

"Did she look high?" I asked.

"Not at all."

"Did you talk to her?"

"Yeah."

I was missing something. "What about?"

"Just stuff. You know, catching up."

"How long have you known Ashley?" The atmosphere was tenser, the fear in my gut increasing. I looked at Donovan, seated again behind his desk, arms resting on the top, hard brown eyes riveted on his twin.

"A while. A few years."

"How?"

He shrugged. "We've hung out before."

"You know a guy named Flash? Ashley used to run around with him. He's a drug dealer."

Donovan didn't move a muscle.

"I know who he is," Lucas answered.

"Was he here that night?"

"No."

"How do you know Ashley?"

"Look, I've done some stuff in the past I'm not proud of."

What the hell did that mean? Was he a drug buddy of Ashley's? One of her johns?

"You know anything about GHB?"

"What do you mean?"

"Ashley's son died of a GHB overdose. You ever see Ashley do any of that? Here, or —"

"No."

"What about you? Have you ever —"

Donovan cut me off.

"Lucas is working very hard to get his life straight. Part of that is working for me. He needs to go set up the bar for tonight."

Lucas moved toward the door. "Yeah, I gotta go start stocking. If you see Ashley, let her know I'm thinking about her."

"I will."

After Lucas left, Donovan walked me to the door. "I'm sorry we couldn't be more help."

"It's fine. You were very helpful. I'm sorry if I pried too much. I didn't mean to offend you, or your brother."

"Lucas is going through a difficult time right now."

"Oh. I'm sorry."

"Me too."

"Can I ask one more question?"

"What?"

"In the club, are drugs a big problem?"

"Sure, we have a few people who show up under the influence. And Lucas is real good about cutting people off when they've reached their limit. The bouncers usually call them a cab. I don't allow drugs in here, but we can't always catch it. More than anything, Ecstasy is an issue."

"I see." I thanked him for his time as he walked me down the stairs. Some early customers were already in the club. A girl, long black hair reaching all the way to her Daisy Duke shorts, sipped a tall drink as she chatted with the guy fixing the speaker. Another young man with long, shaggy, blond hair and dressed in casual business attire sat at the bar. His finger traced the rim of his glass. He and Lucas stopped talking when Donovan and I came through the door. Lucas waved to me from behind the bar where he was stacking bottles of imported beer in a cooler. Under their gazes, Donovan and I crossed the dance floor to the door and he showed me out.

According to Lucas, Ashley hadn't been high. And, of course, her drug screens had been clean. She'd been here three Saturdays ago, but had nothing to drink. Could she have gotten the G here and kept it for later? I doubted it. If Ashley was going to use again, she would have done it immediately, not squirreled it away. So what had I learned from coming here? Not much, other than Ashley and Lucas knew each other, and that Lucas was a drug user. Or in recovery.

It was a quick trip to Avondale, where I parked in my usual spot in front of Ashley's. Her upstairs neighbors were on their balcony, a barrel smoker filling the air with the aroma of hickory and pork. They raised beer cans to me as I walked to her door. I fished out Brandi's key and unlocked it.

I jumped inside my skin as the door opened. Al Mackey was standing at Ashley's battered dining table, flipping through her mail.

CHAPTER EIGHTEEN

Al and I spotted each other at the same instant.

"Holy crap, you scared the shit outta me," he said, once he saw who it was.

"Same here. What are you doing?"

"Dee sent me down to look and see if the bills was paid. I don't see none. What're you doin' here?"

"Same thing. Ashley asked me to check on the bills."

"Hell, if I'da known that, I coulda saved me a trip."

"Sorry."

"Ah, well." He tossed the handful of flyers and envelopes on the table. "Least the ball and chain will quit her bitchin' about it."

Never mind that the ball and chain provided the beer in your belly and the sexually explicit clothes on your back. I walked to the table and thumbed through the pile he'd just dropped. Grocery ads, three catalogs, some coupons, and a credit card offer. "Looks like someone paid them, anyway."

"Yeah." Al waddled over and opened Ashley's fridge. Over his shoulder I could see what was inside. Not much. Some pickles, mayo, a small hunk of cheese, and a Tupperware container. Zander had cleaned her out.

Not finding what he wanted, he closed the door. "Well, I guess I'll be headin' back."

"Yeah. Me too."

"Can I ask you something?"

"Sure."

"You know if Ashley had any life insurance on that kid?"

That kid. Disgust rose in my throat like bile. "I don't think so. Most people don't carry policies on children."

"How come?"

"Well, the purpose of the insurance is to provide for your family should anything happen to you. Children normally don't die suddenly, and they don't have income that needs to be replaced." I felt like I was lecturing to a kindergartener.

"What about insurance for her?"

"I believe Ashley has a policy." We'd discussed it at one of her intervention meetings, and had made it a goal. Just in case something were to happen to her unexpectedly. Although I hadn't envisioned Ashley being poisoned by the juice in her own refrigerator.

"She won't need hers now, now that the kid's gone, right?"

"Why?"

"I was just wondering. I thought maybe if she'd had some insurance on the boy we could give some of it to that drunks' home, since — what's her name — the big black one — helped so much with the funeral and all."

"Nona."

"Yeah, Nona."

"No, as far as I know there's no insurance for Michael."

"Too bad. Maybe Ashley could cash in hers."

"I don't know." If she did, I hoped Al would be the last person to know about it.

"Well, I'll see you."

I nodded. "I'll lock up."

He exited the apartment, beer belly leading the way, and pulled the door shut behind him. I peeked out the front blinds and saw him cram himself into a rusty Dodge Colt, his stomach jammed against the steering wheel like a clown in a tiny car. The sight made me chuckle.

Ashley's apartment was still a wreck. I folded the blanket on the couch, then draped it over the back. Emptied the ashtray and cleared the coffee table of wrappers and empty fast-food bags. Took out the trash. Washed a stack of dishes in the sink and left them to dry in the rack. Why the heck I was cleaning up after Zander, I had no idea. I just knew Ashley had been through enough without someone trashing her space. Even though she wouldn't see it again for nearly a year. If she found a way to hang on to it.

When I was finished, I laid the dishtowel on the counter. Ashley's room was neat, the bed smooth under a double wedding-ring quilt. Her clothes hung in the closet, as if she were due home any minute. I opened the door across the hall from her bedroom.

Michael's sky blue sheets were unmade, just as he must have left them the morning he died. The pillow on the toddler-sized mattress was still indented from his little head. Toys were scattered all over the floor. Matchbox cars, trains, a plastic dump truck. I sat on the bed, put my hand in the small hollow in the pillow and talked to him.

After a while I turned off the lights and locked the door behind me.

Rush hour was winding down, the sun sinking over west Birmingham. At home, my message light was blinking.

The first call was from some solicitor. The next was a surprise.

"Miss Conover, this is Alexander Madison. I understand you met my wife at a function this afternoon. I'd like to talk to you in person. Tonight, if possible. Please call me back."

He left a number. An 879 prefix. Mountain Brook or Homewood. His voice revealed no emotion.

So the first question was how the hell did he get my number? As a person who took children away for a living, I tended to piss people off occasionally. Once, I'd even been threatened at gunpoint. I was overly careful about my privacy for the sake of my own safety. Then it hit me. Kelsey. Karen had probably called Kelsey at Our Mothers Have Wings and asked for my number. Kelsey was friendly, but not so bright. And the Madisons gave a lot of money to her organization.

She surely wouldn't let a little request like a phone number stand in the way of a generous donation.

I listened to the message again, then called the number. A teenage-sounding girl answered, and I asked for Alexander Madison. He came on the line, all business.

"Mr. Madison, this is Claire Conover. I got your message."

"Yes, Miss Conover. Thank you for returning my call. I was hoping we could get together this evening. For drinks?"

I could have been any of his chaps he was asking around for a Scotch, instead of the woman who knew his greatest secret.

"Certainly. Where?"

"How about here? I'd rather not discuss this in public, as you might imagine."

Yeah, I could imagine. Still, going to his house wasn't my safest option. He continued, "Say, in forty-five minutes? Would that be convenient?"

I couldn't think of a decent excuse not to go. "Fine."

He gave me directions. Off of Cherokee Road, near the Country Club in Mountain Brook.

Interesting. Figuring that my current outfit wouldn't impress anyone, I changed to business attire, the same pink suit I'd worn that morning. A little wrinkled, but it would do. Then I picked up the phone again.

Toby answered after the third ring. We chatted for a minute until Royanne came on the line.

"Hey, what are you doing?" I asked.

"The kids are making Play-Doh spaghetti, I'm making the real thing. What are you up to?"

"I've just been summoned to Chez Madison."

"No kidding?"

"No kidding. I saw Karen at a luncheon today. She knew about Michael."

"Whoa."

"Yeah."

I summarized the earlier events for her, and the phone call.

"What do you suppose he wants?"

"I don't know. I wanted you to know where I was, just in case. Because you know what's going on."

"You're making me nervous."

"I think I'll be fine."

"You'll call me the second you're done?"

"Yep."

"What time are you supposed to meet him?"

I checked my watch. Six thirty-eight. "Seven fifteen."

"If you don't call me by nine o'clock I'm gonna ring your cell phone off the hook."

"Sounds good."

She warned me to be careful and I left for the Madison's. I took Shades Crest Road through Vestavia Hills, passing my father's house on the way. His car was gone. I crossed Highway 280 and entered the city of Mountain Brook.

Mountain Brook was an old town with old money. A city of Ivy League educations, country club memberships, and last names with numbers. Women who lived here spent their days playing bridge and tennis and were commonly known as Brookies. The course of my career had brought me into these homes, too. Child abusers weren't limited to one social class.

I found the Madison's street without difficulty and turned onto a long, uphill drive. Woods enclosed the property, and at this time of year all of the neighbors were hidden by the trees. At the summit of the drive were a large mock-Tudor house and a detached three-car garage. A crisply edged lawn was being watered by an automatic sprinkler system. I parked in the circular drive and walked to the walnut-stained front door, next to which sat a picture-perfect planter of geraniums. I rang the bell.

I wouldn't have been surprised if a butler opened the door. Some stooped old servant with an appropriate butler name like Jeeves or James. Instead Karen opened the door, in the same white suit she'd worn earlier, but her eyes were a little more swollen and red.

"Come in," she said. No other greeting.

I followed her into the house. Lamps were on here and there since the sun was almost down. Karen led me to a living room at the rear of the house. Had I seen it in a decorating magazine, I would have poured over the picture, coveting the antique sideboard and marble-topped end tables. The sofa, armchairs, and drapes were done in a blend of prints of apricot and gold, the fabrics lush. I thought about Zander, flopping around and guffawing on Ashley's sofa. I doubted anyone had ever done that on this furniture.

A pocket door sealed the room off from the rest of the house. Karen closed it behind us. Alexander Madison was standing at a sideboard when we entered, mixing himself a martini. The crystal decanters held various liquors that gleamed in the lamplight. He turned when we entered and held out his free hand.

"Miss Conover. Thank you for coming."

We shook hands. "You're welcome."

"Would you care for a drink?"

"No, thanks."

"Nothing? A Coke, perhaps?"

"I'm fine, thanks."

The contrived hospitality was driving me nuts. "What did you want to talk with me about, Mr. Madison?"

"Please, have a seat."

I sank into one of the armchairs. He and his wife sat next to each other on the sofa across from me. A united front.

Alexander continued. "I understand you are aware of our son's problem."

"The child he fathered, you mean?"

"That, and his addiction to drugs."

I nodded.

"As you might imagine, the situation is quite awkward. I run a substantial corporation, and should the news of his problem get out, it could do damage. To me, to my employees, and to my family. Do you understand?"

Cut the supercilious bullshit and get to the point, I wanted to say. Instead I said, "I understand. What is it you want, Mr. Madison?"

"I was going to ask you the same question."

"I want to find out who killed Michael."

"His mother."

"She was clean."

"She had drugs in her home."

"Maybe they were Zander's."

"He says not. And if you repeat that accusation in public, I'll sue you for slander."

The threat rolled off his tongue too easily. This was the message I was supposed to hear.

"Mr. Madison, I told your wife this afternoon that I have no intention of telling anyone about Zander's involvement in this case. I'm not going to put it in the DHS record, nor am I going to leak it to the public."

"And in return?"

"What do you mean?"

"What do you want?"

What the hell? Did he think I was trying to extort money from him? That he'd have to pay for my silence? Through my incredulity, I sputtered, "Nothing."

"Nothing at all?"

"No, of course not. Your private lives are no one's business. Believe me, I know what it's like to have your name dragged through the media. I'm going through it now. I may lose my job. I wouldn't wish all this on my worst enemy."

For the first time since walking in, I saw Alexander relax. The brow underneath his neatly combed gray hair smoothed, a tightness around his jaw slacked. Karen had been sitting with her legs crossed, her fingers laced around her knee. Slowly, the whiteness faded from her knuckles.

Over their shoulders, I saw the door to the room move. Just a fraction, enough to catch my eye. I thought I saw a thin, tan shoulder through the crack. Kaylin, listening in.

"Thank you." Alexander said. "We're trying to get Zander some help. He's gone to rehab in Arizona. A highly reputable place. Perhaps they'll be able to help him."

I studied Alexander Senior's tie for a moment. If I ratted out Zander and he found out about it, he'd never speak to me again. I weighed the options, wondering who would be the better ally. I moved my gaze from his perfect half-English knot to his face and said, "Mr. Madison, Zander's not in Arizona."

His brow wrinkled again. "He's not?"

"Not as of Tuesday. He was at Ashley's apartment."

"He was?"

I'd thrown him a curve ball and he was reeling. "I'm sorry, he was. That's how I found out he was Michael's father. I went to Ashley's apartment to see if I could find some clue as to what happened to Michael. Zander was there. He was high."

"And he told you he was the child's father?"

"No, he didn't. I guessed. They looked alike, he and Michael. As a matter of fact, they both resemble — resembled — Karen."

Karen's shoulders began shaking as she put her hands over her face. Alexander made no move toward her, made no attempt to comfort her. God, what had having a son like Zander done to these poor people, to their marriage? Or maybe it was the other way around.

I opened my purse and found a small notepad and a pen. On a sheet of paper I wrote a name and phone number, then folded it in half and offered it to Alexander. "This is the name of a local psychologist. He's very good. He's treated a lot of families that are dealing with addiction. I think he'd be able to help you understand what Zander's going through, to help you understand your role in it. Help you set the right boundaries. He might even have some fresh ideas about how to get Zander to try to save his own life."

Alexander took the paper, opened it, and read it. For the first time since my arrival, I caught the hint of smile. "Dr. Christopher Conover. No relation, I presume?"

"He's my father. And he really is very good."

"I'll bet."

Both of them walked me to the door and shook my hand before I left, trust instead of suspicion shining in their eyes. Once on the road, I called Royanne on my cell.

"Was it ugly?"

"At first."

"What did he want?"

"To warn me not to tell anyone about Zander."

"Well, duh."

"And to see if I was going to hold it over their heads."

"Really?"

"Really. But I think it ended well."

"All right, then." I heard her yawn. "I'm glad you're okay."

"I'll call you later."

My stomach let out a loud grumble. I dropped into Baker's and picked up a pepperoni pizza on the way home. My diet, especially lately, consisted mostly of fat and cholesterol. I admonished myself and promised to do better. Tomorrow.

Four slices later, I dialed Dad. We exchanged some news before I said, "A guy named Alexander Madison may call you soon. I referred him and his wife to you today."

"Okay."

He didn't say any more about it. No surprise about the well-known name, or questions. I knew even if Alexander and Karen called him, he'd never tell me. He was sworn, just as I was, to keep our clients' information confidential. And we Conovers kept our word.

CHAPTER NINETEEN

My cell phone woke me up the next morning, its shrill song summoning me from the depths of deep sleep. I rolled over and grabbed it, hit the talk button, and mumbled something that sounded nothing like hello.

"Morning. I woke you up. I'm so sorry. I'll call back."

Grant. I struggled to sit up in the tangled sheets. "No, it's fine. What time is it?"

"Ten after ten."

"You're at High Tech?"

"Yeah. I hadn't heard from you so I thought I'd call. Do you know what movie you want to see tonight?"

I ran a hand through my mussed hair. "I haven't had a chance to see what's playing."

"Well, look if you get a chance, and I'll bring a newspaper with me just in case. Do you want to eat first?"

"I don't care. Whatever you want."

We discussed tonight's date, finally deciding Grant would pick me up at my house at six thirty and we'd see a movie first. We hung up and I unwound my way out of my sheets and plodded my way into the kitchen, brewed some strong coffee, and ate a breakfast of cold pizza. The best breakfast in the world. Just not the healthiest.

Guilt prodded me. I had all day to do something to counteract the effects of this horrible diet. I've never been much of a gym girl, much preferring nature's hills to artificial ones created by a treadmill or a StairMaster.

I put my hair up under a baseball cap. Dressed in heavy twill shorts, a heather gray long-sleeved shirt, thick socks, and hiking boots. I found my small backpack in the hall closet and loaded it with two liter-sized bottles of water, some granola bars, a small towel, my trail map, insect repellant, and sunscreen. I grabbed my walking stick from behind the door and locked up.

Oak Mountain State Park was five exits south on I-65, almost ten thousand acres of outdoor recreation smack dab in the middle of Birmingham's urban sprawl. Among the park's amenities were a golf course, camp sites, horse stables, a BMX track, and, of course, hiking trails. I thought about which one I wanted to hike today as I drove. The trails all had names, but most people referred to them by the colors of the blazes that were marked on trees along the way.

I parked the Honda at the mouth of the North Trailhead. It was a bit less crowded than the one near the park office and picnic areas. As I shouldered my backpack, two mountain bikers unlatched their gear from a rack on the back of their SUV. We exchanged hellos and pleasantries until they got helmets on and pedaled away toward the red trail, the one most commonly used by bikers.

I entered the woods, the mouth of the trailhead an inviting portal into the shade. I met four other hikers coming down the mountain. It was just after one, and the lucky morning hikers had already done their miles in the cooler hours.

I decided to do South Rim, otherwise known as the blue trail. It started out as a difficult hike from this end of the ridge, with a brief, steep climb that eased up another five or six hundred feet over the next two miles. Once at the top, I'd be rewarded with gorgeous views of the double-ridged mountain. My plan was to hike the blue trail toward Shackleford Point Trail, marked in white. No way I'd do the whole loop, since it was six miles long. An ambitious hike to say the least, especially since I was getting such a late start.

I started up the hill, planting my walking stick ahead of each step. The path was well maintained, clearly marked, and wide enough for comfort. Underfoot, a soft mixture of mulched pine bark and leaves was interspersed with tree roots that made handy footholds. The underbrush of ferns, briars, and ivy was well cut back, making it less likely that hikers would take a tumble. White oaks, sweetgums, and flowering dogwoods all graced the trail, and the tall long-leaf pines gave the air a clean scent. Mockingbirds and squirrels chattered high in the canopy.

Hiking the South Rim gave me little time to think about anything but making sure one foot was in front of the other. My thigh muscles tensed and relaxed, and after a while my whole mind was focused on nothing but the rhythm of the walk. Plant, step. Plant, step. Breathe.

After some time, I passed the first connector to the Red Trail, hearing some bikers talking loudly over the whirring of their tires somewhere down the track. An hour into it, I stopped to rest on a low fallen tree. I took one of the water bottles out of my pack, drank half of it, then wet the towel and wiped my sweaty head and face. Zipped the pack up and started again.

Plant, step, plant, step. I hiked past a steep clearing dotted with pink-blooming mimosa trees that sloped down to a valley. The views of the mountain were just up ahead, and for a short time I enjoyed the relative peace of the woods.

The quiet was broken by the sound of another hiker behind me. A solo. Not uncommon, Oak Mountain was a popular place. His footfalls tromped through the dead leaves accompanied by heavy breathing. He, or she, was having a hard time.

I rounded a boulder. At the end of the turn, the smooth stump of a dead pine jutted up from the ground, a perfect place for another rest. I sat, the hazy sunshine flickering through the leaves, breathed deeply, and pulled out the water bottle.

The footsteps behind me grew closer, to within ten yards, then halted.

Weird. There really was no place to rest around that particular curve. No fallen trees or small rocks. It was a strange place to stop. Whoever it was obviously hadn't hiked this trail before and didn't know the good resting spots. I listened for sounds of his kit opening. Water gurgling.

Nothing. I took one last swig of my water, put the bottle back in my pack, strapped on the backpack, and hit the trail again. Sure enough, the footsteps started when mine did.

You're being paranoid, I told myself. Just because some pissant slashed your tires. You can't let one incident make you afraid all the time. There were probably twenty-five hikers or more on various sections of this trail today. Just because there's one who doesn't want to overtake you doesn't mean you're being followed.

The footpath leveled out as it followed the top of the ridge. This part of the trail was easier because it wasn't as steep. I passed another connector that led to the red trail, but didn't see any other people. I hiked on toward the connector that would take me down from the blue trail. Along the way, I'd stop at my favorite overlook. To get to it I had to climb up a steep outcrop of boulders. At the top was a large, flat rock that hovered over a broad view of the mountains to the south. Below the rock was a sharp hundred-foot drop to a wooded ravine. Being on the edge of the precipice gave me a delirious sensation of floating at the edge of the world.

I turned off the trail to the short path that would take me to my spot. The footsteps behind me stopped again.

I was starting to get seriously annoyed with whoever it was. Yes, other hikers had just as much right to be out here, but this stop-start-stop thing was getting on my nerves. I wished whoever it was would just pass me and get on with it. Unless, of course, the person was following me on purpose. Ridiculous. Or was it? I needed to find out.

Feeling stupid even as I did it, I left the short path to the overlook and doubled back through the forest to a copse of trees that bordered the blue trail. When I'd made the turnoff to the short path, the other hiker had been some distance behind, thirty yards or so by the echo of his steps. I hid behind a thick white oak and waited.

The footfalls came closer. I could hear breathing again, more ragged. Whoever it was had no business being this far out on the trail when they were that out of shape. It sounded from the clomping of the steps like a man. A big man.

He came into view and my heart dropped, then sped up to double time as I caught sight of wild brown hair and beard.

Jimmy Shelton was following me. He was ill-equipped for the trail. I saw no evidence of drinking water, and the dark blue jeans and black T-shirt he was wearing were too hot for this time of day. His tennis shoes were wrong, too. He was heaving with the effort of every step.

I moved a bit, quietly, as he drew near, making sure I was well hidden by the trunk of the tree. I'd have preferred a bit more cover, but this part of the park was more pine forest than anything, the tight canopy not allowing smaller bushes to thrive. I squatted and pressed my face to the rough bark of the oak. Large black ants crawled around the base of the tree, toward my face. I waited.

He was within feet of my hiding place now. Eyes forward, thinking I was somewhere up ahead. As he passed, my breath caught as I saw something in his right hand. Silver and sharp with a black handle. A knife.

I held my breath. An adrenaline rush accompanied the realization that I was in serious trouble. My heartbeat thundered in my ears. I felt dizzy. Too scared to move.

Jimmy kept walking. I crouched, stock-still. I couldn't stay here forever. Soon he would realize I wasn't ahead of him. Then what would he do? Would he notice the short path to the rocks and check to see if I'd gone there? My stomach turned sick as images of what could have happened flashed in my mind. If I'd gone to my rock, I would have been trapped. Caught between a man with a knife and a hundred-foot plunge. Had that been his plan all along? To force me off the edge of some cliff so it looked like a hiking accident? Or to find a relatively deserted section of trail and stab me to death? Hiding my body in the woods somewhere to rot. I hadn't told anyone where I was going today. It could be hours before anyone figured out I was missing.

I breathed short and shallow. Jimmy was fifty feet away from me now. The turnoff to the short path was another thirty feet or so ahead of him. I quickly weighed what few options I had.

I could head back down the blue trail the way I came, but hiking the blue in reverse would be tough. Too many steep downward inclines. No way to go fast. And when Jimmy figured out I wasn't in front of him, he'd probably turn around to try and find me. It was too much of a gamble to try to get back to the red connector I'd passed earlier. No guarantee I could outrun him. So going back was out.

The connector ahead would lead me to the red and white trails. But any second now Jimmy would be back on the blue trail, searching for me. So my route to the connector was cut off.

Or I could wait him out. He couldn't last much longer in this heat with no water or food and would have to go down the mountain. Surely he'd leave before dark, when the park closed. I didn't relish the thought of spending the night out here. My clothes were cotton. Breathable, but not the best material for keeping warm. July nights weren't cold, but eighty-something degrees was a lot cooler than it sounded when sleeping on the ground without a blanket. We still had a good five hours of daylight left. No way he'd last that long.

Or, I could bushwhack it. Head straight down the mountain off-trail. If I could make it to the red trail, I could get back to the North Trailhead where I'd started, or hike the other way to the office and find a park ranger. Or maybe someone on the trail who had a cell phone. I'd neglected to bring mine. I'd give anything to have it now.

At the moment, the last option seemed like the best. Jimmy wouldn't expect me to leave the trail at this point. With my boots, I was better fitted to cross the gulleys and streams between here and the base of the mountain. I peeked out from behind the oak and, not seeing Jimmy, crept across the trail and into the dense forest.

The leaves were more slippery than on the man-made path. And louder. I tried to shuffle, rather than walk, hoping I'd sound more like some wild animal than an escaping hiker. I didn't dare turn around, fearing I'd see Jimmy behind me, knife raised.

The slope quickly became steep. It wasn't long before I fell, the hillside too angled for me to stay upright, even with my stick. I landed on my ass and slid that way for a while, until the slope leveled out a bit before a ravine. The ravine had good cover in the form of a fallen tree. I stopped, lying on my stomach behind the low tree, thankful the ditch wasn't full of nasty water. I inhaled the scent of the moldy leaves an inch from my nose as I lay quietly and waited, listening.

Nothing that sounded like a man. I heard a few birds cawing. A tree branch somewhere cracked and fell to earth. A slight breeze rustled the leaves. That was it.

After I listened for a minute or so, I sat up. Unshouldering my pack, I unzipped it slowly, and dug out the map. I found the place on the trail where I thought I'd gone off the marked path. The trails were basically loops, each stacked on top of the other at different elevations. The blue trail was at the highest elevation. So as long as I headed down, I should run into some other trail. Or if I didn't want to chance it, I could go west where I was pretty sure the red trail snaked near the connector I'd passed earlier.

I listened a few more minutes, making sure no one was near. Sat up, drank some water. I had a liter left. I followed the ravine west, hopping from rock to rock when I could to minimize the noise. Stopped occasionally to look around and listen. When the ravine narrowed and ended just below a sharp cliff, I turned downward again, sliding on the steep slope until I came to a clearing.

The clearing made me nervous because I was visible. I ducked back into the trees, figuring I was maybe a few hundred yards from the red trail. The topography was more level here, but I was moving quickly, and the heat and exertion were taking their toll. I felt nauseous and struggled to keep the water in my stomach. I snuck through the trees, wishing I had eyes in the back of my head, praying Jimmy and his knife wouldn't appear any moment. I just wanted to be where there were people. Anybody.

Finally, the forest became less dense and I came upon a wide path that bore the unmistakable signs of being man-made. I stayed to the side of the trail, trying to remain hidden, until—thank God Almighty—a family of hikers came my way.

I waited until they passed, then eased out of the woods and followed them. I was totally turned around after bushwhacking my way down. I had no idea where I was, so I was surprised to see yellow blazes painted on the trees. Somehow I'd managed to find my way to the Foothills Trail. Now I just had to figure out which direction I was going.

I followed the family at a reasonable distance, listening to the three of them chat about things they'd seen on the hike. The two kids were maybe twelve and eight, both boys. The youngest one was full of questions, the father patient in his answers. They glanced behind them when they heard my steps, nodding and calling hello.

I'd hiked this trail before, most recently last fall, so after a few minutes I was able to get my bearings and knew that we were headed back toward the North Trailhead. To my car.

My legs were aching with the effort of what had become a three-hour-plus hike. My clothes were streaked with dirt from lying face down in the gulley. Leaves were clinging to my socks and I was damp with sweat. I stank, and could think of nothing that would be more wonderful than safety and a cool shower.

As we approached the trailhead, I began to walk quickly, ready to get out of the woods, out of the park, and home. At the mouth of the forest was a kiosk filled with park rules, maps, and information.

Jimmy was leaning against the kiosk, breathing hard.

CHAPTER TWENTY

I gripped my walking stick tight, preparing to use it as a weapon if I had to. Jimmy hadn't seen me yet. He was still a good distance away. I could see his bushy profile as he stared at my car in the nearby parking lot. The hiker father and his two sons were several feet ahead of me, and all of us were on a course to walk right past Jimmy in less than a minute. I jogged to catch up with them.

"Excuse me, sir?" I said, loudly enough to be heard by anybody within a mile of the trailhead.

The father stopped and turned. Jimmy, at the sound of my voice, stared dead at me. Keeping a peripheral eye on him, I said to the father, "Can you give me a ride to the office? I need to find a park ranger."

Jimmy's muddy brown eyes darted back and forth. I had about half a second to question what the hell I'd just done. Suppose Jimmy whipped out the knife and came after all of us? Had I just put this poor family at risk from a slasher?

"Sure. Is there a problem?"

The three of them wore similar quizzical looks on their faces. Jimmy, hearing my request, took off for his truck at just short of a run. I watched him go. The father, no moron, noticed and asked, "Has he been bothering you?"

"Yeah, actually."

Jimmy's driver-side door slammed. The truck struggled to turn over, then started. Jimmy squealed the tires as he sped out of the lot onto the road, tobacco-blue smoke spewing from the tailpipe.

I sucked in a deep breath that ended in a sigh of relief. The four of us walked toward the parked cars as the man asked, "Do you still want to report him?"

"No, he's gone. I'll be all right."

Kid number one, the one who looked about twelve, cried, "Hey, he dropped something!" He sprinted toward a small black object on the ground. It was a pouch of some sort, sealed with a snap. He picked it up, opened it, and unsheathed the knife I'd seen in Jimmy's hand earlier. The blade was shiny, four inches long, a deep groove running the length of it. The tip was very sharp.

"Whoa, cool!" the kid said.

Dad reached his side and gently eased it out of his son's hands. "Careful, Dylan." He turned the knife over, examining it. "It's a Buck knife, like hunters use." And a handy way to slash someone's tires, I thought. Could I have been wrong about Flash?

Kid number two asked, "Can we keep it?"

"No, Austin."

Austin gave a little "Awww," in protest. The father offered it to me, and I took it. Feeling the weight of the handle made nausea creep into my stomach again. I was woozy.

The father said, "I think you should report this."

I probably should, but I really didn't want to try to explain my relationship with Jimmy to the rangers, or the police. I thought for several seconds and said, "I don't think they could help, now that he's gone."

"But if he's bothering people in the park—"

"I know who he is, and what he wants. I'll be careful."

The father looked at me like I was about to get a lecture. He changed his mind and asked, "Are you sure?"

"I'm sure."

"Okay. Well, just in case—" He reached a tanned hand into his back pocket and brought out his wallet. From one of the little leather pockets he extracted a business card. "Here's my card, if you need me to talk to the cops or anything."

"Thanks," I took it and read it. Bob Cooper, it said. He sold surgical equipment. "And thanks for your help."

I shook his hand and said good-bye to the boys. I unlocked my car and followed their SUV out of the park. At the main entrance I took a right and made my way to Cahaba Valley Road. To go home, I should have turned right toward the interstate, like the Coopers had, but instead I turned left. I drove toward Highway 31, then turned north. I wound my way through the combination business-residential area known as Riverchase, driving around in what were essentially circles until I was convinced that Jimmy wasn't following me.

Then the shakes started. And dry mouth. More nausea too. A silly, delayed reaction to my earlier fear. God, I could have been killed. My heart rate jumped to full speed again. I drank the rest of the water and willed myself to calm down. You're safe now, I thought. But I was too scared to go home. I made my back to Highway 31 and from there to Royanne's nearby house.

Thankfully, her minivan was in the driveway. So was Toby's pickup truck. It was five o'clock. I parked behind the van and knocked on the front door. She opened it, and her eyes went wide.

"Christ, you're a mess."

I was. The sweat that had soaked my shirt was dry, but I was still smeared with dirt. I had leaves in my hair in addition to the ones clinging to my socks.

"I know."

Royanne opened the door wide, inviting me into the cool house. I could hear the voice of Dora the Explorer coming from the TV in the living room. Royanne led me back to the kitchen where she was prepping a chicken for dinner.

"Where have you been?"

"Oak Mountain."

"Doing what? Rolling around on the horse track?"

"Do I smell that bad?"

"You don't smell good."

"Thanks. Can I use your phone? And your shower? And maybe borrow an outfit?"

"What's going on?"

"It's a long story."

"Roast chicken takes an hour."

"I had a little run-in with a guy on Oak Mountain. He might be following me. I need to call Grant. We have a date tonight and I need him to pick me up here."

"Wait. Slow down. What? What do you mean you had a run-in with a guy? What guy? Did he hurt you? Oh my God."

My best friend was quickly escalating to full-blown panic. "I'm fine. He didn't touch me. He didn't get a chance. Can I use the shower?"

"In a minute. Do you know what he looked like? Tell me what happened."

I tried to explain my afternoon rationally. "Okay, I went for a hike in the park. About an hour or so into it I noticed someone following me. Someone I knew. He had a knife. I got off the trail and down the mountain, but I saw him again at the trailhead. By that time I was with some other hikers. He left, but for all I know he followed me to the park in the first place, and he could be at my house." Damn, the trembling was starting again.

"Someone you know? Like a client?"

"Yes."

"You should call Mac. And the police."

"I can't"

"Why not?

"Because."

"Oh Lord. Here we go again."

"It's someone from the case I'm not supposed to be looking into."

"You mean it was —"

"No one you know," I said, meaning the Madisons.

"But someone from that case?"

"Yes. Now can I take a shower?"

Toby, hearing us from the other room, wandered in. "Hey, girl," he said. He made a move to hug me — the big sweetheart always greeted me that way — but I held out my hand. "Don't. I stink."

"She sure does," Royanne added.

Toby shrugged. "Okay. How long till dinner?"

"About an hour," Royanne answered.

He asked, "You staying?"

"I can't. I have to get cleaned up and go on a date."

Toby smiled. "Have fun." He poured himself a soda out of a two-liter bottle. He offered me some, which I declined, and went back to the living room to join the kids.

"You have to call the police." Royanne picked up where we'd left off.

"No. He didn't do anything. I don't have anything, really, to report."

"I'm going to get Toby to follow you home."

"No, Grant can do it."

"Promise me you'll call the police if he's at your house."

She was in full mother hen mode, one of the things I loved about her. "Oh, I will. Don't worry."

Royanne slid the chicken into the oven and led me upstairs. I showered in the master bathroom, using her coconut-mango shampoo, then her blow dryer. While I styled my hair, she rummaged around in her bureau for something that would come close to fitting me. We were the same height, five foot four, but I was a size ten, and Roy was easily an eighteen or a twenty.

I waited, wrapped in a green towel, while she found a pair of denim shorts with a drawstring. "Here, try these." I slid them on, tied them tight, and hoped they wouldn't fall off. She tossed me a T-shirt. BIRMINGHAM FINANCIAL, it read. YOUR HOMETOWN BANK. The whole outfit was yards too big.

"It'll do," Royanne said.

"I appreciate it."

I called Grant's cell. "Hey, what's up?"

"I have a little problem."

"You're canceling our date?"

For a half-second, I considered calling tonight off. Maybe I wasn't up to a social occasion. But I didn't want to inconvenience Toby by asking him to follow me home.

"No, I just need you to pick me up at a different place."

"Oh, okay."

"I'm at my best friend's house." I gave him directions, and he said he could be there in fifteen minutes.

I took another look at myself in the mirror. Pitiful. Royanne brought me a plastic grocery bag to put my smelly outfit in, then she and I sat on the deck and had a beer while we waited for Grant.

We chatted about the Madisons for a while, as I gave her a more detailed version of what had happened at their house on Friday night. Then, through the sliding glass door, I heard the doorbell ring. Toby answered it and led Grant to the deck.

I rose as he joined us and introduced him to Royanne. He shook her hand as they sized each other up. Royanne had to crane her neck to meet his gaze. I held the waistband of my shorts in a death grip.

"Have a seat," Royanne offered. "Would you like a beer?"

I wasn't in the mood for the verbal dissection that was about to spill forth from my friend. I knew that look on her face. Grant was in for it. "We'd better go," I said to him.

"Okay, whatever you want." His attention was diverted by the fact that I was wearing an outfit four sizes too big. "Is something wrong?"

"I'll explain in the van."

"Okay."

I focused on Royanne. "Can I leave my car here and get it tomor-row?"

"Sure."

She and Toby walked us out to Grant's van, Toby chatting with Grant like they'd been friends for years. Toby was a good old boy, and had that effect on people.

In the van, Grant asked, "So now are you going to tell me what's up?"

"Remember on the Fourth, when I told you about the case? Michael's case?"

"Sure."

"Remember I said that Ashley, the little boy's mother, had a mysterious boyfriend who showed up at the jail the day I went to see her?"

"Yeah."

"The boyfriend was following me around Oak Mountain today with a knife."

"Good Lord."

"Take a left here."

The direction I'd given was opposite from the way to my house. He didn't question it, and turned as I asked.

"What did you do?"

"I got off the trail and lost him in the woods, until I got to the parking lot. He was there, but by that time I'd found some other hikers."

"Jesus."

"Yeah. I'm afraid he may have followed me from my house. I wanted somebody with me when I went home. So I went to Royanne's."

"Then where are we going now?"

"I want to drive around for a minute. Make sure he's not following me. I think I lost him before, but I want to make sure."

"Poor thing. He really freaked you out."

That was true. The shaking had stopped, but I couldn't ditch this horrible sensation that I was being tracked.

"You shouldn't be alone tonight, Claire. Why don't you stay at my apartment? Or I can stay with you? On the couch," he finished mildly.

That might not be a bad idea. Not that I was going to get a lot of sleep, but it might be nice to have some company. I shrugged noncommittally and directed Grant to Highway 150, and from there up the Lakeshore extension. I scanned every direction, with Grant's help, for a black pickup. It wasn't until we were on a more or less deserted stretch of the four-lane road that I was convinced we were alone. Grant took a right at West Oxmoor and within a few minutes we were in my neighborhood. As he pulled into my driveway, I was fiddling with the drawstring on my shorts so that I wouldn't give him a full moon as I slid out of the van. As I tied a tight bow, Grant asked a question.

"Exactly how many men do you have stalking you?"

"What do you mean?" I asked back, looking at him.

He nodded toward the house. "That man is sitting on your stoop again."

CHAPTER TWENTY-ONE

Oh, Christ. Kirk Mahoney was the last thing I needed right now. But on my stoop he sat, as unwelcome as a pimple on prom night. This time with a plastic grocery bag beside him.

"Damn." I muttered. What was I going to do now? I needed to talk to Kirk, but I didn't really feel like introducing him to Grant. The less Kirk knew about my personal life, the better.

Grant rescued me from having to make some awkward excuse. "I'll tell you what. Why don't I go to my apartment and pick up a change of clothes? You can talk to what's-his-name. I'll be back in thirty minutes. You'll be okay with him here, right?"

"Yeah, okay." I picked up my clothes and slid out of the van. I turned to face Kirk, clutching my shorts again.

"What do you want?"

"That's the second time you've shown up in that van. Who is he?" Kirk jumped down off the stoop and made his way down the concrete path to meet me as Grant backed out. I could think of little else except getting into the house and making sure no one had been there. And getting out of sight.

"None of your business."

"Touchy, aren't we? Can I come in? I want to talk to you."

I was hurrying past him at a race-walk, keys out. I slid the key into the doorknob and motioned him inside, closing the door fast behind us, then locking it. Once inside, I scrutinized the living room. Nothing seemed disturbed.

Kirk began, "What —"

I held up one finger to silence him while I continued my search. Checked to make sure the door to the carport was locked, then the back door. Looked in the pantry and all the closets. Under the guest bed and under mine. Kirk followed me from room to room, confused.

"What are you doing?"

"Making sure no one's here."

"Why would somebody be here? And why are you wearing those huge clothes?"

I was at the end of my emotional rope. I could not spend another second talking to anyone, or explaining anything. "Can you give me a minute? I'm going to go change." I found some clean underwear, shorts and a top, then locked myself in the bathroom. I wet a pink washcloth with warm water, and, leaving the water running, pressed it to my eyes. I took deep, deep breaths to ward off the sobs. It didn't work. The shakes were back, worse than before. I wet the washcloth again and pressed it to my face. Breathe. Breathe. I was tired. Tired of being scared, tired of grief. And my legs hurt like hell.

After a few minutes the hysteria passed and I felt more in control. I washed my face, changed, and put Royanne's clothes in the wicker hamper to be washed. Took one last deep breath and went out to face the reporter in my living room who thought I was a paranoid schizophrenic.

He was sitting on the couch, watching CNN. I eased down beside him. "Hi," I said, limply.

"You okay?"

"No, not really."

"I didn't think so."

I was drained. "What's going on?" he asked.

"I had a little incident today on Oak Mountain. Somebody threatened me."

"God. What happened?"

"I can't really talk about it."

"Why not?"

"Because."

"Because of your work? Was it one of your clients?"

"Yeah, sort of."

"Did you call the police?"

"I'll take care of it. You said you wanted to talk to me."

"I wanted to say I'm sorry. I was rude to you on the phone. I feel bad."

"It's okay."

"I brought you a peace offering." He handed me the grocery bag, which had been sitting on the coffee table. In it was a six-pack of Michelob Ultra.

For what seemed like the first time that day, I smiled. "Thanks."

"You look like you could use one, too. They're probably a little warm. Let me go put them in the fridge."

"Pour me one, while you're at it. The glasses are to the right of the sink."

He came back, carrying two pilsner glasses of beer. It was a little tepid. I didn't care.

Kirk said, "You must get threatened all the time by your clients, no?"

I thought back to the few times it had happened. The tire-slashing incident last week, the one I'd blamed on Flash. Now I wasn't so sure. The client who'd left the lovely note spray painted in orange on my car. I'd put her kids in foster care. The police didn't have a whole lot of trouble discerning whodunit. She'd been hanging out in the parking lot every time I left the office for nearly a week before committing the crime, screaming threats and obscenities as I walked out. She'd been charged and forced to pay restitution. She was now in a mental institution, and her kids had been adopted.

I'd been held at gunpoint too, while executing a pickup order, by a father who wasn't too keen on DHS taking his kids away. Luckily the standoff didn't last long. The police officer I was with called for backup and within five minutes the house was surrounded with SWAT officers. Daddy made the right decision and put the gun down before anybody got shot. Their mother had custody now, but he had supervised visitation. He'd actually sent me a letter of apology later.

So why was this so different? What was it about today that had me so incredibly shit-scared? Because Michael was murdered. This was different because someone was dead. And I could be next.

"Hello?" Kirk said, pulling me out of my musings.

"Sorry. Yeah, I mean, threats do happen. This was different though."

"How?"

"It just was."

"Man, you're a tough nut to crack."

"What do you mean?"

"You don't share a lot. About anything."

"I can't, about my cases. You know that."

"Yeah, but you know, I don't put everything in the paper."

"Ha! Sure you don't."

"You think I'm that untrustworthy?"

"I think you want to sell papers. Get the big story."

"I—"

"Come on, admit it."

A sheepish grin. I thought it was adorable until I caught myself.

"See? I was right."

"I have to get the big stories. That's the only way I'm going to get where I want to go."

"Which is?"

"One of the big weekly mags. *Time* or *Newsweek*. Or *U.S. News*. One with real resources for investigative reporters. Another year or two with a big daily like *The News*, and I'll be ready to move on. Or maybe I'll freelance. I'm not sure. I want to go where the action is, across the globe."

I sipped my beer, thinking of Kirk dressed in camouflage in some war-torn Middle East country. I shuddered. "Sounds dangerous."

"So does your job. But you still do it."

"Because I love it." I said it without thinking, and realized the impulsive statement had come from the heart. I wanted to keep my job.

"So who's the guy in the van? Is he your boyfriend?"

I shrugged.

"What does that mean?"

"I don't know."

"You don't know if you have a boyfriend?"

"He's going to be back here any minute."

"So I should go." He drained the last of his beer and put the glass on the coffee table. We made our way toward the door.

"Before you go, I want to ask you something," I said.

"Shoot."

"Can you look into something for me? There's a company here, a local one, called Eclipse Entertainment. Run by a guy named Donovan Grayson. He owns a bar called Kaleidoscope, along with two or three others. Can you see if there is anything fishy going on with them?"

"Why? What do you think is going on?"

"Maybe nothing."

"What do I get out of it?"

"If there is something, then you get a story."

"I meant from you. You'll owe me a favor." There was that grin again.

"Kirk—"

"What?"

"No more kissing."

He laughed. "I'll dig around a bit and call you next week. Bye."

I locked the door behind him, then knelt on my loveseat to peek out the front blinds. Kirk drove a dark silver Infiniti G35 coupe. I watched him roar down the street, then sipped another beer while I waited for Grant.

It was almost dark before he got back. He knocked on the door softly, and I unbolted it for him. He was holding a bag from Movie Gallery and two medium pizzas from Papa John's. "Sorry to be so long. I didn't think you were up for going out, so I brought dinner. I got one pepperoni and one cheese, okay?"

"Okay."

"You like sci-fi?"

I did, actually. "Yeah."

The movie was pretty good, humans-versus-robots with plenty of action. When it was over, we found an Indiana Jones movie on Showtime. By the end of that one, it was after midnight and Grant's head was nodding to his chest. I reached over and ran my hand through his curls, the natural copper highlights glinting in my fingers. "Why don't you go to bed? The guest room has clean sheets."

" 'kay"

I leaned over and kissed his stubbly, sun-browned cheek. "Thanks, for staying tonight."

He reached a hand around the back of my neck and pulled me close for a tender kiss on the lips. " 'Night."

"Good night." I watched him pick up his small duffel bag and walk down the hall to the guest room. The door closed and I suddenly realized that I was a bit let down. Kirk would have tried harder to get me into bed with him. Pulling my mind back from bedroom fantasies, I considered going to sleep. But thoughts of Jimmy were waiting in the darkness. I channel surfed, trying to concentrate on TV, but instead finding my mind replaying all of the events of the past week and a half. So I picked up a pad and pencil.

I am a compulsive list maker. Can't live without them. From the grocery list on the magnetic pad on the refrigerator to the to-do list on my desk at work, lists run my life. They help me think clearly. This list started with ASHLEY HENNESSY.

Claims she did it. I still didn't believe it, and she wouldn't tell me why she was willing to take the blame for her son's death. Would she have killed him for Jimmy? Because he didn't want kids? Did Jimmy threaten to leave her if Michael wasn't out of the picture? Did Ashley love Jimmy so much that she'd kill her only son? No way.

Next, JIMMY SHELTON. A big unknown. How much influence did he have over Ashley? Did he want her, but not her son? He was dangerous. Dangerous enough to follow me into the woods with a knife. The thought made me want to check the doors again.

Then there was ZANDER MADISON. Michael's dad. Not exactly a responsible guy, but not really a deadbeat either. Seemed to love Michael. Even provided for his son in his own way. I'd seen a lot worse. But Zander was dependent on his family's wealth to support his drug habit. What would he do for drugs? Anything, probably. Including kill his own son, if his parents told him to?

ALEXANDER AND KAREN MADISON. Powerful. A family used to getting their way and with a whole lot to lose. Including control of a huge corporation. But also desperate to get help for Zander. I thought about the love I'd seen in them for their son. Would two parents with so much concern for their child be capable of murdering a toddler? Their own grandson? My instincts said no. Careful, though, I told myself. You might be wrong. That made me uneasy. Self-doubt wasn't something I was used to. Not until this case.

I studied the list so far. AL MACKEY, I wrote next. Had a history of hurting his own daughter. In debt up to his eyeballs and had gone so far as to directly ask about life insurance for Michael and Ashley. A scumbag. But a murderer for money?

GREGORY BOWMAN, AKA FLASH. He was in love with Ashley, and he'd stalked her before. Unstable was an understatement, especially when he was high. I was fairly sure he'd been the voice of the threatening message at work. Reacted rather violently to the idea that he could be Michael's father. But Ashley had never asked him for child support because she knew all along who Michael's dad was. What motive could he have for killing Michael? None. But Ashley? Possession. He could have tried to kill Ashley for dumping him. If I can't have her, no one can. That sort of twisted, abusive logic. I'd bet he knew how to get his hands on some GHB if he wanted to.

Then I wrote OTHERS. A question mark after that one. Ashley had lied to me about knowing the identity of Michael's father. What else was she lying about? Who she was hanging out with? Was she staying clean? If she wasn't sober, she sure knew how to fake a drug screen. Who knows what kind of partying she'd been doing behind my back?

KALIEDESCOPE. Another question mark. A hangout for Ashley and her friends. A club whose name always seemed to come up when GHB was the subject. And Ashley knew the bartender.

So, what now? My brain was being sucked into an undertow of exhaustion. I studied the list. I'd just have to do what I did with every other list. Tackle each item one by one until I was done. Until I was satisfied that I had answers.

It was after one. I yawned an enormous yawn and closed the notepad, then curled up under a chenille blanket on the couch. *The Empire Strikes Back* was on one of the cable channels. I knew it by heart, watched it anyway. I fell asleep while Luke Skywalker was on Dagobah and dreamed of a man with Darth Vader's voice, except he had long, bushy hair and a beard.

I woke with a start to the sound of someone opening my carport door.

CHAPTER TWENTY-TWO

The carport door had a distinctive squeak, and my eyes flew open when I heard it. Sunlight filtered through the closed blinds and made a pattern on the hardwood floors. I jumped up like someone had poked me with a pin.

My father was closing the door behind him. He looked to the couch where I sat, hair tangled and eyes puffy. I started breathing again and tried to get my heart rate down. The grit in my eyes had grown overnight to the size of pebbles. I rubbed them. My legs ached.

"Good morning. You're sleeping late."

"What time is it?"

"Nine thirty."

"Oh."

My father suddenly noticed something and started. I followed his surprised gaze to see Grant, standing in the hallway outside the bathroom door, wet. His glasses were steamed over. All of his important parts were wrapped in a pink towel.

"Hello," my father said.

"Hi," Grant said, with a nod. He turned quickly and ducked into the guest bedroom.

"New friend?" Dad asked me.

"He's the guy I met at the computer store."

"I see." There was an edge to my father's voice. His liberalism didn't extend to wanting to know any details about his daughter's sex life. Or that I even had one. "Something wrong with his place?"

"I asked him to stay. It's a long story. And if you are going to let yourself in to *my* house, you have no right to make snide comments. Next time, knock."

"Sorry."

I shouldn't have been short with him. "Me too. He slept in the guest bedroom, by the way."

"It's none of my business."

"It's okay."

Grant, dressed, walked into the room. I introduced him to Dad and they shook hands. Awkward. Probably would have gone better if my father hadn't seen him in a towel.

"I came over to do some edging," Dad said. "I guess I'll get started."

"Thanks."

I ran a hand through my hair and walked, sore and stiff, to the kitchen to make coffee.

Grant said, "What are you going to do today?"

First item on my agenda for tomorrow, Monday, was to get to the jail to see Ashley, but in order to do that I need to get some things done at work. I had several home visits to schedule and court Monday afternoon. Not to mention the ever-present pile of pending paperwork. "I'm probably going into work."

"You going to be okay? I told my parents I'd come down today, but if you need me —"

"I'll be okay."

"What about tonight?"

"If I get nervous, I'll call you. Or go to my father's."

Grant and I had coffee, then we decided on breakfast before going to get my car. We waved to Dad as we pulled out of the drive. After satiating ourselves on biscuits and gravy and grits at a nearby restaurant, we made our way to Royanne's. I knocked on the door and let her know I was taking my car, said good-bye to Grant with promises to call him, and drove downtown to work.

There were enough cars in the parking lot to make me feel somewhat safe, but nonetheless I compulsively checked behind my back as I entered the building and signed in with the weekend security guard. I spent an uneventful afternoon doing paperwork, and at four thirty left for home. At my request, the guard walked me to my car.

I picked up the ingredients for vegetarian spinach lasagna at the Piggly Wiggly and called Grant on my way to my father's. He was still at his parents' house and declined my invitation to join us for dinner. I parked behind Dad's hybrid, as usual, and lugged the groceries into the kitchen.

"What's all this?" he asked, poking through the bags.

"Dinner." I started unloading the groceries. "Unless you had plans?"

"No plans. I was just going to heat up some soup and watch *60 Minutes.*"

"Can I stay the night here?"

"Why?"

"I don't want to stay at my place."

"Why? Stop fussing with the damn groceries and tell me what's going on."

I stopped and faced him. "I may be in a bit of trouble." Leaning against the harvest gold countertop, I told him about the stalking at Oak Mountain yesterday.

When I was finished, he stormed, "You know, I've never liked your job. I keep saying that I want you to come into practice with me, and I mean it."

"I know, but I'm not giving up. Not on my job, unless the A.G.'s office presses charges and I get fired. I'm not giving up on this case. I owe it to Ashley. And myself. But most of all to Michael."

He studied me a moment, then his pastel blue eyes took on a distant expression. He said, "I remember when the other Freedom Riders and I left that May. We knew there'd be trouble, maybe even some of us would be killed. Then, when we got to the bus station and saw that huge mob and no cops in sight, I was sure of it. But we went ahead, anyway. Because we believed what we were doing was right. Your grandfather thought I'd gone crazy. He didn't believe in desegregation, or understand why it was so important. Maybe worth dying for."

"Then you get where I'm coming from."

"I get it. But I'm still worried."

I kissed the scar on his cheek. "Don't be. I'll be careful."

We spent a companionable evening eating and watching TV. Dad drove me over to my house so I could get something to sleep in and something to wear to work in the morning. I went to bed early, snuggling into the concave twin mattress, wrapped in the tattered pink and green floral comforter that I'd dreamt under for so many years as a teenager. Someday, my dad might get remarried and his new wife would turn this space into a fashionable guest room or office. For now, I'd relish the sensation of safety infused from the familiar stuffed animals around me and the cotton candy-colored paint on the walls.

I slept deeply and the alarm clock buzzed way too soon. After leaving Dad a thank-you note, I went to my eight thirty staff meeting, then to the court to file my addendum for the one thirty dependency review. By eleven, I was circling the jailhouse, looking for a place to park. No luck. After deciding to spend the three dollars it would cost to put the car in a garage, I made my way into the building and through security. The guard recognized me now, but still made me do the whole routine, walking me through the metal detector and making me leave my things. I went to the second floor as before, perched and waited until Ashley was escorted in.

When she saw me, she rolled her eyes. Whatever sympathy I'd been nurturing toward her transformed instantly into anger. She picked up the handset and said, "What now?"

"How do I get in touch with Jimmy?"

"I told you, you don't."

I was pissed as hell, and I didn't care if she knew it. "Damn it, Ashley. That son of a bitch followed me around Oak Mountain State Park Saturday with a knife. He might have killed me. I want to talk to him. Because now he has a problem."

"Claire, it ain't what you think."

"Then what is it?"

"Just leave it alone. Please. I'm beggin' you. You're just gonna get hurt."

"By Jimmy? I want to talk to him."

"No."

"Give me a number. Or an address. I'm going to find him."

"Don't. He's not dangerous."

"Then why was he tracking me on a hiking trail with a knife? Listen to me. You tell him if I even see him near me again, I'm going straight to the police."

"But it ain't what you think."

I'd had enough of her lies. I slammed the headset down in the cradle a little too forcefully and stood. Through the glass I heard her yell, "Wait, don't be mad! Please!" The guard, not liking the shouting, came over and gripped Ashley by the elbow. "Please!"

I caught a glimpse of her over my shoulder as I marched for the door. I didn't stay to watch the guard take her back. I took the stairs to the security station, my heels clicking loudly on the concrete steps. I retrieved my car from the garage. The money I'd wasted to park just so I could get nothing from Ashley was another needle of anger that stuck in me.

I drove north and found a spot at a meter two blocks away from the Top of the Hill Grill. It was busy, full of lunch patrons, and I had to wait until I could get a seat at the counter. Brandi flew from the window to the counter to the tables and back. Another waitress, a new girl, was doing the same thing. So the manager had replaced Ashley. Life was going on without her.

An elderly couple paid their tab and left, and I slid onto one of the vinyl-covered stools they'd vacated. Brandi saw me, nodded, and a few minutes later took my order. "I need to talk to you," I said.

"Way busy. Can you wait?"

I checked my watch. It was five to twelve. I had court at one thirty. "For a while."

I ate, then bought a newspaper from a box outside the restaurant and read it while the surge of diners receded. Kirk didn't have an article in the paper today. I skimmed the editorial page, which was full of comments about rising water prices and, mercifully, not entirely full of criticism of DHS.

Brandi finally had a few minutes of down time at one. I had to leave for court within fifteen minutes, so I made it quick. "I need to talk to Jimmy. Do you know where I can find him?"

"He hasn't been in here since Ashley went to jail. Didn't you ask her for his number?"

"I just came from the jail. She won't tell me how to reach him."

"Weird."

"What's weirder is that he followed me out to Oak Mountain Saturday, and he had a knife on him."

Her eyes widened under the royal purple-streaked hair. "No shit? Why?"

"I don't know. I need to know what he's up to. You said before that he worked in one of the buildings around here. Did he or Ashley ever say which one?"

She fiddled with one of the earrings in her right ear as she thought. "I don't think so. If they did, I can't remember. I know it's close to here, 'cause he walked over for lunch. He used to come in his uniform. A burgundy shirt, something blue on the pocket."

I nodded. It was the same shirt he was wearing when I first saw him at the jail. However, it didn't help me much. I prompted Brandi again. "Anything else you remember? Anything at all?"

She thought some more. "Sorry. Ashley was like, real private about him. She never really talked about him, you know?"

"Okay. Thanks anyway." I paid my check and once again left her a big tip. She promised to call if she remembered anything. Out on the sidewalk, I looked around. The Top of the Hill was on a busy street. Within blocks of here were a hundred huge buildings, including the art museum, the Alabama School of Fine Arts, Boutwell Auditorium, the courthouses, BFB Bank, the jail — the list went on and on. As much as I'd love to canvass all of them in search of Jimmy, it was impractical.

I hoofed it back to the Honda, and arrived at Family Court in West End three minutes late. I wasn't worried since most of the judges didn't start the afternoon docket on time anyway. I hung my badge around my neck, cleared security, and climbed the large marble staircase to the courtrooms on the second floor. Judge Myer was hearing my case today. The family I was working with sat in the waiting area. The ten- and eight-year old siblings who were in my custody were ecstatic about seeing their mom. The foster parent kept a watchful eye from a distance.

I pulled the family into one of the glass-fronted conference rooms to talk to them confidentially. For the biological mother, I outlined the contents of the report I'd submitted to the judge, reminding her that although I was proud of her progress, the kids would likely be staying in foster care for another few months. It was a little too early for them to go home, and I didn't want her to be blindsided when Judge Myer ruled. Mom took it well, said she understood, and the family went back to the waiting area while I sat in the courtroom, whispering with my colleagues who were there on other cases. Finally, at ten after three, the clerk called my case. Judge agreed with my recommendation to leave the kids in their current placement, and as he ruled, the kids' mother started to bawl. Then the kids started, too.

Judge Myer signed his order, and I shooed the family into the hallway where I attempted to calm everyone down. I praised Mom again for her progress, telling her it wouldn't be long until the kids came home. She needed to stay sober and away from the man who had sexually abused her daughter. The kids needed to mind their foster parents and do well in school. I'd just about gotten the situation stabilized when one of the D.A.s stuck her head out of the courtroom door.

"Claire? Judge wants you in chambers."

Judge Myer's office was behind his courtroom. He was seated behind a traditional wooden desk. He had a head full of blond hair and a round face, which often fooled people into thinking he was younger than he was. I knew he was pushing fifty. He had slipped off his black robe, and was now in shirtsleeves with his tie loose. The robe hung on a hanger on the back of the door to the courtroom. A crimson-matted degree dominated the wall space behind his desk, and Tide memorabilia decorated the room here and there.

"How are you?"

"Fine, Your Honor, thanks."

"You sure? Teresa called me last week about the A.G.'s office requesting the Hennessy records." Judge Myer was one of the few people who'd earned the right to call Dr. Pope by her first name. "She also mentioned you were a little worried about your job."

"Well, yeah, a bit."

"Don't be. It seems like there isn't a day that goes by that someone doesn't question my rulings. If it isn't the attorney general, then it's the appellate court. They usually hold up. I reviewed the Hennessy record before we sent it to Montgomery. We did a good job on that case. You do a good job on all your cases. I heard you outside a minute ago, talking to that family. You know how to relate to people, and you treat them with respect. We need more social workers like you."

For some inexplicable reason I was almost moved to tears. "Thanks," I said, hoarsely. Judge Myer was a good judge. He didn't let emotion cloud his rulings. He was fair. He listened to those around him and took everything into consideration, even if he disagreed. What he'd said meant a lot.

He came around the desk to give me a reassuring squeeze on the shoulder. "Don't worry about the A.G.'s office. It'll blow over."

"I hope you're right."

I sat in my Honda in the parking lot for a few minutes, enjoying a warm sense of pleasure at the judge's words. He didn't think I was a failure. Now I just had to prove it to myself.

I checked my office voice mail remotely, to make sure there wasn't anything urgent that needed to be taken care of before I left for the day. Twenty minutes later I parked my car in front of Ashley's apartment.

Connections, Mac said many years ago while he was training me. Look at who the family knows. Most child abuse is committed by someone familiar. A stepparent, an uncle, a coach, a family friend. Talk to everyone who spends time with that child, and get a feel for them. In other words, do what I do best.

Michael's death was no different. Ashley knew who did this. I thought about my list, sitting by the phone at home. Who on that list had done this to him, and what was I missing? It was time for a more thorough look around the crime scene.

Mail overflowed out of the box next to Ashley's door. I collected it and brought it inside. The apartment was still clean, as it had been when Al and I were here, which meant Zander hadn't been back.

The only sounds were the faint hum of the refrigerator and the click and whir of the AC cutting on. I surveyed my surroundings, deciding what to do. I started in the kitchen, looking through the drawers for an address book. Nothing. I wandered to the hallway, searched a small closet that produced nothing but sheets and mismatched towels. In Ashley's bedroom, I went first to her closet. Clothes, shoes, a shoe box of junk that revealed souvenir Mardi Gras beads, a get-well-soon card, a pen, some old photos of herself, and a broken watch. I put it all back and rummaged through the nightstand.

In the nightstand's drawer were vitamins, a bottle of lotion, some ibuprofen, and some expired children's cough syrup. No address book. Damn. Talk to me, Michael, I prayed. Help me out here, angel.

I went back to the living room, my gaze settling on the framed collage of pictures I'd seen the day Michael died. I studied them closely. Especially the second set. There was the picture of Dee, as before, and of Brandi. But now I could look at the photo of the three guys on the couch and put names to faces. Zander was the one at the end, laughing, a plastic cup raised in a toast to no one in particular. Next to him was —

Whoa. Lucas Grayson. I almost didn't recognize him with hair. It was dark and straight, like his brother's, but not as receded. It'd been shoulder length before he shaved it all off. If it wasn't for the Icarus tattoo, I wouldn't have recognized him at all.

Next to Lucas was another young man I'd seen before. But where?

With Lucas. Sitting at the bar at Kaleidoscope. The blond guy with shaggy hair, dressed in business attire the day I met Lucas and Donovan. Drinking a cocktail while Lucas stocked the bar. I wondered who he was.

I took the picture frame down, placed it on the worn table, then pried up the little metal tabs holding the mat in place. I untaped, carefully, the picture of the three guys. I went back to the shoe box and retrieved one of the old pictures of Ashley. I used the tape to fix Ashley's picture to the mat and replaced the mat in the frame, then hung it back up.

I had just slipped the photo into my purse and was heading for the door when it opened and in walked Zander.

CHAPTER TWENTY-THREE

Zander saw me, purse on my shoulder, and his expression went cold. "What the fuck are you doing here?"

"Checking on things for Ashley. What about you?"

"That's none of your damn business." He noticed the mail on the table, walked past me, and began to sort through it.

"What's with you?" I asked.

"You sold me out, bitch. Told my parents where I was."

"They're worried sick about you."

"So? What do you care?"

"They care. That's what matters."

He was flipping through a sales circular but listening to me nonetheless.

"C'mon, Zander. You know you can't go on like this forever. Sooner or later, you're going to kill yourself, or, God forbid, someone else. Your parents want the best for you, to get you help."

"They're dragging me to some shrink."

"So take advantage of that. Use the help to try and figure out where your life is going."

"I know where my life is going."

"It's up to you."

"Fuck you."

I couldn't think of a thing to say to that, so I left.

On the way home, my mind was occupied with Zander. I felt for his parents. The struggle ahead of them was going to be a long one, trying to get him straight. In order to focus my thoughts elsewhere, I called Grant on my cell.

"Hey," he answered. "How are you? Any sign of that guy?"

"I'm okay, and no, no sign."

"You want me to come over tonight?"

I really didn't. I was tired after the long day, and I wanted some peace and quiet. A long bubble bath and a good book. "I'm pretty tired."

"Oh, all right then." A note of hurt colored his voice. I felt a twinge of guilt.

"I tell you what," I said, "How about a date Friday? Maybe we can go for that dinner and a movie we missed Saturday."

"That sounds good." We small talked until I pulled into my driveway, and he stayed on the line as I went inside, just to be safe. The house was undisturbed, but I checked it carefully, as before. I spent the night soaking my still-sore body in the tub and slept lightly with a butcher knife within arm's reach.

On Tuesday morning Mac plopped a new case on my desk that had come in overnight. Interviews with the parents and three children ate up the morning. I decided to leave them with their family with some intense counseling services in place. I made the therapy referral, and, stomach growling loudly, went to find some lunch.

It was quarter to two when I got to the Top of the Hill Grill. Brandi and her new coworker were chatting companionably, wiping tables. I knew the grill stopped service at two, and the girls washed dishes until four.

"Hey," Brandi greeted me.

"Hey. Is it too late to eat?"

"Nah, you're fine. What can I get you?"

The special was a patty melt, which sounded delicious. But my clothes were getting tighter so I decided to be good and ordered the grilled chicken salad with light dressing.

Brandi stuck my order in the window and rang the little bell. I pulled the picture of the three guys on Ashley's sofa out of my purse and laid it on the sticky countertop. Pointing to the blond mystery man, I asked, "Do you know who that is?"

She glanced at the photo. "Oh, sure, that's Trey."

"Trey who?"

"Dunno. All I know is his name's Trey. He's a friend of . . . of, of Ashley's."

"And he's also a friend of Zander's."

Her gaze went everywhere but to my face. "I'm not sure who you mean."

"Yes, you do. I know about Zander. I met him at Ashley's apartment." I lowered my voice to barely above a whisper and added, "He was Michael's dad."

Brandi, knowing the game was up, nodded slowly. "I always told Ashley she should tell you. She felt real bad, not telling you. She hated lying to you. But Zander, and Zander's daddy, they didn't want no one to know. They didn't want a DHS record. They were so afraid you were gonna find out."

"Was it Zander's drugs that killed Michael?"

"I don't know. Ashley won't say. But that's what I think. Zander's fun to hang out with, don't get me wrong, but he's a fucked-up mess. I'm surprised, what with all the shit he does, that he's not dead yet. Ashley's been tryin' for months to get him to go someplace for help. She loves Zander, really. He was good to her, you know? At a time when she needed it."

"You think she loves him enough to cover up for him?"

Brandi nodded again. Another late customer entered the diner. The other waitress, getting a signal from Brandi, seated him and took his order. I thought about what Brandi had said, then asked, "But what about Jimmy? I thought she and Jimmy—"

"She loves Jimmy. She's in love with Jimmy. But she and Zander have, had, a baby together. She'll always have feelings for him, you know what I mean? Maybe I'm not making any sense."

She was making sense. I thought about the guy I'd been with

throughout grad school. We'd even lived together for a while before our jobs took us in different directions. He was married now, with a kid, but we still exchanged rare e-mails and Christmas cards. I would always care for him. But go to prison for him?

And it still didn't explain why Ashley's current boyfriend was trailing me around with a knife. He certainly didn't owe anything to Zander. Was Jimmy so much in love with Ashley that he'd actually help her cover up for her ex-lover?

The little bell rang and Brandi delivered my salad. It didn't smell as good as the French fries now cooking in the kitchen, but I dug in anyway. Brandi wiped the counter. Between bites I asked, "So who's this Trey guy?"

She shrugged. "Some friend of Zander's. I've met him twice. His real name is Something-Something-Something the Third, but they call him Trey."

Something-Something-Something the Third. Well, that was helpful. But I bet I knew who could tell me Trey's identity. I put the picture back in my purse and finished the salad. Brandi refilled my drink, and at my request poured it into a to-go cup.

Outside the grill, I surveyed the area as I had last time. I needed to go back to work. I had to start a chart on my investigation from this morning, and follow up on that referral. Instead, I took a walk. To clear my head. I walked south for a few blocks, taking note of the larger buildings in the area. Took a right just before the historic Tutweiler Hotel, between it and the old library building, and then into Linn Park. The park was the headquarters for many events in the city, including City Stages, the big music festival held in June, and the local Race for the Cure in October. On race day, the trees in the park were tied with huge pink ribbons in memory of breast cancer victims. My brother Chris and I bought one every year for Mom.

I passed the fountain and reached the north side of the park, facing the Birmingham Museum of Art. A bench sat near the towering glass front doors to the museum, and I was ready for a rest. The temperature was typical for July, in the mid-nineties. I wiped perspiration from my forehead and sipped the rest of my watery drink. The temptation to go into the air-conditioned museum and browse around the collections was almost too strong to ignore. I finished my drink and tossed it into a nearby can. A gaggle of students from ASFA made their way down the sidewalk, on the way to their campus in the next block. They reminded me of Zander's younger sister, Kaylin. I wondered if she would head down the same dangerous path as her brother.

Okay, enough time wasted. The chart from this morning wasn't going away, and the sooner I got it done, the sooner I could go home. I strolled up the sidewalk on the east side of the park, in no hurry. I was going over everything about Michael's case in my mind again when I saw him.

A man, walking toward me, in a burgundy shirt with a blue logo on the pocket. It wasn't Jimmy, but I was fairly sure it was the same shirt that he wore that day at the jail. The guy in the shirt was younger and trimmer than Jimmy, in his mid-twenties. As we closed in on each other, I saw he was a handsome guy, with thick blond hair and blue eyes that stood out against his tan skin. In his right hand was a bag from Sneaky Pete's hot dog shop.

I still couldn't make out the logo. As he passed me on the sidewalk, I said, "Excuse me, sir?"

He stopped, gave me a half-smile that revealed stained teeth. "Yeah?"

"Could I ask where you work?"

He nodded straight ahead of him, behind me. "The convention center."

I turned around. Beyond the interstate overpass, the sprawling, brown-brick complex took up a solid city block, more if you counted the parking decks that surrounded it and the mammoth hotel next door. A fight had been raging year after year among city leaders about whether to replace it with a domed stadium. I fell in step with Sneaky Pete and asked, "Do you know a guy named Jimmy Shelton?"

"Oh sure, I know Jimmy." Sneaky Pete had a country accent that I placed from the plains, in the southern part of the state.

"Is he working today, do you know? I'd love to say hi to him." And stick a knife up his —

"He's there. C'mon and I'll find him for you."

We approached the elevated section of I-59/20, and as we walked underneath it, I had to shout to be heard.

"What do you do?"

"Our department sets up all the stuff for the meetin's. All the A/V and the chairs and such. We got the full crew on today. Got a huge meetin' of foot doctors comin' in. I guess they got a lotta pi'tures of feet to look at."

I stifled a giggle and asked, "So that's what Jimmy does, too?"

"Yup."

I followed him to the main entrance of the center, over the intricate pavers in front, and through a large door. We climbed a flight of stairs. Miles of teal-patterned carpet stretched everywhere. Sneaky Pete led me to the guts of the building, to a small office whose occupant was out. A collection of brown clipboards hung on the wall. He pulled one down and checked the schedule. "Jimmy's in the East Hall, upstairs."

"I can find him."

"You sure?"

"Yeah, thanks for your help."

I went back to the main entrance hall. An upward-bound escalator to the East Hall was on the right, shut off. The downward one, also off, was on the left. If I had any sense at all, I'd turn around and leave. Go back to DHS and do the paperwork that was waiting on my desk.

I started to do just that, but at the last minute turned around and climbed the metal stairs of the escalator. Halfway up, my legs started to shake, and I didn't think it was because of the lingering soreness from the hike. What could he do to me at his work? Surely he didn't have another knife on him. And I didn't think someone would fail to notice if he made some attempt to harm me here. Still, I felt like I was poised to poke a big dog with a stick.

The East Exhibition rooms were at the top of the escalator. Several, identified by letters. I started at *D*, poking my head through double doors that revealed rows of teal-cushioned chairs and screens for slide projectors. When I got to *K*, I found him.

He was lining up chairs, taking them four at a time from a large stack. He turned around when the door opened, and what I could see of his face under all that hair registered surprise.

I stepped inside, letting the heavy wood door swing shut behind me with a booming thud. I stood in front of the door, my butt leaning against the metal push-bar that opened it. Jimmy was fifteen feet away, a chair in his hands. I stood ready to run if he came at me.

"What are you doing here?" His deep voice shattered the quiet room.

"I want to know why you followed me around Oak Mountain with a knife."

"I told you to stay out of it."

"Why?"

"You can't do anything to help Ashley. She wants you to leave it alone."

"I want to know who killed Michael. I want to know who Ashley is protecting. Is it you? Or Zander?"

"It doesn't matter. Leave it alone. I mean it. I'd hate to see you get hurt. So would Ashley."

"By you?"

He sneered. "If that's what it takes. A little visit to that cute little black and white house of yours up in Bluff Park."

My body went icy, like I'd taken a polar swim. I fought to steady my still-shaking legs and said, "If I see you anywhere near me, I'll call the cops." I hoped my voice was more forceful than it sounded to me.

He laughed, a short jeer that echoed in the room. "You do that."

The door behind me suddenly swung out, throwing me off balance. I stumbled sideways and caught myself before I fell as a woman in a black suit and scarf entered. She carried one of the brown clip-boards. "Oh, sorry," she said, watching me right myself. "Didn't see you there. Jimmy, I need a word."

"See you around," Jimmy said with a glare that bore right into my brain.

I left Jimmy and the woman and made it outside in a flash. By the time I reached my car some six blocks away, I was soaked in sweat and breathing hard. The bastard knew where I lived.

I punched a number into my cell phone. "I need a favor."

CHAPTER TWENTY-FOUR

I went back to work and tried to concentrate on putting together the chart regarding the family I'd seen this morning. I had to redo two forms because I wasn't paying attention. After documenting the interviews, scheduling the intervention meeting for tomorrow, and following up with the therapist, I left the office at six, still uneasy and with only half my mind on anything I was doing. As arranged, I met Grant at High Tech.

I knocked above the logo on the front door. Grant emerged from the back office and unlocked the door with a key to let me in. I followed him back to his desk, where he put his bookkeeping away before tailing me back to my house.

He hadn't asked any questions on the phone when I told him I needed a place to spend the night. Hadn't asked any questions when I'd arrived at the store, and without comment entered my house first to make sure it was safe. He waited patiently while I packed an overnight case, threw in the list of suspects I'd made, and locked up.

Grant lived in an apartment complex near the mall, two minutes from his shop. A people stable of a hundred units, high on a hill, shielded from the commercial traffic below by a long drive and lots of trees. He lived on the third floor.

He gave me the fifty-cent tour. The place was definitely function rather than fashion. White walls. Minimal furniture. A big-screen TV in the living room. Two bedrooms, one an office that held trestle tables like the ones he worked on at the shop, full of computers. They hummed quietly. A bookcase, black, with thick tomes on mysterious subjects such as C and Visual Basic and Dot Net. In the next room lay a king-sized mattress set, no frame, unmade navy sheets and a brown bedspread. A clock radio was plugged in next to it. A dresser spilled clothes from every drawer.

After the tour we sank down on the leather couch. Grant picked up a fancy remote control that looked like a handheld PC and used it to turn on the lamps. "You okay?"

I wasn't. I wanted desperately to be home and for all this to be over. I wanted Michael alive, happy, and playing, and Ashley working and doing well. I didn't want awful men threatening me and I didn't want to have to look over my shoulder twenty-four-seven. I didn't want to feel like I had failed. And I hated burdening Grant with an un-invited house guest. I teared up before I could stop myself.

He scooted over and wrapped both arms around me. My cheek rested on his shoulder and my face pressed against his neck. He pat-ted my back and shoulders and said, "It's okay, it's okay," until my fit subsided.

When it was over I sat back, wiped away tears, and apologized.

"What happened?" he asked.

I told him about Jimmy and our conversation earlier. Grant said I was an idiot for seeking him out. I agreed. Grant brought me some toilet tissue from the bathroom. "Here. Why don't you get cleaned up a bit and get comfortable while I make us something to eat?"

I locked myself in Grant's bathroom. A plain, clear shower curtain enclosed the tub. His hairbrush and shaving kit lay on the counter, and that was it. I washed my face with cold water and studied my re-flection in the mirror. My blue eyes were pink and puffy, my nose red, and my skin splotchy. Nice. Claire, I said to myself, you really owe this guy. As soon as this is over, go out and buy yourself a hot new dress, get your hair and makeup done, and take him out for a steak.

I stripped off the clothes I'd worn to work and stood in a hot shower for twenty minutes, lingering with Grant's shampoo and soap. I brushed my hair and put on the shorts and T-shirt I'd brought with me.

Grant was frying bacon and eggs when I joined him in the kitchen. Two TV trays were set up in front of the couch, with paper napkins and forks. "Hungry?" he asked.

The smell of the bacon was getting to me. "Yeah."

I poured us each a glass of water from the pitcher in the fridge and we dug in. After supper, Grant put in a movie. By nine thirty I was sinking ever lower into the sofa. Grant went into his bedroom. He returned carrying a striped comforter and a pillow, wearing cotton shorts and a navy T-shirt that fit tight across his shoulders. The sleeves hugged his arms halfway down his biceps. He shut off the television, put the pillow gently under my head, and tucked me in.

"Need anything?" he asked.

Boy, did I. I leaned toward him and said, "How about a kiss good night?"

I slid his glasses off and put them on the floor next the sofa. Several minutes later, I began to ease his T-shirt up and over his head. He stopped me, catching my hands in his. "Not tonight."

"Why?"

He found his glasses and slid them on again, then brushed my cheek with his hand. "Good night."

I heard the click of his bedroom door shutting as I closed my eyes.

The next morning I awoke to the whine of an electric razor. The hollow, ashamed feeling was still with me. I drifted back to sleep and woke a few minutes later to the aroma of brewing coffee. I threw off the comforter and padded my way to the kitchen. Grant was dressed for work, in khakis and a polo with his store logo on it.

"Coffee?"

"Yes, please."

He handed me a full mug. "Cream and sugar?"

"No thanks." I sipped the hot, rich liquid as Grant stirred his. "Thanks for letting me stay last night."

"No problem."

"I'm sorry about —"

"Don't worry about it."

Before he left for work, Grant made me promise to meet him that evening. I got ready and faced a challenging day head-on. First on the agenda was the intervention meeting regarding the case from yester-day. I refereed a room full of people including parents, kids, grand-parents, a teacher, and the therapist I'd contacted. Everything was going fine until one of the grandparents commented that the bruises never would have happened if her daughter hadn't married the stu-pid sumbitch in the first place. Then the yelling started. I sent the kids out of the room and got everyone calm by announcing that I was about three seconds away from putting the kids in foster care. That shut them up.

The meeting lasted four hours. After it was over, I ate lunch and hid in my office all afternoon, documenting the family's intervention plan, nursing a headache, and only coming out of my tiny space to meet with Mac for an hour. There was no word from the A.G.'s office yet. It was still too early.

At five I took the Red Mountain Expressway to Highway 280, jammed with commuters bound for home. I turned into Mountain Brook. The parking pad at the top of Karen and Alexander Madison's drive was full of cars, so I parked in the street. I rang the doorbell and Karen answered, dressed in a Roberto Cavalli print dress. She looked gorgeous.

"Hello. What are you doing here?"

I could hear the buzz of conversation behind her as a uniformed caterer passed by with a silver tray of canapés. "I want a word."

"We're having a party. I'm afraid I can't right now."

"I'll only take a second." I nodded toward the garage. "We can go in there."

I leaned against the bumper of a Cadillac Escalade, flanked on one side by a Porsche. The other space was empty. I took out the somewhat sticky photo I'd filched from Ashley's apartment and pointed to it. "That's Trey, correct?"

"That's right. I don't know who the other young man is."

"What's Trey's last name?"

"Baxter. He's a friend of Zander's. You can't possibly think he has anything to do with Michael's death?"

"Why not?"

"Oh, that's ridiculous. We've been friends with his parents forever."

"When you say he's a friend of Zander's, does he —" I trailed off, searching for the right way to phrase my question.

She picked up on what I was fishing for. "No. He doesn't have the same — problems — as Zander has."

It irked me that she couldn't bring herself to say "addiction." No wonder it was called the elephant in the living room. "You're sure?"

"Yes, I'm sure. Trey is doing very well, actually. He graduated early with his undergraduate degree, and has already completed his Ph.D. He's only twenty-six. His father was a doctor, you see."

There was a stiffness to Karen's expression as she spoke and a strained quality to her voice. Pain. And envy. Lots of envy.

"I see. What's Trey do? For a living?"

"He and his father, Walt, started a business together. Some kind of medical research facility. Walt was a GP here for years and always wanted to go into the research end of medicine. He sold his practice and founded BaxMed with his son. I don't know why you are so curious about Trey. He couldn't have had anything to do with Michael. I doubt he even knew about him."

I bet he did. "Trey's just a nickname, right? What's his real name?"

"Walter. Like his father. Walter Arlington Baxter, the third."

No wonder he went by Trey.

Anxiety distressed Karen's face. She continued, "You aren't going to tell him about Zander and Ashley, are you? Trey? Or Walt and Mary Ann?"

"I don't know."

"They don't have anything to do with this. Please don't."

"They don't know about Zander's problems?"

"They do. Well, some. They don't know how bad he's gotten. Trey might."

"I see. I won't talk to them unless I have to, I promise." I thanked Karen for her time, and she repeated that she didn't see how any of this was going to be helpful. I didn't either, but didn't say so.

On the drive to Grant's apartment, I thought about Trey. For someone who was squeaky clean, he sure hung out in some strange places. Like Ashley's apartment. And Kaleidoscope, where I'd seen him with Lucas. Karen claimed he didn't have the same "problem," but I wondered. Maybe he was just a recreational user. I'd seen people over the years who could use drugs only on occasion, without spiraling down into the hole of hardcore addiction that some did. If he used casually, could it be GHB?

I didn't want to go back to Grant's apartment after what I'd done last night. My face burned every time I thought about it. I had embarrassed myself. Embarrassed him. But this morning he'd insisted I come back.

When I got to his place, I found he'd ordered pizza again for dinner. So much for working on my diet. I vowed to do better once this case was over. Whenever that was. After we ate, I studied my list of suspects while Grant took care of some work on the phone.

I added TREY BAXTER to the list, along with a question mark. Looking at the list made my head go soft. I had no idea where to go next, or what to do. Despite the confusion, I felt like I was onto something. But what? What could Trey Baxter and Zander have to do with Jimmy? Damn it. What was I missing?

What would a detective do? Look at motive, for one. Only everyone on this list had that. A detective would also look for opportunity.

Jimmy was my number one suspect. Chasing me around with a knife definitely put him in the "killer" category. He had motive if what Brandi said about his not wanting children was true. As Ashley's boyfriend, he had access to her apartment and could have put the drug in the juice. What didn't ring true was Ashley's reaction to him. She'd gotten clean, straightened her life out, and done it all for Michael. Why stand back and take the heat for Jimmy if he was her son's murderer? She wouldn't have allowed it to happen, and she wouldn't forgive Jimmy if he was behind Michael's death. She'd be furious, not all lovey-dovey with him as she'd been lately.

Al Mackey wanted money, and could have tried to kill both Ashley and Michael for the life insurance. He had access to Ashley's apartment. But could he have gotten his hands on GHB? He was lazy and stupid, and somehow I doubted he had the connections to drug dealers. But Flash did. So did Zander.

Would Zander kill his own child? In order to save his family's reputation? He had both motive and opportunity. That led me to another question: Why now? Why did Michael, and possibly Ashley, have to die now? Michael had graced this earth for two years before his death. If Zander wanted to get rid of Michael, why not when he was first born? Or before. Maybe he could have convinced Ashley to go through with the abortion.

Alexander and Karen Madison had found out about Michael's existence the Friday before his death. That might explain the timing, why Michael died when he did. If they were going to get rid of him, they'd do it as soon as possible. I hated to think it, but the Madisons were now at the top of my list of suspects.

"You okay?" Grant's voice interrupted my musings. "You look puzzled."

"I am."

"Listen, I have to go out for a while. That was one of my clients on the phone and their server just went toes-up. I've got to go fix it. It may take a while. Are you going to be okay by yourself?"

I didn't really want to be alone. "I think I'll go to my father's."

"I'm sorry about this."

"It's okay."

I called Dad on my cell on the way to his house. He was out, but I let myself in and found a bottle of wine in the fridge. I was on my third glass when he entered the den dressed in his *gi* and sweaty from his Tae Kwon Do class. He helped himself to a glass of wine.

"How are you?" he asked.

"Okay."

He chuckled.

"What?" I asked.

"I suddenly had a flashback of you and your brother doing math homework at the kitchen table. Whenever you had a problem you couldn't solve, you'd get this crease between your eyebrows and clench your jaw. It was so cute."

"What on earth made you think of that now?"

"You've got that crease, and you're about to break your teeth."

So I was.

"What's the problem?" Dad asked.

I outlined the stream of thoughts that I'd had at Grant's. Who I suspected and why.

"It wasn't the Madisons," he said.

"How do you know?"

"They're devastated over Michael's death. They wanted to be part of his life."

"You mean, you—"

"And that's all I'm going to say."

CHAPTER TWENTY-FIVE

"Dad, if you know something about this —"

"Like I said, that's all I'm going to say."

He walked into the kitchen, put his wine glass in the sink, then came back to the bar in the den and poured himself a bourbon and water. "You want something stronger?"

"No, the wine's plenty." My thinking was muddled enough without liquor. Dad had just taken away my number one suspects. I believed what he said about the Madisons. It was the first time he'd ever hinted at anything in one of his therapy sessions, and he was never going to reveal any more than what he had just told me. I had to trust him.

"What's the matter?" he asked.

"I was almost convinced that they were behind it. I don't know what to do next."

"I think you're right to look at the timing. Try to piece together what happened that night."

He was right. I knew where I was headed tomorrow. Now at least I had a direction.

Wednesday was busy, spent on the road doing home visits with clients. Between stops, I called *The News* on my cell phone.

"Mahoney," he answered after the first ring.

"It's Claire Conover."

"Hi. I was just thinking about you."

"Nice thoughts, I hope."

"Very."

I let the flirting slide. "What'd you find out?"

"Eclipse Entertainment, owned by Donovan B. Grayson. Business license applied for three years ago, liquor license the same year for a club called Kaleidoscope. Since then Eclipse has applied for and received licenses for three other places. Grayson's opening another place this fall, and that one's a restaurant."

He wasn't telling me anything I didn't already know. "Anything weird about him?"

"I called a contact with the police department. They've had a few incidents at some of the bars owned by Grayson, but nothing really major. A couple of fights at a hip-hop club called Flow, but only one that got really ugly. Occasionally his bartenders will call the cops when drunks get out of control. Like I said, nothing they're likely to lose their license for or anything."

"No drug busts?"

"Not that I could find. So what's the big story?"

"I'm not sure yet."

"But there is a story?"

"I think so."

"Okay, until then you owe me one."

We hung up and I went to my final two appointments. When the last one was over, I went to East Lake. I parked in front of Dazzle's house, feeling more than a pang of guilt that I hadn't called before now to see how she was coping. I rang the bell and she answered.

It was bedlam inside. Thomas the Tank Engine and his friends blasted out of the television. One little boy was playing with some sort of toy that played tinny music at full volume, and two girls were shrieking and chasing each other around the room. Another smaller boy wailed in misery.

"Lord Almighty," I said.

"Jus' let me run an' change Lil' Jeremy's diaper. Go on in to the kitchen, and I'll be righ' there."

I sat at the stained table and, wondering how Dazzle was able to tune it all out, kept an eye on the kids for a few minutes until she returned. Lil' Jeremy had stopped crying. Dazzle wiped his tear-streaked face with a napkin, handed him a section of graham cracker, and sent him to the living room with a loving swat on his behind.

"Can I get you somthin'? A Co-cola? It's hot enough out there to melt steel."

"Some water would be great, thanks."

I waited until she handed me the tall, cool glass. She joined me at the table and I asked, "How are you holding up?"

"Aw'right, I sup'ose. I did that thing you tol' me about." She nodded toward the other room. "Me and some o' their mammas took 'em all to the park last Friday. We talked a lot 'bout Michael and then we sent him some balloons up in heaven. Some o' 'em drew him pictures. We talked about how he had wings now and was an angel. I do alright mos' days, until I see somethin' that reminds me o' him. Like his favorite toy or somethin'.'"

I knew how she felt. I reached over and squeezed her hand gently.

"You seen Ashley?" she asked.

"Yes, a few times."

"How's she?"

"I think she's doing okay, all things considered. That's why I'm here. I wanted to ask you some questions about her."

"How come?"

"I'm trying to put together exactly what happened the night Michael died. I know you told me how he was Monday, before he went home."

"He wasn't sick or nothin'. He musta got into the drugs after he got home."

"What about Ashley? Did you notice anything about her that was different? Did she say anything unusual?"

"Lemme think, now. She was jus' like she always was, I'm sure. She got here a little after ten. Michael had colored her a picture outta one o' the coloring books. Just scribbles, you know, but he was proud o' it. He was sleepin' when she got here, on the couch. He was the last o' my babies to get picked up that night."

"How did Ashley seem? Did she act different? High? Or drunk?"

"Oh, no. No. I'da never let her leave if she was."

"What kind of mood was she in?"

"She seemed a little tired, but the poor thin', she worked so hard. Said she'd had a long day. Now that you mention it, though, Ashley had a real bad day that Friday."

"What do you mean?"

"I hadn't thought 'bout it till jus' now, but when she picked Michael up Friday, it was like she weren't herself."

"Go on."

"She always lit up when she come to get him, you know. All smilin'. She'd say how's my big boy and pick him up and give him big hug."

"And Friday was different?"

"She looked upset 'bout something. I asked her how her day went and she said not so good."

"Upset how? Like she was angry or scared?"

"Jus' upset. I thought maybe she'd gotten into trouble with her boss at work. That kind o' upset. Troubled. But by Monday she seemed aw'right."

I knew Ashley's bosses at her second job, and had never seen them upset anybody. So something had happened Friday night or Friday afternoon. I found myself clenching my teeth again as I realized that Friday was the day that Karen Madison had found out about Michael.

"Does tha' help?"

"Maybe, Dazzle. Thanks. If you think of something else, please call me. Oh, one more question. Was Ashley wearing her uniform those days when she picked Michael up?"

"She didn't wear no uniform for her night job."

"Was she dressed different than usual?"

"Naw, jus' jeans and a blouse, like always."

So she wasn't dressed to go out. Likely she was telling the truth about having been at work Monday night, instead of out partying. But I was going to double-check.

Dazzle walked me to the door. I had another referral for her sitting service and told her about the family briefly. She had room for the little girl, and I said I'd give them her number.

It was four twenty. I rushed down Oporto-Madrid Boulevard, cut through Crestwood and Mountain Brook Village to the suburb of Homewood.

Taylor Maids was sandwiched between a dry cleaner and a shop that rented party supplies. It wasn't much more than a narrow, linoleum-tiled room with asbestos green walls and a couple of desks. The owners, Liz and Trish Taylor, were sisters-in-law, happily married to two brothers. Several years ago, when their respective nests grew empty, they turned their twenty-plus years of homemaking experience into a cleaning business. But they did it with a twist. They exclusively hired women who were trying to get back on their feet. They worked closely with Nona at St. Monica's, The Harbor downtown, and the local battered women's shelters. As long as the women didn't have a history of stealing, Taylor Maids would do everything in their power to help them stabilize their lives and become independent. They'd hired more of my clients than I could count, and I needed an army of Taylors and people like them.

Liz greeted me when I walked through the door. She, like the actress whose name she shared, was the more flamboyant of the two, fond of elaborate hairstyles and lots of makeup. She also chain-smoked.

"Claire Conover! How you been, girl?" she asked in her husky voice. An ancient television on Liz's desk played a seventies sitcom. She turned down the volume.

"Fine, Liz, thanks. How are y'all?" Trish, the mousier one, was quietly working at a desk near the back of the room. She did more of the behind-the-scenes work, like scheduling and bookkeeping. She waved to me.

"Good, good. Busy. Damn shame about Ashley and her son. Me and Trish went by the jail last week. We cashed her last check for her and put it in her commissary account. She looks pitiful."

"I know."

"You coulda never have convinced me she was using again. Never. She showed up to work right on time, always. Never missed a day. Never called in, like they do when they're dope-sick or hungover. I'da never believed it till I saw it on the TV. Right, Trish? We saw it on the TV."

"Right." Trish murmured.

"No complaints from your clients, about Ashley?" I asked.

"No! Never, I tell ya. She was one of our best girls, right, Trish? I tell ya, I was shocked beyond belief."

"Did either of you notice anything different about Ashley that day? Or that week?"

"No way. You know how I am with my girls. I love 'em all, but I don't let 'em get away with nothin'. If there's a problem, we take care of it, right, Trish? We take care of it right away."

"Mmm-hmm," Trish said, still bent over her paperwork.

I didn't doubt it. Taylor Maids had excellent boundaries. A strict hierarchy and a strong set of rules. They had to, to stay in business. Otherwise the girls would take advantage.

"Where was Ashley working the night Michael died? Did she have the same clients every week? How does that work?"

"All of my girls have some clients that are regular. It depends on what the client wants, see? Most big offices, they want cleanin' every night. The full job — empty the trash, dust, vacuum, clean the bathrooms. Ashley, for example, every night she did a law firm here in Homewood. Fielding, Kendall, and Morris. She's been doing them every night since she started for us a year and a half ago, right, Trish? They never had no complaints about her. Then, after she did the law office, she might go do for a smaller client. Some small offices, they only want someone in once a week to do the vacuuming and such."

"How do you keep track of where the girls go?"

"That's Trish's department. She keeps the master schedule. The girls look at the master to see what office or building to go to. Then they take a work order sheet with 'em, to the job. That's like a check-list of what they done, what time they got there, and what time they left. Then Trish uses that to bill the client for the hours, plus a fee for supplies and equipment."

"Where was Ashley the night before her son died?"

"What day was that?"

"Monday, June twenty-seventh."

Trish turned around from her desk and pulled down a thick red binder from the top of a lateral filing cabinet. I walked closer to her desk so I could see. She flipped to a tab, then turned a few pages. I stood in front of her desk and read upside down.

The page was a photocopied form, filled with Trish's neat, block writing. She scanned the list of names until she came to Ashley's. She read across and said in her soft voice, "She cleaned the law firm, then went to one of our once-weeklies, CitiCorps."

"What do they do?"

She shrugged. "I think they're city planners. Or architects, maybe."

"What about on Friday? The twenty-fourth? Where did Ashley work?"

Trish flipped two pages back and scanned it. "Same law firm, as usual. Then she had a new client. Another once-a-week. BaxMed."

CHAPTER TWENTY-SIX

Holy God.

"Does that mean anything?" Liz asked.

"Maybe," I said, trying hard to cover my surprise. I quickly memorized the upside-down address of BaxMed. They were on Eleventh Avenue South, near the university campus. "Who cleans their offices now?" I asked Trish.

Liz answered, "Nobody. They cancelled their service right after Ashley was arrested. Me and Trish figured they saw the story on the news and got the idea that we'd hired some kinda child killer. I guess they thought they couldn't trust any of our girls. I called them and tried to smooth it all over. Talked to Dr. Walt Baxter myself, he's the owner, but it was a no go. He just said they wouldn't be needing us anymore. Oh, well. What're you gonna do? Right, Trish?"

"Right, Liz."

"You just can't convince some people," Liz finished.

I thanked the ladies and asked after another of my clients.

Back in my Civic, I checked the time. Five twenty. I called *The News.* As expected, I got Kirk's voice mail. I left him a message asking him to call me on my cell.

I wanted to go home. To be alone and to think. But unbidden images of Jimmy with his knife and Ashley's fear-twisted face kept me from feeling easy. My phone rang. The caller ID said it was Grant, from the shop.

"You headed here?" he asked.

"I was just debating that. I think I'll go home."

"That's not such a good idea."

"I'll be all right."

"Famous last words."

"That's not funny."

"This whole situation isn't funny. At least let me come over."

"No. Really. I just want to be alone for a while. I've got some things to do too."

"Then I'm going to call you every hour."

I laughed.

"I'm serious."

"Fine, call me if it'll make you feel better."

"It will."

"Okay."

"I'm only doing this because I care about you."

That threw me. I didn't know what to say. Before I could piece together a response, he hung up.

My house was still standing, undisturbed. I checked it over, cell phone in hand, ready to dial 911 if needed. Several messages were on my answering machine. Two from Dad, asking me to call him when I got in, one from a friend, and two from Royanne, wondering where the heck I was and confirming lunch for tomorrow.

I called Dad and checked in, did the same with Royanne. I called my friend and we chatted for a while, then I sorted the laundry and washed clothes. Precisely an hour after I got home, the phone rang. Grant's cell.

"You okay?"

"Yes. Are you really going to do this all night?"

"Maybe not. I think I have an idea. I'll see you in a little bit." He hung up before I could protest. Twenty minutes later, I heard a vehicle pull into my driveway. I peeked out the window and saw Grant's minivan. He hopped out, a box in hand.

I met him at the door. "What's that?"

"Something I remembered." He put the box down on the dining table. SMARTHOME was printed in blue letters across the top. He opened it and took out a rectangular white motion sensor, a box with a keypad, and a small keyring remote.

"What's all this?"

"It's an alarm system. You can get them for about a hundred bucks online. I bought this when I first opened High Tech. I used it until I could afford a real security service. I had it in storage at the shop." He surveyed the room. "This detector will sense motion in a range of about twenty feet. It'll go off if someone comes in. All you have to do is turn it on before you go to bed."

"It's a loud alarm?"

"One hundred and thirty decibels, so, yeah. And," he pulled out the white keypad, "this is already programmed to call my cell phone if it goes off. It's an auto-dialer. I just need to hook it to your land line." I watched as he positioned the motion sensor on an occasional table, and plugged the little box into my phone. "There. Just switch it on with the remote when you go to bed. The beam goes all the way across this room, so if anyone comes in here, you'll know about it. Just don't forget to shut it off before you break the beam in the morning."

"You're a genius."

I gave him a grateful hug and felt his long arms pull me in. He kissed the top of my head. "You sure you don't want me to stay? I don't mind."

"I know. I just want some time to myself," I murmured into his chest.

He held me for a few minutes longer. Then, "I meant what I said on the phone. That's why — the other night — why I didn't — I want to do this right."

Suddenly, so did I. "Me, too."

He left after a long, sweet kiss good-bye. I switched the alarm on before going to bed, and it did make me sleep easier in between thoughts of what my next move in Ashley's case should be.

The next morning, on my way to work, my cell phone sang.

"You rang?"

Kirk. "Hi. Can you look into something else for me?"

"For this mysterious story that is going to surface someday?"

"That's the one."

"Shoot."

"BaxMed. It's some kind of medical research firm —"

"Oh, yeah, one of Joey's."

"Who's Joey? The owner's a Dr. Walter Baxter."

"What, you don't read my newspaper?"

"I read all the articles destroying my career, thank you very much."

He laughed. "Joey Renzi is one of our reporters. He's doing a series of articles on Birmingham's biotech industry. BaxMed is one of them. The article ran a couple of weeks ago." Now that he mentioned it, I did remember reading something about a biotech firm, probably the same day as Kirk's article quoting my name.

"Gee, I guess I had my mind on other things. I can't imagine what. Can you get me copies of the articles?"

"You want the whole series?"

"Sure. And anything at all on BaxMed or Dr. Walter Baxter."

"You got it. I'll bring them by your office."

"No! Are you nuts?"

He laughed again. "Oops. Sorry, I forgot. So, you'll put the red flag in the flower pot, and we'll meet in the parking garage down the street?"

"Don't you dare start calling me Deep Throat."

He did have a point, though. My paranoid self didn't want to be seen walking into the newspaper building, and he sure as hell wasn't welcome at the office. We needed a place, downtown, close to both our workplaces. "I'll meet you at the main library."

"Where?"

"In the mystery section, of course."

"What time?"

"Five?"

"That works. When am I going to get this story of yours?"

"When there is one. I promise."

We hung up as I arrived at work.

Russell walked in, his usual cup of coffee in hand. Before he could start his daily ritual of checking his messages and returning calls, I asked, "How's Heinrich?"

"Fine."

"Are y'all busy tonight?"

He put the handset back down on the phone. "Why?"

"Got time for drinks?"

Eyes narrowed, he asked, "Why?" Boy, he knew me.

"I wanted to talk to Heinrich about something."

"What?"

"I just have some questions to ask, that's all." I wasn't even sure what those questions were yet. "About the university. He's getting his master's in chemistry, right? I want to ask him about some things."

"I guess we could do that. Let me call him and see."

A few minutes later, Russell hung up the phone and said his boyfriend would meet us at the office at five thirty. That didn't give me much time to meet with Kirk and get back here.

Our secretary came in with a new case for Russell. He left while I was catching up my case narratives. At ten till ten, I left for the jail.

All the glass cubicles were filled today, so I had to wait a few minutes until someone left before claiming my own uncomfortable stool. The guard brought Ashley in. Her hair was pulled back today, and it looked brittle. She looked thinner than the last time I'd seen her. I could only imagine how bad the food was here, if she even felt like eating with all she'd been through.

She sat down and grabbed her handset as I picked up mine. After the way we left things last time, this was going to be a bit awkward. I was over the anger. Now I just wanted answers.

"Hi," I began. "How are you?"

"I'm okay."

"Do you need anything?"

"No. Are you still mad at me?"

"No. I wasn't really mad. Just frustrated."

"Same thing."

"No, it's not. Ashley, I'm trying to help you. I can't for the life of me understand why you don't want to help yourself."

"There's nothing you can do."

"But if you know something that can get you out of prison —"

"What for? What do I got to go home to? Mikey's gone."

"There's your mother. And Jimmy."

"Jimmy'll wait for me."

"I know where you were the Friday night before Michael died."

"So? I was at work. And Monday. All day, like always."

"Friday, you were at BaxMed. That's Trey Baxter's company. You knew him through Zander, didn't you?"

The moment the words were out of my mouth, her expression turned to raw fear. Like I'd just pulled out a gun and aimed it right between her eyes. I pressed on. "Did something happen there?"

She was making an effort to stay composed, but I could detect a slight tremor as she clutched the handset. "I cleaned for them, yeah."

"Ashley, I don't get it. Why did Michael die now? What happened that someone tried to get rid of you, or him?"

"I relapsed."

"No, you didn't. Don't give me that. Something happened, and I think it was at BaxMed. If you tell me, I can —"

The fear flashed again in her eyes. Her knuckles around the phone were white. "Claire! No! Promise me you'll stop. Please!"

"Why? What are you afraid of?"

"Death."

She was serious, and it stopped me cold. "Whose?"

"Mine. Yours. Please, please let this go. They'll kill you."

"Who?"

"I'm not sayin'. If we shut up and leave it alone, no one will get hurt."

It sounded like she was repeating a line someone had said to her. "Who threatened you?"

"Please, Claire. Please don't do this. Mikey's already dead because of me. I couldn't live with it if somethin' happened to you. Please."

The begging was getting to me. "Okay."

"You'll drop it?"

"Yeah."

"You promise?"

I opened my mouth to say yes, but couldn't do it. I owed it to Michael. Once I gave my word about something, it was law, and I couldn't honestly say I was going to stop. I couldn't lie to her. Ashley saw my open-mouthed hesitation.

I muttered, "I'm sorry," and hung up the receiver. I turned my back on Ashley and started for the elevator. She was leaning on the cubicle, yelling through the glass. Before the guard grabbed her arm, she screamed, "Don't! It's not worth it!"

CHAPTER TWENTY-SEVEN

I went back to work, my mind a jumbled mess of thoughts. Over my whole mood lay a blanket of apprehension. I was close to something dangerous. Mac popped his head in to check on my crazy case from the other day, and I asked him about the attorney general. He said there'd still been no word, and there probably wouldn't be for another week or so.

Beth, one of the receptionists downstairs, buzzed me. "Royanne wants to know if you are going or what?"

"Oh, hell. Tell her I'll be right down." I packed up my stuff and raced to the elevator. Royanne was in the lobby, chatting with Beth and Nancy and fanning herself.

"There you are. I was about to die in that car."

"I'm sorry. I lost track of time."

Pablo greeted us at Los Compadres with a big smile. I think he was relieved to see that we'd patched things up. He seated us and brought us our drinks. I picked up a tortilla chip and nibbled a corner.

"You're awful quiet today."

"Sorry. Just distracted."

"I've got to make a decision about Madison Accounting Services. This afternoon. My boss is really pushing me to do this loan."

"I'd go ahead."

"You mean —"

"I don't think Alexander Senior had anything to do with Michael's death. Or Karen."

"That's a relief. I really kind of like Old Man Madison. And this deal is going to launch his company to the next tier. He won't do so bad either, financially. What about Zander?"

"He's the wild card. I'm not sure what role he might have played in all this. I don't think he put the drug in the juice, but I bet he knows who did. Anyway, as far as he's concerned, it's over. Ashley's in jail, so he's off the hook. Oh, and by the way, it looks like he might be getting some help for his addiction."

"Well, that's good."

"I hope he can quit."

"Me, too. So how's the Geek God?" she asked.

At the mention of Grant, my memories quickly flashed back to the other night and what he'd said yesterday. I felt my face grow warm.

"Good Lord, you're blushing. Is it that serious?"

"Yeah, I think maybe it is. I like him a lot."

Royanne grinned from ear to ear. "'Bout time."

"Yeah, well, I've been a little bit messed up because of this case. Hopefully he can overlook that."

We ate our usual lunch and Royanne dropped me off at work. "See you next week," she said as I shut the door to the van. I went to one quick appointment and worked on paperwork in the afternoon. Russell was there when I got back from the home visit. "We still on for drinks?" he asked.

"Yeah. I've got to run a quick errand, but I'll meet you here at five thirty."

At quarter to five I left for the library. I parked in the small public lot behind the building and entered the towering, angled glass structure through the back door. I made my way to the mystery section and was browsing through a book about a woman who solved mysteries dealing with gravestones when someone behind me whispered in my ear, "Follow the money."

I jumped. "Jesus!"

"Sorry."

I put the book back on the shelf and faced him. "God Almighty. You scared the shit out of me."

He was chuckling, standing so close I could smell his cologne again, mingled with the slight scent of starch from his light pink shirt. Pink was really his color. His gaze traveled over my body once before meeting mine.

"And I said no Deep Throat jokes."

Amusement sparkled in his blue eyes. "Sorry. Here." He handed me a manilla folder with a small stack of photocopied articles. "When do I get my story?"

"Soon."

"Uh-huh." He hadn't moved and we were inches apart. "When do I get to take you to dinner?"

"Never."

"Never? Never-ever?"

"I can't be seen with you. You know that."

"Is that the only reason?"

"Yes. I mean, no."

"Which is it?"

"That's not the only reason."

"Then what is?"

"Kirk —"

"Is it minivan man?"

"Yes."

"Oh." For a second I swore I saw real disappointment in his eyes. He leaned to me and barely brushed his lips on the skin just in front of my left ear. He whispered, "You'll let me know if it doesn't work out." Then he left.

I stood there, a bit tingly, and took a couple of steadying breaths. I waited until I was sure he was gone before leaving the library. I tossed the folder into the front seat of my Honda and called Russell's extension from my cell. He and Heinrich met me in the parking lot of the DHS building.

We decided on Fuel, the pub-like bar Grant and I visited on the Fourth. We found a table in the back and I ordered a Riesling. Both Russell and Heinrich were politically active, and they caught me up on their latest events as Russell sipped his Cosmo and Heinrich his dark brown beer. Then Heinrich asked in his thick German accent, "What did you want to speak to me about?"

"Do you know anything about drug research?"

"A little bit."

"Let's say I have an idea for a new drug. What happens?"

"It depends. Are you employed at a large drug company?"

"I'm just some girl with a biomedical degree."

"Ah. First you have to set up your business. And find funding."

"How does that work?"

"Here in the U.S., large drug manufacturers sponsor most clinical trials. They have much money. Sometimes researchers get grants from the National Institutes of Health. Smaller companies may use a combination of a sponsor and an NIH grant."

"For?"

"First you have your overhead, of course. Your lab, doctors, staff, and such. Then you need money to pay the participants in the study."

Russell asked, "The patients get paid?"

"Oh, yes, often they do. They may get paid a stipend, plus their travel costs and expenses. It depends on the study. And many times, doctors get money too. The doctors that refer the patients get compensated."

"I didn't know that."

"It takes a great deal of cash."

"Okay, so let's assume I'm able to raise the money, through a sponsor or whatever. Then what?"

"Then you would develop the drug and do preclinical studies. Experiments on animals to prove that your drug is safe for the people to take. If you succeed in this part, then you go on to clinical trials."

"And then you can sell the drug?"

"After you finish the three phases of the clinical trial and the FDA approves it."

"Three phases? That sounds like it takes forever."

"It does take time. But it is necessary. Companies test for side effects, safety, and to see if the drug is effective. They also compare your drug to medicines already on the market, to make sure it would work better than the ones already out there."

"That's a long process."

"And yet, there is always a need for improvement. There have been drugs on the market that have been pulled off because they were not safe."

"Who regulates the safety part of it?"

"It depends. Either the FDA or OHRP."

"I've heard of the FDA. What's the OHRP?"

"The Office of Human Research Protections. Why do you want to know about all this?"

I answered his question with a question. "Have you ever heard of a company called BaxMed? They do drug research."

He shook his head. "No. I know of a few biotech companies at the incubator, but that is all."

"Incubator?"

"The university has a biotech incubator. They help start-up companies. Are you thinking of investing in this BaxMed?"

"Oh, no. I just wondered how they worked, that's all. It has to do with work, so I can't really go into it right now."

Russell asked, "Is this the case —"

"Yes."

"Why?" Russell asked.

"Because there are still questions to be answered."

Russell muttered, "Fool," under his breath.

Heinrich, confused, asked, "I want to go into pharmaceutical research when I get my master's, so if you hear they are good, please do let me know."

Heinrich had been in this country for ten years, but occasionally talked about going back to Germany. As the bartender brought me another glass of wine, I asked Heinrich about his future plans and inadvertently started an argument between him and Russell that blew over quickly. They'd been together eight months, and it looked to me like they were getting more serious. I hoped so. Heinrich had been good for Russell. A stabilizing force.

We finished our drinks, and I paid the bill before we left. In the small parking lot, I thanked Heinrich for the information and told Russell I'd see him tomorrow.

In my car on the way home, I thought about my theory. Ashley goes to work at BaxMed Friday night. She sees someone at their office. Trey, perhaps. They have a fight about — what? Michael? Zander? Or something at BaxMed? Whatever it is, it nearly gets her killed, and scares her half to death. Time to find out more about that company.

I U-turned in a gas station and took Lakeshore to Mountain Brook. By the time I pulled up to the Madison's house, it was almost eight fifteen. I could see lights burning at the back of the house. I parked on the drive, empty today, and rang the bell.

Karen answered the door. "You again?"

"Sorry. I know it's late." I studied her for a second. One of her eyes was drooping slightly, and she'd slurred her greeting a tad. She'd been drinking. "Can I talk to you for a minute?"

She let me in. "Come on through to the back. Alexander and I were just having a celebratory drink." Or two or three.

"What's the occasion?"

"I'll let Alexander tell you." She ushered me into the apricot and gold room we'd met in before. Alexander was relaxing in one of the upholstered chairs, a glass of neat amber liquid on the marble table at his side. He stood when he saw me, but it took some effort. "Do come in," he said. "Would you care for a drink?"

"No, thanks." The two glasses of wine I'd had at Fuel were more than enough when I was driving. "What are you celebrating?"

Alexander answered, "I got the funding today to take my business to the next level. A big move. You'll be reading about it in the paper."

"Congratulations." And to you, Royanne, I thought.

"Thank you. What can we do for you?" He motioned for me to sit down and I complied.

"I wanted to ask you about BaxMed."

Karen asked, "What about it?"

"How are they doing?"

"Why? What do the Baxters have to do with anything?"

"I'm just curious."

Alexander answered. "Walt's having the time of his life. He was a doctor here for years, but he was always interested in research. Now, with his son on board, they're doing very well."

"Are you an investor? In BaxMed?"

"Not anymore. I helped them with the initial start-up costs. Helped them get going with a little loan. Walt's paid me back already."

"Why aren't you an investor? Do you know how BaxMed is financed?"

"I think he has a sponsor. I don't know who. One of the larger drug companies, I would imagine. I don't think he needs my money. Besides, Walt and I don't like to mix business with friendship. I'd rather have him as a fishing buddy than a business partner."

"But things are going well?"

"To my knowledge, yes. Why?"

"I don't think it's anything. How's Zander? Is he home?"

At the mention of Zander's name, both of them stiffened. Alexander answered, "No, he's not here. We don't know where he is."

"Oh. Well, tell him I said hello when you see him." No wonder Zander was angry. His parents griping at him to get clean when they were piss-drunk by eight o'clock on a Thursday. Who's to say which addiction was more acceptable?

Karen walked me to the door. Once I was out on the stoop, she said, "Claire—"

"Yes?"

"I wanted to thank you. We're seeing Dr. Conover again tomorrow."

"I hope he's helping."

"He didn't tell you?"

"It's confidential. He never would."

"It is helping. Alexander and I are seeing things differently. Patterns we've never seen before."

 "Hang in there. I know it's hard, but it's worth it."

I took a left at the end of the long driveway and made my way to Highway 280. Traffic was still quite heavy, so it wasn't until I'd made the turn onto I-459 and was under the bright lights illuminating the on-ramp that I noticed the truck.

A ten-year-old black pick-up truck. Jimmy was back.

CHAPTER TWENTY-EIGHT

At least I thought it was Jimmy. In the twilight it sure looked like his truck. I hit the interstate bypass at sixty-five miles an hour, then accelerated to seventy-five. The truck matched my speed, easily. The cloverleaf of the I-65 junction was two exits away, and I opted to take it north. The truck followed me. I sped up again, this time to ninety. The truck's speed kept pace.

Now I was sure it was Jimmy. He hung back, not making any attempt to run me off the road or overtake my car. I needed a safe place to go, now, before he did whatever he was planning. But where? The Birmingham Police Department was in the middle of downtown. I didn't want to risk getting off the highway, where I could get stopped by a traffic light, giving Jimmy a chance to get out of his truck and come after me. So the city streets were out. I weaved in and out of cars, one eye on my rearview mirror. This was getting dangerous. I was overdriving my headlights and it was getting darker. I slowed back down to seventy-five. So did he.

I took one hand off the wheel and took my cell phone out of its pocket in my purse. Should I call 911? What would Jimmy do when the police showed up? Would their arrival, lights flashing, force him to make his move? He might even disappear. And then what would I say to the cops?

Where the hell was a state trooper when you needed one? I zipped between two cars and crossed three lanes of traffic, but Jimmy didn't back off. We were coming up on Malfunction Junction. In an instant I decided to take I-20 eastbound, and from there to where it intersected again with I-459. Maybe Jimmy would figure out that I was onto him — leading him around in a great big circle — and go away.

Still clutching my cell, I got into the right lane to exit and merged into heavy oncoming traffic, cutting off an eighteen-wheeler. The driver honked two long blasts. Jimmy was still behind me, three car lengths back. The convention center flashed by in a blur, and the skyscrapers of downtown towered on my right. I wondered how many people were in those buildings, maybe even watching the traffic go by, with no idea that one of the tiny cars was in trouble. I passed the exit to the airport and stayed on I-20, passing through suburbs east of the city. My speed was a steady eighty miles an hour, yet Jimmy made no move to overtake me.

As I made the wide turn to get back on the bypass, my cell phone rang, sending another shot of adrenaline pumping through my body. Grant's home number was on the screen.

"That guy is following me again." My words came out on top of each other.

"What? Where are you?"

"Near Liberty Park."

"I'm calling 911."

"No, don't. He hasn't done anything yet."

"Come here. Come here right now. If he follows you, we'll call the cops."

That actually wasn't such a bad plan. Grant lived close to an exit. "Okay."

I sped to the Galleria exit, taking the flyover to where it hit Highway 150. I had to make it through three traffic lights before the entrance to Grant's apartment complex. The first was green, and I sped through it. So did Jimmy. The next turned yellow as I approached and I floored it through that one. So did Jimmy.

I could see the last light up ahead. It was red. I barely slowed at the intersection, wheels clipping the curb in front of a gas station on the corner. I climbed the long drive and went through the brick signs that flanked the entrance to the apartments. Jimmy was still three car lengths behind me.

He stayed behind me as I entered the cluster of buildings. I spotted Grant, standing in front of his building waiting for me, and parked as close to him as I could. He met me as I put the car in park and got out.

"Where is he?"

"In a black pickup. There." In the orange glow of the streetlights, I could see his bushy profile as he cruised between the rows of cars.

"Let's get inside," Grant said, taking my arm.

We climbed the stairs two at a time. Inside, he locked the door with the deadbolt as I peeked through the mini blinds at the lot. Jimmy had parked one row away from my Honda, keeping his eyes on it. I was breathing hard.

Behind me, Grant called 911. He reported there was a man who had been stalking his girlfriend in the parking lot of his apartment. He described the truck and the man inside, then thanked the person on the other end of the line and hung up.

We waited, both peeking out the window, until a white Chevrolet SUV with HOOVER POLICE DEPARTMENT in gold and blue on the side entered the lot. It idled behind Jimmy's truck for a minute before a uniformed officer got out. He tapped Jimmy's window with his flashlight and spoke with him. Jimmy's headlights came on and he eased out of the space and toward the exit. The police SUV followed.

I collapsed onto the leather sofa. "Thanks."

"You need a drink."

"Amen. Have you got any wine?"

"I don't think so. I've got some beer."

"That'll work." While he was in the kitchen, I picked up my keys and my purse from where I'd dropped them near the front door.

"Where're you going?"

"I need to get something out of my car."

"Oh, no, I don't think so. I'll get it. Here." He crossed the room with a sweating cold Killian's and traded me the beer for my keys. "You're staying right here. What do you need?"

"There's a folder on the passenger seat. A plain manila folder with some photocopied newspaper articles in it."

"I'll be back in a minute."

Grant returned with the folder Kirk had given to me at the library. "This it?"

"Yep, thanks."

I curled my feet under me and sipped on the beer. Grant got his own Killian's and a laptop and joined me in the living room, stretching his bare feet out in front of his oversized chair. With the click-click-click of his typing in the background, I browsed the articles.

They were in chronological order. The first was a small article, dated five years ago, from the Local News section. RESPECTED LOCAL PHYSICIAN RETIRES, the title read. It was just a fluff piece announcing that after twenty-seven years of service to the Birmingham area, Dr. Walter Baxter, a specialist in internal medicine, was selling his practice. It quoted several patients he had treated over the years, telling how much he meant to them, blah, blah, blah. No pictures. I put it aside.

The next article had run in the fall, two years ago. DOCTOR EXPERIMENTS WITH RESEARCH SIDE OF MEDICINE. A brief article about the incorporation of BaxMed, owned by former Birmingham physician Dr. Walter Baxter. He was quoted about the exciting promise of medicines for the future, stating that new and more effective drugs were being developed every day. How he'd gained a greater interest in the research side of medicine since his retirement. His son, the article mentioned, was about to complete his graduate degree in pharmacology. Dr. Baxter hoped to have him on board soon. The story delved a little into the fact that Dr. Baxter was seeking sponsors for his company's research. Nothing new there.

Next was Joey Renzi's four-part series that Kirk had mentioned. The pieces were paper-clipped together. The first one ran on the nineteenth of June. Birmingham had thrived for decades as an industrial steel city, but like other urban areas was moving toward a more modern, service-based economy with an emphasis on health care. The article talked about the university's role in the change.

All this was interesting, but not very helpful. I skimmed the rest of the article, and, not seeing anything about BaxMed, put it aside. The following Sunday, June twenty-sixth, Joey had profiled a company called Field Genetics. Nothing about BaxMed there, either.

The next article was dated July third, the same day Kirk's story naming me as Michael's social worker appeared in the paper. No wonder I'd forgotten it. It was all about BaxMed. Complete with a color picture of a smiling old man standing next to a plaque-style sign affixed to a yellow brick wall. He was tall and thin, dressed in a lab coat and a neat shirt and tie. He had a full head of gray hair, and his tanned face was deeply lined. The caption read, "Dr. Walter Baxter is one of Birmingham's pioneers in the pharmaceutical industry."

The first paragraph reiterated what I already knew about BaxMed's founding. There was no mention of Trey. The next outlined what the company was working on. They planned to specialize in psychopharmaceutical drug research for mental health disorders. BaxMed was optimistic about the trials of their new medicine for attention deficit hyperactivity disorder, currently being tested under the name Focanix. Early results held hope that it had fewer side effects for its users. The company was also in the early stages of testing a new drug, named Alerox, for patients suffering from narcolepsy and cataplexy.

A grey sidebar box defined the disorders, ADHD being a disorder first visible in childhood whose symptoms included distractibility and hyperactivity. Like I didn't know what that was. It seemed like half the kids I took into custody had it.

Narcolepsy was a sleep disorder, characterized by excessive sleepiness during the day, uncontrollable falling asleep, and in some cases, cataplexy, a sudden loss of muscle control, especially when in extreme emotional states.

I said, "Huh," and threw the stack of articles onto the couch beside me.

Grant looked up from whatever he was working on and asked, "What is all that stuff?"

"Just some articles I thought might help me understand this case better."

"And did they?"

"No, not really. Can I use your computer? I want to look something up on the Internet."

"Here," he said, passing me the thin laptop. It was smaller than a hardcover book. "Use this one."

"You have a wireless network set up in your apartment?"

He gave me a half-embarrassed grin. "Yeah. You want another beer?"

"Sure."

Grant went to the kitchen, returning with two more Killian's. I thanked him, balanced the computer on my knees, and pulled up a search engine.

First, I entered "BaxMed." Got a one-page Web site that wasn't much more than the electronic version of what I'd just read in the article. I thought for a minute, then entered "ADHD." I got over sixty million hits. No time for that.

I skimmed the BaxMed article again and typed "Focanix." I got a few hits, nothing that I didn't already know. I typed in "Alerox" and got the same result.

Grant was watching me hit the keys with a soft look on his face. I caught his expression out of the corner of my eye and asked, "What?"

"You look sexy when you type."

I laughed. "God, you are such a geek."

He smiled.

I back-browsed to the search engine again and entered "Narcolepsy." Fewer hits, only about four million. I scrolled the list for a minute and finally clicked on a fact sheet at narcolepticsupport.com.

The site gave an overview of the disorder. I clicked on a menu box under "treatment." It listed several drugs used to treat narcolepsy. One was also an ADHD medication, Ritalin. So it made sense that BaxMed

was working on the two disorders together. It seemed they over-
lapped. Maybe one of the two meds they were researching could be
used to treat both conditions. A newer medication, Xyrem, was on
the market for narcolepsy too, I read. Its active component was—

Holy cow. Gama hydroxybutyrate. GHB.

So far, despite some public concern for the safety of the drug, it
had shown enormous promise. Especially in treating the cataplexy
part of narcolepsy. I read the rest of the site so fast my head started to
spin. I put the laptop next to me without closing it.

I got up and paced the room. The pieces to this puzzle were flying together so fast I could hardly think.

Grant watched me wearing out his carpet and finally asked, "You
okay?"

"Fine, fine. I think I may have figured out why Michael died. And
who killed him."

Grant peeled himself off the chair and picked up the laptop. The
BaxMed articles were underneath it. He put the computer down on
the couch and studied the photocopies.

"BaxMed? You don't think the Baxters are involved, do you?"

I stopped pacing. "Yeah, why?"

"Because they're my clients."

CHAPTER TWENTY-NINE

"Your clients? Are you serious?"

"Yeah, I've worked with Dr. Baxter ever since I opened the shop. Remember I said I used to work for an insurance company? I used to install and maintain billing software in doctors' offices. When I decided to hang out my shingle, I contacted all the doctors I had worked for and told them to call me if they needed anything. Dr. Baxter called the next week and hired me to put in the PCs for his new research firm. What do the Baxters have to do with your dead client?"

I started pacing again, ignoring his question. "Can you look at his computer system?"

"Sure. I do periodic updates on his software. Why? What's he done?"

"I think his son may be involved in Michael's death."

"Trey? How?"

"You know him?"

"I've met him once. Stop that pacing and tell me what's going on, for God's sake."

I didn't stop. "Ashley, she's Michael's mom, remember?" He nodded. "Ashley had two jobs, one in a restaurant and one cleaning offices at night. Four nights before Michael was killed, Friday, she worked at BaxMed."

"So?"

"So Michael died of a GHB overdose. One of the drugs that BaxMed is developing is very similar to GHB, to treat narcolepsy."

"Isn't that where you fall asleep all the time?"

"Yes. So, here's what happened. Ashley goes to work as usual on Friday night. She goes to BaxMed to clean for the first time and sees Trey. She recognizes him."

"Why would she know him?"

"Because he's her baby's father's best friend. There's a picture of him in Ashley's apartment. And her baby's father is a big-time drug addict. I'm betting that they all used to party together."

"Oh, but —"

"So she gets to BaxMed and sees Trey — or sees Trey doing something — I mean, think about it. You're making GHB, right? Or something very close to it. Granted, it's for a legitimate reason, to treat this disease. But what's to stop you from making up an extra batch and selling it on the street? Or to your friends? Or —" I could barely breathe with the realizations hitting me. "Or in your other friend's nightclub?"

"And you think Ashley didn't know what Trey was doing before she saw him that night?"

"I don't know. Maybe not. I'm willing to bet she does now, and that's why her son died. And why she almost died. Can you show me what's on BaxMed's computers? Is that illegal?"

"No, it's not illegal. Just very unethical."

"So is killing a two-year-old."

"Right. Come on."

He led me back to his office, unfolded a chair and set it next to his. His monitor was the biggest one I'd ever seen. I watched as he logged onto his system, then into BaxMed's.

"What if there's a password?"

"There is, but I know it. I do their upgrades."

"What if they've changed it?"

"There are ways. Be patient."

He hit a few more keys and suddenly we were looking at a menu of the contents of BaxMed's server. "What do you want to look at?"

"I don't know." I hardly expected to find a signed confession, although that would have been lovely. "What do you think?"

"There's a ton of document files here." He clicked and read several of them. "It looks like some letters and applications to the FDA, trying to get approval for tests."

"This could take all night, even if we knew what to look for."

"Let's check out the books."

"You can do that?"

"Sure. Watch." He pulled up QuickBooks and logged in a password.

"How did you do that?"

"I told you, I upgrade their software. I have my own set of passwords. Let's see —" He studied something called the main checking ledger for several moments. I'd never used the software and had no idea what I was looking at.

"There's an initial deposit of six hundred thousand dollars from Dr. Baxter. A few checks going out to Edgewater Properties. I assume that's for the rent, then a check to me —" He scrolled down. "A lot of big checks to medical supply companies. Then some checks to about twenty different people."

"That must be the study subjects." I told him what Heinrich had said about people getting paid in clinical trials.

"Then another deposit from Dr. Baxter for another six hundred grand. Whew, that's one point two million he's put into this. I bet that's most of what he got for his former practice. And it goes fast." He scrolled down some more. "Here's another deposit. From Global Holdings of Birmingham. I wonder who they are."

"One of Dr. Baxter's friends told me he had a sponsor. I guess that's them."

"It looks like Global Holdings has been depositing a steady stream of a few thousand dollars every week into BaxMed. It's what's keeping them afloat at this point. Barely."

We looked through more documents on the Baxter's server, correspondence and reports, and some statistical data about the medicines they were developing. We didn't understand the stats much. And we didn't see anything immediately incriminating. After a while, Grant starting yawning.

"You should go to bed," I said.

"What about you?"

"I think I'll stay up a little longer."

Grant logged out of BaxMed's system and loaned me a T-shirt to sleep in. It came almost to my knees. He kissed me good night and I curled up on the couch under the same striped comforter as before. I spent most of the night browsing through TV channels, not really watching, but not able to sleep. Mental pictures of Michael wouldn't let me rest. I finally drifted off about three thirty.

Grant kissed me awake — which was nice — at seven. He handed me a hot cup of coffee and sat in the living room with me while I sipped it and tried to get my mind together after only three and a half hours of sleep.

"So what's the next step?" he asked.

"I'm going to talk to the police. First I've got to go home and get something to wear to work."

"Maybe I should go with you."

"No, that's okay. I'm not going to be there long. You can go to work."

"You sure?"

"I'm sure."

I changed back into the clothes I'd worn yesterday, brushed my hair, and locked Grant's door. I scanned the lot carefully for Jimmy's truck, but I didn't see it. He was the only part of the equation that hadn't come together. What in the world could he have to do with BaxMed? If my theory was right, maybe he was one of Trey's customers. It wouldn't be the first time an addict like Ashley had hooked up with another addict. Many romances bloomed in recovery. Maybe Jimmy had relapsed and was protecting his dealer. Still, he didn't seem like a user. At least not of GHB. I'd never seen him high, and he didn't have that strung-out-and-desperate look I was so familiar with. Then why would he want to kill me? To keep Ashley's secret?

Maybe. Perhaps Ashley wasn't safe in jail. Maybe by uncovering what she'd been hiding, I was endangering her. Whoever had threatened her might be able to get to her in prison. But if Jimmy killed me, the secret was safe. I hadn't thought of that before, and it gave me the creeps.

Noticing the time on the dashboard clock, I pulled my cell phone out of my purse, searched through the calls received, and dialed Kirk's cell. I could hear traffic in the background when he answered.

"I need one last favor," I said.

"Boy, they're really piling up. I'm going to get something good."

"Do you know how to find out who owns a certain company?"

"Sure, at the courthouse. That's Investigative Reporting 101."

"I need to know who owns Global Holdings of Birmingham."

"Global Holdings of Birmingham. Gotcha. They're here in Jefferson County?"

"I think so."

"I'll stop by the courthouse on my way to the office."

"Okay, I'm running late to work, so call my cell."

Speaking of running late, I called my secretary to tell her I'd be there in an hour.

I still had a touch of the willies as I pulled into my carport. I checked the carport door to make sure it was still locked, then the sliding glass door at the back. All was secure. I detoured to the mailbox before letting myself in the front door.

I threw the mail on the table and went to take a shower, activating the little alarm with the keyring remote as I went down the hall. Out of my closet I grabbed a pair of jeans and a black V-neck top and set them on the bed. Today was Friday, and we were allowed to dress down a bit, as long as we didn't have to testify in court. I didn't have court today, just a home visit in the afternoon, and a huge stack of vouchers to tackle so my kids could get back-to-school supplies and uniforms. Registration time was soon upon us, and things were going to get busy.

I showered quickly, dried my hair, and went to the bedroom to dress. I heard my cell phone beeping from inside my purse, lying on the bed next to my clothes. I had a message.

Kirk. "Call me. I'm at the courthouse," was all it said. I dialed his cell.

"Sorry. I was in the shower," I said.

"Wait. Let me just hold that image in my mind for a minute."

"Kirk—"

"Okay, okay. I know. Global Holdings of Birmingham is owned by Walter Arlington Baxter."

"Which one?"

"Huh?"

"There are at least two."

"Hang on." He came back on the line after a minute. "The third. Walter Arlington Baxter the Third. Hey, is that the BaxMed kid?"

"Yep."

"So what's it mean? What's DHS got to do with BaxMed?"

"I'll let you know. I'll call you later."

"Claire—"

"Trust me."

So Trey Baxter owned the company that was financing his father's research company. That made no sense at all. Why form a company? Why not just give the money to his father? Unless, of course, the money was coming from an illegal source. Like drug dealing. Trey could deposit the cash into the Holdings bank account, then give it to BaxMed. That was money laundering, right?

I stripped off my bathrobe and dressed. I needed to call Brighton. I didn't know if he could act on any of this information, since what I had wasn't exactly evidence. More like a theory. A theory I was pretty sure he didn't want to hear. After all, he had his man. Or woman, as the case may be. Maybe once I told him what I knew, and what I suspected, he could lean on Ashley for the truth. If she wouldn't give it to me, maybe she would tell him.

I was sliding into a pair of black clogs when the alarm screamed. Every nerve in my body jumped and my hands flew to my ears. My first instinct was to run and shut the horrible screeching thing off, but then it hit me.

Someone was in my house.

I ran to the bedroom door, slammed and locked it. Pressing my ear against the door, I heard two men.

"Shut that fuckin' thing off." I didn't recognize that voice.

"There's no button."

Lucas Donovan, the bartender from Kaleidoscope.

"She's back here."

Out. I had to get out. My bedroom had one window that opened into the back yard. I ran to it. Ripped off the curtain, unlocked the window, and tugged on the frame with all my might. It didn't budge. I grabbed a lamp off the table next to my bed. Tore off the shade and used the base to shatter a pane of glass. Shattered the next and tried to break out the wooden grid.

"She's in here!" the first man shouted.

I broke out the third pane as one of the two men kicked in my door with a loud crash. The alarm was still blaring. I tried to force myself to scream. But fear had frozen my throat.

"Oh, no, you don't," Lucas said. He lunged across the room and grabbed me around the waist. I fought as hard as I could, kicking and punching him as he tossed me onto the bed.

I landed on my back and rolled over. Got up on all fours before Lucas got my ankles and pulled me onto my stomach. Terror vibrated through me. A buzzing in my head mixed with the scream of the alarm and the thumping of my heart.

Lucas straddled my back as reality seemed to grow distant. I didn't want to live through whatever was going to happen next.

"Hold her still," the second voice said. I whipped my head around to see Trey Baxter at my side, long blond bangs hanging over his face. His brown eyes were intense, focused. As I struggled some more, Lucas gripped my arms and held them to my sides.

Trey had a needle. With an orange cap.

"No," I said, weakly.

"Don't worry," Trey said. "It's just something to put you to sleep."

"Permanently?" I squeaked.

He chuckled.

Trey shoved the sleeve of my shirt up. I twisted, trying to free my arms, but Lucas was too strong. I felt a pinch as he sank the needle into a vein.

Within a few seconds my body felt heavy, as if my flesh had turned to steel. Lucas got off me. I tried to say something, anything, but my mouth wouldn't work. I thought about my father. My brother. Grant. My last thought was a prayer.

Please, God, let that autodialer doohickey work.

CHAPTER THIRTY

I floated into a semiconscious state. Came to the realization that I was lying on my right side, on a mattress of some sort. A blanket over me. I wasn't dead.

Then I felt the pain. A headache worse than any I'd ever had in my life. Searing. No hangover had ever been this bad.

I forced my eyes open. I was looking at some kind of plastic railing. On the railing was a keypad. Up. Down. A red button with a cross. A clear plastic tube went from my arm to an IV bag.

I was in the hospital. If I was in the hospital, I was safe. I had vague, fuzzy memories of the last several hours. I remembered flashing lights, shouting. A dim recollection of a ride on a stretcher. Then nothing but darkness.

"She's awake." Dad, sounding relieved.

I struggled onto my back and tried to sit up. A gentle male voice said, "Hang on, I'll help you." It was strange to hear that voice in person. Chris, my brother.

He came to my side and worked a button. The bed under my back rose until I was upright.

My gaze focused on the faces in the room. My father, baggy-eyed, stubble rough on his face. Grant, frowning with concern. Mac, with that exasperated expression I knew so well. Chris and Royanne.

"Uh-oh," I said.

My brother the nurse knew exactly what was about to happen. Chris shoved a pink banana-shaped plastic tray under my chin just as

I gave a mighty heave and spewed out a thin, vile stream of greenish liquid.

The first wave passed and I looked at the crowd, their worried expressions now layered with disgust. "Can I have some privacy please?"

"Oh, sure."

"Yeah."

"Let's get out of here."

Everyone left except Dad and Chris. The second wave of stomach cramps hit and Chris left to get someone. When the nausea subsided again, I asked Dad, "What happened? How'd they find me? Who found me?"

"Maybe you'd better rest. We can talk about this later."

"No. I want to know what happened."

"Your boyfriend —"

"He's not —"

"Well, if he's not he damn well should be. He saved your life. Him and some guy named Jimmy Shelton."

"What? Jimmy —"

"Just listen, okay? When the alarm went off, Grant tried to call your cell phone, then your phone at home. When you didn't answer, he raised all hell. Called 911 and had the police meet him at your house. At the same time another 911 call came in. It was that Jimmy guy, saying that two men had broken in. When the police got there and busted through the door, they were discussing what to do with your — with you."

"With my body."

"Yeah," he said, his voice thick with emotion. "They were talking about how to make your death look like a suicide."

I remembered Dad's revelation about his client twenty years ago. And his grief over my mother's death. I didn't want to think about what he would have gone through if I hadn't been rescued. I was suddenly flooded with such sadness and guilt I could hardly stand it.

"Dad, don't. Please. I'm all right."

He cleared his throat and pulled himself together. "Anyway, the two guys were arrested. The cops called an ambulance and you were brought here."

"Where am I?"

"St. Vincent's."

"How long have I been out?"

"Almost fourteen hours." He checked his watch. "It's ten twenty Friday night now. Those two guys injected you with a huge dose of Valium. They also had pills and a bottle of booze, to leave with your body."

Chris and a nurse with a cute haircut and apple cheeks came in. She had a syringe in her hand, and the sight of it made my stomach tighten. But there was no needle, just a port that she plugged into my IV cord. As she plunged the medicine in, I asked, "What is that?"

"Phenergan. For the nausea. It'll make you sleepy."

"Oh, good, I need more sleep."

She laughed, tossed the syringe into a red trash can, and left. Dad said, "Detective Brighton also stopped by. He wants to meet with you when you're feeling a bit better."

Grant peeked in the door. "You okay? The nurse said she gave you something to help."

I nodded and held my hand out to him. He came in and took it.

"Thanks," I said. And here I thought all heroes looked like Indiana Jones.

He kissed my hand gently as I fell back to sleep.

I woke up nine hours later when the nurse came in to get vitals. I felt much better. The headache and the nausea were gone and I was ravenously hungry after almost twenty-four hours with nothing to eat. I ate the hospital breakfast of eggs, bacon, grits, and a biscuit and sent Dad to the cafeteria for more food. The doctor discharged me Saturday afternoon. I spent two nights at Dad's, he and Chris waiting on me hand and foot as I rested in my old, familiar bed.

Monday morning I drove myself downtown to Police Headquarters.

A large mural covered the side of the brick building, depicting four children of different races, arms draped around each other. The Birmingham Pledge against racism was painted next to the children. *I will treat all people with dignity and respect,* it said, *knowing that the world will be a better place because of my effort.*

I asked for Brighton at the desk. I was taken to a narrow room. The walls were stark white and the only furniture was an old, coffee-ringed table and some plastic and metal chairs. Brighton met me there and taped my statement about what happened the day I was attacked, including what Grant and I had discovered about BaxMed and Global Holdings of Birmingham. Then he asked me to wait. He returned with a typed transcript of what I'd said and had me sign it.

In the hallway after the interview, I saw a uniformed officer escorting Ashley to the room I'd just left. She stopped next to me and rested her head briefly on my shoulder. It was the closest thing to a hug she could give me, considering the fact that her wrists were handcuffed in front of her. I waited until she finished talking to Brighton.

While I waited, Zander arrived. He looked miserable. Pale. Ill. I wondered if he was detoxing. He went in after Ashley and gave his statement. Afterward, the three of us met in the hall.

"Are you okay?" Ashley asked me.

"I'm fine."

"I'm so sorry," she said. "I tried to warn you."

"I know. Let's not talk about whose fault it was. I should have listened to you. Told the police. Backed off."

"I'm glad you didn't. Now they got them, and they can't hurt no one else."

"Why did Michael die?"

"I went to work Friday night, to clean BaxMed. I finished the lobby and went down the hall to do Trey's office. I knew Trey, see. He and Zander were friends. When I was usin', we all used to hang out together. Anyway, that night I heard Trey arguing with his father. They're fighting, so I go into the office across the hall to clean instead. I tried not to listen, but I could still hear them. Trey's daddy said something about the money not covering it all, and Trey said well, what do you want me to do, Dad? I'm doing the best I can. Then his dad said they needed to step it up. That's what he said, step it up. Trey said the new nightclub would help. They'd be able to distribute more G and X that way.

"Trey said he would bring in more money, and to give him time. His daddy left, and I guess after that Trey heard me cleaning in the other room. He asked me how much I overheard, between him and his dad. I said I didn't hear nothin'. He said I better not have and if I didn't want to die I'd keep my mouth shut. I wasn't going to say nothin' to nobody. I knew he meant it. But then, Tuesday, my son died. I was supposed to die too. They didn't want no one knowin' where the money to support their company was comin' from."

I said, "So Trey Baxter was manufacturing GHB and Ecstasy in BaxMed's lab?"

She nodded. I looked at Zander. He added, "I knew Trey was dealing. Lucas sold the stuff for him at Kaleidoscope, and some of Donovan's other bartenders did the same at his other places. Donovan didn't know about it, but I think he suspected something. Then Trey used the profits from his dealing to boost BaxMed. He funneled the money through a company called Global Holdings of Birmingham. Get it? GHB. He used to brag about that. He thought it was funny."

I asked, "You knew he killed Michael?"

"Trey came over to my house on Monday. He had some G and some vodka with him. We had a few drinks, I did the G, then he waited until I passed out. I think he took my keys, and my car, to Ashley's and put the GHB in the juice."

"Zander, why didn't you tell someone?"

He pressed his lips together. "Trey gave me shit for free. I needed —I wanted the drugs. Ashley was clean. They couldn't control her like they were controlling me. She would have turned them in, too, if they hadn't threatened her, right?"

Ashley nodded again.

I had lots of questions. "Why'd they need the money from illegal drug dealing? Why couldn't BaxMed just find a sponsor? An investor? A large drug company to help with costs?"

Zander said, "No drug company would've picked them up. The trials of the ADHD medicine weren't going well. Not that it harmed anyone or anything, it just wasn't any better than what's already out there. Trey knew it, but he wanted to keep BaxMed going. His dad had already sunk his life savings into the company. And I think Trey wanted to be legitimate, eventually. Produce a drug that really could help people."

I asked Ashley, "I don't get what Jimmy had to with any of this. Why was he threatening me? Why'd he slash my tires?"

"He didn't. I think that was Flash. He'd been callin' me again, trying to get back with me. He hates you. He blames you for breakin' us up. It's stupid, 'cause you saved my life. I wanted to save yours. I made Jimmy promise to protect you. I knew you were gonna be stubborn and not give up. Jimmy was supposed to keep you from getting hurt."

"And you let me believe he was out to kill me. Ashley—"

"I wanted you to be scared. I wanted you to quit. Now, I'm glad you didn't. Now my baby has justice."

I studied Michael's parents, seeing them together for the first time. I realized that Michael had been a perfect blend of the two. He'd had his father's hair and eyes, and his mother's cheekbones and fair skin.

Zander buried his head in his hands. "He killed my son. I was his best friend, and he killed my son. I should have stopped him."

I didn't know what to say to that, except, "I'm sorry."

Kirk got his story. Several, actually, in the weeks after we were interviewed by Brighton. I secretly filled in the blanks, on occasion, in exchange for his not using my name. He kept his word. He wrote about the systematic dismantling of BaxMed and the FDA investigation. He covered the investigations and indictments of Trey Baxter, Dr. Walter Baxter, and Lucas Grayson. The long list of charges against them included murder and attempted murder. Attempted murder of me. I could barely get my head around that.

I met with Mac and Dr. Pope on my first day back at work and related the whole story. I assume that Dr. Pope had a word with the state office, who quietly had a word with the attorney general. That's what I guess, anyway, because nobody ever told me anything. The only clue I had that the official investigation was over was when I got an e-mail from Mac that said to close the Hennessy file and send it to the file room. Business as usual. I was grateful to still have my job.

Ashley got out of jail and she and Jimmy sent me a wedding invitation a week after her release. I went, huge gift in hand, and thanked Jimmy in person for saving my life. Al and Dee were at the wedding, all smiles. Al couldn't take his eyes off the decorated box set out to collect cards and cash for the newlyweds. I never found out if the box made it home with Ashley and Jimmy. I suspect not.

A week and a day after I nearly died, Grant and I went on the dinner-and-a-movie date we'd planned forever. He stayed the night, but not in the guest room.

The evening after that, Kirk called me ahead of press time and read the next day's headline to me over the phone. SON OF PROMINENT LOCAL BUSINESSMAN FOUND DEAD OF OVERDOSE, it said. Kirk said the paramedics found a crack pipe lying next to Zander's body, along with an empty bottle of stolen pills.

Dad and I went to Zander's funeral, along with Jimmy and Ashley and hundreds of others, at St. Luke's Episcopal Church. Karen and Alexander Madison both shook our hands like robots as we arrived. The only member of the family who showed a hint of emotion was Zander's little sister, Kaylin. She cried throughout the whole service.

As the priest eulogized Zander, it gave me some comfort to picture him with his son in some sort of heavenly afterlife. In a green meadow, perhaps. With a pond. Feeding the ducks like Mikey loved to do. Holding hands and playing together. Neither of them lost any longer.

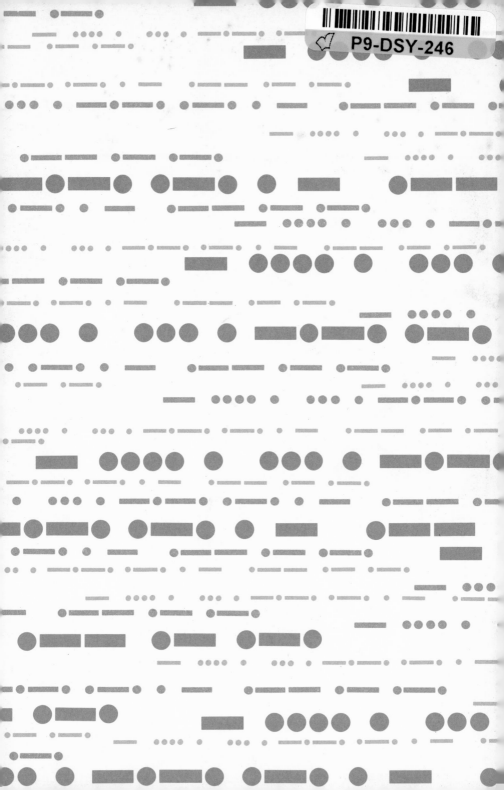

UNDERCOVER GIRL

THE MACMILLAN COMPANY
NEW YORK · BOSTON · CHICAGO
DALLAS · ATLANTA · SAN FRANCISCO

MACMILLAN AND CO., LIMITED
LONDON · BOMBAY · CALCUTTA
MADRAS · MELBOURNE

THE MACMILLAN COMPANY
OF CANADA, LIMITED
TORONTO

ELIZABETH P. MacDONALD

UNDERCOVER GIRL

THE MACMILLAN COMPANY

NEW YORK 1947

PRINTED IN THE UNITED STATES OF AMERICA
BY THE VAIL-BALLOU PRESS, INC., BINGHAMTON, N. Y.

INTRODUCTION

By Major General William J. Donovan

Wartime Director of the Office of Strategic Services (OSS)

The great majority of women who worked for America's first organized and integrated overall intelligence agency, spent their war years behind desks and filing cases in Washington, invisible apron strings of an organization which touched every theater of war. They were the ones at home who patiently filed secret reports, encoded and decoded messages, answered telephones, mailed pay checks and kept the records. But these were necessary tasks without the faithful performance of which an organization of 26,000 people, with civil and military personnel, could not be maintained. Upon the discretion of their performance depended the security of the organization.

There were some, however, who had important administrative positions and others with regional and linguistic knowledge of great value in research, whose special skills were employed in exact and painstaking work such as map making, cryptography and research.

Only a small percentage of the women ever went overseas, and a still smaller percentage was assigned to actual operational jobs behind enemy lines.

The author of this work was one of those who went overseas. She carried out an important and effective assignment for which she was qualified by natural talent, knowledge of the people, and intensive training. She epitomized the devotion to duty of the group of women in the Office of Strategic Services.

With humor but with comprehension the author describes a phase of warfare little known or understood in this country. Indeed our people did not become aware of it, and its implications, until the Nazi machine applied it against us in the strategy of World War II. It is an unorthodox aspect of warfare which, by moral and physical means other than the truly military, seeks to break the will of the enemy to resist. For varying purposes its techniques may be and are used equally effectively in war and in peace. In one form it endeavors by indirect and subtly planned rumor and propaganda to subvert people from allegiance to their own country. It is essentially a weapon of exploitation. If successful it can be more effective than a shooting war. For that reason it is vital in defense to counter its effects by using the same methods against the enemy. The direct method of doing this was under the jurisdiction of the Office of War Information (OWI). The indirect method was under the Office of Strategic Services (OSS). Each served its purpose. They were most successful when working together.

This work in the China Theater and in Southeast Asia was done by a branch of OSS under the name of Morale Operations. The author was a very effective operator in this unit. Acting on the assumption that the enemy would more readily believe rumors coming from within his own country and from his own people, the Morale Operations branch succeeded in inducing surrenders, defections and a lowering of morale.

Betty MacDonald knows how this was done. Reading her book should give a better understanding of the way in which a strategy of disunity and confusion can be carried out against us in time of peace and yet how it can be guarded against by an alert and informed American public. This is the message behind the lively good humor of this book.

WILLIAM J. DONOVAN

ACKNOWLEDGMENTS

Notes and meditations on this book are still being found in bureau drawers from Waikiki to Marthas Vineyard, but most of them have finally been collected in *Undercover Girl*.

There were many who generously shared their first-hand experiences in the Office of Strategic Services with me. Without the help of these people, particularly Major General William J. Donovan, I could never have constructed the serious framework for this book..

There were other patient ones who doggedly corrected my spelling and patched up my fractured syntax, particularly *New York Times* man Gilbert P. Bailey, who understood because he wrote a book once himself.

And there were also those who applied cold packs to my hot forehead and vice versa as the seasons changed and the book began to grow thick enough to weigh in on the bathroom scales at one pound plus. Just about that time, when something dire happened to my apartment lease, the *dea ex machina* arrived in the form of a sterling and severe Aunt Marj, who turned over her Connecticut place to me with strict injunctions to "write a book."

I'm particularly grateful to the following patient, considerate people who helped me collect material and contact other OSS alumni:

Richard P. Heppner, O. C. Doering, Jr., J. Russell Forgan, Dr. Justin O'Brien, Mrs. Barklie Henry, Miss Marjorie Peet, John Shaheen, Foster Hailey, Charles E. Cuningham, William A. Smith, Mrs. Walter J. Mansfield, Mrs. Arthur J. Makholm, Lucius O. Rucker, Roger Starr, Alfred T. Cox, Dr. Cora Du Bois, Rosamond and Thibaut de St. Phalle, Roland E. Dulin, Colonel Gustav G. Kraus, Dr. Henry A. Murray, Robert J. Wentworth, Herbert S. Little, Dr. Richard S. Lyman, and Duncan C. Lee.

GRAND CENTRAL STATION, 1947

ix

CONTENTS

CHAPTER ONE

MATA HARIDANS

I AM certain that Jane Foster and I were not exactly the types the Joint Chiefs of Staff had in mind when they decided to mobilize women for total war. On the home front they needed efficient clerks and stenographers to relieve men for active duty. Overseas, they wanted well regimented females, preferably in uniform, who would create no morale problems and would obey orders without question.

Jane and I filled none of these qualifications, but luckily we were members of a lenient, quasi-military organization which forgave us our idiosyncrasies and eventually harnessed the pixies in us. That organization, the Office of Strategic Services, was elastically conceived to utilize people like ourselves, together with hundreds of more serious-minded women who did heroic things such as parachuting behind lines, arranging secret air drops in enemy-held territory or risking their lives to transmit intelligence over clandestine radio sets.

The very thought of jumping out of an airplane terrified us. At the slightest suggestion of torture, we knew we'd tell all, including names and addresses of our grandmothers. We also had great difficulty in keeping a secret, and were considered as definite security liabilities by everyone who came in contact with us outside our immediate associates—people like ourselves who were employed to produce psychological warfare material.

Because our lives had been completely unregimented until the war, we started work at the Office of Strategic Services with a deep unconcern, which bordered on irreverence, for the military method of getting things done. We flippantly maintained that chains of command, finished staff work—even reports typed in triplicate under separate buck slips—were bureaucratic methods of prolonging hostilities. Thinking back on it now, I realize that any good psychologist could have told us that we were a trifle awed, as women usually are, by the vast army machine into which we were gradually integrated, and the way men went about making war.

For the most part, OSS was a serious-minded organization initially set up with three branches:

R & A—a research and analysis department that prepared area surveys and intelligence studies for operational groups;

SI—a secret intelligence branch which infiltrated enemy lines and sent information back to headquarters;

SO—a sabotage branch which organized guerrilla bands and carried out irregular warfare in Axis territory.

As the organization grew in size and scope under the imaginative administration of Major General William J. Donovan, many appendages were added, including MO—the Morale Operations branch, which dealt with "black" psychological warfare.

Donovan's men had a great deal of difficulty in selling MO to hardheaded commanders in the field. MO was not taught at West Point or Annapolis, yet in theory it predates the classic military doctrines of Clausewitz and dips as far back in antiquity as the incident of the Trojan horse.

MO was the art of influencing enemy thinking by means of "black" propaganda. It was a method of sapping morale comparable to the sapping of city walls in medieval warfare. It was subtle propaganda, ostensibly coming from within the enemy's own ranks. Hence, because of its supposed source, the material did not carry the stigma usually attached to "white" psychological warfare material originating from standard government sources such as the Office of War Information.

MO operators were taught to handle their trade in hundreds of tricky ways. They faked newspapers or clippings supposedly printed in enemy territory. They issued false orders to confuse military leaders, and distributed leaflets supporting underground unrest in Axis countries. They manufactured rumors suggesting such calamities as the collapse of the German home front, insanity of leaders, and instilled false hopes among enemy soldiers which would lead to gradual disillusionment. MO "freedom" radio stations, allegedly manned by rebels, preached lost causes, pricked enemy hopes.

For example, medium-wave broadcasts in October, 1944, from a fictitious MO station, Radio Paris, were so effective that French newspapers carried front-page stories on them. These black broadcasts were beamed to Germany from "commanders" of undesignated German towns in the path of advancing Allied armies who announced they were going to resist the scorched-earth-policy retreat orders and were preparing to deliver their towns intact to the Americans. They urged other German commanders to do likewise. United States Twelfth Army group monitors considered the first broadcast so important that they woke General Bradley up in the middle of the night with the news.

The production of MO material called for imagination, coupled with area and ethnic knowledge, and a certain amount of artistic ability. Since no one person could fill the requirements, one type was hired to complement another, and there developed an odd and pixylike band of characters in OSS referred to as "MO Types." These types played with ideas in much the same trial-and-error manner as the atom-bomb scientists; but it was difficult to estimate MO results. Even the best interrogators could not determine just what made a Japanese surrender: starvation, loss of blood, disease, temporary insanity, or that phony and purely coincidental MO clipping in his pocket discussing results of a new American secret projectile upon his homeland.

Jane and I first met during the winter of 1943, in the secret fingerprinting room at OSS where we shared a grimy towel together. Her bright Irish smile encouraged tentative friendship feelers, although I had been warned by the OSS personnel officer just twenty minutes before not to discuss anything with anyone. I asked if she were just starting her job here with OSS.

Jane looked around cautiously. The finger printer was at work on another pair of hands.

"My first day here," she said furtively out of the corner of her mouth.

Then, as if chancing everything on my being an honest American girl, she edged closer.

"Look," she asked, "just what kind of an organization *is* this?"

I had been wondering the same thing myself. It was the first job I'd ever had where the employer hadn't described the kind of work I was being hired to do.

Several weeks before joining OSS I had met a tall, friendly, elfin-faced major at a Department of Agriculture exhibit I was covering for the Scripps-Howard feature service in Washington. Completely charming, he was at the moment interested in the display of chicken-feather-lined sleeping bags the department's Beltsville scientists had developed. He seemed to have stepped out of the fifth dimension, with his one kewpie-like curl swirling below his overseas cap and his dancing blue eyes inviting, or rather provoking, small talk. It was quite natural to tell him that I'd been a newspaper reporter for six years; that I had worked a stretch on the west coast and in Manila, but mostly in Hawaii. I had been at Pearl Harbor. No, I didn't think island Japanese were disloyal. In fact, I spoke some Japanese because I had lived with a Japanese professor and his wife in Honolulu for over a year while I covered the war.

The major suddenly focused his intense blue eyes on me. Had I ever considered working for the government? Would I like to make a great contribution to the war effort? Sorry he couldn't explain the type of work, because it was secret; but he knew I could qualify. Meanwhile, fumbling in his briefcase, he fished out three government application blanks.

"Fill them out immediately and mail them to the Office of Strategic Services. Time is of the essence," he whispered dramatically, and disappeared before I could demur.

I explained all this briefly to Jane. It turned out that she had been hired under similar circumstances which involved whispered overtures, through a third party, while she was still working on the Netherlands East Indies desk of the Board of Economic Warfare. Since raids by one government agency on another were frowned upon, Jane took the initiative and resigned from the BEW, overcome by a great curiosity to find out how her knowledge of the Malayan language, her art training in France, Germany, and New York, her four years in Java could change the Allied war effort in the Far East. To this day, she still gleefully tells friends, she has never discovered the answer.

On the day we met each other, we were instructed to report to the security office, where the tone of our secret service organization was tactfully and tastefully set with such posters as "Button Your Lip" or "Someone Talked." There were also printed memoranda on the walls and desks, asking if the safes were secure and all secret papers put away, and admonishing people to turn out lights, save fuel and paper.

My first impulse was to drop a curtsy to the security officer, a gruff second lieutenant with a dead cigar in his mouth who looked as if he had just been recruited from a detective agency. He was seated at a desk before a large poster of a pink ear upon which had been superscribed: "The Enemy is Listening."

"You girls please raise your right hands and solemnly swear . . ."

He spoke so rapidly, the cigar bobbing in his mouth and mushing up the words, that we missed most of what we were solemnly swearing to; but the gist of it was something like a sorority oath that we would never—repeat—never reveal what went on behind the OSS velvet curtain.

Completing this ritual, the lieutenant slouched confidentially across his desk and fixed us with what we later learned to identify as the "security officer eye."

"OSS is an undercover organization authorized by the Joint Chiefs of Staff. We are anonymous. If people ask you what you do here, tell 'em you are file clerks. People aren't interested in file clerks— not enough to ask questions. Remember, there are enemy agents at work here in Washington. They are here to listen to people who talk. One slip from me for instance, and a dozen OSS agents would be snuffed out within forty-eight hours behind lines in France. What branch you girls in?"

"Morale Operations."

The security officer snapped back in his chair, drew a deep breath. Then he exploded.

"Propagandists! Your branch—I'll tell you right here—it has the worst security record in the organization. Girls, for my sake, see if you can't set a good example. At least remember to put top-secret papers in a safe place at night. Always think, maybe my brother's life, or my sweetheart's, or great-uncle Harry's depends on me putting this paper back in the safe! Every time you do this, girls, you save a life."

Then, because he felt so strongly about MO, the man spent half an hour not in line of duty telling us how essential it was to keep our lips buttoned and to take things seriously, in spite of what went on in MO.

When we left the room I felt cowed. Surely I didn't have the power over human destinies that this man with the cigar seemed to think. It was as if I had taken the veil, henceforth to be wed forever to this strange and terrible organization. Furthermore, I began to develop the complex that whatever I said, no matter how trivial, was immediately picked up by radar and transmitted to the security officer.

After our lecture, we were told to report to work at once. The only hitch was that we couldn't immediately locate our new offices. The personnel branch had assigned us to a definite number in Que, a rambling, haphazardly designed temporary office building shaped, I was convinced, like the letter Q. We walked down long corridors lined with offices identified only by numbers. Through a few open doors we saw that the rooms were decorated with large pink and purple maps of Europe or Asia and marked with pins which were removed each evening, according to the security rules we had just been learning. When we finally arrived at our number, we found an empty suite of rooms in which an irate workman was ripping telephone extension wires out of the walls. There was no one else.

"They're always moving, from one building to another—and taking their damned phones with them," the man muttered petulantly. He couldn't tell us where MO had gone, but he was certain someone would be back for the phones. It seemed that all OSS branches moved at least once a month as the ever growing wartime agency began to burst its narrow confines at Twenty-sixth and E streets like some plumpish lady who was unable to contain her expanding girth in the circumference of last year's girdle.

We tracked down MO for an hour. The OSS campus sprawled down a steep hill, bounded on one side by a wonderfully odoriferous brewery, on the other by the Naval Hospital. There were five main buildings in the group, with Que at the bottom of the hill. We climbed a long flight of steps to South Building, passed the Administration Building where General Donovan had his offices, went through an underground tunnel that linked the Central and North buildings and here, on the top floor of North, we stumbled upon the MO redoubt. The branch had been relegated to a single, long drafty room piled high with freshly moved desks. At the far end of the empty office we saw our major perched precariously on a chair top, tacking a large map of Asia to the wall.

As we approached him down the obstacle course, I began to wonder how a new civilian recruit should address a major in the United States Army: Should I click heels and salute? shake hands? use the Girl Scout grip? In all my OSS service, I never did discover the approved protocol. I managed a sloppy introduction, not sure whether I was correctly quoting from the OSS indoctrination manual, or reenacting something in the movies.

"Elizabeth MacDonald—reporting, sir."

Jane coasted. "Foster, also."

The major stopped his work, looked down upon us, and beamed.

"Welcome, girls—we're informal around here. Good to see you two. Hand me a tack till I get Manchuria anchored, and we'll talk business."

That is how we started work. The major led us into his inner

office, set apart from the larger room by a plywood partition, unlocked a safe, and took out a document entitled, "MO Manual, Revised."

The manual, he explained, had been prepared by members of the
European branch, long since departed for the field, and it had been
bequeathed as a sort of heritage to the newly formed Far Eastern
section of MO. He left us with it while he went off to lunch.

In the months ahead, that dog-eared mimeographed handbook became a bible to me, opening up a completely new approach to life
in which suddenly everything that had once been forbidden now
became a way of thinking in wartime.

. . . morale operations include all measures of subversion, other
than physical, used to create confusion and division, and to undermine
the morale and the political unity of the enemy through any means
from within, or purporting to emanate within, enemy countries; or
from bases within other areas where action and counteraction may be
effective against the enemy . . .

That was the introduction, the objective. To accomplish the task,
we hitherto law-abiding Americans were authorized to contact and
manipulate underground groups and *agents provocateurs;* initiate
rumors—either the subversive variety designed to play upon emotions and attitudes, or the deliberate deception; forge misleading intelligence documents, falsify proclamations, print subversive false
leaflets! It was all carefully worked out in the manual—a fascinating
set of rules for enemy deception.

The only unpardonable sin in the manual was to "blow cover," or
reveal the origin of MO material or personnel!

Psychological Warfare was an integral part of the German blitz-
krieg, the MO branch of which had paid off handsome dividends in
the drive into France, we further learned. Nazi agents preceded the
armies with rumors, forged documents and false newspapers pro-
claiming widespread German victories, and the collapse of England.
MO rode best in the wake of defeat, when countries lost faith in
their soldiers and leaders.

To be most effective, black operations behind lines should be coordinated with white efforts at the front. For example, an attempt
on Hitler's life could be factually reported by OWI in a leaflet drop;
but all the implications of a discontented home front, a wavering
general staff, a rebellious underground could be handled from within
enemy territory by alert rumor mongers on the MO pay roll.

We were just concluding the section on "preparation of incriminating documents" when the major returned, carrying with him the uprooted telephones. He launched into a brisk lecture on MO procedure.

"Morale operations are most effective when they are planned as part of common campaigns conducted by undergrounds and integrated with actual military operations and Allied strategy," he began a discourse that he gave to every recruit who walked into his office. He was a sort of Pandora, opening the forbidden box containing MO pandemonium.

"Take an example—if we knew the Allies were going to make a landing at Shanghai, we could plan a series of deceptive rumors to throw the Japs off—let them think we're aiming at Formosa. Then we could try to disrupt Jap-puppet relations. We'd plant evidences of treason. Our black radio net could send out 'compromise' code messages—deceptive information purposely planted to mislead them in an easily broken code. We'd hint about puppet defection in clandestine leaflets. Tell the Chinese the Japs are going to raze their city in the event of an attack. Tell the Japs their puppet troops are planning to revolt . . ."

In MO work, the major continued, we must not restrain our imaginations. Out of twenty wild schemes there might be one that would really work—and save lives. Whatever projects were developed in the Washington laboratory were checked by a board of Far Eastern experts who passed on the feasibility of the ideas. They were people like the celebrated Japanese scholar, Dr. Serge Elisséeff of Harvard, Dr. Raymond Kennedy of Yale, Eugene Dooman of State, Charles Nelson Spinks of the Office of Naval Intelligence.

"Of course, all our stuff is based on concrete intelligence reports. Our two analysts over here—Marjorie Severyns and Mildred Turner —collect material from OSS branches, Federal Communications intercepts, and other sources, and route it to everyone in the office."

The major led us over to Mrs. Turner, who was just slapping a pink routing slip on a cable marked Top Secret. It was the first time I had ever seen a Top Secret message, and I warily lifted the cover sheet to learn that Burmese agents preferred to be paid in opium. (This fact stayed with me as gospel truth until one day I met a Burmese agent in Calcutta who told me *he* preferred to be paid in Parker 51's.)

"It takes all kinds to make an MO team," the major was saying to

us as he started introductions around the room, which was now becoming peopled.

My impressions of the MO types I met during the next few hours
were vivid impacts of rare, strange personalities selected at grab-bag
random from all corners of the world, for many reasons. Together
they fitted into the over-all jigsaw picture. Apart, they were odd-
shaped pieces with no apparent *raison d'être*. On the first day in
that long, noisy room I met a Chinese artist, a Thai missionary, a
newspaper reporter, a Shanghai business man, a private detective, the
producer of the Lucky Strike Hit Parade, a girl graduate from
Hunter with a degree in international law, an Olympic broad-jump
champion, a lawyer from New York, a dog fancier, a renegade American in British navy uniform who was also a black-belt holder in jiu-
jitsu, a traveling patent medicine salesman, and a Japanese-American
who had fought with General Donovan and the Rainbow Division in
World War I.

By the time the desks had been sorted, I saw the group settling
down to a pattern, clustering like convention delegates around maps
of their particular areas. Behind a pile of Thai newspapers, moodily
staring out towards the Potomac, sat a heavy, rather handsome middle-
aged man whom the major introduced as Dr. John Holladay, a medical missionary from Thailand. At an adjoining desk sat another missionary, elderly Miss Lucy Starling, who handed the major a program
for the establishment of an underground near Chengmai, Thailand,
prefacing it with the request that she be allowed to "jump in" and
teach the natives how to use demolitions.

"Dr. Holladay," the major explained to us as we walked on, "is
having trouble realigning his past life as a man of God with his present
occupation in MO. Lucy Starling, on the other hand, can't wait to
get back. She's learned everything our schools can teach about guerrilla warfare. You should see that lady strip a machine gun! First
time she shot it, she had the jumps for a week. She's taking up judo
now—look at her! She only weighs 105 pounds! And she's sixty-five
if she's a day."

The boys in the services were off in another part of the room, arguing, when we arrived, about the relative values of the Army, Navy,
and Marine Corps post exchanges. Two naval lieutenants, Doug
Bonamy and Roy Squires, were holding out for the superior salted
almond bars at the Navy commissary. Marine Lieutenant Charles
Fenn, whom the major introduced as "our lad who walked out of

Burma with Stilwell," said that the Marines got the best chocolate marshmallow creams. Captain Max Kleiman, the major's Japanese linguist who had just returned from Port Darwin where he'd been an interrogator for the Air Corps, leaned silently back in his chair and smoked a cigarette, Japanese style, down to the last quarter-inch.

"The Air Corps," he muttered cryptically, "gets walnut fudge!"

It began to remind me of a Gilbert and Sullivan opera, especially when a middle-aged nisei sauntered up, thrust his hand out and said:

"I'm Tokie Slocum. Are you in favor of liquidating the Japanese emperor, or can we use him later for a figurehead?"

At that time, no one seemed to make much more sense than I did. Looking back on it now, I can appreciate the major's vision in hiring his odd assortment for the jobs ahead. Lieutenant Roy Squires, a hard-headed business man with years of experience in Shanghai, was one of our first MO men to be sent into the field of China, where he operated alone for over two years, building up a strong anti-Japanese, pro-American feeling in Foochow. Here he was instrumental in causing rickshaw strikes, anti-Jap demonstrations and a spontaneous welcome parade for the first United States troops to march through the streets of the little Chinese city in May of 1945.

Doug Bonamy, a good executive and radio man, went to Burma where he helped build the first Freedom Station in the Far East at Chittagong.

Charley Fenn was sent into French Indo-China to launch rumor campaigns against the Japs near Hanoi. Max Kleiman and Tokie organized, trained, and delivered the first contingent of Japanese translators, interpreters, writers, and technicians to India for OSS.

The war ended before Lucy Starling jumped into Thailand; but the major's man of God, Dr. Holladay, finally overcame his doubts and parachuted into Chengmai, his former parish, bearing some of the blackest MO ever perpetrated against the ancestry of the Japanese emperor. Dr. Holladay assuaged his conscience by using a medical clinic which he set up in the jungles as his cover for being in Thailand. He also stirred up good will towards America at the same time he dispensed our atabrine and paregoric to the natives.

Of course the major, like everyone else in the war, had to make use of the material at hand. When he made mistakes, he chalked them up to experience and started over again. Mr. Earp was a fine example of early MO trial and error whose own ideas were usually far too theoretical for practical purposes, but whose imagination primed others to produce truly effective material. Mr. Earp was the man who made MO and Japanese foxes synonymous terms of nonsense throughout the CBI theater. The fox story was a legend passed down to each recruit and was received with varying degrees of credulity. Some accepted it as a legitimate MO approach to a problem. Others, like Jane and myself, got the uncontrollable giggles.

Mr. Earp's theory was that the Japanese have been afraid of foxes since mythical times, when their *inori* stories tell of foxes with werewolf powers. He believed that by playing upon their superstitions he could induce the Japs to surrender. To dramatize his idea, he staged a dawn demonstration off Long Island to which he invited General Donovan, General Hugh A. Drum, and other dignitaries. The group went out in the middle of the Sound, accompanied by Mr. Earp and two snapping, snarling foxes which had been previously immersed in phosphorus. Mr. Earp told his shivering audience to imagine that it was Burma, and that Japs were crouched in dugouts ashore. He then released his two foxes which made a glittering parabola as they tumbled into the water. Instead of swimming ashore to run along the beaches and terrify the Japs, the foxes swam out to sea and were never seen again.

Mr. Earp came to visit us in Washington every Saturday from New York, where he had his own offices. Jane and I were both on the *qui vive* the day, soon after our indoctrination, when he arrived bearing a stuffed fox in a paper bag which he wanted to try out on Tokie to see if he had any "throwback reactions." Mr. Earp was a pleasant man with an elongated, foxlike face, curiously pointed at the chin. He wore the very expensive clothes of a dollar-a-year man, affected an ivory cigarette holder and bow tie. He had lived in Japan in 1919 and had maintained contacts with a group of Japanese friends of that vintage.

As the staff gathered round, he began to produce MO material from his brief case with the quiet pride of a Fuller Brush salesman. His first selection was a black tube, shaped like a saxophone mouthpiece.

"It's a snake call for Wingate's Raiders," he told us. "The Raiders creep up on a Jap position, blow one of these gadgets. The Japs think they're surrounded by snakes. Confusion—panic—then surrender! Simple device. You can purchase this whistle for $4.50 at any sporting-goods store."

So saying, Mr. Earp took the snake call, blew into it, and produced a singularly unimpressive sound: "Sh-h-h."

He then pulled out a leaflet. On one side was a picture of Tojo, quite intoxicated, surrounded by geisha. On the reverse side was a Japanese soldier on Guadalcanal, his intestines unraveled on the beach.

Someone asked Mr. Earp what was "black" about the leaflet. It looked like an OWI job.

"The picture of Tojo is a fake," Mr. Earp hastened to explain. "I cut him out of an official photograph and pasted him in between the girls, painted drinks in their hands, bags under his eyes, and rephotographed the whole thing."

While we were all forced to admit that it was an admirable forgery, Tokie spoke up with the authority invested in him as the only Japanese present.

"If I were a Jap soldier," he said, "I'd feel that Tojo has a right to enjoy any teahouse party he could afford. I'd just envy him. He's too high up on the social scale for me to criticize him anyway."

These frequent transmigrations of Tokie into the mind of a Jap soldier brought down many an MO trial balloon, as Mr. Earp himself agreed, ruefully putting Tojo away in his brief case.

Mr. Earp was a familiar figure in the offices for about two months after I started to work. Despite his flights into fancy, he contributed a great deal to our experiments in sonic devices which OSS researchers were developing on the theory that soldiers in the jungle become supersensitive to sound. Certain sound effects—the chatter of a machine gun, the buzz of a plane, whispered commands—were recorded on wire and a portable machine was devised for use in the jungle. A spool of these noises, together with one Mr. Earp made on cries of Japanese women and children, authentic Jap ghost voices, and of course fox snarls, were tried out one dark night in the Virginia woods for the benefit of certain OSS communications officials whose branch was to operate the mechanism in Burma.

Everything went well until Mr. Earp pulled his surprise act and rose in the darkness like a phoenix, wearing a phosphorescent skeleton costume which he had slipped on during the demonstration. The colonels were routed. Unfortunately, Mr. Earp, like his foxes, was never heard of again after their report went in; but shortly afterwards a large carton of snake calls arrived for him from Abercrombie and Fitch.

My first week with MO was spent in trying to identify myself with the quixotic group. I was assigned to the Japan desk and told to work with Captain Kleiman, whom I discovered in the throes of a violent conflict with the security office. The captain had obtained some seven Japanese aliens to help produce MO material. Security refused to allow him to keep them in Washington because they represented a possible threat to national defense. Taking his Nips to New York, Captain Kleiman established a print shop in the heart of the metropolis, acting on the security adage that if you want to avoid detection, set up shop at Times Square. The printing establishment was carefully guarded. Iron bars were placed with sinister precision at the entrance, which was on the seventh floor of a busy office building. It was then decided that the Japanese might create too much suspicion if they used the elevator. The security officer decided they should use the fire escape. Scarcely an hour after the staff reported for work the first morning, Captain Kleiman received a call from the FBI checking on several reports that "mysterious Orientals" were seen climbing the side of a building on Thirty-ninth Street. After that the Japanese rode in the elevators.

Meanwhile, fresh recruits were arriving daily, including a newspaper friend of mine from Hawaii named Leo Crowley who was so thoroughly indoctrinated by the security office that not a flicker of recognition registered when we met.

Gradually I began to remember people and their first names. By the end of the first week I was considered a member of the old guard. In recognition of this, I was allowed to participate in an office conspiracy against a newly commissioned lieutenant, Gordon Auchincloss, for whom we forged a set of orders packing him off to Peoria, Illinois. (Gordon, who later experienced some soul-trying months in China establishing a black radio station, once confessed that he wished he had gone to Peoria in the first place.)

Jane and I had been in MO for nearly two months, absorbing the amazing new concept of subversive warfare and planning for the day when we should be ready to launch our campaigns in the field, thereby bringing the war in the Far East to an earlier conclusion than even the Joint Chiefs of Staff could hope for at that time.

We stumbled on our formula for driving the Japs out of Greater East Asia quite by accident one noon hour when we were standing in line at the OSS cafeteria and Jane casually mentioned Indonesian "love curry." Her chance remark launched us on our first field trip, an expedition upon which we swore each other to secrecy since it ended in such complete ignominy.

A "love curry," Jane informed me, was a concoction Indonesian girls cooked up to get rid of their faithless Dutch lovers in the days before the Republic. Into the curries they put tiny, indissoluble hairs which grew at the base of bamboo clumps. The hairs worked their way through the intestine walls and caused death through hemorrhage.

"And why not revive it for MO?" Jane asked.

We spent our lunch hour plotting a "bamboo death" campaign. We would present the idea to the Jap soldiers in Indonesia, Burma, and Thailand through a medical leaflet issued by the Jap high command in which the legend would be explained. We would cast suspicion on native eating houses. "Love curry" symptoms could be described to the hypochondriac Jap soldier in a general way that would lead him to believe that simple dysentery and indigestion were the beginnings of hemorrhages.

Jane would do a series of drawings on simple sabotage in the digestive tract, tracing the course of the deadly splinters into and through the colon walls with fluoroscopic clarity.

"Of course, if I could make sketches from the original bamboo—" Jane mused. "How about going down to the Botanical Gardens?"

After lunch we borrowed a large kitchen knife from the cook, gathered up sketch pads and pencils, and were off to the Gardens. We passed the guards at the gate without any trouble although I was uncomfortably conscious of the knife handle which protruded from my purse. There was no one in the sweltering greenhouses as we walked between the rows of palms, tree ferns, and potted orchids towards a clump of bamboo. When we reached it, Jane began to sketch the shape of the knifelike leaves and knobbed stalks.

But we were both eager to see the hairs that brought death to so many Dutchmen. Edging in like jungle fighters, we crept through the underbrush on hands and knees. At the base of a large clump I reached out for a dead sheath and peeled it down to the ground. It was full of dust.

"It's too old," Jane whispered. "Try a younger one."

I grasped a green shoot, rubbing my hands down the under bark. Suddenly I felt the tiny barbs. Jane handed me the knife and, with what I fancied was the sure, firm touch of a Dr. Kildare, I began to scrape the stalk. We were flat on our stomachs in mulch and dry bamboo leaves when we heard a distinct cough. With some difficulty and in utter confusion we inched out backward on all fours.

"Lose something, girls?" The guard's tone was frigid.

In spite of Jane's hastily constructed story that we were a couple of art students, the man took the knife away from us and told us to leave the premises immediately. Our only consolation, besides the bamboo splinters imbedded in my hand as evidence, was the over-all feeling of pride that we knew the security officer would take in us for not "blowing our cover."

The war in the so-called forgotten Burma theater was hitting the front pages with a new Jap thrust towards Imphal, when the MO staff met its first Man from the Field, Colonel Carl Eifler, who spoke to us at a regular Monday meeting one blustery March morning.

The impact of Colonel Eifler and his work had a sobering effect on our chair-borne group, even before he appeared. Colonel Eifler, our major told us, was a fabulous, powerful man of action whose super-human energy was responsible for the establishment of the OSS base in northern Burma—Detachment 101. The colonel had walked into the Burma jungles alone to befriend, recruit, and train a guerrilla band of Kachin natives. Then he had established headquarters in Assam, where he developed a small corps of Americans into a hard-hitting group which produced a major part of the intelligence for General Stilwell's north Burma campaigns and led Kachin raiders against Jap lines of communication and supply dumps.

There was an undercurrent of excitement as the group met to hear Colonel Eifler's story, and to see the movies which he was to show on agent training and air drops in Burma.

Everybody but the colonel was there promptly at nine o'clock. After a fifteen-minute wait the major's phone rang. He muttered a few words none of us could catch, then beckoned to me.

"Go down and escort Colonel Eifler to this meeting. The guard won't let him in because he doesn't have an OSS badge!"

I found the colonel striding up and down the reception room. For the guard's benefit he turned savagely to me and explained that when he left for the Burma jungles OSS didn't have badges.

The guard ignored him. "Can you identify this man?" he asked me.

It would have been a wonderful opportunity to hood my eyes like Sydney Greenstreet, shrug contemptuously, and say, "The man is evidently an impostor!" since I'd never seen him before in my life. Shelving this impulse, I assured the guard that Colonel Eifler was a bona fide member of OSS and just back from the front. As we were about to leave the guard spotted the colonel's film container.

"What's in that package, sir?" he demanded.

Short-tempered by now, the mighty colonel blasted: "Enough plastic to blow you to hell, and I have a good mind to set it off!" However, he was forced to bow to Army regulations, open the pack, and explain the contents of the reel. Then the guard told me to sign a visitor's pass for one colonel and metal container, and we proceeded to the MO room.

Here for three hours we listened as the colonel described the founding and work of 101. To me the most fascinating part of his exploits dealt with the Kachins who lived in North Burma. These people, when the colonel arrived there, lived an autonomous, simple village existence and wanted no part of the white man's war. It was up to the colonel to change their minds, which he did by actual legerdemain, tricks of magic he had found handy during his work on the Mexican border patrol when he needed an innocent means of striking up acquaintances.

Armed with his .45 and magician's kit, he started out to recruit Kachins. Through native runners he sent word to the various village headmen that he was arriving to perform feats of magic for them. And while Jap patrols were seeking out the mad American colonel, sometimes only a few miles away, Eifler set up his show in the village square. He made coins disappear. Flowers grew out of pots before the eyes of the astonished audience. He drew cigarettes from the ear of the headman. Upon the symbolic climax, the colonel claimed most of his recruits. He fired his .45 into the air, and from the sky dropped a headless miniature Jap soldier. Through the interpreter he explained that this was a sign that the Kachins should join forces with the great white father in fighting the Japs. Eifler's prestige and his groundwork in North Burma enabled 101 to build up an army of 8,500 natives by the end of the Burma campaigns.

After the lecture the room was darkened, and we viewed the first films of this top-secret base in Assam. The heat had spoiled some of the shots, but we could distinguish the rolling, mushroomlike trees in the jungle photographed through the wing struts of the colonel's own L-5. The plane flew low over even, well trimmed tea plants, and we saw a neat compound where the secret 101 base was. Hidden behind the façade of tea plantation houses, GI's bare to their waists were instructing Kachins to assemble machine guns.

"The Japs would give a lot to see these films," Eifler commented.

The camera took us inside a thatched *basha*. Here men were poring over a map, locating a secret air-drop area where supplies were needed by an advance unit.

The next shot showed a camouflaged C–47 on a secret air strip. Natives were loading her with cylindrical tins of supplies, drop chutes and ammunition. The plane took off, and we were in the cabin now, watching the Kachins and Americans slip into their parachutes.

"It's their first jump," Eifler said when the doors opened and there was nothing below but jungle. The plane crossed what looked like a low valley, and on a bluff far to the north was a distinct white **T**. The drop clearing was defined only by the marker; without it the jungle appeared to engulf everything in its tide of trees. The jump-master began to call out numbers.

"Watch carefully," the colonel interrupted. "You'll see one chute that didn't open. We lost that boy."

There was a shot of a twisting figure plummeting earthwards to be crushed under the weight of a parachute that should have borne him to safety. It was the last frame on the reel. Someone flashed the lights on, and we were all back in Washington. Only the colonel seemed an anachronism.

When he departed, an unusual silence fell over the MO office. Eifler had been out there; he had seen Japanese soldiers; he had set up an intelligence net. His work was vital, of use to someone.

Going back to my desk, I took a good look at the map. Washington, I noted, was about 15,000 miles away from the nearest Jap outpost. So were the materials we were producing, I decided, looking at the long rows of filing cabinets in the major's office. Was his office, then, a graveyard, and were those green steel coffins the official repositories for MO ideas, alphabetically buried under such headstones as "Rangoon, Rumor Plan for" or "Shanghai, Infiltration of"?

My question was answered by the major's own redheaded secretary when I passed her desk. She was in the process of ordering still another cabinet, and she turned to me aggressively as if I were partially responsible.

"There won't be any more room left in this building if you people continue to produce material," she scolded. "If I were the major I'd just join the Marines and get away from all this."

Her glance took in the large outer office, where I could see Tokie at work, probably assassinating the emperor for the hundredth time in a spectacular palace plot on paper. Near by was Jane, drawing pictures of Indonesians under the heel of Jap militarists or, possibly, Jap militarists under the heel of a united Indonesian underground. Lucy Starling and Dr. Holladay had their heads together, busy on rumors that the Japs were going to steal the precious Emerald Buddha from Bangkok. And there was my own typewriter, in which a half-written leaflet on surrender waved gaily like a white flag.

On an impulse, I decided to take up this problem of Sisyphean endeavor with the major, face to face. Ignoring the MO paraphrase that hell hath no fury like a channel spurned, I walked past the major's aide and confronted him in his den. Away from the group, he suddenly looked terribly tired. There were blue circles under his eyes, and his ashtray was studded with half-smoked butts. My entrance surprised him, but he managed a smile.

"Well, Betty, what's on your mind?" he asked.

I told him, and he sat for some time before answering. Then he began:

"Can you keep a secret?"

I nodded and fervently hoped that I could. He continued in a quiet, authoritative voice:

"I have been told to recruit personnel for five major rear echelon bases—New Delhi, Colombo, Calcutta, Chungking, and Künming. I have also been ordered to recruit field teams and mobile printing units to be sent into Burma, Southeast Asia, and China. We'll be able to send a first small unit into Burma soon because of the work Eifler has done in setting up a detachment which reports to an American general. But 101 is still pretty small, and the emphasis in Burma is placed on sabotage and intelligence.

"In India the head of the British intelligence there, not so very long ago, told General Donovan that the door to India was closed to OSS. To this the general replied, 'We'll come through the transom.' That's exactly what we're doing. Infiltrating slowly. We aren't too welcome, as you can see. It's a British theater, interested in the lost British empire on the periphery of India.

"In China we are committed to work with the Generalissimo's secret service chief, General Tai Li, under a pact known as the Sino-American Cooperative Organization signed back in April of 1943. We must take orders from the Chinese, and they are not too happy to have us snooping around behind the lines, possibly uncovering certain things about Communist and central government relations that would prove embarrassing. So I'm marking time. I'm trying to keep everyone's morale up, and it's tough. All I can ask is that you have faith . . ."

Suddenly I felt very devoted to the major. It was the first time the veil of red tape had been withdrawn from the military. It was comforting to discover that even generals had their problems.

CHAPTER TWO

CLOAK AND DAGUERREOTYPES

Most government agencies have a quiet dullness about them set to the labored, slow pace of government work. The Office of Strategic Services, however, never seemed to settle into the dignified boredom of the Washington white-collar strata.

Jane and I often tried to type our organization, but with little luck. OSS was volatile, fluid, heavily endowed, beloved of President Roosevelt; it possessed an imagination which generated right from the blue-eyed Irish major general in charge of it; it was charged with excitement because of the very nature of the work; yet it was staffed with amateurs like ourselves who were told to use common sense in carrying out directives. The personnel office once boasted that every nationality and every occupation was listed on its pay roll; there were also members of the Canine Corps, carrier pigeons, and an elephant on the records.

We had been told during indoctrination that General Donovan regarded the OSS primarily as a central intelligence organization which collected, either directly or through existing government agencies at home or abroad, pertinent information concerning enemy countries, the character and strength of their armed forces, their internal economic organization, their principal channels of supply, troop morale, relation to their allies.

The hazardous work assigned to the other colorful operational arms of the organization—the sabotage of enemy installations, organization of guerrilla resistance and waging of irregular warfare—was of secondary importance compared with the main job of gathering intelligence and transmitting it to the proper authorities.

In Washington, the administrative and research offices of OSS sprawled beyond the original five assigned buildings and occupied at least ten additional buildings throughout the Capital to carry out OSS functions. A very high echelon planning group acted as a sort of governor to keep the booming agency on an even keel, and to pass on all programs submitted by the branches. Once a plan was approved, all necessary equipment, such as ammunition, agent radio sets or field presses, was furnished by the OSS Services Branch; personnel were checked by the medical and screened by the psychological clinics. Everything pointed towards getting a few men into the field. It was a quiet process, like osmosis, once the men reached their destination. They flowed through a porous underground to mix behind enemy lines, and from that time on they were bound by only the invisible radio impulses to Washington headquarters.

There were times, however, when both Jane and myself became slightly cynical. There were so many people in Washington headquarters and so few in the field that it was like the elephant laboring to produce a field mouse. (However, we were to learn the wisdom behind our forced sojourn in Washington later, when the seven months' training we received in MO became evident in our more mature efforts in the field.)

In our early attempts to categorize our organization, we established two major listening posts—the ladies' washroom and the ten o'clock coffee line in the cafeteria—either of which might have been profitably tapped by enemy agents or spies from the Washington Merry-Go-Round. I suppose there had to be some escape valves for all the excitement in OSS, and it was hard to go from day to day without mentioning some phase of work to someone. It was like holding a Quaker meeting, Jane once said, when everyone was bursting to blab.

In the washroom we learned extraneous bits of gossip, usually about the movements of OSS people to overseas posts. From the same sources we also heard colorful rumors about famous personalities hired by OSS. An alert secretarial staff was always spotting such people as Jumping Joe Savoldi of Notre Dame and Actor Sterling Hayden at the same lunch table. Rumors that Marlene Dietrich had been sighted were as regular as MacArthur communiqués. One young giddy had been taking supersecret dictation from Movie Director John Ford, head of the OSS Field Photographic Unit, and had been warned to make only one copy of the report and to forget what she'd typed.

"And do you know what I said to him?" she confided to the ladies in the washroom. "I looked him straight in the eye and said, 'Commander Ford, who do you think I am—the Informer?' "

By far the most remunerative post of the two was the cafeteria at coffee time where Jane and I did our best listening between the hours of ten and noon. To further classify the organization, we divided the employees of OSS we met in the cafeteria at this time into three groups: the sip-and-runners; the ten-minute tasters; and malingerers, like ourselves. It was as good a way as any to classify people, we figured, and we were learning that everything had to be classified. We excused our own absenteeism on the ground that we were able to do our best MO plotting over the coffee cup. Too, by talking with other employees of OSS, we slowly began to piece the work of the organization together like a large, colorful, and somewhat crazy quilt.

Among our favorite sip-and-runners was pretty, intelligent, and efficient Margaret Griggs, one of the first women hired by OSS. When we met her she was in charge of all secret intelligence files, but her spare time was used up in recruiting women specialists for key jobs. This chore was a holdover from the days when General Donovan turned the entire business of hiring women over to Maggie with the vague injunction that she was to "get the right types to work in OSS."

"In the beginning," so the legend runs, "there was Maggie Griggs."

As the Eve of OSS, Maggie had many anecdotes to tell of the early days in the Garden when there were only thirty-five men and two women. Now there were two thousand women and five times that many men, and a large personnel office had taken over the routine job of hiring *en masse*.

However, in the days when quality counted, Maggie worked on the theory that the general's idea of the right-type OSS girl was a cross between a Smith graduate, a Powers model, and a Katie Gibbs secretary. This type, she soon discovered, was particularly difficult to obtain because at that time the WAVES, WACS, and Marines were offering fancy uniforms and high adventure to the girls of America. Maggie, on the other hand, couldn't even tell her recruits what they were hired to do.

"So I took the women where I found them—and the first batch came right out of the Social Register," she told us. "Much of the work required a knowledge of a European language and familiarity with terrain in France where many of them had vacationed. These women didn't have to know office routine, so I had to hire civil service girls who did. The CAF's handled the steno work. The outcome, as you might imagine, was an undeclared war between the CAF's and the Café societies!"

After Maggie's explanation, Jane and I began to understand why the columnists had taken to referring to OSS as Oh So Social and Oh So Snobbish. However, General Donovan later defended the blue-bloods he hired—Roosevelts, Morgans, Vanderbilts—as well as Maggie's café society women, on the ground that Park Avenue could produce as good second-story men as the Bowery.

Maggie assured us that the class rivalry was all but forgotten now, and that the work itself had become a common leveler. She still maintained that the best women leaders came from the upper strata, from the groups accustomed to managing large social gatherings or benefits, who were sure of themselves and who didn't care about money.

"But those early feuds! Made the Kilkenny cats look like pikers. You should have seen the fur fly when one of our dowagers blue-penciled a twelve-page report, changing a little steno's Afrika Korps to Africa Corps and muttering about the girl being illiterate!"

It was the stress of her special recruiting work that made a sip-and-runner out of Maggie. She seldom became flustered, but one particular morning I saw her in an unusual state of perturbation. This is what Maggie had to do that morning in her own words:

"The Message Center wants a girl math shark. Research and Analysis wants an expert on Guam. A colonel in Africa wired for a combination secretary-seamstress to sew agents' clothes so they'll look 'of the country.' Visual Presentation wants an artist to help decorate the London war room. Cartography wants a girl with steady hands to retrace lines on captured maps. And MO, bless them, just called up for a lady varityper. What, may I ask, is a varityper?" Then she was off with half a cup of coffee still steaming.

Another sip-and-runner was one of General Donovan's secretaries who always entered the cafeteria in a rush, sat rigidly before her coffee, as if her dictation pad were perched on her knee, gulped hastily, and was off like a wild thing. The general, we gathered, was a hard taskmaster. From bits of information which she charily dropped, we also discovered that he was an avid baseball fan, that he had one more medal than General MacArthur, and that one of his code names was Sea Biscuit!

"And he certainly lives up to his code name," she informed us. "He only sleeps four hours. The rest is work, work, work. He reads a page of a book at a glance—photostatic mind. He can remember the names of everyone from the janitor to the Chinese consul, and he even pronounces them right! He wears out five stenos a day, dictating without a stop, composing on his feet. And in the middle of a sentence, if a corporal in the Canine Corps should walk in for a friendly chat on dog training, the general would drop everything he was doing and listen to the man as if he were President Roosevelt himself."

Once, over what we considered for her a particularly long and intimate cup of coffee, the general's secretary drew out a carefully folded piece of paper from the inside of her wallet as gingerly as if it contained the name of the agent assigned to assassinate Hitler. At the top of the small piece of note-pad paper was printed, "The White House Executive Offices." In the center of the page was scribbled, "OK—FDR."

"It was in the general's wastebasket," she confided, "attached to a memorandum the general sent the President. I'm keeping it as one of my prize souvenirs from OSS." (I put this bit of incidental intelligence down as one of the many things I learned at OSS as part of my general education—what happened to F. D. R.'s memoranda!)

Perhaps because he was one of the most restless executives in Washington and was always boarding planes for all parts of his far-flung empire from England to China, few people on the campus had a very clear picture of the man who ran OSS.

Those among his inner zone of confidantes swore that he was one of the men of the century.

Hadn't the President placed great faith in his ability when he sent the general to Great Britain in 1940, ostensibly to study the German Fifth Column, but actually to observe how the British would withstand the blitz? And hadn't the general returned to tell America that the Germans couldn't lick England, when almost everyone else believed the contrary?

Wasn't the general one of the first advocates of the Mediterranean as a theater of war to "pull the Germans off balance" on the continent, and hadn't he made the first negotiations with Weygand to establish American fifth columns in Morocco, Algiers, and Tunisia?

Wasn't the general, then, one of the few Americans who knew what modern warfare meant, foresaw its global character, and realized how totally unprepared we were?

And wasn't the general one of the few men capable of conceiving and implementing OSS when the President told him to start from scratch and organize an intelligence clearing house for those some ten million words of strategic intelligence that poured into Washington daily from scores of government sources?

These were the valid questions posed by the general's close associates who accepted his genius for long-range planning and his ready grasp of broader situations.

There were also complaints, however, from those who stayed behind in Washington and felt that their absentee landlord relegated too much authority to too many people. One area desk head once commented that if the flag at OSS were raised and lowered, like President Roosevelt's, every time the general packed his flight bag, it would require a full-time color guard operating on day and night shifts. And oddly enough, even without the flag, the organization seemed to sense the general's presence at home by the sudden spurt of activity, the signing of papers, the release of personnel to the field which seemed to get blocked like a log jam during his absence.

To me he remained an enigma. I sometimes caught glimpses of him rushing up the steps to his office in a flurry of unheard trumpets, flanked by brief-case-carrying aides. I often wondered why they called him Wild Bill, since his demeanor suggested a benign gentleness, emphasized by an almost bashful smile which was quite disarming. I could sense his immense energy from the way he swung his tall, penguin-shaped body quickly out of a car or led his hovering aides by several lengths down the corridors.

Occasionally the general had sudden impulses, probably harking back to his days with the Fighting 69th in France, and orders would go out to all branches to "dress up" its military personnel, report for inspection or small-arms training. Once I was walking with an MO sergeant, thoroughly unversed in the ways of the military, when the general's sleek, black two-star limousine passed us. The sergeant failed to salute. The vehicle stopped. A naval aide leaped out, took down the sergeant's name, branch, and serial number, and popped back into the car. Neither of us saw the general (who actually wasn't in the car), and nothing ever happened to the GI; but the incident so startled the sergeant that for days afterwards he saluted every car that drove by, including taxis.

Once General Donovan paid the MO offices a surprise inspection visit, marching briskly through the door as his sergeant yelled " 'Ten-n-ntion" into the startled staff room. A few of our lads had the presence of mind to leap to attention; others ignored the procedure until they saw the two stars twinkling from the visitor's shoulder and bashfully arose. I didn't know whether to salute or stand with hand over heart or sit quietly like a lady. In the end I was so flustered I forgot to shake hands with him as he passed my desk and peered at my work. I could see that photostatic mind of his making a mental note of the message on the paper in my typewriter that started out, "Dear Mother and Dad."

One of our longest established friends among the ten-minute coffee tasters was Sergeant Timothy Horan, the self-styled "man most likely to be broken to a corporal any day now." Tim was a Message Center mole who spent long hours in an underground office coding and decoding classified messages to and from the field.

"We are the lifeblood of OSS," Tim would tell us, striking a heroic pose. "If we snafu, you'll all bog down and fall apart!"

When we asked him why, he sank into a "security silence," ordered another cup of coffee, and hedged:

"We know what Eisenhower has for dinner. We know why Madame Chiang Kai-shek is feuding with the G'issimo. We know the name of the girl agent in Belgium whose work is referred to as Operation Mattress! We even know where gas coupons are printed. And we keep our mouths shut."

A thorough pixy but a brilliant one, Tim had been one of the many young men spirited out of college by selective service and picked up by OSS because of his I.Q. and his precocity for things cryptographic.

"All men in the Message Center, with rare exceptions, were recruited from Dartmouth," Tim revealed. "At first they were suspicious of Harvard men like me. To get the job, I had to sing three choruses of Eleazar Wheelock and wear green undershorts. The girls who work with us are mostly from Smith or Holyoke. They must have a lot of gals at those schools who do nothing but work crossword puzzles or play bridge or chess. Those kind make the best crypt teasers."

Cryptography required a special type of mind adept at working out puzzles. It took Tim about three weeks to master the code systems developed by OSS, which were rated as some of the most complicated ever devised during the war.

"No one outside the chosen few is ever allowed in the Message Center, of course. It's the most top-secret place in OSS—it's underground and the crypto equipment there is worth well over $500,000."

Tim admitted that girls were better at the long year-in, year-out grind at the center than men, who were subconsciously influenced by desires to leave State-side office work for overseas duty.

When we asked him about the pressure of handling "hot stuff" in the confines of what he called the Black Chamber, he shook his head gloomily.

"You develop a terrific sense of responsibility. Look at me! I'm tongue-tied at cocktail parties because I'm afraid if I say something interesting it will be from a cable I've read, and not from the papers.

One gal in the office mesmerizes herself when she types up cables. She says she never remembers a thing she types! And the married men are afraid of talking in their sleep! One lad says he'll never be able to go to another Dartmouth prep-school football game. Some of our code keys are based on their songs!"

One of our more serious-minded ten-minute quaffers was Julia McWilliams, who worked in a special office called Registry. Julia said very little about her job more than that she had the "top-secret twitch" from filing so many secrets from so many people. Registry, as Jane and I gathered, was a sort of OSS brain bank into which went the distilled reports of the Research and Analysis branch; the real names of agents operating behind the lines; itemized amounts of expenditure for agent work, pay-offs, and organization of undergrounds; locations of OSS detachments around the world and implemented plans of operations of all branches bearing the Joint Chiefs of Staff stamp of approval.

Julia, we agreed, was just the type of sensible, high-minded woman with a highly developed security sixth sense who could be counted upon to conceal, and not reveal, top-secret information. The most we were ever able to pry from Julia was the pertinent fact that "eyes alone" messages from one high echelon officer to another were filed in folders marked with yellow tabs.

By far our favorite malingerer was Jan, a charming German-American MO type who was one of the few persons left in the European branch in Washington. Jan had a sweet smile which lighted up his long, tender face with a neon glow. His voice was soft, and he had a charming continental habit of getting us coffee refills—which our American confreres did not, operating on the assumption that we were all on the single standard in the cafeteria line.

Jan always greeted us with a slight bow. "Girls, girls, I'm glad to see you," he would say with a slight accent. "I've had a wonderful MO morning."

He always had astounding announcements to make at coffee. Sometimes it was a rumor wired that morning to London about Hitler's latest epileptic fit. Once it was an exposé to the Germans in France of a series of "surrender passes" which the Italian soldiers were printing for themselves in Italy.

One morning he announced pleasantly that he had "sterilized half the male population in Berlin" in a medical leaflet dropped by our planes during a recent raid on the German capital.

"In the confusion, the Germans couldn't tell who dropped the leaf-lets," he explained. "They were copied from formats of other infor-mation throwaways produced by the Nazi medical corps, but our 'black' ones informed the Germans that the nervous reaction to Allied pattern bombing was causing sterility and ordered the men to go to bed immediately after the raid with their wives. 'If nothing happens, see your doctor at once,' we warned them. Then we went into a lot of medical hocus-pocus about what happens to the reproductive sys-tems through terror, malnutrition, and the new-type Allied bomb."

As he talked, Jan brought the fingertips of his right hand together with those of his left hand, forming a digital arch upon which he rested his chin. His eyes were usually half closed, as if he could better reach for English words by inward concentration. There was some-thing of a benign Mephistopheles about him. (Years later we were to hear that Jan was one of the MO civilians employed to "smoke out" the German soldiers in American uniforms when von Rundstedt at-tempted his last counteroffensive against the Allies at the Bulge. Jan had reportedly captured one of the German MO agents sent to de-moralize American troops near Bastogne, when he posed as a fellow German spy and innocently asked the direction to American head-quarters in German. He was probably smiling softly as the Nazi agent answered his $64 question and got a bullet in the skull.)

On one particularly bright summer morning Jan was awaiting us to say that he had just received some top-secret MO recordings, Operation Pancake, from London which he wanted us to hear. But since it was all classified, we must first obtain our major's permission. Jane and I assured him it would only be a matter of minutes, and started out in search of our branch chief.

The major's adjutant informed us that we could find him at an informal meeting, and suggested we go to the room, send a message in, and get our answer. We had already dashed down two flights of steps in the MO building when Jane discovered she had forgotten to take down the name of the building. We were both positive, however, that it was the Administration Building.

The guard at this building passed us when we insisted that we must get in touch with the head of Morale Operations at once. We de-scended a stairway which was plainly marked Restricted Area and found ourselves at the beginning of a long, badly lighted corridor. At the farther end a muted whir sounded like a stutter of a teletype machine. We proceeded cautiously but never once doubted that the major would be located, like the White Rabbit, at the end of the tunnel. We followed a girl ahead of us into a brilliantly lighted room, ventilated by a single blower, where some thirty persons at tables were working on what seemed to be crossword puzzles. No one looked up as we entered, and we passed into a smaller room where a girl and two men were seated at the teletype machines.

The sudden realization of where we were struck both Jane and me at the same time. We pivoted sharply and began to walk rapidly out of the Message Center—the inner sanctum which according to Tim had never been penetrated. Although no one paid any attention to us, I was as nervous as an enemy agent might have been if someone suddenly had given him the combination to General Marshall's safe. I tried not to look at the crypt pads and kept my eyes on Jane's blond head and slinking shoulders, directly in front of me. We reached the door just as a man in khaki, with a very familiar, pale, bespectacled face walked in. He gave Jane a piece of paper, saying, "Will you handle this immediately?" turned, and was gone before either of us realized that he was General Donovan's naval aide.

Jane held up a thoroughly illegible memo, and at the bottom was a larger, illegible scrawl which we recognized as "Donovan" (the general seldom signed his first name).

My only thought was to give ourselves up to the first responsible person we saw; but suddenly out of the glare of lights loomed the familiar red head of Timothy Horan. The next second he was pushing us unceremoniously out the door.

In the safety of the hallway he gasped: "My God, girls, do you realize where you've just been?" His tone implied more amazement than anything else at our ability to penetrate the secret Message Center.

Then Jane held up the Donovan communiqué. "General Donovan's aide thought I worked here," she explained.

Tim snatched the paper from her, glancing at the signature, and cautioned us not to mention what it said. When Jane told him we couldn't decipher it anyway, he nodded.

"Very few people can. We have a special decoding team that works on the general's handwritten messages. Even then we have to send back the typed copies for him to verify. He has the hastiest hand-writing . . ."

That day was marked with more security violations than any two normal people amassed during their entire stay with the organization. We next blundered into another restricted area in a second basement in South Building, guided by the familiar clatter of a rotary press.

"Maybe he's down here producing leaflets," I told Jane as we walked into a room where a grimy GI in T shirt was reading a galley proof still wet with ink.

"You girls want proofs?" he asked, thrusting his copy toward us.

This time we couldn't read what he gave us because it was printed in German, but Jane had just enough smattering of the language to explain that it was some sort of manual on arson for German factory workers.

We told the man, after we had carefully perused the proof, that we were looking for the MO branch chief. He grabbed back the copy, muttering something about "expecting some German language people to read proof."

"There isn't any major down here anyway, unless he's in the darkroom next door," he added. "But I doubt it because they're developing some agent passport photos and they wouldn't even let General Donovan in."

Before he got around to asking how we got in, we fled up the stairs and into the sunlight. This time we phoned for the correct building and were informed by an icy adjutant that it was the MO building all the time!

Again we had the nervous feeling of violating another secure area because the major was attending a meeting in a basement room where there was no secretarial anteroom. An armed guard sat at a small table directly outside the door, reading a comic magazine.

"Just knock," he told us. "If they want you in there they'll tell you. If they don't you can cool your heels out here."

We knocked. Someone inside growled "Come in," and we timidly opened the door. The room was crowded with officers around a long table upon which had been piled an odd assortment of weapons. Our major spotted us almost immediately and invited us in. A few quizzical eyebrows were raised, but the major glibly put everyone at ease.

"Show these MO girls some of the gadgets, and get their reaction," he suggested.

A pleasant, round-faced captain at the end of the table reached for a .22 to which had been attached an elongated black tube at the end of the muzzle.

"New OSS silencer," he told us with a certain note of pride in his voice. "Shoot the .22, and the only sound you hear is a click."

Then he produced what looked like an ordinary pen-and-pencil desk set in an onyx stand.

"This is a device we worked out to protect agents who are unarmed and who might be surprised by a sudden visit from the Gestapo. The pencil contains one bullet and is fired at close range, so."

He held the deadly instrument close to us in much the same casual manner as a professor might point a pencil while talking.

"It goes off with a slight noise. We haven't perfected it enough yet to guarantee against backfire. As often as not your hand is shot off."

We tried to look pleased with the lethal little toy, but I for one felt a surge of relief when he replaced it in the stand.

"Then there are the usual run of limpets to attach to sides of ships, vehicles, and tanks to blow them up. And here's a time pencil we developed that is placed in the cargo of ships and timed to go off at sea. It is fairly effective, as it consumes itself so that no one can trace the cause of the fire."

We handled the narrow tube he threw across the table to us with dainty hands, wondering when something in the room would detonate and blow us all up to the third floor.

"Now here's something in a noisemaker we call the Hedy Lamarr," he grinned, holding up a round object about the size of a lemon. "Agents use it to distract attention if they're in a tight spot. Or if they just want to create panic in a theater or an office. Listen, and you'll see what I mean."

To our consternation he pulled the cap out, tossed the mechanism into a wastebasket and there was a split second of silence, just long enough for me to inch in a quick prayer. Suddenly there was the long screech of a falling bomb, a loud explosion, and a flash of yellow flame, which expended itself in the metal wastebasket.

"Just like an air raid, don't you think, girls?"

We nodded in quick agreement, and I wondered why the racket hadn't caused a major stir on Capitol Hill. (Later I discovered that the room was soundproof.)

"Here's something you girls might find useful out in the Orient where they say 'face' is everything," he continued, as if producing a particular plum just for us.

"It's a nasty little vial we've nicknamed 'Who, me?' It contains an odor about ten times as offensive as a skunk's. Simply splash it on an enemy official in a crowd, and he can't appear in public for days. The scent clings to his clothing and his person. Imagine what would happen if someone squirted some of this on Tojo?"

I found myself thinking rather nastily that if any agent ever got that close to Tojo he should use a long knife, but I remained silent in the midst of so much sudden death.

After several other demonstrations, we finally obtained the permission slip from the major. We backed out of the room, thanking the captain and telling him how exciting it had all been; but no one else looked up as we left. The group had gone back to their searching examinations of the weapons with all the ardor of a small boy over his first electric train set.

By the time we returned to the cafeteria it was noontime, and an S-shaped luncheon line was winding sluggishly around tables like a large tapeworm. Jan, we surmised, had been evicted. We tracked him to his office, where we found him chuckling over a newspaper clipping.

"This should make our security office turn handsprings." He tossed us a story from a Washington paper which reported that the Italian underground was seething with revolt, based on an anti-Fascist radio program which American monitors had picked up in New York.

"We've monitored Italo Balbo again," Jan informed us. "That's our MO black radio gang in Tunis with Eugene Warner. They have a hotheaded Italian named Salerno working for the station whom they keep locked up in a room writing anti-Mussolini speeches. They beam the programs over a portable transmitter to the Italian mainland. Italians who hear the speeches have become devoted to Salerno and his bombast. They think he's a disciple of General Balbo, the liberal whom Mussolini banished from Rome. The ironic thing about Salerno —he's a renegade Fascist himself. He'd do anything to make a dishonest dollar!"

Jan began to sift through a stack of sixteen-inch recordings stamped: "Operation Pancake—Top Secret."

"You know how black radio works, of course. It's based on the same MO principles of deception as the forged order, the falsified document. It can be simple 'jamming' or the use of ghost voices to spoil an important enemy broadcast through artificially created static on the same wave length. It can be a Freedom Station, supposedly manned by discontented rebels within enemy territory. It can be a program of slanted news, slipped in so close to the regular enemy wave length as to be confused with the genuine program."

Jan lifted the lid of a play-back machine and began to change a needle.

"These records I'm going to play will illustrate how MO can be the handmaiden to white propaganda—and how admirably adapted to this technique is the feminine mind! Who knows better than a woman how to use the poison darts of slander—the razor-edged rumor? Break a man with the twist of a phrase! Change an attitude of mind with a well placed snicker!"

I bristled a bit at this burden he hinted we all had inherited from Eve. I still harbored the newspaper reporter's disdain for the high-pressure advertising man, and saw in MO the fine tracery of his handiwork—packed propaganda designed to foist products upon the fifteen-year-old mind by a cheap use of emphasis, repetition, and the singing commercial.

"Women aren't the only experts," I argued. "Advertising has gone to war, Jan. Repeat a plausible falsehood until it sounds true—place emphasis on 'our side' with plenty of fanfare for the people running the show—"

Jan nodded affably, but he didn't argue.

"You know, sometimes I imagine myself floating on a pink cloud. Down below there are two wars going on: one, in the dirt and mud where men are shooting it out; the other, in men's brains, where words and ideas are used in black or white ways to gain control of minds and emotions. The second war employs morale-sapping techniques, heavy barrages of facts and figures. You'll find lies, too, buried like hidden mines in the verbiage—"

Then Jan told us how black radio warfare between the British and the Axis began back in 1940 when they started operating a medium-wave-length station, Sender Nord, which broadcast unexpurgated war news to Germans who presumably wanted to get away from the Goebbels presentation. The next year they changed their cover, or fictional *raison d'être*, and the station became a one-man show dominated by an imaginary corporal named Gustav Siegfried Eintz, a foul-mouthed, earthy Falstaffian character who slandered the German hierarchy with half-truths and cabaret gossip picked up by agents on the continent. After Gustav had ranted for about eight months the British decided to expand and again change cover. In 1943 they obtained a $200,000 Lend-Lease transmitter which blanketed the air over Europe. The new station, Soldatensender West (abbreviated in the best government style to MB), operated in conjunction with a short-wave station carrying the same programs, known as Deutscher Kurz-wellensender Atlantic, which used slanted newscasts and speeches.

Director of MB, Sefton Delmar, was a legendary character among Allied propagandists around the world. Delmar (before the war, the German political expert for the London *Daily Express*) spoke flaw-less German and was intimately acquainted with Nazi leaders. Around the MB studios he was known as "The Beard" because of the untrimmed whiskers which grew down his chest. He weighed about two hundred pounds, was six feet four inches tall, and allowed his expansive paunch to flow out and over the loose dressing gown he invariably wore on duty.

The production methods used in black radio followed a fairly universal pattern. Latest intelligence—including German magazines, newspapers, radio intercepts, and prisoner-of-war interrogations—was rushed daily to Delmar and his experts, who sifted through them and formulated a program of both "spot" and long-range thought warfare. Propaganda was directed against the German Army, Navy, and Luftwaffe on the lower echelon level where petty graft, inefficiency, and war weariness were charged. As the war progressed propaganda was later leveled at the German home front, at small-town officials, black marketeers, and slackers.

"OSS has been working with MB during the past year through Operation Pancake," Jan explained. "We supplement the heavy British subversive propaganda with music and barbed entertainment —the way American radio sells commercials with music and laughs."

He turned to a wall map of Great Britain over his desk and pointed out several red-tipped pins stuck in an area roughly ten miles from London.

"This pin here is where Pancake's staff is located, in a guarded area —as British security calls places in England where secret government projects are located.

"The village is Newton-Longville. People who live in districts such as this, which borders the twenty-five miles of wooded, hilly country near the Duke of Bedford's estate, become aware over a passage of time that no evacuees from bombed-out cities are billeted with them, that no one can rent in the neighborhood. Knowing this, they develop a special sense of security and tacitly refrain from discussing what goes on in the neighborhood."

By such security innuendos Jan commanded our silence, flattered us with what we hoped was his belief in our ability to perpetrate MO, and at the same time enlightened us on what was being done in other theaters.

Pancake's MO staff, we learned, lived in a thatched cottage called "The Grange," a small cell of the much larger mother organization of MB offices and studios which nestled in camouflaged security against a pastoral English countryside.

Members of the staff, in addition to three cats and a French poodle, were the American script writers, Ira Ashley and Charles Kebbe.

Then there was an Irish boogiewoogie artist, Pat O'Neil, who adapted orchestral arrangements for the Grange singers with the help of a German prisoner-of-war violinist, Mr. Zimmerman. The German expert and adviser was Rudolf Bernauer, a former entrepreneur, and his wife was hired as Grange chaperon. Corporal Manny Segal, a former sound-effects man, was the Most Indispensable Man in the cottage, filling in with everything from bird calls to an imitation of a bass viol.

Stars of the show were four pretty girls whom Kebbe and Ashley recruited in London entertainment spots. Trudy Binar, one-time Miss Czechoslovakia, who was a motion picture star of some repute on the continent, sang German songs with a saucy Czech accent that Germans enjoyed, as Americans enjoy a singer with French or Latin accent. Elisabeth Carroca, an Austrian *femme fatale* with strawberry curls and a tanned skin, was billed on Pancake programs as "Lisel, the Moonlight Madonna," because of her sultry voice. A pert little redhead with a flair for comedy, Hildy Palmer, was discovered in a chorus line of the musical "Something for the Boys" and was booked in all Pancake comedy roles. (She made such a hit with Talent Scout Kebbe that he later married her.) Agnes Bernelle, daughter of the Bernauers and a favorite on the Hungarian and British stages, was signed up as "Vicki, the Girl with the Pin-Up Voice."

Jan told us that since the Grange artists could produce only two recordings a day for MB, and one Music Hall program a month, their work was supplemented in New York, where Marlene Dietrich, Sig Arno, Jarmila Novotna, and other artists recorded cleverly twisted lyrics under the vague impression that the songs were either for OWI broadcasts or for the use of the Special Services branch of the Army when it invaded Germany and took over Nazi stations.

"Here's the way they put over songs to the German Army," Jan explained, switching on the play-back.

The room was filled with music—a Glen Miller recording of "Stardust." We all sat back and listened until somewhere in the middle of the recording a husky German voice began to sing the lyrics.

"The American vocalist was dubbed out, and Carroca's voice was slipped in for the re-recording. If you have a German audience, you have to have German words, Petrillo or no Petrillo," Jan reminded us.

"And now for Vicki—she's her own disc jockey. She's so popular with the soldiers that she actually received fan mail through an agent drop in a neutral country! Her greatest single achievement was bringing about the surrender of a Nazi U-boat captain who heard her program when she accidentally announced that the captain's fiancée had married another man! Of course it wasn't true, but the captain was so discouraged—he'd been out at sea for months and had been on the run—that he surfaced and surrendered. He said Vicki's program was the straw that broke the camel's back! On this disc she is telling the German soldiers to forget how badly the war is going and to relax and listen to their requests—all of which are nostalgic, homesick pieces sung by Carroca."

Vicki was supplied with a mythical mailbag which seemed to produce anything she wanted it to. Her first bit of MO was performed on "that brave little garrison near Arras" whose commanding officer, Vicki had just been informed in a letter from Essen, was about to become a father. Jan explained that part of this information had been obtained from a prisoner interrogation. It was learned that the commander at Arras was from Essen. Morale at Arras was low because the men stationed there had not been granted home leave for over two years. When Vicki's announcement is made, the men will presumably wonder how their commanding officer wangled leave to go home and have a baby, the translation explained. (Jan failed to mention the effect the news would have on the C.O.)

Vicki then plunged the knife in again and turned it slightly. She read a letter from a mother who had been unable to contact her son on the Italian front because of the complete collapse of the postal system "along with everything else." The German mother wanted Vicki to reassure her son that those rumors about the Russians being in the suburbs of Berlin were unfounded.

Vicki used actual names and locations of soldiers. She also had access to the vast MB files of home-town German papers, obituary notices, wedding and engagement announcements, and other information that added the flavor of authenticity to her work.

We next heard selections from a Grange Music Hall production in which the Pancake artists became a group of village amateurs playing for a German garrison.

The MB announcer ended a news program to say that he was now transferring controls to a small town somewhere in Germany. There might be technical delays, he warned, as he asked Herr Bürgermeister to "come in." After some well placed static Mr. Bernauer was heard:

". . . and we are proud of the spirit of our men who may soon have to give up their lives for the Fatherland . . ."

The show was crisp with slanted entertainment and barbed jokes.

Hildy gave a short speech to reassure the German *Fräulein* back home that their men were having a fine time with the girls at the front. Carroca sang a song about wealthy Germans who were deserting the country, taking with them their fortunes and leaving the unfortunate poor to the bombings. The program finished with a throaty, lonesome love song by Carroca that didn't need any translation. Even in Jan's unlovely Washington office the music conjured up honeysuckle and moonlight, and I was suddenly glad *I* wasn't a German soldier, crouching in some bombed-out beer parlor listening to Carroca's seductive siren song.

Even Jan sighed as he took the record off. "See how it works?"

The professional quality of Operation Pancake awed me into polite silence. I left for lunch with the feeling that our newly spawned Far East branch could never compete with European MO. After all, on the continent we were fighting people who reacted to the same brand of emotional stimuli as we did. In the Japanese we were dealing with an Oriental people who were exasperated with a Marx Brothers comedy and went into gales of laughter when Clark Gable kissed his leading lady. The Jap coating of Western veneer was not yet dry—and beneath the glazed surface was still the inscrutable East. What sound, basic campaign could MO wage against soldiers like the Japs on Guadalcanal who led a banzai charge yelling: "Down with Babe Ruth!"

I suppose it would have helped to know that just seven months later both Jane and I would be writing copy for a very effective black radio station deep in the Burmese jungles. But on that hot June day there was nothing ahead but the long lunch line at Que Building, and from where I stood I could see that the chocolate fudge cake was already gone.

CHAPTER THREE

TRAINING THE SPLIT PERSONALITY

It takes hot, humid July weather to wilt Washington back to her colorless role of a small-town world capital, spawned in the swampy bottomlands of the Potomac without benefit of culture or tradition. When Constitution Avenue becomes a mirror of heat, and squirrels lie spread-eagle on their bellies panting under the cool White House porte-cochere, the hybrid American city seems to take off her store-bought clothes, unloosen the stays of her corset, and sink into the summer doldrums.

A definite feeling of lassitude clung to me one hot July evening when I left the office and decided to walk home to Georgetown along the Potomac, where a slight breeze usually fanned across the parkway. There was a hush of late sunset on the river, and the quietness was emphasized by an occasional gull's cry which seemed to hang in the summer air as if possessed of shape and texture.

I found myself thinking, with a detached sense of guilt, that the war had been raging on for three Julys now—at a very safe distance from me somewhere over the horizons. The same sun that now colored the Potomac with a coppery brilliance had been slanting into sandy foxholes in the Marianas, and on Mitscher's silent armada bearing down on the Philippines; it would soon light the darkness on the other side of the world where men were burying their dead within the walls of Siena, and soldiers were killing behind the ancient, root-matted hedgerow barricades on Normandy farms.

In the past two months the Far Eastern branch of MO had been busy, sometimes jousting windmills, sometimes producing material of academic interest to field commanders in Burma and China.

The major, who had left for the field late in May, wrote back from China that things were looking up. General Tai Li and the Chinese had agreed to the establishment of a forward base at Foochow with Lieutenant Roy Squires in charge. The British had approved the plan for a small MO unit to operate in Ceylon under a joint psychological warfare board composed of Dutch, British, and Americans. An intelligence gathering unit would also be established for MO in New Delhi, where the headquarters for China-Burma-India were located.

In Washington, the feel of the staff for MO work improved with experience. Black methods used in the European theater were carefully studied and analyzed; the problems of waging thought warfare against the Japanese were discussed constantly, and our thinking was enhanced by prisoner-of-war interrogations which were coming in from MacArthur's theater and from Burma. More and more we began to realize that our big problem with the Jap was to induce him to surrender, to crack through the fanatical indoctrination he had received since childhood.

From a pathetically small amount of intelligence dealing with his ideology and morale, we learned that the Jap believed as doggedly in the doctrine of the Greater East Asia Co-Prosperity Sphere as we did in the Atlantic Charter. He believed that Japan was engaged in a life-and-death struggle, and that the armies of the emperor were champions of the downtrodden Oriental countries which, until now, had been exploited by Western capitalism.

This doctrine made good sense to the Jap, and he wanted to believe it. Western idealism about the Four Freedoms was not geared to his background or culture. Would MO have to wait for an eventual Allied conquest of Asia and ride in on victory when thought warfare could be waged at its best? Or could we undermine the Jap while he still held Asia by playing on his vulnerable emotions and his lack of confidence in Japanese versus American science and production, by turning his puppet peoples against him? We were all anxious to demonstrate the power of MO. It depended now upon the major to arrange the methods of getting our material to the field and disseminating it behind the lines.

The heat that arose from the anachronistic cobblestone streets of Georgetown on this particularly sultry afternoon only intensified the odd combination of torpor and restlessness inside me. I turned off the towpath from the antiquated Chesapeake and Ohio Canal and passed the yellow clapboard house that had once been George Washington's office—the only building I had ever seen in which he worked instead of sleeping. Then I turned the corner from the poplar-colonnaded street toward the little bandbox house where I was living with my aunt.

She was at the front door waiting for me, and something about the way she adjusted her nose glasses suggested that things had not followed their placid course that day.

"The least you could do," she chid as I stumbled for the cellar-coolness of the front parlor with its drawn shades, "would be to tell me that you're leaving next Monday for India!"

I thought the heat had been too much for her; but then I saw that her chin was quivering in genuine distress.

"A strange man phoned from OSS. He wants to rent your room when you go!"

Suddenly the Washington apathy was dissipated. The whole thing began to fall into a familiar OSS pattern. I hurried out to the hall telephone, assuring my aunt that it might be a very clever ruse to clear me out of my room.

The man at the transportation office who answered the phone was sorry, but no confidential information of that sort could be revealed over the wires. Didn't I know that the security office tapped all MO phones on the alert for just such security leaks as I wanted him to make?

Then, *sotto voce*, as if the security office wouldn't catch everything he said, he added: "Just relax. You won't get off Monday anyway. You have to go to school first!"

At the office the next morning, after a sleepless night of tossing and conjecture, I read the cable from the major announcing theater commander approval of "number three air priorities for MacDonald to New Delhi, Foster to Ceylon."

"Of course," the adjutant calmed me down, "you'll have to attend Assessment School, where they'll check on your emotional stability. Then you'll get a three-day course in Far East orientation work and a few added courses in small arms and OSS weapons at the farm. You start your immunizations today, put in for your passport and equipment. And there's a field trip they're thinking about sending you and Foster on down to Richmond . . ."

In the next three weeks, which I spent in the never-never land of OSS Training Schools, my secret dreams of becoming a *femme fatale* were systematically punctured, one by one, and I faced the inflexible truth at the end of my training that I was not the stuff that a Mata Hari was made of, with or without black satin décolleté evening gown. As one instructor put it, I was an open-face-sandwich type, with enough imagination to conceive a plausible MO cover story, but with absolutely no histrionic ability to carry it out as an active agent.

My first dismal failure as the American Girl Spy started when I boarded the train for Richmond, Virginia, to participate in a top-secret student training course "designed to test students in operations of actual value in the field including cipher, clandestine meeting, tailing, interrogating, opinion sampling, and residence search."

My typewritten sheet of secret instructions—reduced to an uncomfortable wad of thick bond paper which pricked tender flesh beneath my brassiere where I had discreetly concealed it—told me that I must arrive at the Broad Street Station in Richmond with an unbreakable cover story, shake any agent who might be detailed to follow me upon arrival and secrete myself somewhere in the city before contacting the head agent at the John Marshall Hotel!

I'd spent hours on a cover story. First I was a Gallup Poll worker. Then I decided in favor of an OPA snooper until I realized I needed some sort of credentials. Next I was a college girl off to write a thesis on Patrick Henry. I finally became an insurance company representative after a happy remark my aunt dropped about a distant cousin she used to have in Richmond named Raphael Green, a journeyman printer who had gone out West some fifteen years ago. She had received Christmas cards from him somewhere in Oregon until about the time of Pearl Harbor. Since then she hadn't heard from him. For all she knew he was dead, and as far as my cover story was concerned, he *was* dead.

Out of the make-believe atmosphere in the MO offices, in a shabby, hot day coach with worn plush seats, little doubts began to sift through my mind like the soot that was sifting through the open windows of the train. What if Raphael were still in Oregon, busy as a beaver every Christmas, sending cards to his journeyman printer friends in Richmond? Maybe he had a wife and eighteen children on the dole. I tried to dismiss my worries by imagining Raphael dead these many years, his body discovered over an old flat-bed press somewhere in Oregon. I was presently aware that an odd sort of schizophrenia was developing in my mind. I was no longer Elizabeth MacDonald, a former newspaper reporter. I was Eileen O'Brien, an insurance agent, looking for the missing kin of one Raphael Green. With this gradual switch of personalities, all sorts of problems arose. What should I do if I met Jane on the train, for instance? Should I ignore her? or maybe slip her a note in a matchbox threatening to expose her to the Dies Committee as a common spy? What if someone were even now "tailing" me from Washington? Perhaps he—somehow I never considered the possibility of a lady tail—was that man in back of me hidden behind the newspapers? He was, I noted ominously, *smoking a large black cigar!*

Once this spy complex started operating, it was impossible to curb. I tried to act nonchalant as I handed the conductor my ticket. What would people around me think if they knew I was about to penetrate Richmond! No one paid the slightest attention, however, as I debarked and plunged into the rather grimy capital of the sovereign state of Virginia. I was still under my self-induced cloak-and-dagger spell when I gave the cab driver the whispered order to take me to the Y.W.C.A.—and hurry! Here, I imagined, I should be safe from male trailers.

Once inside the respectable foyer of the Y with its ubiquitous bulletin boards littered with health programs, I began to relax. The wren-like lady at the desk was so solidly a Helen Hokinson type that under the influence of her absolute congruency I signed my own name to the register and thus immediately jeopardized my cover.

My next security break occurred five minutes later at the telephone, which was firmly anchored to the front desk. After registering, I had just time to call the head agent and announce my presence, according to instructions. He sounded as if he were talking through his nose when he replied:

"Repeat your cover story to me."

I told him about Raphael and then, lowering my voice, admitted signing my own name to the register. The voice then told me to repeat after him the following instructions:

"Obtain locations of all defense plants, radio stations, newspaper offices, water and power systems together with proposed methods of penetrating them."

I muttered the words back to him while I felt like a worm covered by the darting birdlike eyes of the Y.W.C.A. secretary.

"Now repeat the following opinion-sampling question which you are expected to ask during your search for Green: 'Is it fair to ask German-American Bund members to bear arms against their mother country?' "

I tried to race over "German-American Bund," but I knew Madame Sherlock behind me hadn't missed a trick. Then the agent told me to start work first thing in the morning. If anything went wrong, I was to contact him at the John Marshall Hotel.

That evening I skulked around the Y.W.C.A., apprehensively studying a wall map of the city and noting the location of the vital installations. Word, I was certain, had been passed on to the night clerk, a thin, mousy, twitching girl with large horn-rimmed goggles which seemed to follow me like periscopes all over the foyer.

I tucked a rough sketch of target areas and a list of print shops in my purse, hailed a cab, and directed the man to drive slowly around the ironworks. I was working on the theory that the less suspicious you act, the better. As the driver circled the rather ugly edifice for the third time, he turned around to inquire why I didn't want to see something historic, like the state capitol that Jefferson had designed, or the life-sized marble statue of Washington.

"You can get all the dope about the ironworks at the public library," he added brightly.

It took me some time to gather up enough courage to direct the cab to my first print shop, and I faltered as I entered the noisy little building with its familiar smell of ink and click of type. It just wasn't in my nature to dissemble when the nice old foreman ambled toward me from the back room, wiping his hands on his black leather apron, his spectacles stuck on the top of his bald head.

"Howdy, miss," he greeted me affably. "What can I do for you?"

I tried to speak quietly but had to shout against the clatter of the presses.

"I'm from Washington," I fumbled, trying to imply that such a statement might imply something official. "Just want to get some information on an old-timer in the printing trade—Raphael Green. Ever hear of him?"

The man cocked his head quizzically, readjusted his glasses, and exploded:

"Now what's that old coot been up to?"

When I didn't answer from sheer tongue-tied confusion, he continued:

"Why, sure I know Raphael! Odd duck, but right as a huckleberry. He was out West for some time, and then he signed aboard a ship as a printer—set menus and ship's news and things. His boat was torpedoed some place in the Pacific just after Pearl Harbor, and a tanker picked him up in a lifeboat, half dead. He was some hero when he hit Richmond, let me tell you. Saw old Raph the other day, drunk as a hooty owl as usual. Yep, there's an odd one. What's he done, did you say, miss?"

Somehow the truth at this point sufficed. "Didn't do a thing." I explained lamely. "He has a cousin up in Washington who hasn't heard from him in some time and told me to look him up."

At this point I could see no way of introducing the opinion-sampling question about German-American Bund members. I just scribbled down Raphael's address from the foreman, left as quickly as possible through trays of type and odd bits of machinery and arbitrarily nominated Raphael Green the man I least wanted to meet in America.

When I warily knocked on the head agent's hotel room, it slowly swung open a few feet and I found myself staring into the freckled face of Red Crowley. Behind him glowered the square Irish features of Robert Wentworth, a former Boston newspaperman now working in MO. They ushered me in seriously and refused to allow any burst of friendship on my part.

"What happened?" scowled Wentworth.

I explained briefly, and then produced my sketches of the iron-works, which they ignored.

"First you immediately blow your cover," began Red, "and then Foster loses the agent she's trailing when he disappears into the men's lavatory and escapes through the window!"

At that critical moment I was saved by the telephone bell. Red answered it and told somebody that he didn't think Jake's Saloon and Quick Lunch Counter was such a hot idea.

"You can sample the same opinions over a chocolate malt at the drugstore, and you know it," he added testily.

Jane and I spent the next two days correcting student reports and helping Red and Bob with their paper work. During that time we learned something about the Richmond Project.

"We cooperate with Army intelligence officers and sometimes with the FBI, who are training their student agents to pick up suspicious characters," Bob explained.

"We try to do everything possible to point the finger of suspicion at our MO lads. Sometimes Red or I slip the OSS men incriminating cipher messages or plans for defense plants, and then we tip off the Army G-2 to have their students nab our men. We try to make our agents say suspicious things—the way Red did to you when he made you repeat instructions over the phone. In Jane's case, we made her a finger woman to get experience in trailing suspects. The opinion-sampling questions we give are deliberately provocative, designed to arouse the suspicions of even the most lukewarm patriot. We try to get you into trouble, and you try to keep out of it."

Upon my return to Washington from the Richmond Project, I had the uncomfortable feeling that I was in disrepute in the better spy circles, and that guarded whispers preceded me down the corridors of Que Building—"There she goes, the MO type who blew her cover!"

Hence I considered my next training assignment to Assessment School a definite challenge. Assessment (or S) School was a sort of mental clinic, I was informed, in which a group of nationally famous psychologists and psychiatrists screened all candidates for overseas assignments in "live" situations and examinations such as the British War Office Selection Board used at country estate parties to select officer candidates.

"What they try to do out there," our friend Jan told us guardedly when we put the question to him over our morning coffee, "is to explore your personality: What will you do under major pressure? How do you make friends? What situations frighten you? What goes on up here?" And he tapped his forehead solemnly with his coffee spoon.

After talking with Jan, I approached the S School problem with the stubborn resolve that I would be brave and diligent in all legitimate mental or physical exercises, but no Herr Doktor was going to find out what went on in *my* subconscious! I would be on the alert for all sly projective tests that sought to lure hidden repressions out of the cobwebs of my past. If presented with those tricky Rorschach ink blobs and asked what the shapeless forms conjured up, I'd discreetly prune all my answers of any possible Freudian connotation. If asked about sex—well, perhaps I could think up something as apt as that schoolmarm did who asked: "What business is it of S School whether I've slept with a man? I can still spell, can't I?"

Unfortunately I emerged from S School completely broken, tricked, exposed, everything revealed including my belief in Gremlins, after my character weaknesses and subconscious desires started to appear like measles under applied psychological pressure.

Assessment School was conducted at a 118-acre estate near Fairfax, Virginia, which belonged to the Willard Hotel family in Washington. As our station wagon drove under the porte-cochere of the colonial mansion and a tweedy group of instructors met us on the sweeping veranda, I had the illusion of a fancy week-end party with perhaps a fox hunt thrown in.

The S School staff greeted us informally—there were six students in our group, including Jane. The dean of the school was Dr. Henry A. Murray of the Harvard Psychological Laboratory. On his staff were Dr. Richard S. Lyman, famous neuropsychiatrist from Duke University who later admitted that he had "neither the heart nor the mind to flunk any woman student"; Dr. James A. Hamilton and Dr. Robert C. Tryon, cofounders of the S School project which had been originally planned to remedy complaints about mental crack-ups in the field, and several junior staff psychologists including Kippy and Buster, who I later discovered must have studied in the Olsen and Johnson school of applied psychosadism.

We were immediately told about S School routine. The staff knew who we were although we had been told to assume student names and covers. They had all our branch reports. Therefore, when we took tests, we were to be ourselves. Among the other students we should be expected to maintain cover. It was permissible to ferret out anything we could about our confrères. We could break and enter their rooms, listen at keyholes, question them at meals. At the end of our course we should be asked to evaluate one another in a confidential report to the faculty. We should be graded on our powers of observation and conversely upon our ability to maintain our own cover.

The business of becoming a split personality should have been a fairly simple job in a small area where everyone else was playing at the same game, and when I arrived at S School I fondly imagined that the flippant, brash soul of a stenographer named Myrtle had transmigrated into my body. The first mental hazard I met was Jane, who had selected the student name Betty and the cover story that she was a former newspaper reporter. In this situation, I constantly broke cover by answering her student name. I could never remember to respond to Myrtle, the first test of an alert agent. Neither could I continue to live in the same body with Myrtle, whom I was beginning to loathe at the end of the three-day course. She even broke me of the habit of chewing gum!

On the drive out to S, I had slyly tried to size up our little group:

There was one other girl with us who seldom joined in our discussions. Her student name was Annette. She spoke with a foreign accent, seemed high-strung and unusually thin, and had large black eyes.

There was a quiet, thoughtful pipe smoker named Ronald who gave off an aura of thorough, industrious research.

Butch was a thick-necked, short enthusiastic lad with a crew haircut and a tattoo on his arm—Ronald's antithesis in appearance and actions. After covertly studying his powerful, muscular hands I arbitrarily catalogued him as a taxicab driver, or perhaps one of those safe-crackers OSS employed for special sabotage jobs. I readjusted my deductions about him twice during our acquaintance. Before supper on our first day at S School he accompanied Jane and me on a stroll through the grounds and confided that he was an amateur ornithologist. On our walk he called attention to several bird calls: the piercing note of the ruby-throated grippe, the warble of the double-breasted fit and the indigo nuthatch, the excellent trill of the triple sec and dove-tailed cote. It took some time to catch on to Butch's ornithological nonsense, and his sprightly humor was somehow incongruous to my preconceived notion of him. Ten months later when I reported for duty in Künming, China, I met Butch again, a Navy medical-corps man serving with troops along the Yellow River bend. He recalled S School to me by puckishly mentioning that he had been out trapping that *rara avis* known as the yellow-bellied Nip.

The last member of our class was lithe, swarthy Paul, whom I smugly suspected of being in the Navy because he wore black pumps while all the other men wore Army issue shoes. That night at supper, however, my pat deduction was upset completely when Paul said grace for the group at table. After that I took it for granted that he was a clergyman, and during the three hectic days ahead I found in Paul a willing Father Confessor. In my final analysis of the students, I described him as a kindly, understanding man of God whose religious convictions made it difficult for him to dissemble. Scarcely a week after those condescending words, I met Paul back in Que Building when I attended a showing of a midget agent movie projector, built like a stereopticon to give native agents a more vivid idea of how to commit acts of sabotage. The man demonstrating the machine was Brother Paul, who winked slyly at me when they introduced him as Lieutenant Commander John Shaheen, one of New York's experts in the field of public relations!

During our stay at S, Jane and I shared a charming little colonial bedroom furnished with incongruous Army cots; Annette occupied the adjoining room alone, and the men were segregated on the top floor. After retiring that first night, we discussed the feasibility of breaking and entering their quarters. We both had the same aversion—"like walking into the men's lavatory," as Jane put it. Although we considered leaving Kilroy messages pinned to our dainties in case the men did snoop through our room, they seemed to be just as reluctant to enter our quarters.

We also spent some time discussing our fellow students—one of the few forbidden pastimes at S, since we were supposedly making our own deductions. Jane added to our communal fund of knowledge that Ronald, the professor, had volunteered to give her watch the adjustment it needed. We had nothing on Annette yet, but when we looked in on her to say good night she was reading *Popular Mechanics*.

That night, stretched out on an Army cot in a strange room permeated with the fragrance of Virginia honeysuckle, I thought of Alice and the Caterpillar in reviewing first impressions of S School and the students. I visualized Dr. Lyman, like the venerable caterpillar with hookah in hand, asking me *who* I was, from atop his mushroom. As Alice said, it was all very confusing. I had known who I was when I got up in the morning; but, like Alice, I must have changed several times since then.

As if to emphasize this chimerical condition, Jane said, "Good night, Myrtle"; and for at least the tenth time that day I failed to respond to my student name.

Sometime during the night we were awakened by what sounded like an explosion, followed by a scream. Our insouciance was typical of most Americans untouched by war—the sound was too far away to have any connection with us, and later we learned that Annette was the only one in our group who recognized the sound and inquired about it the next day. I thought maybe someone was blasting. Jane said it sounded more like a blowout.

"And you'd probably scream too," she sleepily reminded me, "if *your* last good tire went blooie."

Just before I went back to sleep I was conscious of a scratching somewhere near our beds. Jane told me the next morning that I had mentioned "mice in the room" with monotonous regularity for at least ten minutes. Although I knew that I occasionally muttered in my sleep, the thought never bothered me until the last day at school, when we found out that our room had been wired for sound and that all our confidences had been heard, including our sleepy reaction to an actual demolition charge which had been set off in a near-by field to test our reflexes.

Mass and individual tests began promptly after breakfast the next morning, when our faculty began its elusive task of charting our personality attributes—our emotional stability, social relations, integrity, initiative, and leadership, in a series of some thirty-two examinations.

The tests proved several things conclusively to me: (a) I was not a leader; (b) I should be a total failure as commander of a machine-gun company, having annihilated by well placed crossfire a small group of men I was given to command—on paper; (c) it was impossible to split my personality, and by the end of three days everyone knew I wasn't Myrtle anyway, because I could only type with two fingers.

It was in testing my leadership abilities that I ran sniveling from the field to the comforting arms of Brother Paul. On the lawn in front of the main building was scattered a set of five-foot and seven-foot poles, wooden blocks with sockets into which poles were fitted, and pegs to hold the poles and blocks together. With those I was told to build a five-foot cube with seven-foot diagonals on all sides. I was given two "helpers," Kippy and Buster, who I later learned were junior psychiatrists especially trained to obstruct. Kippy's role was to do nothing until he received a specific order; Buster's was to heckle and make clumsy mistakes. They immediately found my sensitive spot—"She probably can't work out a simple math problem," I distinctly heard Buster whisper to his pal.

Nothing went right after that. They reminded me constantly that I had only ten minutes to do the job, and snickered behind my back until I began to wonder whether my petticoat showed or I had a run in my stockings. At the end of the period I had worked up a bitter hatred for S School, OSS, and all round and square objects. I was both humiliated and furious when I left the boys with the result of my mathematical calculations—a sort of tinker-toy tower of Pisa which they scathingly dubbed "Myrtle's Folly." In the week preceding, Dr. Hamilton told me later by way of comfort, Kippy and Buster had whittled another student, a one-star general, down to size on the same project when they told him he probably couldn't hold the rank of sergeant in the Army!

As the tests progressed, I felt more and more like a full-blown moron. I had no idea how many tires I should need to drive over the Burma Road with mileage given. When handed a brief case containing suspicious documents, I could find nothing that made sense including the floor plan of the Pentagon Building, which had always baffled me anyway. Asked to search a room and describe the occupant from his belongings, I could only resurrect a reasonable facsimile of Dr. Murray himself from the clues—a half-consumed pint of bourbon, railroad ticket stubs from Cambridge, suit from Brooks Brothers, neatly darned socks, and a copy of *Harper's*. To this day I wonder just who that missing man may have been (S School instructors never revealed his identity, and all the students had a different idea about "him").

I fell neatly into the Thematic Apperception Test trap which Dr. Murray had carefully devised at Harvard for blabbermouths with literary yearnings like myself. We were handed five dramatic pictures and given five minutes to write our own interpretation of each one. On rereading my rather sordid interpretations of suggestive pictures, I realized how cleverly the tests had drawn out hidden thoughts, how I had written myself and my desires into each situation.

Jane, on the other hand, rebelled completely. She told Dr. Murray the Apperception Tests were not applicable to her because she was an artist and knew the works of the men who painted the pictures. Besides, such subjects were not meant to tell stories. Painting was painting. Literature was literature. One art doesn't interpret another. A picture emphasizes visual qualities! Only after Dr. Murray rooted through an old copy of *Cosmopolitan*, clipped five illustrations from as many stories, and presented them to my artistic friend, would Jane take the test.

Our last night at S was especially designed to liberate our libidos through several quarts of bonded bourbon which were brought out before dinner to celebrate the end of the school and ease the tension. Dr. Hamilton also announced that we were to participate in a discussion of the topic, "What Are We Fighting for?"—a subject which elicited as many answers as there were people in the room. The discussion was led by Dr. Hamilton, who, with adroit questions and implications, brought out the background of the students. We found it almost impossible, under alcohol and an interested audience, to maintain complete cover. Myrtle died a sad death on the debate floor that night when I started my own impromptu speech by recalling not without a touch of bravado a remark of Mr. Litvinov's about World War II at a press conference I had covered shortly before Pearl Harbor.

Annette, lapsing into excited French after several drinks, said we were fighting to overthrow Hitler and to free Europe. Butch thought it was a war based on unequal balances of trade, and Paul maintained it was a clash of basic ideologies. Ronald, who I still hoped would blossom out in true professorial splendor, had several drinks too many, incoherently mumbled something about democracy, and ended up telling everyone how to train Doberman pinschers to come to heel.

I think Jane and I avoided most of the hazards of the bourbon course and came through slightly above par because we ended up making a sandwich supper for the staff, students, and lads on KP who had joined our party.

The next morning after breakfast we were told to write an assessment of our fellow students. My only accurate picture was of Jane, which Dr. Murray said didn't count anyway. I was absolutely off about Paul and Butch. Ronald, whom I put down as a possible professor who couldn't drink well, later turned out to be a dog trainer assigned to the OSS Canine Corps in Burma. Annette, as I partially suspected, was a French agent. Several weeks after she left S she was dropped behind enemy lines in Belgium as a radio operator. She had been a member of the French resistance movement from its inception and was rated, I later learned, as one of the most apt agents to pass through the portals of S School.

I returned from Assessment School with the feeling that my mind, shorn of all pretensions, was an open book to whoever was in charge of sending people overseas, and that I should soon be notified that I was being dropped from the OSS pay rolls as a low-grade moron.

"The S School reports are 97 per cent right," the major's aide told me glibly the day I returned to work—by way of preparing me for the worst, I was sure. "We never see the confidential reports here, of course—only the school recommendations—but they seemed to think you and Foster passed pretty high in your own fields. Just keep MacDonald away from anything involving higher mathematics, they tell us."

Passing in S School was the high spot of my OSS schooling. After that everything, including dynamite and booby traps, was anticlimax. Our last training took place at the Congressional Country Club several miles outside the Capital, which had been taken over by OSS as a relatively safe location for practical demonstrations in mine laying, arson, small arms, and close combat. Here, as a sideline, MO students were also taught how to work multilith machines and small-agent offset presses.

For three days we drove out to the "Farm," packing so much material into a few hours of lecturing that, at the end, classes began to fuse into kaleidoscopic impressions which still come back to me in the monotonous tones of instructors who demonstrated death and destruction week after week to recruits until the meaning and import of their words seemed lost on the instructors themselves. As one lusty character said, at what he considered a safe distance from the girls in the class, OSS mechanical weapons commit every atrocity in war except rape. And certainly, any of the adventuresome spirit of the Bloomer Girl evaporated after our first brush with death in the demolition class. It happened the day the instructor took a piece of TNT, tossed it toward Jane, and said: "Here, catch!" The instructor grinned when she missed it and several people rushed for the nearest exit.

"Don't be afraid," he teased. "You've got to understand about the stability of things like plastic and TNT . . ."

I was still shaky during the next class on the Country Club fairway, when Major William Fairbairn lectured to us on the use of the knife and small arms in close combat.

"Shoot your .45 at a crouching position from your hips," explained the famous authority on sudden death. "Don't take sight at eye level —you don't have time. The object is to stop your assailant. Hit him anywhere. Aim the gun the way you'd point your finger at your target. Same thing with a submachine gun . . ."

It looked fairly simple as the major manipulated his Thompson submachine gun after some fifty years of practice with weapons. It was a different story when I took hold of the weapon and the MO ballistics expert, Lieutenant Norman Sturgis, gave me the same instructions.

"From the hip, now," he told me as I gingerly grasped the gun. "Remember—it's loaded. Shoot straight ahead towards number three green—"

The Thompson submachine gun acted something like a bucking fire hose, and once I touched the trigger I found it physically impossible to release my grip. The force of the gun began to turn me slowly in the direction of the lieutenant, but luckily the stream of bullets stopped before I went too far; the machine clicked and was silent, and my whole body seemed to list noticeably to starboard. The fairway ahead was chewed with .45 bullet holes.

After that introduction to America's greatest contribution to the World War II arsenal, I went back to the club and directed all my attention lovingly to a two-and-a-half-pound offset agent press of bright aluminum. It didn't work well, but I had it under control.

Jane and I began to feel equipped to handle any emergency after we had finished classes in the care and shifting of the jeep, the monitoring of short- and medium-wave foreign broadcasts, the setting up of agent networks on paper, orientation courses in Malay, Thai, Burmese, Japanese, and Chinese culture.

We were smugly applying ourselves to our toilet preparatory to leaving the Country Club for the last time, when we learned once more that in OSS you can't be prepared enough. It happened when I pulled the overhead chain in the ladies' latrine and the room suddenly seemed to explode in noise and smoke.

We had been introduced to our first booby trap!

While Jane and I were attending indoctrination courses with other MO selectees, our papers had been processed through the State Department; and on the eve of departure in July, 1944, we received special passports enabling us to pass through territories held by the British, French, and Chinese. Our immunization shots ranged from smallpox to plague. We had attended extracurricular lectures on everything from Sex to Military Protocol, and as a last friendly gesture Lieutenant Thomas McFadden, a brilliant, patient lawyer in our office who spent most of his time keeping MO running on an even keel, drew up our wills for us.

Into an extra foot locker to be shipped by sea, had been stowed all the Army issue equipment that a busy Services Office could collect, including a helmet, sleeping bag, thermos bottle, flashlight, machete, medical kit, mosquito gloves, leggings and bars, fatigues and a poncho. Into the locker also went our "operational equipment": several boxes of squash and tennis balls which the major wrote would be of value in trading with the British; trinkets such as lipstick and cigarette lighters for the "natives," although the ones I met all had their own; several long evening gowns which the personnel branch whispered were *de rigueur* at official functions; face lotions and potions for the rigors of the field, and a book that OSS Visual Presentation Branch sent around entitled, "This Is No Picnic."

The rest of my gear—a year's supply of clothes—I stuffed into a flight bag and hoped that it would weigh in at sixty-five pounds.

It was not until the adjutant handed me a set of mimeographed orders marked "Confidential" that I realized I should actually be on my way in the morning and, with luck, would be in New Delhi within the week.

"The major returned yesterday from India," the adjutant told me privately, after instructing me for the third time not to lose my orders or show them to anyone, on pain of court-martial.

"Be at the airport half an hour before take-off. The major will meet you there and explain your work to you. And *don't lose your orders. Sew 'em in your corsets or something.*"

CHAPTER FOUR

MOTHER! INDIA!

THE major, browned from the Indian sun and flashing a velvet CBI patch on his shoulder, strode into the Washington airport at the appointed hour to find Jane and me rooting out feminine gear from the bulging pockets of our B–4 bags.

Everything had gone wrong from the minute we arrived at the airport and had questioned the ATC flight clerk's privilege of inspecting our confidential orders.

"It's only natural," he told us acidly, "for someone to look at those orders if you are going to travel fifteen thousand miles on them at government expense."

Somehow we both had the idea that our orders should be seen only by General Harold L. George of the ATC, President Roosevelt, or a member of his cabinet.

Once the clerk had wheedled them from us, he made a notation in the log and continued his nasty show of authority.

"OSS girls bound for the wars, eh?"

With the shadow of the security office still darkening our lives, I repeated the required formula that we were research analysts employed by the United States Government.

"Don't give me any of that cloak-and-dagger stuff," he snapped. "Anybody wearing those special GI Hamilton watches—and traveling under shush-shush orders—is OSS! C'mon, girls, weigh in. Y're allowed sixty-five pounds."

We had both made the mistake of just hoping that our flight bags would pass inspection. The result of our wishful packing, as the clerk was swift to point out, was that we were an easy forty pounds over the weight allowance.

He looked at the scales, smirked and pointed to a partially empty anteroom. "Cast off, girls."

It was a frustrating task, and the major's arrival only added to the confusion of trigger-quick decisions we were forced to make. The major patiently seated himself and held our jettisoned dresses in his lap while he explained something about our overseas job.

"You and Marj Severyns will set up a Morale Operations unit there," he began with me. "Marj will collect MO intelligence from British and American sources, and you—well, you'll work on all MO production out of Delhi for China and Burma."

The major might just as well have appointed me ambassador to Ruritania. MO production facilities in New Delhi were nonexistent! There wouldn't even be an office until Marj and I arrived to set it up!

"You'll probably meet up with Marj en route," he continued blithely. "When you get to Delhi you report to the commanding officer of Detachment 303—Lieutenant Colonel Harry Berno. And you're getting the best secretary in MO—Grace Mullen."

I sat down heavily on my disemboweled flight bag, trailing stockings and underwear.

Retracing the conversation back to production, I protested: "What do I use for a language staff? paper? presses? typesetters? Who disseminates it?"

He gave me his "ye of little faith" look and put a firm hand on my shoulder.

"Elizabeth, I just have the feeling you can find a way, once you start operating."

It was a flattering challenge, and it stopped me, momentarily. Once away from the spell of the major's ebullient personality, however, I brooded halfway around the world on not having pinned him down to more specific commitments.

Having dispensed with me in so many words, the major then bestowed upon Jane the title "MO Desk Head for Malaya and Sumatra." She would carry out the job under the guidance of Dr. Carlton Scofield, who was now acting chief of MO in Ceylon.

Unfortunately, we had little time for further conversation. We weighed in again at sixty-five pounds, leaving a tidy pile of gear with the major. The loud-speaker called our flight number, and we saw an ATC attendant start our depleted bags on their long trip to India. At the ramp, the major managed to slip in a few words on the glum political picture we were to face in the Far East.

"Psychological warfare is one of the best ways to reach people whose contact with the outside world has been shut off since Pearl Harbor," he reminded us.

"The Japs, we know, have been telling these people that, under the new Greater East Asia Co-Prosperity Sphere, they've attained independence that they'll never get under the British, or Dutch, or French. They've told them that the Atlantic Charter principles are empty words. They've told them that Asia is for the Asiatics. Now— what can we tell them? The British and French and Dutch won't mention the word 'independence' in their appeals to colonials. Instead, they talk of the return of the good old days before the Japs came. They ask the natives to protect property left behind by their white masters when they fled. That's bad psychology. Just a while back a directive came out from London, I understand, specifically banning references to the Atlantic Charter in psychological warfare. And India herself is a big white elephant that Jap propagandists have been pointing to across the Bay of Bengal as a fine example of white imperialism. So—until policies get straightened out there, our common target will have to continue to be the Jap."

Somehow the snarled conflicts of empire were too much to contemplate now. Always irrelevant at the wrong time, I was imagining instead what Tojo would think if he could see Jane and me walking up to the plane, tennis rackets under arm, bound for the front to fight the Imperial Japanese Army with pad and pencil!

Once I lost sight of the major's confident, friendly face and the plane door was bolted shut, a wave of doubt concerning my new job swept over me, intensified by my inherent distrust of airplanes. Jane and the assorted civilians and service personnel looked perfectly nonchalant as the motors revved up. As protective covering, I tried to assume that "set subway stare" I had seen on the faces of New Yorkers as they jolted along their mole runs. It would probably take them, I told myself, all their workaday lives to ride as far on the IRT as I was going in five days on the ATC. At that moment, however, I would have gladly changed seats. After all, their work was cut out for them, as simple as punching a time clock. And here I was—hurtling through space toward a nebulous job, equipped only with ideas, to be implemented by my own opportunism, and all of it classified "Secret"!

I adjusted my seat belt with studied unconcern, crossed my fingers, and went through all the take-off rituals to insure a safe flight. Then, as we became air-borne, that war-worn cliché came out in spite of myself.

"This is it!"

Our plane came to a bumpy landing at Miami, which was a deserted resort town in those days catering chiefly to servicemen. We were both quietly perspiring as we climbed aboard the shuttle truck destined for the Floridian Hotel. With us in the back seat was a civilian in a comfortable white linen suit who immediately opened the conversation by asking Jane if she worked for OWI. She replied guardedly that she was "with a government agency."

"Not a research analyst by any chance?" His question was almost in the form of a password.

"We're both research analysts," she replied warily.

"Me too," he grinned. "What do you do?"

It was surprising in the months ahead how the OSS brotherhood unerringly searched its members out like some underground fraternity, all over the world.

"We're MO," I blurted out, forgetting for a fleeting instance the security truism that the driver of any vehicle might be in the pay of somebody's Gestapo. Our friend looked first at Jane, then me, and shook his head in quiet disapproval of my indiscreet technique.

"I'm Herman Harjes—security office!" he whispered.

After the initial shock of shaking hands with a member of that dreaded branch, Herman proved to be quite human and very handy during our few days' sojourn at the Florida Port of Embarkation. He knew all the best spots in Miami and was on pleasant terms with all head waiters of any importance. Herman was a husky, phlegmatic *bon vivant* who approached the problem of being a security officer intellectually.

"The best way to maintain cover is to act like a typical American businessman on a buying trip. Smoke cigars. Slap people on the back. Wear your Elks tooth." (And Herman, who later worked on the million-dollar Hump smuggling-ring case in India, looked indeed like the Man from Main Street.)

Miami's fashionable Floridian Hotel was still structurally plush, but all the attributes of wealth and distinction had disappeared as soon as ATC installed a corporal behind the front desk and sent the carpets, napery, and dishes off to storage for the duration. There were still the swimming pool, palm-fringed walks through tropic gardens, and prewar postcards for sale at the PX recalling the era when the Peacock and Crystal ballrooms were the last word in décor. Now everything about the place was utilitarian, from the slot machines in the lounge to the loud-speakers on the wide verandas that announced plane flights.

The camaraderie which developed at a Port of Embarkation was pleasant but mercurial. Two State Department girls from Cairo and a flight nurse from Sicily bunked in my room overnight; a GI mechanic from Barrackpore treated me to a coke at the pool; an Army major on his way to London went deep-sea fishing with me one morning. Then, when I thought about them again, they had already been guided through the busy narrows of the POE, caught in the tides of personnel flowing east and west.

On our second day at the hotel Jane and I were joined by Marjorie Severyns and another security officer, Lieutenant Edmund Lee, in what looked like a concerted effort on the part of that branch to keep MO under close surveillance. Marj was a slender, bright young girl with a piquant, dimpled face. A native of Sunnyside, Washington, she had been graduated from the University of Washington several years after me. She had good organizational ability, was efficient and capable, and had majored in international law.

Lieutenant Lee, a lawyer in prewar life, was a good-natured traveling companion who almost immediately became the object of our attention when we learned that he had been allotted an extra eighty-five pounds' weight allowance to transport a submachine gun and ammunition and had some fifteen pounds extra to spare. This he offered to split among the three of us, and the result was a last-minute buying spree at Miami resort shops. It was probably the first time salesgirls were asked to weigh purchases before they were bought.

In a studied attempt to remind us that there was a war on, ATC officials organized a series of briefings to add some austerity to our Miami playground.

The opening words of the medical lecture had an embarrassing effect on the three of us when we were ushered to front-row seats at the open-air class with some seventy-five men.

"Anybody here wanna get a venereal disease?" barked the medical officer. And his glance seemed to linger on us as he searched the audience for a raised hand. No one would own up. "Then, wherever you go, stay away from native women—and men," he added as a conspicuous afterthought.

Some of my distrust of airplanes was dispelled during a "ditching" lecture given by an enthusiastic young officer who started out his talk:

"Now, *when* your plane goes down, there's nothing to worry about . . ."

His synthetic charm made the adventure of escaping from a plane seem so alluring that I half hoped I should be among those lucky few flying ATC who would be permitted to use all' the life-raft paraphernalia which modern science had designed for the care and feeding of downed airplane passengers. With my feet planted firmly on Florida soil, I could see myself calmly, quietly preparing for ditching:

Brace myself against the seat. Relax. The first jolt wasn't going to be so bad as the second, the man said. Then action stations. Inflate Mae Wests. One minute to leave the ship. Into the rubber life raft with its complete assortment of sails, oars, compass, flares, seasickness pills, even a container of yellow chemicals to spread like an oil slick on the water and attract rescue planes which would be out within half an hour. Meanwhile, stretch out, throw a fishing line over the side, get a tan . . .

Somehow the whole picture changed for me as soon as my feet left solid ground, and I could never recapture that yearning to "prepare for ditching" on the entire trip across.

Our vacation came to an end on the third day, when we were told to take our baggage to the inspection room for a last-minute security check to be certain we weren't smuggling butter or Parker 51's out of America. Marj and Jane passed inspection and a sergeant was about to check me off and continue with Lieutenant Lee when he opened my typewriter, and a small packet of what I considered irrelevant MO material dropped out of the case.

The sergeant untied the package and spread out several small micro-film rolls of Japanese newspapers. There was also a small manual on Jap type faces, two wooden "chops" or seals of the Japanese High Command captured on Kiska, a street map of Tokyo with certain areas marked in red pencil. The sergeant suddenly began to act as if he'd caught Tojo's Girl Friday. He called the security officer over, and they studied the display in serious, baffled silence. Behind me I heard Lieutenant Lee take a deep, agonized breath.

"What've you *got here*, Tokyo Rose?" The captain finally accosted me with a sneer. I was probably his first "case" since the POE opened and he was determined to make the most of it. Quite a group of curious bystanders had gathered around, and I began to feel a certain guilt induced solely by the captain's attitude. I further snarled the situation by saying that it was "just stuff you wouldn't understand about anyway—"

"Yeah. Then what's the map marked up for?"

Just then Lieutenant Lee shoved ahead of me.

"I'm an accredited OSS courier," he said fast and authoritatively. "I'll take these off your hands, captain. I'll be responsible. No trouble at all." And he quickly swept the material into his brief case and pad-locked it before the captain could protest.

Once outside, he turned with the How-could-you-be-so-stupid? look that security officers often assumed around me.

"Just what was that map marked up for, Mac?" he asked me.

I explained that it was the only street map of Tokyo I could get, and a tourist friend of mine had given it to me. The red marks were just where he'd found the best bars in and around the city!

"And anyway," I persisted, "none of that stuff was classified. The Japs published the papers. They knew what was in them. And that type-face manual was printed in Yokohama."

Lieutenant Lee began his lecture patiently.

"Suppose we nabbed a Jap with copies of the New York *Times* and *Mirror* in his suitcase. And a manual on American type faces. And photostats of General Marshall's signature. And a map of Washington? What would we deduce? Something fishy—right? Even though none of those articles were marked secret. Now—suppose when we land in India a Jap agent stole your typewriter and sent its contents to the Japs in Rangoon. The stuff might not make sense, but Jap intelligence would be on the alert for some sort of monkey business, wouldn't they? And don't ever forget it—the success of all OSS work depends on surprise!"

Lieutenant Lee's lecture again put the fear of the security office in me. That evening when the ATC duty officer subtly remarked how little time we had left to write a last letter home, I began to wonder whether it was safe even to say goodbye to my parents, par-ticularly since all the stationery at the hotel was plainly marked, "Air Transport Command—Miami Beach," and we had been warned not to mention the location of our POE. But there was too much of the ham in me, as in almost everyone else, to resist that final grand gesture, that underplayed adieu.

I had in mind a simple little note, something like the memo "To Lucasta on Going to The Wars," but I knew Dad would see through any heroics on my part. Closing my eyes, I could picture him quite plainly, doing his bit for the war effort along the sunny Waikiki beach promenade with an amiable group of civilian defense shore watchers who spent their hours on duty playing cribbage under a leafy hau arbor "waiting for Nips who never came in" as Dad put it.

Dad was a jovial, semi-retired Honolulu newspaperman with an unbridled sense of humor. As a sort of Falstaff of the Fourth Estate he would hold court for hours under the arbor, regaling cronies with newspaper anecdotes. Over a period of years he had acquired a cynicism common to many newsmen that resulted in a deep unconcern for any institution, including the military, that dared take itself too seriously. He delighted in heckling me about OSS, and his letters contained sly allusions to my new occupation. He apologized for not being able to obtain the latest plans for a series of air bases on Oahu. He made constant references to my "Japanese connections." Once I discovered a small packet of sand in the mail—an example, Dad explained, of what was at the bottom of Pearl Harbor! I had several worried notes from Mother in which she cautioned that my father openly referred to me as "that spy."

"So you're going overseas to do psychological warfare!" he had commented in his last letter. "Has MacArthur been informed? Does Nimitz know? Into the breach, my girl, with split infinitives and dangling participles! Fracture their syntax beyond all recognition. It serves them right!"

Out of the letter had fallen a little gold cross. Dad wasn't all bluff.

In the end I couldn't think of a thing to write that wouldn't break security, so I just scribbled on a postcard that they wouldn't hear from me for several weeks, but not to worry.

The next day was Sunday. I was taking a leisurely pre-breakfast stroll through the gardens when I heard quick steps on the gravel path behind me and a major wearing chaplain's insignia caught up with me and nodded cordially.

"You won't make chapel if you don't hurry," he reminded me, and I followed him meekly, like the truant officer, to his open-air pavilion facing the sea, where coconut fronds hung down to form a symmetrical laced pattern of green against blue sky.. I was the only woman among some thirty men who stood up to sing, when a soldier at a squeaky field organ began to play "Onward, Christian Soldiers." It sounded strangely exciting, this marching church music which rolled out and across Biscayne Bay.

The call came after breakfast when the PA system cleared its throat with a jangling series of static noises:

"The following will report to the transportation desk at 1300 hours."

As the names were called, about twenty-three people in addition to our little OSS group left the porch where they were lounging and went to pack their gear. I waited till the end, but Jane's name was not listed. The prospect of splitting up was the only regret I felt at leaving Miami. It also meant a last-minute diving into Lieutenant Lee's luggage to remove her new dresses and underwear, an action which took place in the foyer of the hotel under the bemused stares of transient GI's.

Jane saw us off at the field, and it was many long months before we met again. She trailed us the next day and was in our wake until she hit the Gold Coast, where she was "bumped" and spent a week in the bush studying native art. Her trip from then on was filled with a series of time gaps, when she disappeared into the blue. Finally, two weeks later, we had it on good authority that she had reached Ceylon after a circuitous trip through India.

During our own uneventful flight across the keys at twilight and over the sea toward Puerto Rico, Marj and I were invited forward to sit in the copilot's seat—an honor which ATC crews paid Very Important Personages, or VIP's, as we came to know the term, and the lady passengers. To this day the enormous panel board with its myriads of darting arrows, gauges, and throttles will be one of life's more complicated mysteries; but on each trip I made I was invited forward to admire the gadgets, which only amazed me by their complexity and left me with a deep-seated reverence for the fellow at the controls who knew what they were saying to him.

I soon discovered that the excitement of seeing new places was vitiated when traveling with the Army. Stopovers in Africa and Arabia might just as well have been on a milk run between Chicago and New York. The Army had placed its stamp of uniformity on every refueling depot from Miami to Karachi, India. There were the same heavy dishes in the mess halls, the same smooth asphalt runways and casual, competent American boys in identically greasy fatigues to service the ship. There were even the same candy bars at post exchanges. The scenery was shifted only on the walls of the clubrooms. Across South America we found lush American versions of Carmen Miranda painted over the bars. Tall negro women with Ubangi lips who looked something like Harlem hepcats followed us across the Dark Continent from one mural to the next. In Arabia there were sloe-eyed, Varga type Shebas, and in India, the lithesome GI version of a sari-clad memsahib.

Sometimes our position, as we moved across the world, was revealed by the natives working on ATC air strips. There were dark-skinned Portuguese, lanky Sudanese the color of freshly poured fudge, turbaned Arabs, thin-legged Indians with betel-stained teeth.

Animals also identified the country. With the exception of the ubiquitous GI dog, we saw baboons, toucans, and cockatoos which ATC ground crews had lured from the encroaching jungle near the strip at Belém, Brazil; sooty terns roosted on the plane wings at Ascension Island in the middle of the Atlantic; tawny camels, with skin that looked like the drawn top over an apple pie, gave us a lippy look at Maiduguri in the bush country at the edge of the Sahara; a giraffe at El Fashar coquettishly kicked up his heels when Lieutenant Lee blew a smoke ring at him; ridiculous small gray donkeys at Khartoum gravely carried their long-legged passengers.

Continents below us gave off general impressions of color and contour. South America sprawled immense and green, with convoluted jungle. The Africa we saw was a vast stretch of brown and red prairie where stockaded villages looked like an outbreak of ringworm on an old, wrinkled face. Motionless tawny desert tides met the brittle blue stationary waters of the Red Sea and Arabian Sea as we neared India and the gateway to the Far East, and only on the ground did details emerge again, and the desert acquire sand, the jungle, leaves, like the sudden discovery of earth's capillary system.

Natal is one of the few brief stops en route to New Delhi that I remember with any degree of clarity, because it was at this colorful little Brazilian settlement that I met the only wolves I have ever known who came in on instruments.

By the time we'd hit a few tropical fronts as high as 10,000 feet, shared stale flight lunches and emerged from the plane stiff and miserable at wild, cold hours of the dawn, Marj Severyns and I had exchanged all the confidences necessary to cement a working friendship for the long months ahead.

Consequently we operated as a team when we stepped down from the plane at Parnamirim Field after a tiring flight over the continent. Here, two personable young officers greeted us and asked if we were the OSS girls aboard. Lieutenant Lee, directly in back, commented tartly that if there were any other girls aboard the ship working for OSS, they were hiding in the belly tanks. The men ignored him and began to press us for dinner at the club, a trip to Natal, which is usually off limits to transients. Thinking back on the grim meals we had had in the past twenty hours, we both agreed rather eagerly, especially when they added that they would drive us right over to the nurses' quarters, where hot baths were already drawn.

I felt like a guilty Cinderella as we were escorted to a staff car and saw the male passengers climb wearily aboard a large open truck for the uninviting transient tent city at the base.

On the way to our billets we learned how our escorts operated. They were the two public relations men for the field and were notified well in advance by ATC radio operators when VIP—diplomats, generals, congressmen—were expected. They were then able to roll out the carpets and arrange parties. To break the monotony, they also arranged with the radio operators on the side to be notified when any women passengers were aboard.

"We got word half an hour before you arrived," one of the boys explained. "The operator flashed the message: 'Two crows aboard—pipe the gams.' That meant you were OSS. OWI girls are owls, the Red Cross, goneys—nurses are wrens."

Although the baths were refreshing, Marj and I agreed while we waited for our escorts that all we really wanted to do after our long trip was to eat and "hit the sack"—one of the many GI phrases we were beginning to acquire. "I get tired from the noise of the engines," Marj said, "—that and just sitting and never really relaxing." And we made a firm decision to stage a polite sit-down strike after dinner and pull out all the stops about being frail females, without taking into consideration the fact that there hadn't been a white woman through Natal since Paulette Goddard, a full month ago. Our wolves were set for a gala evening.

"We'll go over to the club for a few drinks," one of them announced before he even walked through the front door.

"Then we'll go into Natal, half an hour away. It's moonlight—brings out that old-world charm."

"Dinner at the Grande—"

"Dancing at the Ideal Club—"

"Drive along the beach. We'll buy some of those Brazilian pineapples—sweetest things you ever tasted."

Flattered as we were by our first brush with the American male away from home and mate, Marj and I continued our protests. We were tired and sleepy.

"We can promise you," one of them finally said, in a cautious Can-you-keep-a-secret? tone, "that your plane won't take off till ten tomorrow morning. We know. We're on the inside. Have to know those things. One of your motors needs a complete overhaul . . ."

We saw Natal by moonlight. We dined on the terrace of the

Grande Hotel, where our escorts tried to impress us with their mastery of a few Portuguese phrases and brought a wide-eyed gazelle of a boy waiter. running to our table with warm beer. We ate pineapple and walked the waffle-patterned tile. sidewalks while our escorts told us of the hardships at Natal, the difficulties of entertaining VIP's, the inconvenience in observing malaria prevention rules on the post, and the delicate matter of taking a bottle of Skat along on dates.

It was nearly one o'clock when Marj and I finally threatened to walk home if our friends persisted in one more warm beer at the Wonder Club—a noisy den filled with British, Brazilian, and American fighting men.

We reached our billets suffering from what Marj described as wolf-combat fatigue, undressed, fell into bed, and tucked our mosquito nets in after us according to malaria warnings tacked on the front door. No sooner had we stretched out than a heavy knock rattled the door.

"Severyns and MacDonald—your flight leaves in thirty minutes. Report with your baggage immediately at the terminal!"

Marj and I were the only ones aboard who didn't worry about finding Ascension, that island of 34 square miles, 1,450 miles out across the Atlantic—somewhere midway between the bulge of Africa and South America. We slept from the time we were air-borne until we raised Ascension late in the afternoon and floated down through pink puffs of clouds to the black landing strip that Army engineers had blasted out of lava rubble in the record time of ninety-one days. We bounced to a rough landing as brown cinder cones and fungus-covered *aa* clinkers rushed by the plane in a blur of brown and gray. Far down the runway, at the edge of the island was a fluttering, moving blanket of white terns disturbed by the arrival of our ship. (The terns, a hazard to planes, were later eliminated from Ascension by a transient OSS ornithologist who suggested the simple expedient of breaking their eggs!)

The engines were cut. The cessation of noise brought about a relaxation. How integrated the whir and throb of the plane had become to my body!

The door opened, and a young lieutenant popped his head inside. "You are now on Ascension Island. Transportation is provided at the terminal." Suddenly he noticed us. "Um-m-m. My friend and I will escort the ladies to their cabana!"

Lieutenant Lee looked at us and then leaned over to ask us in a confidential voice if we'd like a couple of his Mickey Finn capsules.

"It's a handy little harmless knock-out pill OSS developed for agents when they get cornered. Just slip it in your escort's drink. You'll cheat a fate worse than death!"

While we didn't need the pills, someone should have posted us on the Ascension Kiss Gag. We were initiated later that evening, after our escorts had shown us the single tree that grew on Ascension's air field, had jeeped to the beach where Paulette Goddard bathed, and had introduced us to the rock-happy bartender who kept twelve wrist watches in a foot locker, wound them each morning, and worried all day until he returned to find out which had gained, which had lost time.

We were in separate jeeps after dinner when our friends took us home to the cabana, a pleasant little modernistic villa by the shore. My lieutenant parked his jeep ominously in the shadow of the cabana walls, switched off the ignition, and fumbled for his cigarettes. It could have been any place near the ocean—Coney Island, Jones Beach, West Los Angeles. But it was on an island in the middle of the Atlantic, and here I was, the victim of war, on my way toward the front where female stock goes up with the law of supply and demand.

"You smell good," he sniffed, sidling closer. "What kinda perfume?"

It was that familiar "lonely boy" approach, and I blamed Marj for tempting me to douse myself in her Blue Grass to get rid of that "slept-in" odor our clothes had aboard the plane.

"Been twenty months now since I've talked to a girl. I'm going to write my wife about tonight. She'll understand. You know, I even think she'd thank you if you'd let me kiss you good night!"

H'm-m. Was it Mother, or the OSS Overseas Handbook for Girls, that had warned me of lonely soldiers? Oh, for the gift of a glib tongue!

"Been nice—showing you around tonight. Get so lonely here. Just to talk to a woman. Been real nice, tonight—"

Here was the conversational break I'd been waiting for.

"Yep, terribly nice, really. But I do need sleep—"

Then I made the mistake of facing him, and he was agile enough to plant a resounding smack squarely on my lips.

Once inside the sanctuary of the cabana, I learned that Marj had been accosted with the same tale of loneliness and hunger for a goodnight kiss. Later we learned the Kiss Story was the hardest to resist. But the men on Ascension Island never told their victims that just over the hill on the other side of the Rock was a British cable station, complete with very charming women who often gave teas and dances for American soldiers stationed on Ascension!

"Don't look now," the flight clerk cautioned as we took off in an early-morning flurry of terns at the end of the runway, "but we're heading for a pass in the mountain straight ahead that's strewn with the wrecks of planes that didn't quite make it."

With this thought in mind, we pulled through the notch in the hill over the graveyard of planes and swept out across the ocean for the African Gold Coast.

We'd been flying about two hours when I suddenly realized that I had left my nightgown hanging in the bedroom at the cabana. Lieutenant Lee assured me that it would be impossible to turn back at this point, what with the high cost of aviation gasoline and the evident hurry of some of our passengers to get to the war.

Hours later, when the long white beaches and palm-fringed shores of the Dark Continent had been raised, our sly security officer slipped me a piece of paper upon which he had scrawled a bit of doggerel.

"To the tune of 'She Had to Go and Lose It at the Astor,'" he added.

> She had to go and lose it on Ascension
> In spite of words of warning from her mother.
> What she lost is far too delicate to mention
> On the Rock, where one good tern deserves another.

Customs clerks ticked off Accra, Maiduguri, then Khartoum on the banks of the Nile on our passports as we flew across Africa. On our way from Khartoum to Aden, Arabia, we crossed the Red Sea riding the crest of a typhoon which struck Aden an hour after we landed, ripped roofs off the barracks, and caused thousands of dollars' damage to the little refueling station whose adobe walls and thatched roofs disintegrated beneath the steady downpour of rain that followed the wind.

At Aden, one of the plane passengers was berated by an alert post censor for attempting to divulge ATC routes in limerick code. Lieutenant Lee told us that the lad had written home to his wife telling her, among other things, that "he'd just left a place which was the scene of a very confusing incident in Limerickology." The censor, unfortunately, was a limerick student and returned the letter to the passenger with the following notation:

> To that wise guy en route from Khartoum,
> We censors are hep to your rune!
>   We know all the tricks,
>   Like those sly limericks
> Which refer to Bombay and Khartoum!

The air was still turbulent on our flight over to the island of Masira, last stop before India. As we approached the field the flight clerk came aft to tell us we should be "stacked" for about ten minutes. Other planes were circling the field, awaiting landing instructions. Far below us the Masira air field, ringed with twinkling lights, was barely visible through the pelting rain. The control tower searchlight, like some gigantic windshield wiper, swept back and forth as if trying to clear the atmosphere. Our plane circled wide, banked, returned, circled again. Occasionally she would shudder, caught by a freakish crosscurrent of wind, and then the engines seemed to roar louder in protest as we bucked through the sky.

We had been over the field about seven minutes when it happened. Our plane suddenly side-slipped, and we hurtled earthward with the speed of a crippled elevator descending from the top of the Empire State Building. Luckily all seat belts were fastened, but the flight clerk, walking the aisles, was knocked cold against the forward compartment. I recall distinctly the tiny beads of perspiration oozing from the back of Herman Harjes' neck, who was seated directly in front of me. Herman was near the window and I saw his hand go up automatically to his face as if to ward off some invisible blow that never came. Then there was a loud roar, and our plane plummeted. We came out of the drop so quickly that my head jerked back. We then leveled off at what seemed only a few feet from ground and came in fast for a rough landing. When the crew walked out of their compartment every face was ashen. Herman leaned over and asked the pilot something I didn't catch. But everyone in the plane heard his reply.

"Yes, those bastards in the control tower—gave us the same altitude to come in as they did another plane—coming in at right angles!"

As we left the plane Herman told us he had seen the green lights of another ship almost parallel to our own running lights. Only the split-second thinking of the pilot saved our lives.

My knees began to shake several minutes later, and I was thankful no lives depended on *my* reflexes. There wasn't the usual joking and talk as the rest of the passengers debarked, either.

Marj and I sat up front with a driver in the truck assigned to take us to the mess hall, but our breathless account of the landing made little impression on him.

"Never a dull moment on Masira!" he shrugged. "The boys have to keep things lively around here, or they go nuts!"

To illustrate his point he stepped the truck up to sixty, and raced through the darkness. While Army drivers are generally conceded to be a reckless brood, the one we drew that night must have been president of the Sudden Death Club. When he finally came to a shrieking stop before the mess hall in a hiss of burning rubber, someone yelled from the rear that two full colonels had fallen off the truck on one of our two-wheel turns. At this juncture the driver evidently decided that things on Masira were lively enough, and his truck was out of sight when the colonels hobbled up, muddy and livid. No one in the mess hall seemed to know who the driver was.

"Probably some cowboy pilot they grounded," the mess sergeant told the colonels, who were already composing letters to the War Department and President Roosevelt.

The remaining 580 miles to Karachi were nervous, bumpy ones. Our bad weather continued, and a heavy dust storm was rolling across the Sind Desert as our plane sat down at the modern airport of the Gateway to India.

Perhaps we were numb by now to the dangers of air travel. Possibly the spirit of Kismet had descended upon some hardier souls as we loosened our safety belts at Karachi. But at the end of this 15,000-mile journey most of us felt exactly like Lieutenant Lee when he dropped his flight bag on the airport apron, looked around at the brightly lighted terminal, and shouted:

"Mother! India!"

CHAPTER FIVE

32 FEROZ SHAH ROAD

IN MY dream my feet were encased in a block of cement. Then, in the infinitesimal time it took me to veer into the realm of consciousness, I saw that it wasn't cement at all, but a cold, soggy Army blanket wadded at the foot of the bed. There was a steady plosh-plosh on the cement floor of rain seeping in from outside. I stretched stiffly and felt beneath me a taut, wet canvas. The bed was not a bed, but an Army cot. I was on a porch that was somehow shut off from a noisy driveway by a quivering bamboo shade. A desk fan on a reading table was blowing the sultry air away from my face. For a split second my senses wavered again. I was in some asylum for the cure. Then I remembered. I was in New Delhi!

Events of the previous evening flashed through my foggy mind: the long wait at Drigh Road, Karachi, while an Indian civil servant prodded my flight bag, inspected my passport, and gave me a letter certifying that I worked for "Messrs. O. S. S."; the sleepy flight in a bucket-seater, and our landing at Willingdon Airport, Delhi, at three in the morning in a steady, heavy downpour; that sour greeting from the sergeant behind the terminal desk, "My Gawd—more women!"

With a jerk of his thumb, he had directed us toward the front door and the rain. "Bus leaving now for the Taj—that's where you women report."

Water leaked through the covered truck as we climbed aboard, and splashed up through the flooring. It wasn't a cold rain, but it didn't smell like a clean rain, either. Later, when I saw how it sloshed and drained off the fetid Indian earth, I realized that it was the land itself, fresh, new earth, that gave off such sweet, remembered rain smells in our own country. I had an indistinct impression of the country through the thin drizzle. It was flat, and the streets were wide. After our driver dropped our planemates at a billet they called Wistful Vista, he swung through unlighted back alleys and finally turned in at a horseshoe-shaped road and stopped in front of a low building where a light shone out at a door marked "Billeting Officer."

"They'll take care of you here—I hope," he told us, hauling down our wet bags from the portmanteau. Then he was off, and we were standing on a damp porch where all the night insects in India swarmed in a goatee from a single naked electric light bulb. Inside, we found an Indian asleep on the billeting officer's desk. He wore Army trousers but no shoes; his khaki shirt hung neatly from the chair.

Marj tried the Urdu greeting that she had learned from our GI Handbook on India—"Salaam, sahib"—and the man's snores came to a cacophonic climax. He grabbed his shirt, buttoned it hastily, without tucking it into his trousers—a habit which seemed to be universal in India. Only after he had finished this quick toilet did he sit down behind the desk, look up as if we'd just come in that instant, and say, "Yes?"

In a sleepy but patient voice, I asked for quarters. The man continued to regard us with an air of importance, and again said, "Yes?"

Marj leaned across the desk to his chin level and glared: "Bed—bunk—billet!"

For a minute we thought he had it. His eyes brightened, he smiled. Then he shrugged and said: "Nay mallum." Translated from our GI handbook, that meant he didn't know what we were talking about. Suddenly he smiled again as if struck by an idea, reached for a red fez behind him on a hook and motioned us to be seated. He then departed into the night flourishing a large black umbrella which he flapped open like some large bird of prey. As the wall clock neared four our man returned followed by a fat Indian in a fitted jacket and ballooning white pants. He was winding his turban with a rapid, precise motion as he walked into the room and startled us with his English accent.

"What is it you ladies wish?"

Again Marj spluttered our request for billets. The man nodded, walked over to the board upon which the names of all Taj tenants were posted, and consulted the list. Then he turned to us again.

"Sorry, no extra billets listed. Come back tomorrow when the American officer will be here. He'll help you then."

I was ready to strangle them both with the fat man's turban when a freckled-faced girl in a bathrobe, hair done up in pin curls, pushed through the door.

"What's all the fuss? More pilgrims from Mecca? And no billets, Fazle Huque?"

Our turbaned friend nodded happily as if his responsibilities ended with her arrival.

"Ah—Miss Bond of the Red Cross will help you. She is so clever!"

Fazle Huque inched out of the door, disappeared through the curtain of rain, and we never saw him again. His friend had already started to remove his shirt as Miss Bond led us down a corridor to her quarters. She scouted up a cot for Marj in her parlor, and I elected to sleep on the porch in my clothes, too weary then to worry about mosquitoes.

Miss Bond was gone when I awoke to face midmorning realities that I might even now be incubating malarial germs, that my clothes were damp, and that a man in a turban was standing at my bedside with a pot of tea and the news that the billeting sergeant was outside. I immediately broke all colonial rules of etiquette by thanking him with a smile. I learned later that all communications between master and servant are transmitted by a series of grunts. Any show of camaraderie results in a loss of face. My next *faux pas* occurred when I plugged my traveling iron into the light switch as the impassive "bearer" looked on. I immediately blew out all the fuses in the apartment.

"America, AC; India, DC," he muttered with a shrug. Then he took my dress over his arm, informed me coldly that the dhobi did laundry, and disappeared behind the screen like a bad-tempered jinn.

Marj was conversing with a brash young sergeant when I walked out, some twenty minutes later, in a freshly pressed dress.

"I been telling your side-kick here"—he jerked his thumb toward Marj—"you girls got the last double room in the Taj. Housing shortage is terrific here. You're lucky."

He showed us next door into a pleasant whitewashed room facing a grassy court. In it were two charpoys (beds with a woven twine bottom), two bureaus, and a few numdah rugs.

"First thing, you girls have got to get a bearer," he informed us, checking over a list of names. "Here's one, Ali. Passed by security, too. Worked for a colonel once. Very sensitive type, but clean. I can get him for thirty rupees a month."

It was too much like engaging in black-slave traffic, so we agreed to let the sergeant handle the deal. We *had* to keep up with the British!

"Sure thing," he continued. "Everybody, even the GI's, keeps a bearer. Get the Wogs to shine their brass, keep the billets straight, and when there's an inspection they just about have the Wogs salute for them. We never had it so good!"

In India most foreigners amassed a large entourage of Wogs— disrespectfully so called by Europeans who lacked the patience to use their fuller sobriquet, Westernized Oriental Gentlemen. American girls were no exception. In addition to a bearer, we learned that we had to have a sweeper, who cleaned up the place, a dhobi for laundry, and a dog wallah if we kept a dog.

"One of the girls here keeps a mongoose named Fifi, and the character who cleans up after Fifi is even a lower caste than the dog wallah," the sergeant explained. As far as we could determine, our bearer supervised all these people and occasionally, as a special favor, brought chota hazri, early-morning tea.

Our adviser on Indian affairs then told us to take a tonga outside the Taj to get to the American headquarters on Queensway where we were to report for work.

"Only give the tonga driver half a rupee—no more, or the British will get sore. They say we're overtipping and ruining their economy over here."

The tonga was a top-heavy sulky in which passengers and driver sat back to back, separated by a removable board between front and rear seats. Our combined weight in back caused the driver to ride most of the way into town on the shafts to keep his tiny pony from being lifted off the road.

At CBI headquarters we were directed to the OSS wing, where the noisy shuffling of papers in the anteroom gave the impression that a great deal of work was being accomplished in Colonel Berno's inner sanctum—until I saw a bearer and assistant march from his office with the remains of ten o'clock tea.

Colonel Berno was a handsome, capable-looking young man, a steel executive in "real" life, whose OSS mission in Delhi was to keep on good terms with Service of Supply officers in other branches of the Army and to maintain a steady, uninterrupted flow of intelligence to and from the field through our large communications center.

With our orders in his hand, the colonel motioned us to chairs.

"Just what is this—MO?" he asked.

Before we had a chance to answer he hurried on. "I know—propaganda stuff like OWI does. One word about OWI. You can profit by their example. One of their jobs was to explain America to the Indians —cultural relations business. So OWI here bought up full pages in the Delhi *Statesman;* ran a series of historic stories on how we won our independence. The Indians loved it. Then the British got wise. Accused us of fostering a revolution!"

We tried to explain to the busy man that our target was the Jap soldier, that we were sent out to collect MO intelligence, produce black political warfare material.

And then, for the first time, we ran smack into the cold military reaction about women that dogged me through the war. It was the same thing everywhere—women were at their best during wartime wrapping Red Cross bandages in their own home town! Furthermore, the colonel pointed out, we had no MO equipment and it was against all regulations to go outside channels to obtain supplies.

"OSS girls can help the organization by cementing relations with other branches out here. But don't mix business and pleasure. By the way, I'm having a couple of generals to dinner tonight. Thought you girls might like to come along. We'll pick you up around seven!"

He dismissed us with instructions to report to our office at 32 Feroz Shah Road, off in suburbia where I suspected the colonel hid all those branches of OSS he couldn't explain satisfactorily to his Regular Army friends or the British—branches like MO, the long-haired professors in Research and Analysis, intelligence gumshoes who watched Allied and enemy agents at work in Delhi, cartographers who informed the air force in China on Jap movements.

Our tonga drew up with a wet, squeaky skid at a pleasant-looking private house at 32 Feroz Shah Road. On the outside was a bronze plaque: "Dr. L. L. Smith, American Dentist."

An armed Gurkha at the entrance refused to allow us to enter. "Dr. Smith not stopping." He repeated the phrase mechanically.

Marj flashed the only official-looking document she owned—the certificate of identity of a noncombatant issued in Miami "in case of capture." He studied the fingerprints thoughtfully, ignoring everything else on the reverse side, and finally allowed us both to pass.

We walked out of the rain into a cluttered office where a first lieutenant was making marginal notes on a Japanese newspaper. We fumbled in our handbags for travel orders, but the lieutenant waived all formalities.

"I'm just one of the help—Bill Magistretti," he introduced himself. And from that time on through the many months we worked together, Bill became one of the MO mainstays although he was officially carried on the research table of organization.

We had heard about Bill in Washington as one of the best Japanese scholars in the organization. He had studied in Japanese middle schools and college, where he prepared for the Buddhist priesthood. Watching the war develop from his front-row seat in Japan, Bill decided to return to the United States, where he worked as a civilian with the San Francisco Office of Naval Intelligence at a secret listening post, decoding messages from Sasebo and other Jap military areas. After Pearl Harbor he joined OSS and was sent to India to analyze and study captured material.

One of the doctor's bedrooms had been converted into an MO office with two desks and a filing cabinet on which was a sign reading, "Beware of the kraits."

"Kraits look like worms, but they're deadly poisonous. The bearer found a pair nesting in the cabinet the other day," Bill told us by way of introduction to our new office.

Bill was convinced that MO could be effectively carried out from Delhi once the "brass" was educated to its potentialities. Meanwhile he perched on one of the desks, chewed on a dead pipe, and gave us a fill-in on the situation in the CBI theater since the 1944 Quebec conference.

At the time of that meeting, British and American governments formed an Allied operational command in Burma and India, coordinated with China. This new theater was responsible for land, sea, and air operations against the Japanese in Southeast Asia.

In the beginning the strategists—particularly the British—wanted to mount a large-scale sea offensive with British, Dutch, American, French, and Indian naval units striking Jap positions to the south. However, matériel which CBI expected was rerouted to Europe. Plans were then recast. The Americans concentrated on driving the Japanese from northeast Burma, improving communications with China sufficiently to keep the Generalissimo's country actively in the war.

General Stilwell, as deputy supreme Allied commander under Lord Louis Mountbatten, and commanding general of American forces in CBI, was at the end of a trickle of supplies diverted from Europe. He also faced a delicate political situation midway between the Chinese and British while his troops faced superior Jap forces across fluid Burma battle lines.

"The general," Bill said, "doesn't have any men to spare, and he depends on OSS Detachment 101 at Assam for more than half his intelligence. For instance, we have one group of agents near Myitkyina that has been reporting on all Jap installations in north Burma. There's another team farther south that sends in weather three times daily to the Tenth Air Force. And there's a wild bunch of Kachins that a Catholic priest named Father Stuart organized. His boys saved the Marauders from a Jap ambush. Ray Peers is the colonel in charge of 101—Regular Army man—you'll have to sell MO to him because he isn't too strong for new ideas."

He skipped lightly over China. There, OSS was hanging on precariously under the Sino-American agreement to work with General Tai Li, head of the Generalissimo's secret service, and under a separate cover organization, the Air-Ground Forces Resources and Technical Staff (AGFRTS) under General Chennault's command.

"OSS has one of its most clever women working here in Delhi—Rosamond Frame. You'll meet her. Ask her about the Chinese puzzle."

It was the first time I had heard about the enigmatic Rosy Frame, but our paths were to cross several times before the end of the war.

MO in New Delhi had access to two important intelligence sources. One was under joint American-British command and was called SEATIC—South-East Asia Translation and Interpreter Command. Here American Nisei and British teams worked on captured material. The other equally important intelligence source was the British prisoner-of-war compound at the historic Red Fort, where all Japanese and insurgent Indian prisoners of war were screened.

There were lesser fountains: the British Ministry of Information (BMOI), which maintained a twenty-four-hour monitor service over all occupied areas and supplied us with intercepts; the British Army Aid Group (BAAG), whose advance agents worked in and around Hong Kong, cleared all intelligence through Delhi, and specialized in economic and shipping news from that former British colony. Our own American Joint Intelligence Collection Agency (JICA) maintained headquarters in Delhi. From here men were sent to China and Burma to collect material. (Our girls considered JICA a fine "beat" to cover because handouts to OSS were distributed by its commanding officer, Captain Gene Markey, the film producer.)

"When you piece all their information together, occasionally you get something pretty interesting," Bill told us.

"F'r instance: Because of the growing American offensive in the Pacific the Japs have been secretly pulling their troops out of SEAC. We got the first hint of it from captured documents. Then BMOI picked up a sudden burst of Jap propaganda to conquered areas telling the people that Japan is going to let them govern themselves. The proof? They'll withdraw their troops and leave well trained puppet garrisons, officered by Japs! Then, from agents within the countries, we get a rather ominous sequel to the whole thing—at least it doesn't look too good for the British and French and Dutch: The people in Greater East Asia like the idea of being their own bosses! It's going to be a nice mess after the war."

Bill shifted his dead pipe moodily and muttered, *"Shigata ga nai."*

It was good Japanese for "So what?"

Our own immediate problem—production of MO material— nagged me. The British owned a complete Japanese type font and rotary press in Calcutta where they produced white psychological warfare material. Even if we could use their equipment—and I understood the British weren't too friendly with us down there—would MO be compromised by printing subversive leaflets with the type used in weekly white publications? Particularly since it was old-fashioned type used by a Los Angeles newspaper before the war.

There was an offset press in New Delhi which the British used to produce agent passports and credentials. Hidden away in a stable in the Viceroy's palace grounds, it was operated by a Major André Bicat, but all the material was originally set up for him in Calcutta.

From every angle, the situation looked glum. There was just one faint twinkle of hope—about as bright as the stars on the shoulders of the two generals with whom we were to dine that evening. Surely, generals must perform some useful function in rear echelons. And besides, we didn't need a very large press . . .

After lunch Bill and I visited SEATIC, where a new shipment of captured documents had just been received from Burma. As we drove along in a leaky jeep through a constant, hammering rain I tried to comfort myself with the thought that Japanese morale in Burma might possibly be lower than my own. It was raining there, too, and they didn't even have a leaky jeep!

The fact that Colonel Peers was expected in Delhi within the next four days didn't help much, either. We should make a fine impression —two girls in an empty office with a lot of Washington-spawned ideas. The inconvenience of being a woman, the dank smell of my clothes, the dismal appearance of the buildings of the British rear echelon headquarters only added to my general feeling of futility.

We passed the swirls of barbed wire and entered a series of squat adobe houses where barefoot Indian boys were busy along mud-paved corridors brewing tea over open braziers. Badly ventilated offices were packed with British and Americans—the British in short-sleeved blouses and shorts, the Americans stiffly correct in ties and starched uniforms. We stopped near a room where men were bending over long, crowded work tables. The air was rancid with cigarette smoke. There was a low babel of Japanese and English. On the far wall I saw a Japanese flag and samurai sword.

"American Nisei," Bill explained. "Our GI Samurai."

To me the Japanese Americans in Hawaii occupied a very special niche in the annals of World War II. Before the war their records in the Reserve Officers' Training Corps had been the highest. They were the backbone of the Hawaii National Guard until that day, shortly after Pearl Harbor, when all men of Japanese ancestry were told to fall out of ranks and turn in American uniforms and rifles. They had reentered the service as volunteer labor battalions and had then petitioned Congress to restore their right as American citizens to fight in defense of their country. When their request was granted, a few were chosen for combat. Others, like the boys who bent over the tables at SEATIC, were fighting the enemy with their own precious knowledge of his language, his habits.

I was startled out of this reverie on my favorite minority group by someone calling my name at the far end of the room. Heads bobbed up from work. Suddenly several of the Nisei stood up. The first one I recognized was the second son of my Japanese professor, Saburo Watanabe. Others gathered around: Errol Nagao, who lived only two blocks from our home; Georgie Maeda, whose father owned a sweet-chestnut shop; Wallace Nagao, who earned his way through school working at a Kohala coffee plantation; Haruyoshi Kaya; Harry Ito . . .

A swift, warm exchange of home-town news followed as our little group began to block tea traffic. What was I doing in India? Did I know the Indians made leis like Hawaiians? Would I like to hear their island glee club? Somebody had a can of poi. How about a *luau?* Saburo had a uke. Let them know if they could help in anything . . .

I felt curiously homesick when I finally broke away and Bill escorted me to the office of a British Major Clark, who was in charge of all captured material, including such items as letters, postcards from soldiers' families in Japan, diaries, field manuals, orders, supply books, magazines, newspapers.

Major Willie Clark, Bill warned me, was gruffly pro-American. He was a well educated, smart colonial who had won special honors for his undercover work as a British agent in Malaya when the Japs first overran that area. Willie spoke Japanese better than the Jap prisoners.

We found the major—a slight, dark man in trim gabardine uniform —seated at a desk, with a long ivory cigarette holder clenched between his teeth. He was reading what looked like a Japanese edition of *Spicy Stories*. As we entered, he frowned over horn-rimmed glasses and then began a breathless tirade.

"Now what? I see you are coming to rob me of important documents. And bringing female reinforcements! This time I shall be adamant. Nothing leaves this building!"

After perfunctory introductions Bill ignored the major and strode into a small back room, where he rummaged in a barracks bag. Willie shrugged.

"How does he know about my latest caches?"

I didn't know how to answer that, and our conversation ended abruptly. The major fumbled in his pockets and came out with a package of Japanese cigarettes. By now I realized that he was terribly uncomfortable, or possibly embarrassed and shy. Being a non-smoker, I refused his cigarettes, and he seemed to take affront.

"Captured Japanese cigarettes are better than the vile things we British smoke," he began to apologize. Then his mood veered. "The only advantage of having Americans here is that on rare occasions we sometimes receive their cigarettes."

I tried to explain that I didn't smoke anyway, and he instantly brightened. "Perhaps, then, you'll consider my application for your PX ration?"

I could see I had a bargaining point there. I nodded.

Now, with a wary eye on Bill, he outlined the Burden for the Day. In our long friendship ahead, Willie was never without a Burden.

"I'm working on an intelligence jigsaw puzzle," he began. "Have you ever been to the Philippines?"

When I told him I had spent a short time there he brought out a large photograph album with the insignia of a Japanese infantry unit on the cover. It was the picture story, he told me, of a crack *butai*, recorded by one of Japan's ace camera artists, from the time the company left Yokohama by troop transport until it was wiped out in Burma. Willie identified certain areas where it had been stationed: Balikpapan oil fields, Mandalay, with its temples, Rangoon with inspection by General Homma. An Australian in Willie's section recognized the mountainous contours of the Owen Stanleys and located one picture sequence along the famous Kokoda Trail.

"We know where they were—with the exception of this one spot. I'm sure it's the Philippines—has to be—logical."

He showed me a photo of a group of Japanese soldiers in a motor boat near a wharf. "Mabuhay II" was painted on the prow. At first I looked at the photograph casually. Then I felt as if I'd suddenly stumbled on Tojo hiding in the MO filing case. The picture had been taken at Davao on the island of Mindanao. I identified the Standard Oil Company shed and the nipa shacks along the waterfront. Willie duly inscribed my remarks, first in Japanese, then in English, naming me as the intelligence source. Then, as a gruff reward, he invited me into the back room, where we found Bill elbow-deep in mildewed documents. The place smelled of rancid, unclean things, of moldy leather and papers damp from the jungles.

"I see you are greedily immersed in material we captured in a cholera area," Willie mumbled. "Watch out for fleas and things, lieutenant."

Bill was evidently used to Willie's brand of humor. He continued to study a heavy document.

"So the British finally got the remains of that starving battalion of Japs near Myitkyina," Bill noted. "Suppose it got a big play in the London press. Brave Tommies rout fanatical Japs. Look what this Jap noncom says in his final entry. 'Even mosquitoes can't find nourishment on our emaciated bodies. We've been eating grass and roots for two weeks. No sign of the enemy, but it's just as well. We're out of ammunition.' "

Willie invited me to dip into the sack. I fished out some rather pitiful mementos picked up on the battlefield—pictures of children, good-luck pieces, postcards, brass dog tags, letters. Near the bottom of the bag I felt something solid, and I retrieved a leather pouch with a single five-cornered brass star of the Japanese Army on the flap. I opened the slip lock. Inside were layers of postcards. Willie removed the covering letter and read it.

"Just a batch of cards some C.O. ordered his men to write home before the last battle. We wiped out what was left of this battalion a few days ago. These postcards never say much, just the usual trivia: 'Dear Okasan: I am fine. Eating well. Killing three *beikokujin* daily before breakfast.' "

He drew out several cards. Messages were scrawled in pencil, mostly in unsteady, elementary characters that even I could read. The addresses were printed on the reverse side which had also been stamped with an Army post-office star and a censor's chop. The cards bore no dates or locations.

The idea hit us all about the same time, just after I said what a shame it was that they couldn't be mailed to the families.

"Why *can't* they be mailed to Japan?" Bill fairly ripped the pouch out of Willie's hand. "They've been censored, haven't they?"

While he sample-checked, I picked up his idea. "Erase the original messages! Substitute our own. It could be the first black MO into Japan!"

"It'd be a cinch," Bill agreed. "Our 101 agents can slip this pouch into the Jap postal system that's still working south of Mogaung—there's a damned good chance nobody'll check cards that have already been censored!"

Willie joined in. "Think what the Japanese back home would say if they heard about real conditions in Burma. Their radio still tells them the Imperial armies are marching through India!"

He selected a card at random and read the brief message, about how one Teiji Kano was fighting for the homeland and that therefore all was well. It was written in awkward characters by a soldier with about a fifth-grade education. Willie erased the words, dexterously replaced them with a different message in almost identical handwriting.

"See!" He held it up with a flourish. " 'Where are the supplies from home? Why are we starving in the jungles? Better to surrender than fight without bullets.' "

Bill had already wrapped the cards and container when Willie remembered his earlier threat.

"What would my C.O. say if he knew I was allowing all this valuable material to be stolen by our allies? What authority, lieutenant, do you have to steal?"

Bill ignored the remark but cautioned Willie that he was contemplating cutting down his cigarette supply if he persisted in being an obstructionist.

As we were leaving, Willie sidled up. "If you'll send your jeep around about five this afternoon, I'll come over and help out—with a few friends."

Shortly after five we heard a commotion outside the gates of 32 Feroz Shah and I looked out to see our wary chokidar attempting to hold Willie Clark and some dozen belligerent Nisei at bay. Willie was spitting insults at the guard in Urdu while the Nisei were infiltrating. Bill reached them in time to assure the guard that they weren't looking for Dr. Smith the dentist, and ushered them into the MO office, with the overflow sitting on the porch floor. In spite of a long day at SEATIC, the Nisei said they didn't mind helping out a fellow Hawaiian; besides, they were rather excited about the job.

I explained briefly to them then that we would try to hammer the same message home on each card, like an advertising campaign emphasizing a single slogan. The Japanese were losing Burma because the home front was not behind them. Accuse the folks back home of being slackers. Hint that they were selling the soldiers short. Tell of heartbreak and starvation in the jungle. Accuse the people of Japan of filling their bellies on black-market food, their pockets with war profits.

We divided the cards, and the boys started working. Once Saburo brought over a nostalgic card from a soldier to his wife, who hoped she would tell their son, whom he had never seen, that his father was proud to die for the Emperor.

"It's so sad—I hate to change it," Saburo told me.

I felt a little sentimental myself, but I tried to point out that whatever heartbreak we might bring to one person would be well worth the effort if we could plant a small doubt back home in the minds of the people that Burma was lost and something was radically wrong with their war effort.

He came back later and showed me where he had changed the words: "Don't ever tell our son I died for a lost cause."

Marj and I served coffee and sandwiches from the pantry, and the boys worked on well after nine o'clock at the painstaking task of forgery and deception. We finally called a halt and agreed to meet the following day. With steady application we should finish in three days, just in time to give the cards and translations to Colonel Peers.

When Marj and I returned wearily to our room that night we were met at the door by a strange Indian in a red fez and immaculate uniform who smiled through betel-tinted teeth at us.

"I am Ali your faithful bearer," he repeated, parrotlike, pulling out a sheaf of references which proved he had worked for several American colonels. "One colonel, two generals are here awaiting your arrival for many hours. They are now fooding at Hotel Imperial," he informed us.

Marj and I stared at each other in horror. We had already learned that in the Delhi social whirl it was practically a court-martial offense to stand up a general! Even Ali was upset. He suggested that we allow him to take a chitty to the Imperial tendering our regrets. Marj wrote out a sorry excuse about work, and we both fell into bed.

The room was filled with a heady fragrance from some night-blooming Indian flower that reminded me of jasmine. I drifted off to sleep thinking about Japanese mama-sans marching on the Imperial Palace, brandishing our postcards . . .

We worked for three days on our project until we had completed four hundred and seventy-five cards, with translations for Washington and Colonel Peers. By our dead line we were able to place the lot back in the original mail pouch. To it I attached a brief explanation in correct military terminology.

We had been expecting a grim, craggy colonel of the Blimp variety, but Colonel William Ray Peers was one of those typically young OSS officers, about thirty-three years old, tanned, slim, with a quick smile dotted with a dimple. His friendly southern drawl at first deceived us, but we soon discovered what Bill meant about doing an MO job on him. Beneath his smooth manner we saw that he was not prepared to talk business with a couple of females just fresh from Washington. He started to tease us as soon as we met.

"Need a couple of sirens out in the jungle. How'd you girls like the job?"

We refused to banter. Marj looked at me, and I slowly picked up the sheaf of cards and translations. I wished then that Marj had done the talking because my voice began to tremble when I described the work the Nisei and Bill and Willie had done for us on their own time.

"Colonel, if 101 could get this pouch into the Japanese mails, it would probably be the first black penetration of Japan proper," I concluded weakly.

Colonel Peers stopped smiling and picked up the covering memo. There was a long, uncomfortable pause while he read it, then looked at both of us.

"As I understand it," he said slowly, "you want my Kachins to slip this mail pouch into the Jap postal system south of Mogaung?"

"Yes, sir."

I wondered how people from West Point thought. I wondered if he would humor us with a pleasant passing of the buck. If he could only have seen us working at it! He was frowning now, and scratching his head. He won't take it, I thought, he thinks we're addled females . . .

Instead he picked up the packet, put it into his brief case, and said very seriously:

"Check—I'll get it to the boys first thing tomorrow. You know, it's not such a bad idea—"

We waited at 32 Feroz Shah Road for three days, for news. I could hardly believe it when the Message Center courier arrived with a wire from the colonel himself, from Detachment 101.

"Mission accomplished. Every reason to believe material will reach objective!"

A week later Bill skipped into our office flourishing the Delhi *Statesman*, a sly grin on his face.

"Tojo cabinet resigned," he announced. "Think it could have been black mail?"

CHAPTER SIX

WE MAKE FRIENDS AND INFLUENCE ENEMIES

During my first two weeks in India a gradual change came over me—that almost imperceptible metamorphosis from rookie to veteran. For the first week after my arrival, the most interesting thing about me to the old guard was the nostalgic fact that I was just so many hours removed from "stateside." It always seemed to please jaded Americans with over six months' accumulated foreign service to learn that I had had a glass of real milk about fifty-eight hours ago; that the sun had been shining in Miami last Sunday.

Then, as the new ones arrived in that strange land of drugstores without coke, I found myself talking India with a wise note in my voice. As a CBI veteran who could now make change in rupees and order a burra gimlet with the best of the British, I had become an expert on the American, British, and Indian caste system in New Delhi.

The Imperial Gymkhana Club was super-elect for British colonials, high-ranking officers and specially sifted Americans. Junior officers found sanctuary at the Piccadilly where Rudy Cotton's Burmese orchestra entertained with such specialties as that rage of the early twenties, "Mr. Gallagher and Mr. Shean." The British, when they wanted to get away from the Americans, rallied forces at the pucka Maiden's Hotel air-conditioned ballroom and danced to the grim, measured tempo of a string quartet. The higher-class Indians entertained at the charming, open-air Roshanara Club and didn't seem to mind who came and mingled with them as long as everyone had a good time. And there was always the American Red Cross Canteen— with hot dogs, hamburgers, cokes, and American girls with professional smiles for enlisted men.

Because of the girl shortage, social demands were heavy, and most of the Taj zenana—about twenty-five OSS, Red Cross girls, and nurses —was dated up weeks in advance. The men who couldn't get dates consoled themselves with the thought, "Wait till those crows get back to the states—nobody'll look at them twice." Some of the girls were "brass-happy" and were referred to as "chicken colonel chicks." Others, in patriotic abandon, let it be known that they would date no one but GI's—and flaunted their democracy as if it were some cross they had assumed to save the American Army from itself and from the Anglo-Indian girls.

While I had little trouble establishing a beach head on New Delhi's social front, I discovered that it was one thing to go dancing at the Imperial Gymkhana Club with a two-star Engineer Corps general— another thing to wheedle a printing press from him even after he had been pressed with many burra gimlets and encouraged to talk about the Alcan Highway, World War I, and his wife and children. (My one attempt to obtain MO equipment by such out-of-channel maneuvering did, however, net me some sound advice. "Don't ever come to a general for supplies," I was told by the general. "Go to his supply sergeant. After all, how do you think *we* get things?")

After about three weeks of orientation work on Feroz Shah Road, where Marj and I studied intelligence sources, reports and MO possibilities, and cultivated OSS and British personnel who were all too willing to dispense ephemeral information on the war, the real problems of carrying out a morale operation began to shape up.

Here, certainly, was no Hollywood version, set to Rimski-Korsakov music, of a couple of intrepid American girls alone in the Far East pitting female cunning against the wily Jap, wrapping generals around fingers, in touch with an army of willing native agents who thought nothing of facing the firing squad to carry their white memsahibs' forged documents across the lines. In addition to a repulsive prickly heat rash which banded both our middles, Marj and I were two rather insecure Americans facing each other across empty desks until recently occupied by nesting kraits, and charged with the weighty task, on paper, of "conducting morale operations against the enemy." It had been sheer good luck, with no planning on our part, that enabled us to turn out the postcard project and win a hesitant approval from Colonel Peers and his boys in Burma. From here on we needed, in Washington parlance, "an operational plan and implementation thereof."

Even office supplies were difficult to come by in the impoverished CBI theater, where every paper clip was saved and used again. The arrival from Washington of Grace Mullen, our office secretary, with pounds of carbon and typing paper, typewriter ribbons, incoming and outgoing boxes and that luxurious item, Scotch tape, gave MO more prestige at Feroz Shah Road than a presidential citation. We were known as "those girls with the heavy bond paper." Ours was the only office with a desk calendar!

Consequently, in a theater where every pencil was counted before offices closed at night, it was almost an absurdity to hope for a printing press, although my friend the general said one day, after they had uncrated a complete ice-cream factory unit, he wouldn't be surprised at anything turning up for the American Army in our warehouses.

From Washington we continued to receive those soul-trying memos: "Negotiations under way for shipping press and Jap type."

From American sources "close to the British" came the repeated warning: "Stay away from our cousins until high-level policies have been established for a working arrangement with them!"

From the Japs across the bay in Burma came the only faint word of cheer—their psychological warfare program, too, was bogging down in monsoons and red tape. I read this comforting bit of intelligence in the quarterly report of the Jap propaganda agency, Hikari Kikan, which Willie sent over from SEATIC.

In a program amazingly similar to our own, the Japs outlined plans for intensified black and white campaigns throughout Burma and India, including the establishment of a secret black radio station, "Free Ceylon" with which they planned to incite the Indian population. Like our own reports, the Japs meticulously recorded all successes and failures for the edification of the Tokyo rear echelon. The only difference I could see in standard operating procedure was that they used red carbon paper, Jap typewriters that wrote up and down, and they dated their work in the 19th year of Showa.

The Hikari Kikan report did much to humanize the Nip war effort for me, particularly through the frequent memoranda included in the collection by a certain Mr. Wakayama, a civilian with the Japanese Psychological Warfare section in charge of operating a front-line press. Mr. Wakayama's messages were masterpieces of understatement and frustration in which he repeatedly asked Tokyo for "printing equipment," prefacing his polite requests with subtle remarks that it was impossible to fight the enemy with good intentions. He was also unhappy because the military men would not let him, Mr. Wakayama, a civilian, in on their plans of conquest.

At times like this, war sometimes seemed futile. Mr. Wakayama worked in the office of the *Biruma Shimbun* in Rangoon where a four-page Jap newspaper was printed weekly for their troops. I worked several blocks from the offices of the *CBI Roundup*, a sprightly tabloid for the American GI's. If only Mr. Wakayama and I could have arranged a clandestine exchange of facilities! Then we could have fulfilled our repressed desires to produce something for our respective war efforts instead of fretting in Delhi and Rangoon, each of us developing a neurosis which would doubtless hamper our readjustment in the postwar world.

Acquisition of a printing press and type font was a long-range dream toward eventual success of the American mission. Our immediate problem was to procure a Japanese writer who could do such odd jobs as falsifying Japanese soldiers' diaries, closing them on a sunny note of intent to surrender instead of the usually abrupt manner in which most Jap diaries seemed to end.

Our Nisei translators could not handle any writing which involved detailed composition, since their Japanese language couldn't stand the test. The Nisei thought too much like Americans, and English was their mother tongue. The Japanese they knew had been drilled into them in language schools, or at home where usually an impure, often bad-type Japanese was spoken by an older generation not up on the latest Tokyo idioms. Even Bill Magistretti, well versed as he was in Japanese classicism, did not feel qualified to write black propaganda. He knew his work would have an Occidental cast.

Later, when we needed writers to compose newspaper and magazine articles, we should require someone with journalistic training. In order to reach the Jap soldier, our ideal would be a Jap version of someone like our own Ernie Pyle, someone who could use soldier idioms, understand soldier gripes. Which were the deep-seated grievances that could be played to our advantage? Which were the garden variety peeves without which no GI would be happy, in any army?

The Yenan Communists in China had proved the advantage of using Jap to fight Jap. After capturing Japanese soldiers, they fed them well, clothed them, and treated their wounds. Then they indoctrinated them in the "brotherhood of man" concept and sent them back to their own lines to spread the word that the Imperial Nipponese military system wasn't everything the field manuals said it was, and that the enemy didn't torture prisoners. The ones who stayed on with their brother Communists wrote propaganda to be used against former comrades in arms that touched the nostalgic, sentimental, sometimes mystic, always homesick Jap soldier as only a former tentmate could stir him.

A Japanese prisoner of war, preferably college-educated, would answer our problem. I was determined not to fall into the pitfalls of bad psychological warfare work the Japs in Burma hit when they used one of their own boys with a Y.M.C.A. smattering of English to write the following nostalgic appeal to a British soldier whom they depicted asleep under a tree, dreaming of a thatched cottage, weeping wife in a shawl, her son in wooden shoes tugging at her hand and asking:

"Mom, when's pop coming home?"

Even a willing prisoner of war and a press wouldn't solve everything. There would be innumerable technical difficulties to overcome before we perfected our work, questions involving such simple things as when to use an offset press, when to turn out material on a letter press.

Since the Japs themselves had developed the offset process, we could use it in producing certain magazines, leaflets, documents, and posters. But it was generally agreed by expert typographers that we could not use an offset press to produce newspapers or clippings. Even the most casual Jap newspaper reader would sense some technical error—type leaves a definite dent on newsprint whereas the offset process makes no physical impression on paper.

There were also the worries of using correct paper. Japanese newsprint was a coarser, cheaper grade than that used by American papers. There was quite a difference in Jap typefaces, make-up, reporting styles. Jap news values differed from ours. Any story about the Emperor that missed page one was a social error that might lead the publisher to commit hara-kiri. Because Jap news was slanted, our own black stories had to be subtle. We couldn't criticize the Jap government in a forged news clipping. But we might print a story, for consumption in Burma, telling of the arrest of insurgents at Waseda University who printed antigovernment leaflets—and then quote the leaflets in full to put over our idea.

Meanwhile we were busy enough collecting material for future MO work—diaries, letters, intelligence on specific units in the field, and a card file on leading Japanese militarists in Burma. We initiated rumor sheets with specific objectives in mind, to be disseminated by Burmese agents. We even devised a formula for spreading rumors:

1. Tell the story casually, and don't give yourself away by being overanxious to launch your rumor.

2. If the low-down is especially hot, tell it confidentially.

3. Never speak your rumor more than once in the same place. If it's good, others will repeat it.

4. Tell it innocently, and don't disclose any source that can readily be discredited.

Six weeks passed before we were able to initiate and follow through on our first planned MO project which represented the combined efforts of eight operatives and certain hoodwinked forward units of the Japanese 18th Division in north Burma. JB–1, a code number arbitrarily assigned to the project by Grace, also marked our first successful liaison with the British, and the acquisition of Mr. Okamoto, without whose help we perhaps should never have been able to put over a hoax that we believe resulted in the eventual surrender of a good number of Japanese soldiers.

One morning in late August Marj supplied me with a sheaf of intelligence intercepts that included a military order from the Japanese high command listing the punishments meted out to any Japanese soldiers who surrendered in battle. There was also a report on the morale of the 18th Division in Burma, where food was bad, medicine and supplies exhausted, and news from home was sometimes five months late. The report of Tojo's resignation as premier and the formation of a new cabinet by Koiso had only just reached north Burma, and no explanation was furnished to the news-hungry soldiers.

I considered the facilities we had at hand. Since we had no press, we couldn't produce a news clipping speculating on the capitulation of Tojo; but perhaps we could produce a forged order involving a new policy by Koiso on surrender.

While Tojo was in control, Jap troops were indoctrinated with the fanatical belief that surrender was dishonorable and would bring permanent disgrace to family and Emperor. Upon notification that a Japanese had surrendered, his *genseki*, or birthright, was forfeited; he was declared legally dead, and his soul was barred from fluttering home to Yasukuni Shrine—considered by many a fate worse than death! If recaptured after surrender, the soldier was subjected to penalties ranging from death before a firing squad to banishment from Japan. Who would know in north Burma, I debated, what sort of policy Koiso might have on surrender? Perhaps he might favor the policy of conserving Japanese manhood for the hundred-year war ahead that the Jap propagandists had been promising in order to establish their Greater East Asia Co-Prosperity Sphere.

I typed up a draft of the proposed forgery, addressed by the Koiso government to the Japanese High Command in Rangoon with instructions to disseminate the order to all forward units. The new order rescinded the old war department list of penalties for surrender and announced a new policy. Under certain stringent conditions—when soldiers were hopelessly outnumbered in battle, unconscious, too ill to fight or without further ammunition—it would now be permissible for the Japanese to give himself up to the enemy and demand fair treatment guaranteed under the terms of the Geneva pact.

Concurrently the Japanese government would announce to the homeland that no stigma henceforth attached to such surrender.

This did not mean, of course, that the Koiso government condoned wholesale surrender such as the treacherous mass defections of Italians. Surrender was always the last resort when further fighting was futile.

Once I had reshaped the entire structure of the Japanese Army's basic field manual on proper conduct of a soldier, I faced a definite "iffy" situation. If we found a Japanese prisoner he might be able to forge the order for us, if his calligraphy was above the ordinary. If our own security office allowed us to use the offset press operated by Major Bicat and British intelligence, we should have to get the correct paper and ink. If we procured the necessary material, our forgery on the offset press must resemble Japanese cyclostyling—a process like our mimeographing except the Japanese used a stylus on wax paper and their calligraphy was usually neat and beautifully executed in the difficult "grass" writing that few soldiers could master.

Having once set the *if*'s up like tenpins, I was able, through a set of lucky circumstances, to knock them down fairly easily. Our first and greatest break was the discovery of Mr. Okamoto through a chance remark by Willie that a Waseda University graduate had been captured in Burma and had just recently arrived in Delhi. Several days later, Bill wangled permission from the British at the Red Fort to interview the prisoner.

The morning we set out to visit the Fort, Bill became a sort of genie of the jeep, and aboard his GI magic carpet we left the façade of New Delhi where Occidentals lived in a transplanted European city, and penetrated old Delhi, seven miles away where I became aware for the first time of how some of the three hundred and ninety million Indians really lived.

To reach the Red Fort we drove along a well paved highway that seemed to span past and present between the modern housing project that flanked New Delhi and the nomad tents that were carelessly flung over the green expanse of *maidan* that was part of the old city. It would have almost seemed proper to leave our jeep in the twentieth century and take up our journey in one of the padded camel caravans or jogging bullock carts that were moving slowly toward old Delhi at the approved speed of centuries past. Where New Delhi had been an unnatural transposition of a stiff Western pattern of living on a warm land, the old city seemed to effervesce, like a colorful composition of cellular activity under a microscope, and vibrate with dirt and smells and people who were going about their work unmindful of the war and foreigners who had brought it. (They were also oblivious, I soon noted, to the Occidentals' recently developed sanitary code that man shall commit no nuisance in public.)

Bill twisted his jeep expertly through narrow streets which closed above us in a haphazard utilization of space, where second and third stories hung out over the shops of hucksters, rug merchants, silversmiths, in top-heavy confusion. The jeep horn parted phalanxes of plodding people as we passed on through Chandni Chauk, purportedly the richest street in India, through Kashmir Gate, pockmarked with shell holes of the last great Sepoy rebellion against the British, and we drove up to the massive red sandstone walls of the mile-square Red Fort which towered sixty feet above us. Ahead marched a company of Indian soldiers, swinging along the cobblestones in military rhythm, a sharp contrast to the milling chaos of citizens we had just left. The soldiers' hobnailed British boots clanged across the iron flooring of the drawbridge, and we followed the company under a rusty portcullis through Lahore Gate into the Fort.

Bill pointed out the famous marble pavilions and Pearl Mosque built by Shah Jahan, the Mogul emperor who erected the Taj Mahal.

The ancient splendor was a striking contrast to the drab billets of mud and wood where British and Indian troops were quartered and where the prisoner-of-war compound was located. Here a guard with fixed bayonet passed us into the stockade which abutted the towering walls of the Fort. There were some half-dozen mud-brick buildings in a sandy quadrangle marked by gay hedges of bougainvillaea. Along the shaded paths, British and Nisei interrogators strolled and smoked with Japanese prisoners who wore blue denim suits with POW in large white letters on the backs. We found the commandant, a British major, in a cool, mud-floored office near the prisoners' billets. He was drinking thick tea from a cracked white mug.

"*Dozo—o-haeri nasai!*"

There was something incongruous about a chubby, ruddy-faced Britisher inviting us to enter, in Japanese. Bill kept the conversation

in English—to the major's chagrin, I think, because his otherwise precise speech was punctuated with Jap idioms like lumps in porridge.

The major explained that his college-educated prisoner, Okamoto,
was the smartest one he had interrogated. Sometimes he thought him
almost too smart. Okamoto had surrendered in Burma because he dis-
approved of the stupid loss of life and bungling of the Jap Burma
campaigns. On the other hand, he wasn't particularly impressed with
the Allies or democracy; but he was willing to do anything to help
save further loss of Japanese lives.

The major had instituted what he called a V-2 program among
captured prisoners of war. He attempted to indoctrinate the smart
ones by allowing them to have access to British and American publications and by supplying them with radio entertainment. When he
thought they had got a slant on who was actually winning the war,
he would leave pamphlets on the Atlantic Charter and the four freedoms in strategic places. During this subtle propagandization, Nisei
or British interrogators mingled with the more promising Japanese
and discussed the part the prisoners could play after the war in making over Japan.

If the prisoners were too thoroughly imbued with Jap militarism,
they were screened and packed off to "Shangri-la."

"That's our permanent POW stockade out in the Sind Desert," the
major explained evenly. "We supply them with everything they need
out there—food, quarters, clothes, all according to Geneva convention rules. It's a pity the heat's so bad, though. We have to change
our own guards every other month—"

I must have looked shocked, because the major continued, a little
on the defensive.

"Look what they're doing to our boys at Singapore—hundreds of
British and Australian soldiers dying like flies, building jungle roads,
going crazy, no water, no medicine—"

-Suddenly he lowered his voice to a whisper. A British guard, leading three Japanese prisoners, passed within earshot.

"Most of the Japs say they can't speak English, but you never can
tell. Just the other day we broke up an underground communication
system out in the elephant stables."

He pointed through the open door toward the massive Fort walls
where high, round caves about the size of full-grown elephants had
been carved in the sandstone.

"Shah Jahan used to keep his royal elephants in those pens. We keep
the Japs there. Actually, it's very cool inside the walls."

I could visualize the handsome, panoplied animals swaying back and forth in their houses where some forty diminutive humans with shaved heads now squatted.

The major gulped his tea and wiped his bushy mustache free of a few stray leaves as he explained that Okamoto was quite independent and might be reticent about talking to us. He had only just recently agreed to write scripts for the All India radio programs which were beamed to Japanese-occupied areas. The major thought, too, that Okamoto occasionally had twinges at turning intellectual traitor; but he had volunteered for the work himself. The prisoner said he would do anything to shorten the war.

He then led us through a pleasant garden to a separate house with heavily barred windows up which twined blue morning-glories, a touch which somehow seemed to soften the stigma of a jail. A guard unlocked the door, and we entered a bare white room furnished with an iron cot, blankets, chair, and table. The prisoner was bending over his table, a squat, solid figure in a British gray woolen uniform, with comfortable Punjab slippers on his feet. He looked up at me and stared.

"You're probably the first white woman he's seen in years," the major whispered. I wondered what odd thoughts were going on in Okamoto's mind. *He* certainly wouldn't twitch and think: "First white woman I've seen in years!" Okamoto would doubtless prefer a mincing, almond-faced witch in Bloomer Girl *mompei* at this point. He eventually stood up, possibly recalling Western social amenities. Then he looked beyond me at Bill, squinted, frowned. If it was possible for a Japanese to register emotion, Okamoto did then.

"Biru—Biru Magistretti?" He seemed all choked up.

Bill, too, looked incredulous. "Okamoto—"

There followed a rapid flow of Japanese above the major's head and mine. Finally Bill broke in to tell us in English the amazing coincidence that he and Okamoto had been in middle school together!

From then on, Okamoto became a member of the MO family and was dubbed "Joe" by his American associates. I think Bill convinced him, more than anyone else, that his only hope for a better Japan lay in the years ahead—in education of the children to a new concept of peaceful relations with the rest of the world.

Okamoto was an apt pupil and mastered MO technique rapidly. After a sober study of my Koiso surrender forgery, he said he thought it could be done. He had been assigned to headquarters in Rangoon and was familiar with the correct terminology and format. He was a little concerned about his calligraphy which he said was not as good as it should be. The only seal of authority for the order would be the chop of the High Command in Burma. This we obtained from Willie's captured supplies, in addition to the orange-red ink of vegetable dye used in affixing the chop to the order, and rice paper upon which most Jap military business was cyclostyled.

Our next step was to obtain the use of the British offset press. The forged order could not be disseminated as an original, Okamoto explained, because field headquarters always received copies of the originals. Hence we must further falsify it by producing JB–1 on an offset press since we had no cyclostyle.

Okamoto spent several days perfecting the forgery. When he turned in the finished copy Bill said it looked as if it had come from the headquarters of General Homma himself!

"And now," he ordered me, "put on some lipstick and comb your hair, and I'll drive you over to the Council House where you will negotiate the use of Major Bicat's offset press!"

The Council House, which was the home of the Indian Legislature, was a stately rotunda with spiraling staircases and circular, outer balconies and a floor plan more confusing than the Pentagon, which might account for the trouble the Indian government leaders had in getting together. By the time I reached the major's room I felt something like Theseus in pursuit of the Minotaur. Major Bicat was a jovial, egg-shaped man with crisp red hair and twinkling eyes. I thought I had spotted my first monocle in India when I noticed the small glass dangling from his shirt pocket, but when the major puckishly raised it to his eye I found myself staring through a powerful magnifying glass into his much enlarged pupil, which fixed itself upon me with Svengali-like intensity.

It was a disarming way to start the conversation which I'd been rehearsing for the past half-hour; but when I finally managed to explain about JB–1 the major took the forgery and carefully studied it, upside-down, remarking that Okamoto's beautiful calligraphy looked like "hen tracks" to him. Then he settled back expansively.

"You've come to the right place," he told me, gesturing toward a pile of papers on the floor.

"His Majesty's government pays me to forge documents and pass-·ports and odds and ends for those poor blighters they send behind the lines. In my spare time I make dummy paratroopers for deceptive warfare. Have to stuff them myself, it's so frightfully secret!"

He assured me that it would be a simple job to run off—a matter of a day or so. He seemed rather pleased to get some work that was a little out of the ordinary. I handed over to him ten sheets of captured rice paper upon which to print the order, the seal, ink, and Okamoto's original. We then had tea.

Returning to Feroz Shah Road, I reflected how easy it had all been and how much more gallant the British major had been than some of our own cold military men of the old *Kinder, Küchen, Kirche* school of thought. Would Bicat immediately telephone some top-secret British agent about JB–1? And if he did, what difference did it make? By no stretch of my imagination could I see British Intelligence forwarding the information to the Jap high command.

When Major Bicat delivered JB–1 to our office in an envelope heavily garnished with blobs of red sealing wax and top-secret stamps, we decided to send up a trial balloon before we proceeded. Through Willie Clark we inserted one of the forgeries among bona fide captured material which was routed to a Nisei for translation. Several minutes later the boy rushed to Willie's office, waving the order.

"It's a new surrender policy," he blurted. "It should eliminate a lot of last-ditch fighting. It's an important document!"

Willie then reported back to us that he believed JB–1 was technically and psychologically perfect!

Several days later we placed the forgery rather hesitantly in the hands of the first MO team to go into the field in Burma—a group of four men traveling under the code name Gold Dust, including Major Edward Hamm, 1928 Olympic Broad Jump champion; Major George Boldt, a Seattle attorney; Sergeant Roger Starr, a writer; and Sergeant Robert Salzstien, a former advertising man.

The first news we had had about Gold Dust—several weeks before they arrived in New Delhi en route to Colonel Peers' command—was an announcement of their plans in the shape of a snappy little brochure from Washington presented in Sergeant Salzstien's best advertising patois. The Mission, we read, was terse and to the point.

1. We shall weaken Jap fighting efficiency. Defeat is certain. Resistance means death. Death in futile cause is neither patriotic nor glorious. Therefore: Japs should consider giving up. (Ed. Note: Never use word "surrender" in propaganda—red flag before bull.)
2. Complicate the Japanese Military situation. Make Japanese

soldier distrust his officers; question his orders; lose faith in natives. Make natives distrust Japs, trust us.

AN INTEGRATED, COORDINATED, AND WELL TIMED CAMPAIGN OF THIS NATURE WILL SAVE THE ALLIES TIME, MUNITIONS, AND LIVES.

Gold Dust roared through New Delhi in a great white heat of enthusiasm, the same eager beavers that Marj and I had been before we became acclimated to the slow pace of the Far East. The lads were full of Plans. In their field safe were textbooks on the Japanese Mind and the Burmese Mind and a sample sheaf of projects which they were planning to present to Colonel Peers at 101 as an Integrated Program. (I later learned that Colonel Peers promptly put them all on KP for a cooling-off period.)

Once Gold Dust's crisp Washington enthusiasm had wilted in the damp bashas at Assam, they functioned like a combat unit and through the careful work of Roger Starr, promoted to a lieutenancy in the field, JB–1 was started on its involved way toward the Japanese lines.

Permission to disseminate JB–1 was first obtained from Colonel Peers, who cleared the project with General Stilwell's intelligence staff. Roger Starr was then assigned to work out a plausible scheme to get the forgery into Jap hands. It was imperative that the Japanese believe the document to be a bona fide policy order. Otherwise their intelligence could easily perceive the reason for the forgery. The physical conditions of the Japanese in Burma—lack of efficient communications between forward and rear echelons, low morale, dearth of authentic news from home—all were in our favor. How, then, could we insert JB–1 into their communication system, which, in the fluid jungle front in north Burma, consisted of a series of runners between one outpost and the next?

Roger found the answer one day when he was talking to an OSS Burmese agent, a wiry little killer with the reputation for ambushing and killing more Japs than anyone in the area, meanwhile living among them in an occupied village! Most of his victims were Jap couriers, he told Roger. They traveled alone.

Slowly the plan to infiltrate JB–1 shaped up. Working with the Burmese agent, Roger plotted the death of a Jap courier and the insertion of our forgery in his official pouch by the agent. The Japs would then discover the forgery when they discovered the body.

Roger dispatched the messenger with JB–1 and had no further word from him for several weeks, when he stumbled on the man nonchalantly sharpening his *das* outside a 101 basha. The agent hadn't even bothered to report what he considered such a routine job!

Certainly, he said, he had left the forgery on the courier after slitting his throat from ear to ear—a feat which he graphically illustrated by passing his sharp *das* across his own throat. Then he had been curious to see what happened, so he ambled into Jap headquarters and reported the murder of a courier. He even offered to lead the Japs back to the scene of his crime. He watched the soldiers remove the pouch from the body. He followed them back to headquarters where he saw the company commander open the pouch, and begin to read over the delayed mail. He suddenly seized upon JB–1, the agent said, and started to talk rapidly in Japanese to others in the room. The Burmese said he didn't wait to find out what happened.

Agents used several other indirect methods to infiltrate the forgery through Jap lines; but in order to assure a large distribution a copy of JB–1 was "delivered" to OWI. It was immediately seized by an alert psychological warfare team operating in the triangle in north Burma, and a leaflet was designed showing a photostat of the "captured" order. Our planes papered the jungles and Japs with the news.

Roger later informed us that he believed the forgery had a direct effect upon the Japs' will to resist, particularly toward the end of the campaign when Bhamo fell without a struggle. Many incidents were reported of Jap soldiers feigning unconsciousness, and of prisoners who said they had no objection to the International Red Cross's sending their names back to Japan—a most unusual occurrence. Prisoner-of-war stockades, usually quite empty, became overcrowded with men who voluntarily gave up when surrounded by superior forces. As the Burma campaign closed, reports of fanatical, last-ditch fighting were rare; and it is altogether possible that JB–1, together with intensified OWI and Gold Dust campaigns, influenced the thinking of the Jap soldier.

But when the man with the military mind hammers on his desk and demands a set of figures to prove what MO did in Burma, no one, not even the Japs themselves, can produce anything concrete for the Washington records. The casualties in thought warfare cannot be assessed in factual reports to headquarters. There are no grave crews assigned to count the doubts and troubles planted in men's minds that make them lose the will to fight.

CHAPTER SEVEN

PIXIES ON PER DIEM HILL

OUR report to Washington for September, 1944, modestly listed three "outstanding achievements" for the MO, Delhi Branch:

1. Obtained use of British press facilities in Calcutta through Major Peter Glemser.
2. Indoctrinated four missionaries en route to China for MO.
3. Produced three forged newspaper clippings; falsified ten diaries; inserted faked Tokyo bomb-damage photographs in Jap soldier mail.

There was no space (keep it concise so the boys topsides can read it at a glance) to tell of the Winning Over of Major Glemser, to which Grace attributed the extravagant use of her heady perfume, Tabu; or to relate how we subverted four timid missionaries who were all set to pack their Bibles and go home when they discovered to what depths of perfidy MO could sink. There was also no place in the report to mention our really major accomplishment at 32 Feroz Shah Road: the housebreaking of my white bull-terrier puppy, purchased one day on impulse at the bazaar when I fancied the animal smiled at me. He turned out to be a mentally retarded sort of happy hormone, a pink-nosed, pink-eyed under-vitamined dog called Angel Puss who everyone said should have been thrown back in the developer!

The Winning Over of Glemser constituted a tactical victory for MO, enabling us to proceed with plans for a campaign of long-range subversion against the Japs. But it was nothing to my credit as a diplomat—it was just my MO training, which I am convinced has spoiled me for any constructive work in a postwar civilized community.

Major Glemser, in charge of British white propaganda production in Calcutta, was the ogre whom both British and Americans had warned us against. He was "difficult," OWI people told us, because he belonged to the school of thought which wanted to integrate British and American psychological warfare efforts against target peoples and countries in the Far East. General Stilwell himself had declined for both OWI and OSS on advice from our State Department that such an integration might associate the United States with British colonial aims. The United States must remain free to pursue her own course in foreign policy, he stated. Relations in Calcutta between Major Glemser's headquarters and OWI had deteriorated into a polite exchange of cultural leaflets, with the result that OWI concentrated on working directly under General Stilwell in north Burma where most of their printing equipment was channeled.

Major Glemser was a man of action. A former art editor for one of the Hulton publications in London, he now designed most of the British white propaganda material in India, arranged air drops, contacted the Burmese underground. He had recently initiated a terror campaign, spread mostly by leaflet drop, among Subhas Chandra Bose's Indian soldiers who were marching with the Jap armies toward India. Through this psychological warfare offensive, he was credited with creating enough panic in the ranks to clog the Japanese communication system for two weeks while Indian troops were sent to the rear, banished to hospital duty for the duration.

He was also the man who, working through OSS in Washington a year before, had obtained a font of Japanese type and typesetters from Los Angeles. This feat, we all agreed, was now exceedingly difficult for OSS personnel themselves to duplicate.

Major Bicat's office arranged the interview for me with the major, which took place one rainy Sunday at Maiden's Hotel. I arrived half an hour early to discover the major salving his prickly heat in the hotel tank, a large, open-air swimming pool surrounded by bougainvillaea arbors and haughty, bustling bearers who were preparing the major's afternoon tea in an adjoining pavilion.

I had doused Grace's heaviest perfume all over me, and clutched a carton of operational cigarettes under one arm for the interview. By the time I reached the pool through a maze of box hedges and the rain, my dress clung to me in the wrong places, my upswept had begun to settle like a tired scrubwoman's coiffure at the end of a rough day, and Tabu was everywhere!

A lithe young man with an elfin sort of face bounded out of the tank when I arrived, tossed a soft white cashmere robe on, and told me he was Major Glemser. Then he led me over to the pavilion, where he began to eat sandwiches and drink tea.

"What do the Americans want now?"

The tone of his voice wasn't exactly pleasant, and I explained my mission with much the same trepidation I had once felt when I asked Dorothy Lamour to smile for the press camera when she was wearing bands on her teeth.

"Now let me get this straight," he interjected. "You want the use of our press, type, typesetters, translators—possibly our agent net— and in return, what? Your bright ideas?"

He deliberately stirred his tea while he talked, and the situation was too strained for any quips that came to mind about reverse lend-lease. Here he was—the only man in all India with a Japanese press—and he didn't even *act* like an ally! He spotted the cigarettes just when my upswept fell like a bad omelet.

"Opening wedge—American cigarettes?" he suggested with a faint, bitter edge to his voice.

I often marveled later at the glib, smooth words I heard myself saying in front of Major Glemser. Since that moment, I have never really trusted myself farther than I could toss a small, docile elephant. I was lying most smugly, not believing a word, with no documentary evidence to back up my fantastic statements. I told the major in a frank, flat voice that MO was expecting a shipload of the newest equipment within a very short period of time—new cameras, fast rotary and offset presses, fonts of Burmese, Siamese, and Japanese type, varitypers, newsprint, technicians, photographic supplies, inks, chemicals. It sounded as if all the equipment for the Burma campaign had been left on the San Francisco docks and replaced by this most urgently needed MO shipment.

Furthermore, every new piece of machinery that arrived at Calcutta would be made available to the major's office in case he needed extra press work on his particularly heavy leaflet runs. I was playing on a vague hunch. Sometime ago a friend in OWI had mentioned sarcastically that whatever equipment the British were using in Calcutta was held together with baling wire and bobby pins. My bait of a bright new print shop, complete with air-conditioned pressroom, brought a faint nibble.

"Just exactly when—" He opened the cigarette carton, removed a pack, and began to tear off the cellophane wrapping. "Just when does all this equipment arrive?"

"We've been notified that the stuff left the States—but there's so much secrecy about shipping we won't be able to give you an answer on that till it actually arrives on the Hooghly docks, in Calcutta."

(I crossed my fingers and prayed: "Please don't let the major know that one press has already landed in Calcutta, smashed beyond repair until the technicians arrive—and no one knows where they are!")

Outwardly I smiled and tried to look crisp and efficient, like a woman who might run a cafeteria or a filling station.

The major was very thoughtful for a very long time. I tried to "lift" my upswept with awkward, surreptitious motions as he gazed out toward the pool. I would have given the last three minutes off the end of my life to know what he was thinking. His silence set me to biting my thumbnail in a nervous twitch. But when he finally answered I knew MO's foot was in the door:

"Well—we could use some new equipment. Don't know how long our own presses will stand up under the strain. Even another multilith at our disposal occasionally would help—"

It wasn't so bad after that, and it turned out that Major Glemser was actually quite fond of Americans—on the battlefield. Early in the war, as one of Britain's Desert Rats, he had seen Rommel's men shoot away tank after tank from under the British until they were ready to fight the Nazis with bare hands.

"It looked like our chances of holding Africa were pretty slim, until suddenly equipment started rolling in! American stuff. American city names on boxes of ammo, crated tanks. God, how we loved you people! Over there we fought shoulder to shoulder with you. Then we come out here to fight an ideological war—which is just as important—and we split company."

The major admitted frankly he resented the American attitude in India toward the British. True, the English were carrying out colonial aims as part of government policy. It was the lifeblood of empire. Why should the Americans resent it?

"You can see how suspicion and distrust are splitting us out here," he continued thoughtfully. "If British and Americans, with the same cultural heritage, can become estranged through lack of basic trust, how'll we all get on with the Chinese and Russians after this war?"

Our interview ended with the agreement to use Major Glemser's type for black material between printing schedules for the *Gunjin Shimbun*, his weekly news sheet to Jap troops. We would stick to a common target, the Jap, and try to mesh white and black propaganda campaigns as far as possible through a weekly interchange of intelligence.

"It's not too bad an exchange, actually," he confessed, "because our black psychological warfare section has never really been developed out here."

In the months to come, Major Glemser carried out his promise and gave us every possible assistance in a black propaganda campaign that spread throughout Burma by the end of the war. I was able to assuage my own conscience later by supplying him with spare parts for one of his presses, a large, badly needed paper cutter, newsprint and ink.

Our four missionaries, and their Swiss friend who trained St. Bernard dogs for the famous Hospice in Switzerland, were an incongruous lot when they walked into our office one day in early September and announced that they had been hired by our Washington major, during his last theater visit, to work for the American government in China. That was all they knew. They had remained "under cover" until now, when our security office had finally passed on their credentials.

The head of the little band was a well known Chinese scholar-missionary from Chengtu University, Dr. William Fenn, a rather delicate intellectual who never seemed quite at home in the khaki uniform of the military. Henry Lacy, the youngest in the group, was the son of a famous missionary family in Canton. He was thin, grave and youthfully unprepared for the MO indoctrination course which Marj and I arranged for the group.

"It violates all Christian teachings we are trying to instill in our Chinese brothers," he protested.

Dr. Emery W. Carlson was perhaps the most detached of the group. He was a medical missionary from north China, and his main idea was to establish a clinic somewhere in Honan. Through it he planned to dispense medicine for body, soul, and mind, including MO leaflets.

The most unforgettable character, and the one who most readily assumed the cloak and dagger, was Oliver Caldwell, who could speak seventeen different dialects and had some handy connections with members of a Chinese underground known as the Green Circle. Oliver was of the opinion that MO could be useful as well as destructive and he immediately developed Operation Yak, a plan to infiltrate Tibet and spread democracy through the great Buddhist center in the holy city of Lhasa. He said the priests there had presses upon which they printed religious tracts, and upon which they might even be willing to print a series of MO leaflets against the "false" Buddhism which the Japanese were spreading in Asia. There were a few drawbacks to his project: OSS did not possess a single recruit who spoke Tibetan, and it was almost impossible for Americans to obtain credentials to enter Lhasa, even though they bore gifts from the Great White Father in Washington. Oliver had been intrigued a year before by the Tibetan journey of OSS's Colonel Ilya Tolstoi, who took the Dalai Lama an American watch and submachine gun from President Roosevelt and also mapped out, on the side, an escape route through Tibet from Chungking for the Chinese Government to use if the Japs took Szechuan. According to reports, the Tibetans were apathetic about democracy, and only a few of them knew who President Roosevelt was.

With the missionaries was Robert Chappelet, a former monk from Switzerland who had trained St. Bernards and knew the province of Honan like his own back yard. These two uncorrelated facts were all we could learn from him, except that he thought everyone in MO was crazy.

The first day Marj gathered the missionaries together and explained MO techniques, they showed a definite recoil! If these men were to return to their parishes in China and spread the MO gospel through an agent net of converts, they would have to be shown the light.

Into their required indoctrination reading one day we slipped a "translation" by Magistretti, a document attributed to Kenji Doihara, sometimes called the Japanese Himmler of Occupied China. To any missionary group which had spent years fostering Christianity in China, the Doihara declaration, we felt, would come as a definite challenge to action. In it was expounded his program to eradicate Christianity in Asia and lend all-out support to the spread of Buddhism for political reasons. Doihara estimated that five years of Japanese occupation would forever stamp Christianity out of China!

We marked the document "Top Secret" so that all the missionaries would be certain to read it, attributed the source to "captured documents," and hoped that Magistretti would never see the MO forgery perpetrated under his name.

Once they had digested Doihara, we circulated bona fide intelligence reports on two of OSS's finest agents-of-the-cloth, Thomas Megan, the Fighting Bishop of Honan, and the St. Columban who had spent ten years in Burma, Father James Stuart of North Ireland.

All the missionaries had heard of Bishop Megan, the Catholic priest who had gone to Honan from Iowa twenty-six years ago to build a devoted following among the Chinese in that province. Our recruits were delighted to hear what happened to Bishop Megan and his group which had been trapped behind the Japanese lines after Pearl Harbor. The churchmen fortunately spoke German, and the bishop instructed them to speak only in that language if accosted by Japs. Obtaining bicycles, they pedaled their way through the lines in the guise of German nationals from the Shantung Peninsula, an area which had been German-dominated for years. The ruse worked, and Megan and his men escaped. When the Japs heard of the trick, they set a price of one million Chinese dollars on the bishop's head, dead or alive.

The bishop then organized his own espionage net in Free China and supplied intelligence to the Chinese secret service under General Tai Li. For this work he was commissioned colonel in the Chinese army. Later, as an OSS operator, he supervised his little flock from headquarters in the Yellow River Bend, jeeping across country with carbine strapped over his shoulder, collecting information for the Americans. (It was also hinted in reports that the bishop was an excellent marksman—especially when his duties happened to take him into Jap territory.)

Luckily we had a special assistant to glamorize the already legendary Father Stuart—one of his ardent admirers from Burma, a chap named Bob Rodenburg, on leave in Delhi.

"I'd been sort of hoping for a Pat O'Brien type when I first met the father," Bob told us, "but he turned out to have thinning hair, deep-set brown eyes, slight build. He's an Irishman who speaks Kachin with an Irish brogue. The natives love him—think he's their own special pope and kneel and kiss his hand when he passes through their villages."

The father's hatred of Japs stemmed from his first brush with them shortly after they took Myitkyina and he met a small patrol along a jungle trail. An English-speaking Jap challenged him. Father Stuart, pretending ignorance, stepped forward first and asked if the Japs were Chinese. At this insult, the Jap drew himself up, spat in the dust and haughtily said they were members of the Imperial Japanese Army. He then asked Father Stuart if he were English. Mimicking the Jap, the father indignantly said he was Irish!

"But it was when the Jap said he'd never heard of an Irishman, that Father Stuart really got angry!" Bob grinned.

The Japs allowed Father Stuart to stay on with his Myitkyina parish, and he begged and borrowed medicine, clothes, and food for his Kachins. He became friendly with several Jap officers who taught him to handle small arms. They even procured a pistol from their supply depot for him, which he later used to good advantage.

When Father Stuart decided to become an active participant in the war, he joined Detachment 101 as a leader of Kachin scouts. During his stay at 101 he mastered several American dialects through GI's with whom he worked. He never wore insignia—just khaki shorts and Gurkha hat, and most of the newcomers figured he was another GI. He once told a sergeant from Brooklyn that after the war he was going back to his old racket, running hot cars from Cicero, Illinois, to Gary, Indiana! The Brooklynite was nonplussed when he next saw the father, officiating at Mass.

Maybe it was just wishful thinking on my part, but after the mission group had been exposed to the Nisei, Willie, various boys from the Burma bush, and MO techniques for several weeks, they seemed to assume a more rakish attitude toward their jobs; and hardly a day went by that Oliver didn't report a new nest of Chinese spies in the local restaurants. When they finally left for the field they were equipped to perpetrate any MO crime, from simple sabotage to character defamation campaigns.

The next time I saw them—months later in China—Dr. Fenn, Oliver Caldwell, Robert Chappelet, and Dr. Carlson were leaving by motor convoy for north China on MO Mission Viper, in the company of two male Chinese nurses and a radio technician. Carlson and Chappelet established headquarters eventually at Tantouchen, under cover of a medical mission, set up a small printing plant and disseminated over 18,000 MO leaflets and posters in Loyang and Ichang through a well organized agent net. At the close of the war reports came in on July 26 that Viper was arranging the surrender of some 100,000 puppet troops, virtually all the Chinese who were under arms in Honan Province.

When Henry Lacy left for his post at Meihsien, he was voted the man most likely to succumb to malaria by some of our skeptical, field-toughened sabotage lads. In spite of these predictions, Henry became one of the most successful operators in south China, and not only set up a print shop in the basement of a convent near Canton but caused such havoc in Japanese thought-control circles that they organized special teams to track down the bashful little missionary and wipe out his subversive press.

During the next month our little office was humming with activity and Grace's filing cabinet was gradually becoming stuffed with projects.

On a particularly feverish afternoon the strange officer walked into our room with Colonel Berno. He was confronted with Angel

Puss stretched athwart the front door, Nisei working at improvised desks, Willie sorting through some of his latest contributions of Jap medical kits, uniforms, and evil-smelling documents, and Marj and me smudged from working over proofs from Glemser's office.

"Colonel John Coughlin—OSS chief for China, India, Burma," Colonel Berno announced.

There was an embarrassed silence while we introduced our friends. The colonel's glance rested speculatively on Willie's British pips, on the group of Japanese in a secret OSS area, on the untidy room which I realized must have offended his West Point neatness, and finally upon Angel Puss, who had suddenly begun to fawn on him.

He asked to see our files and studied them silently for several minutes, then waded through the obstacle course to the door.

"These girls do all this?" he asked Colonel Berno, including the people and debris in a general glance which seemed to translate: "How could anyone make such a mess?"

When he had gone, I was ready once again to pack and return to America. My immediate crimes against the American military loomed large as I counted them off: fraternizing with the British; using their printing equipment without official clearance from OSS; breaking rules by allowing Nisei to work in the office; Angel Puss.

Colonel Coughlin, we learned, was planning to move his permanent headquarters to New Delhi from Chungking. He was reorganizing, tightening up his departments, strengthening OSS's new cover organization under Chennault in China, and in general snapping us all to attention.

Consequently, when I received a sealed memorandum from his office the following morning, I asked Grace to open it while I crossed my fingers. She read it twice before I realized what she was saying:

"You are hereby appointed to fill the vacant position of Acting Chief, Morale Operations, China-Burma-India Theater, until a suitable male replacement arrives from Washington!"

There had been acting chiefs in SEAC and China, but never an acting chief for the entire CBI Theater! And now I was it, with some thirty helpers in my MO empire reaching from Ceylon to French Indo-China!

In those days after Colonel Coughlin dropped the promotion bombshell, I must have developed what my father termed a "bureaucracy bun"—an intoxicating feeling of being an executive—although I did the same work as I had been doing and no one, not even Angel

Puss, seemed aware of my new title! The only outward change I noticed in myself was that my usually neat signature could be carelessly scrawled by a busy pen to resemble that of any executive too pressed with details to bother with the fundamental rules of the Palmer Method.

Then one day toward the end of October I walked into my office to learn that, in the best of government tradition, my little paper empire had collapsed, at the end of a long line of collapsing empires, with the split in the China-Burma-India Theater.

The news affected people differently. To General Stilwell it meant reassignment to the Pacific and final release from Chinese and British intrigue. To General Albert C. Wedemeyer, it meant a change of residence from Ceylon to China, where he would command the United States forces in the new China Theater. To Colonel Coughlin, it was a trip back to Washington for reassignment to SEAC. To the Acting Chief, MO, it meant the abolishing of New Delhi as a base of MO operations, moving to Calcutta as of January 1 and setting up shop in that city, which a lengthy memorandum from Washington explained was more centrally located for distribution of MO supplies to the field. Permanent MO chiefs had also been appointed for China, and for India-Burma-SEAC, and would arrive in the Far East at the beginning of the year.

It was only a matter of hours before the acting chief, and handwriting, had snapped back to normal.

During the next two months emphasis was placed on the rather exciting prospect of moving to Calcutta, where a print-shop site had already been rented, where equipment was expected weekly, and where a team of Jap. translators would be located as soon as a secure area had been established for them. Marj had been reassigned to China, and Bill Magistretti had been officially transferred to MO-Calcutta with Grace and myself.

Perhaps the most elated person in New Delhi over the theater split was a girl who had been waiting for permission to go to China since February—Rosamond Frame.

I had first met Rosy about two weeks after my arrival in Delhi at a most incongruous affair—a baby shower, where one doesn't expect to meet undercover girls. The shower was given for a young OSS secretary who had stopped over en route in Cairo to see her husband and who arrived in New Delhi pregnant. (As taxpayers, some of the girls argued that she was a terrible government expense.

Others shrugged and said it was the same thing with soldiers who didn't use Skat in the jungles and were shipped home with malaria— it was all a gamble!)

Rosy was not the Hollywood spy prototype I expected, in black satin evening gown and long, false eyelashes. She was a typical, vivacious, friendly American girl with a quick grin and a naïve way of cocking her head and listening to you intently. When she bounced into a room she was always a distinct contrast to the lethargic Indians around her. She was petite, with curly black hair and a slim, athletic figure. She had the reputation of being dated three weeks in advance, but I later learned that this butterfly cover was part of her OSS beat.

Rosy, born in Peiping, was the daughter of missionary parents and spoke flawless Mandarin. She was charged with watching the large Chinese delegation of "technical ordnance" people who were pouring into Delhi from China. Some of these were considered Jap or puppet agents. Others represented the central government but were employed to keep undercover watch on the activities of British and Americans.

Over the teacups and buzz of girlish gossip, Rosy told me that she hoped to be the first OSS girl to fly the Hump into China. She thought she would probably take off in a few days aboard a special "plush" plane on which she had wangled a seat.

Rosy's subsequent career in Chungking, her adventures with sinister *agents provocateurs* and puppet gunmen had become whispered fables when I met her again in the wartime capital of China. She was one of the most alert, brilliant women OSS sent into the field, a modern Mata Hari who used her specialized talents and education to keep a sensitive finger on the pulse of Chinese puppet intrigue and interpret her findings to the American Government.

Meanwhile, despite topside upheavals, life in New Delhi became increasingly pleasant after the monsoons lifted and the Punjab was plunged into delightfully sunny, crisp autumn with a burst of brilliantly flowering trees and the appearance of itinerant fakirs and their dancing Himalayan bears, their baskets of swaying cobras that always looked bored with the four mournful notes from the master's flute; and the bands of trained canaries that fired toy cannons and threaded beads with needle and string.

There also arrived new litters of chipmunks, leaping and chattering in the banyan tree outside the MO office, spying on us through open windows with bead-bright eyes. (One of the nests, retrieved by Angel Puss, was cozily lined with secret MO leaflets which the expectant mother chipmunk had stolen from our files.)

Autumn brought an increased traffic of camel caravans which passed through the silent streets after dark on velvet pads, swaying, creaking in from long desert journeys to the far-away lands of Iraq and Afghanistan.

Since the Indian social system required it, Angel Puss was now supplied with a special servant who prepared his food and aired his blankets. As part of the expected "baksheesh" the dog bearer ate a third of the dog food.

Angel's terrier instincts developed early in life, and at the age of six months he charged his first herd of happy goats as they danced lightheartedly up the street toward our office. It was a short sortie. Several udders were punctured, and two large rams crumpled under the assault. Following OSS guerrilla tactics, Angel beat a quick retreat, and I was left with the sobbing goatherd and the bill.

As he grew older he brought the wrath of Vishnu down upon our happy home by attacking a stately sacred Brahmin bullock which kicked up its heels and fled down the crowded streets of Delhi, scattering Indians to right and left. Shortly after this incident the Angel caused an old Delhi traffic snarl·by stampeding a specially developed sheep with an enormously fat tail (a delicacy in northern India). The unfortunate animal tripped himself on his tail and was bleating piteously when I unlocked Angel's jaws from the fatty appendage.

The Puss Sahib, as Ali called him, was a haphazard retriever and had to be banned from some of the more secret offices at 32 Feroz Shah Road because in foraging for leftover tea tidbits on desks, he occasionally finished off his meal with a top-secret cable or a list of agent suspects. Some of these he would bring to me with a sly look in his pink eyes; others he would devour on the spot.

My one attempt to teach Angel Puss to ride in the basket of my bicycle ended in defeat. Bill and I pedaled eleven miles out to the Qutub Minar, a monument famous among GI's for diving boys who leaped from the 238-foot tower into a small tank at its base. On the way home in the dark Angel Puss elected to jump from the basket, knocking me and the bike into a telephone pole. Bill hitched us a ride on a passing bullock cart upon which we piled our bikes and the Puss Sahib, who spent the next jolting hour straining to attack the plodding bullock. The motion of the cart was a sort of rumba-jog caused by the solid uneven wooden wheels, and we pitched along the pavement in much the same tempo and rhythm, I imagined, as they did back in the time of the Great Moguls. Maybe, Bill suggested, it was on just such a cart as this that they brought the news to Babar the Great that someone had discovered a place called America.

Angel's other weakness, which I learned at an OSS Thanksgiving party, was for strong drink. During cocktails, he managed surreptitiously to consume several burra gimlets, which sent him reeling off in a stupor. At this same party the head of the intelligence branch in Delhi, Major Philip Crowe, hinted broadly that Angel Puss was the culprit who had made off with the rare Indian ibis which he had shot recently in the Punjab and was saving as a special delicacy for a few connoisseurs of exotic foods. Angel was exonerated when it was later discovered that the ibis had been mixed in with five turkeys in the icebox and probably had been eaten by the *hoi polloi.*

With the improved weather, Americans were utilizing their Sundays to visit the Taj Mahal at Agra, some 120 miles southeast of Delhi. Grace had been the first in our office to make the trip, risking all to see one of the seven wonders of the world in the side car of a courier's motorcycle. Aside from the fact that they ran out of gas twenty miles from Agra, that a tribe of pink-bottomed apes stoned the vehicle from overhanging trees along the road, and that she suffered from motorcycle shakes for the next two weeks, our redheaded office manager recommended the trip by any mode of transportation.

I made it by jeep in the company of two Hawaii-born Nisei, Lieutenant Chioki Ikeda and Captain Richard Betsui, who were en route to China on a highly secret mission. Several months later the trip caused a major flurry in our security branch circles around the world. In typical tourist abandon, the three of us posed before the famous monument for a photograph which I sent home to Dad for Christmas, and which he promptly published under the illuminating caption: "Islanders with Secret Government Agency in India."

Our OSS mission in Honolulu picked up the picture, rushed it to Washington, and thence overseas to China, where my innocent Nisei friends were told that their cover was completely blown and that Japanese intelligence had probably transmitted the picture from Hawaii to Tokyo! Nothing ever happened to them, however, although Chick spent months behind the Jap lines in China.

Our trip to the Taj Mahal required five hours of steady driving across desolate, ancient stretches of country that produced nothing but gray, low foliage which seemed touched by a blight. We knew when we approached villages by the silent black vultures with blood-red wattle necks which wheeled above the mud huts—an air-borne sanitation corps, picking the habitations of humans clean of refuse. Occasionally where the landscape was touched with green and there was some indication of irrigation, we saw peacocks scuttling into tall grass, swishing their cumbersome green and gold tails like café society just coming home when their neighbors were going to work. We flushed a few ring-necked Chinese pheasants and fat, feathery quail, and once Chick pointed out a bleary-eyed boar with curling tusks. Sometimes we saw a yoke of oxen patiently circling a well, while a farmer dipped, then drew out a hide made from the belly of a goat, ballooning with water. Roads in that part of India were arteries that connected pulsating cities and seemed to have nothing to do with a moribund countryside.

The Taj was indeed the "soul of Iran incarnate in the body of India." We remained at the mausoleum until a saffron moon rose over the Jumna and reflected the fairylike beauty of the white marble tomb in the series of pools leading up to it. The building was a marvelous combination of massive foundations, airy superstructures with slender minarets and swelling domes. Our guide led us through a passageway to the underground vault, where the Indian ruler and his wife were buried in richly carved, jewel-encrusted sarcophagi. It wasn't chilly like most tombs. Instead it had a pervasive living beauty, especially where the moving moonlight cut patterns through the pierced marble screens above us. The guide gave us a handful of jasmine blossoms to place on the tombs as we left, and their fragrance filled the small room, a lovely tribute to a long dead queen who had decked herself with jasmine centuries ago.

My rare enjoyment, like all such moods, was rudely shattered. When we left the grounds a roadside Hindu huckster pushed toward us a miniature, birthday-cake replica in plaster of the mausoleum, yelling:

"Buy imitation Taj for memsahib—only fifteen rupees, sahib!"

As the Christmas holidays inched around the calendar, we realized that our days in Delhi were numbered. My own orders had already come through for January 1.

I spent my last night in Delhi at a New Year's Eve party where my Nisei friends celebrated the promotion of one of their heroes, Lieutenant Edward Mitsukada, who'd won his commission in the field with Merrill's Marauders by crawling up to enemy bivouacs, listening to their plans, and returning with the information to our lines.

After the party I walked back to the Taj with him and Saburo Watanabe, who had just been assigned to duty with British troops in the Arakan. Saburo was pretty glum about it because he understood the British treated their interpreters like Indian troops, and not like Americans.

As we scuffed along the dusty lanes toward my billet, we talked about what we would do when the war was won. Saburo wanted to teach music. Eddie didn't know. He thought maybe he should go to Japan with the army of occupation.

"They'll need us over there—we're links between the Japanese and Americans," he reflected.

The new year was an hour old when I crawled into the enveloping softness of my sleeping bag in the outside alcove off our living room, where Marj was already asleep. The air was crisp enough to freeze off the mosquitoes, so that the Army had given us a three months' respite from nets during the winter season. Moonlight filtered through the bamboo shade and made a lattice pattern on the white adobe porch walls. By clumsy manipulation, with one arm out of the sleeping bag, I rolled up the screen and lay back, face toward the moon and the trillions of stars in the Indian sky. Nowhere else in the world had I ever seen quite so many stars all at once, with quite so much space in which to twinkle.

I suppose people were thinking it all over the world: was this new year—1945—to be the year of peace? The Allies were still fighting through the mud in northern Italy. New petroleum jelly fire bombs (wonderful MO material!) were gutting the cities of Japan and Germany. The United States had returned to the Philippines. Its third fleet, larger even than the legendary fifth, roved the Pacific unchallenged.

The last few months had been so busy that only on my last night on Per Diem Hill (as we called Delhi) did I realize how pleasant life had been since that rainy July midnight when I arrived. Since the theater split, all my dreams of broader horizons had been centered on Calcutta, where Washington promised us an establishment of our own that would service the entire Far Eastern theater. Delhi suddenly meant home, now, a temporary war home, and Calcutta loomed up as a strange, unfriendly city of intrigue where even the British admitted the climate was unbearable nine months in the year.

I contemplated our Cinderellalike existence in Delhi, where Ali woke us every morning with a cheery "Salaam" and a hot cup of tea. It was a comfortable, luxurious feeling to know that your clothes would be washed and ironed and ready for you to wear. There was satisfaction in strolling to breakfast where special bearers served you fruit, others poured coffee and the mustachioed major-domo in a cushioned red turban announced that the station wagon was outside to take you to work.

I hoped Dad would not hear about this because I had a guilty feeling that he would never forgive me. My letters home had managed to imply a certain rugged life at the front, where we lived on the fringe of the jungles, fighting off Japs, anopheles mosquitoes and second lieutenants. Dad's letters had been rather touching and sweet. I had let him send me soap and candy, although the PX was stocked with them, just because he said he knew how I should appreciate them. How he would have fumed to see me playing lawn tennis at the Gymkhana Club, dancing under the stars at the Imperial Hotel with someone like the Maharaja of Gwalior, who was short and chubby but nevertheless a maharaja!

But it was the work that made life really worth while in Delhi, I decided. In the last six months we had sent over thirty projects to the field, including a weekly intelligence summary. Although we were listed in Washington as a small unit of three, we actually had some twenty-five people working for us, including the Nisei, Willie, and the staffs of Major Bicat and Major Glemser. Scarcely a week went by that a British courier didn't arrive at our door with large cartons, heavily globbed with sealing wax, containing page proofs and castings which Major Bicat ran off for us on his hand press in the viceregal stables. Marj and I were always tactfully silent about our relations with the "cousins," and to many of our confreres at 32 Feroz Shah Road our methods must have seemed indeed devious and mysterious. Here we were—two women in an office with no visible means of support—producing reams of printed MO propaganda. I was often thankful that OSS was such a secretive organization. People seldom tried to pry information from other branches. We found that a Mona Lisa smile, a cloak-and-dagger gesture sufficed. The oblique questioning ceased.

At introspective intervals like this I sometimes wondered where MO ideas came from. Often I produced nothing for days but just sat and read intelligence reports and captured documents. Then suddenly something began to churn up this backlog of knowledge. Ideas emerged. Some were good, some were bad; but I think most of them were practical. As nearly as I could ascertain, these ideas were the result of a definite mental attitude which I had been developing ever since my indoctrination in Washington.

I never read an intelligence report without thinking, "How can this information be twisted and fed to the Japs?" Every time I thumbed through a Japanese magazine I wondered, "How can this story be rewritten to bring discomfort to the enemy?" I never saw Okamoto at the Red Fort without secretly studying his actions and habits of mind, and wondering what sort of mental torture I could devise for his brothers in Burma.

Some day, I knew, I should have to write a straight news story again, and be a civilized human being. I drifted off to sleep thinking how dull it all would be . . .

Ali awakened me at five with great sobs to tell me I should be leaving in an hour for Calcutta—as far away to him as the shores of North America. The sky was just beginning to become light, and I looked into the living room where Marj was stirring, to see the entire ceiling strung with small American, British, Chinese, and Russian paper flags. Incense was burning on the mantel and small Indian papier-mâché birds and animals were arranged on desks and chairs.

"I am fixing the room for your going away day," he sniffed.

I wondered how much this great show of affection would cost us on Ali's monthly bill; but he was genuinely unhappy to see me go, and the feeling was mutual. Although the language barrier had been almost insurmountable, Marj and I were devoted to Ali, because of his kind, gentle loyalty and almost childlike desire to please.

When I attempted to get out of my sleeping bag, I discovered that the zipper had jammed! First Ali, then Marj tried to pry it free. Grace, roused in her alcove next to mine, flew in with manicure scissors and fingernail file. Nothing budged. Ali rushed for his friend the cook, who arrived in sleepy confusion with a large butcher knife. Just then Grace luckily recalled an OSS commander at the Taj who owned a lock-picking set. We dispatched Ali down the corridors for the commander.

I needed to reach the plane at least ten minutes ahead of time to smuggle Angel Puss aboard. Since Elliott Roosevelt's bull mastiff, Blaze, had ruined canine travel in all theaters, it was necessary to smooth the way with the pilot in advance before secreting dogs aboard, I was instructed.

The commander finally arrived with his instruments, and while Ali wrung his hands and the cook served as a sort of doctor's aid, the zipper churned, rasped, and slid noisily down its track, and I wiggled out in a transparent nightgown, like some breech-born moth.

I climbed aboard the C–47 just in time to buttonhole the pilot.

"Stick the mutt in the toilet and tell the flight clerk," was his muttered, casual reply to my well rehearsed sob story.

Angel Puss was awkward and reluctant, and it took the combined efforts of Marj, me, and the flight clerk to chain him to the toilet compartment.

Just as I had finally relaxed and settled down to a peaceful ride through clear blue Indian skies, the flight clerk sidled up to me in a nervous twitch.

"That full colonel sitting forward—see him?" He jerked his thumb toward the front of the plane as if he didn't dare look around himself.

"Well, he's the ATC colonel who signed the order that no dogs can ride on these planes. If he has to go to the toilet between here and our final stop at Agra, I'll be grounded for the duration!"

For the next fifty minutes whenever the colonel made a move that might indicate he planned to retire to the rear, I jumped up and made for the toilet. When we finally landed at Agra, protocol required the colonel to leave the ship first. We held our breaths as he passed the rear compartment and paused. Distinct whimpers were coming from the tail of the plane. Possibly because there were others behind him, possibly because he sensed the situation and decided to ignore it, he passed on out.

They "off-loaded" Angel Puss at Agra, and I spent a grim half-hour before I found a pilot who was taking a B–25 to Calcutta that afternoon. The lad was a rough, good-natured boy who had been through a lot of bad raids over Germany and had been sent to India to get away from combat missions. He would be glad, he told me, to take the dog with him.

"What's his name?" he asked, patting the pink-eyed Puss Sahib absently.

When I told him, the pilot protested: "No wonder he looks like a bad hangover—Angel Puss! He's Butch from now on, if he's riding with me!"

I didn't bother telling the pilot that Puss never had learned his own name anyway; that it didn't matter what you called him because he wouldn't obey; that for days on end he acted as if I were a complete stranger until I struck a vague chord in his memory and he slobbered all over me with sheer joy of discovery. I felt it would spoil the flyer's simple faith in what the books said was man's best friend. After all, he'd been through so much, over Berlin.

CHAPTER EIGHT

CHOWRINGHEE COMMANDOS

I HAD a preconceived Hollywood notion about Calcutta as our plane circled the fabulous city on the banks of the Hooghly River. It would be a mysterious city of intrigue where international spies traded secrets behind beaded curtains in notoriously wicked places like Margot's, on Kuraia Road.

Calcutta, according to a rough Oliver Caldwell estimate, was a place where security could be maintained exactly five minutes until British, Chinese, and Indian agents known as JIF's, or Japanese Inspired Fifth Columnists, had the name, serial number, and *raison d'être* of every arrival.

Oliver also hinted darkly that people had a strange way of disappearing in Calcutta—like that Chinese bootmaker whose body was found in the Hooghly riddled with bullets.

"And why? Because he took such a long time to fill orders for boots for American and British officers who were going forward, that's why!" Oliver once told me, out of the corner of his mouth. "But this bootmaker was very obliging. Sure—he'd be glad to send the boots wherever the men were going in Burma! A smart racket, until we discovered that he'd send them the boots, all right, but he'd also send news of their positions to the Japs."

I was mildly disappointed in Dumdum Airport, a modern, efficient terminal with no Far Eastern intrigue except a few dusty palm trees at the fringe of the field that looked like parts of a stage set. There was even a Coca-Cola machine at the terminal office where a freckled-faced clerk gave me that playful back-of-the-hand-to-you gesture when I asked him in confidential undertones where OSS was located.

"Lady, OSS breaks out all over this city like the measles. There's R House, O House, G House, Buffalo House, Communications, the Girls' House, and headquarters where your people tell me a colonel called the Great White Maharaja of Tollygunge is C.O."

At that point my faith in the organization was restored when an eavesdropping major appeared from around the coke machine, introduced himself—"Prasenjak—OSS housemother"—and whisked me to a waiting car. He told me to pay no attention to what the clerk said. OSS was doing a fine job in Calcutta, and the Army was just envious because we had better billets.

Among Prasenjak's duties as "housemother" was to warn all female arrivals of the dangers of the anopheles when riding after dark in open carriages, of amoebic dysentery in out-of-bounds Chinese restaurants and of fraternizing with the British.

Dispensing with these amenities in short order, the major then gave me an earthy Cook's tour of the city on our way to headquarters.

"You are now a member of the Chowringhee Commandos," he informed me as we drove down what seemed to be one of the main streets—Chowringhee. It was clean and wide and was lined with ornate mid-Victorian buildings that were the very essence of British propriety.

Commandos, I learned, was that GI term applied to rear echelons from Waikiki to Constitution Avenue, from Piccadilly to Chowringhee, who led a plush existence far from sounds of gunfire.

"We have a real ice-cream parlor at Ferrazini's, steaks at Firpo's, dancing girls at the Hawaiian Club, first-run shows at the air-conditioned Met."

The major became quite ecstatic when he pointed out a new American night club, the Kenarney, which suggested a sort of gaudy second lieutenant's Leon and Eddie's from his description of a ruffled rumba band, spectrum of colored lights, brash murals, and—Tony Martin as the featured entertainer.

The city of Calcutta seemed to sprawl, like Los Angeles, until it lost its original pattern in a thirty-mile maze of suburbs. The buildings had a dissipated look, possibly because the walls sweated and exuded a brown color which settled in dark circles under the windows. Beyond these grave Victorian houses where the colonials lived in cool seclusion, the tenements of the Indians stretched for miles in a wild chaos of poverty and dirt.

The streets were congested with oddly assorted transportation anachronisms. There were stagecoaches with top-hatted footmen, and shuttered "purdah" carriages in which Indian ladies (and OSS agents, I suspected) rode about in anonymous privacy. Bearded Sikhs haphazardly drove their open-air, charcoal-burning taxis between graceful phaetons and carioles drawn by high-stepping horses. Streetcars clanged through traffic, overloaded on the running boards by passengers who saved half a fare by standing up on the outside. Ricksha pullers bobbed along to the rhythmic tinkle of tongueless bells which they sounded against the wooden shafts of their vehicles in lieu of horns. And there were the sway-backed bicycles with as many as four Indians balancing from handlebars to rear fenders—oxcarts, British lorries, American jeeps. It was a situation which the usually tidy Father Time had neglected to clean up in passing from one century to the next in Calcutta.

"You mustn't forget to visit the burning ghats," Prasenjak continued. "They're on the river banks, where the natives burn their corpses on top of a pile of sticks. The body usually only gets half cooked, and then they have to build another fire. The smell is terrific!"

(Calcutta—second city in the British Empire! Center of Oriental mystery and intrigue!)

"It gets pretty cool here nights, and since there isn't any fuel they collect and dry horse dung to burn. There's a special caste that just follows the horses . . ." Prasenjak warmed to his subject.

"And there's a temple of Kali where the Indians splatter themselves all over with chicken blood before they go inside. Kali is a goddess with three hands and a string of little kids' heads around her neck."

(Calcutta! The crown jewel Japan desired for her diadem! Had Hirohito ever seen the place?)

We eventually turned down a winding road through a mosaic of bright green rice paddies to headquarters, where I was to report to Colonel Charles B. McGehee, Calcutta commandant in charge of this OSS Far East supply base.

"We call him 'I'll Never Smile Again' McGehee, since the time he gave a grand opening for the new OSS officers' quarters and invited all the important people in town," Prasenjak confided.

"He'd spent a lot of time fixing the place up, and he even had the gardens surrounded by a high wall to keep people and snakes out, as he put it. On the opening day, we officers hired a snake charmer and told him to plant his cobras all over the yard. In the middle of the party the fakir came up to the colonel and said he was collecting snakes. Some of the ladies screamed, and McGehee went purple and said there were no serpents in *his* garden. So the man sat down, started tooting his flute and pretty soon all his cobras came crawling out from under rocks!"

The Great White Maharaja of Tollygunge was not such a terrifying presence, once cornered at his office desk. He was a round-faced, well fed American businessman in uniform, a former Republic Steel executive through whose portals at Tollygunge passed all OSS personnel and equipment bound for Burma, China, and the South-East Asia Command in Ceylon.

As soon as we had been introduced, the colonel launched into his life and hard times with MO, that unloved, misunderstood fosterchild which had no place in any businessman's cold world of reality. Our press and engraving camera had arrived in bad shape, half smashed in shipping. The Indian government wouldn't grant permission to import our alien Jap typesetters until we had arranged a secure area in which to impound them! Until they arrived, no one could touch the font of Japanese type which was pied all over the floor at R House, where MO production would eventually be handled. R House was in a bad area and only the week before two Indian spies, parachuted in from Burma by the Japs, had been discovered residing next door. To top everything, more MO personnel was expected momentarily from the States. At present, there would be Magistretti, Grace, myself, and a former reporter from Japan and Hawaii named Alwyn Pindar.

I decided our interview was at an end when the colonel bit off the end of a fresh cigar. I rose to leave. At the door he called me back:

"This is a tip I'll pass on for what it's worth. Back home the Washington columnists are riding OSS for allowing British agents to infiltrate the organization here in Calcutta. If I were you, I'd watch my dealings with the cousins—"

All the way back to what turned out to be sumptuous girls' quarters at Harrington Mansions, I mulled over the colonel's warning in the light of all the scuttlebutt I'd heard in Delhi.

It was an open secret that OSS maintained an alert staff in Ceylon for the primary purpose of studying British methods of operating during the war, and analyzing British postwar political and economic aims in Asia.

The boys from Burma hinted that Mountbatten's chief of staff, Sir Henry Pownall, had been dispatched to London for the express purpose of presenting sufficient proof to the British Chiefs of Staff that General Stilwell had shirked his duties as deputy supreme Allied commander. The British wanted the major portion of Lend-Lease supplies routed to Ceylon for their war effort in SEAC. Stilwell, on the other hand, doggedly insisted on sending as much as possible to China to rescue her bogged-down war machine and keep her in the war. To accomplish this, he pushed the Burma Road through to completion over British protests. In the jungles of Burma, I heard, there was little love lost between the British and American soldiers.

As far as I knew, the British made no bones about the fact that they were safeguarding the Empire's Far Eastern colonies. A year or so earlier, I had heard Winston Churchill tell a Washington press group at an off-the-record luncheon that Britain had built Hongkong from mud flats and Britain intended to regain her crown colony. Whether the Americans approved it or not, England was following a specific blueprint in the Far East, and expected every Englishman to implement this blueprint. Meanwhile, that revised World War I MO slogan found many tongues to repeat it:

"England will fight to the last Frenchman, Dutchman, American, Thai, Burmese, Hindu, Moslem, Malay, and Annamite."

And at any cocktail party you'd hear quips like: "SEAC—that means 'Save England's Asiatic Colonies.' "

The undercurrent of distrust distressed me more than any good healthy *sub rosa* political maneuvering. We had been warned in Delhi that the British were past masters at intrigue and had planted spies in all American agencies to piece together information. One blonde British *femme fatale* was supposedly operating against high-echelon personnel in Kandy. Our security branch hinted that gullible American girls were easy targets and went all to pieces at the first sound of a British accent. Through one grapevine I heard that British intelligence kept a file marked "For British Eyes Alone" in which were plotted the day-by-day courses of high-ranking Americans from chota hazri to after-dinner brandy.

What better bacterial culture than this growing distrust could Morale Operations find upon which to work? Didn't our own manual tell us we were to create doubts, seek to split allies, divide, and conquer?

I remembered academic reports we had read in Washington, and they suddenly took on new meaning: *Be on the alert at all times for subversive Axis attempts to split Allied unity.* The enemy never overlooks an opportunity. Don't fancy yourself clever by repeating glib slogans originating from Radio Station Debunk in Berlin—"The War of U.S. Imperialism," or "The War to Make the World Safe for Hypocrisy."

And there had been that all-out radio war on Allied solidarity, in which the Axis nations reported: Australia has surrendered to Washington politics. London played a minor role in the Pacific War Council. British inactivity irks Russia. U.S. Lend-Lease represents a policy of American economic imperialism.

We had countered with stiff announcements of solidarity. We

spoke of the kindness and hospitality shown our troops in Australia, and General MacArthur was quoted as saying that he and his Australian aide, General Blamey, were like "blood brothers." We broadcast an exchange of letters between a British Home Guard corporal and the chief of the United States Army Ordinance, showing English appreciation of Lend-Lease. At home, we even emphasized the solidarity meeting of the CIO and the AFL in Pittsburgh!

It was fairly simple to counteract open propaganda. But how could a whisper campaign be handled, which was far more deadly because it was epidemic in scope, borne on the tongues, in the minds of our own people? Was this CBI ferment possibly a real dose of enemy-inspired MO, spreading under our very noses while we brewed the stuff for enemy consumption? As was always the case in diagnosing a bad attack of MO, there were no symptoms other than mental disturbances.

The eighth floor of a Victorian apartment house, Harrington Mansions, contained a large suite of rooms where some ten OSS girls were comfortably coddled by a corps of Indian servants who came with the flat, rented from a British colonial. The pucka-sahib solemnity was still reflected in the servants' humorless tolerance of American girls blissfully ignorant of the proper scale of attitudes to maintain toward the various kitchen castes.

A commotion in the living room, followed shortly by a knock on my door, disturbed my unpacking that afternoon. It was the bald-pated, glowering, Elizabethan hangman of a head bearer with what he considered distasteful news that "dog come."

I discovered Angel Puss and the pilot in the parlor surrounded by debris, the lad a bit shaken by his recent experiences. Angel looked more Dalmatian than terrier, with daubs of grease resulting from a plunge into the engine while the plane was being checked at Allahabad, the pilot explained.

"He was almost hamburger. As it is, he's a sort of greaseburger. Traveling with that mutt was worse than leading a raid over Ploesti. And as soon as Mahatma here let us into your apartment the dog ate two love birds off that perch, beaks and all!"

I reported for work the next morning at R House, clandestine MO workshop mentioned only in whispers. It was located in a dingy Indian tenement section, a three-story, circular building which the OSS maintenance officer was having "spruced up" a bit with a coat of whitewash. The security officer insisted upon Gurkha guards at the entrance and spirals of barbed wire along the wall. Meanwhile, a family of Indian sweepers for the building had established themselves in the rear, housed in makeshift packing-box debris upon which were stenciled such things as "Press—This Side Up" and "Type Font, Japanese." As far as I know, no one ever apprehended the wag who chalked this appropriate warning on the guardhouse of our Oh So Secret hide-away:

"Spies Keep Out."

The press foreman informed our small staff that it would be at least two months before equipment was repaired and type sorted. The Washington supply officer had forgotten how intensely hot Calcutta was, and most of the chemicals had spoiled on the Hooghly docks. Without them, we couldn't even operate the multilith press, the only mechanism we had that was in fair shape.

Two days later, to add to the confusion and futility at R House, the MO staff was expanded with the arrival of Dr. Ina Telberg, a Russian expert on Japanese battle order; Edward Hunter, assistant cable editor of the *New York Post;* Victor Beals, a commercial artist; and Lieutenant Jack Gilmore, a former private detective from Denver, who later informed me that he had been detailed by Washington to watch MO's British affiliations! Perhaps the most indispensable member of our group at that time was Winifred Jub, a pretty, part-Burmese girl who brewed afternoon tea, interpreted for the Indian help and laboriously opened classified material from Washington which always arrived, security-checked, in two heavy Manila paper folders.

At our first full staff meeting, held in grim Washington tradition amidst a babel of Indian painters, carpenters, and sweepers, Bill pointed out that we still had to work with the British if we wanted to produce material. Not only did they have the equipment, but they had a native agent net which spread down the coast of Burma along the newly opened Arakan front through which the British were pushing toward Rangoon. Later that morning, Bill stood by the telephone as a self-appointed monitor when it was agreed that I should renew acquaintance with Major Glemser, and I asked our operator to connect me with British Psychological Warfare Headquarters. Waiting, I could imagine the operator busily gathering security antibodies around the switchboard. Then a British voice answered:

"Glemsah—heah!"

The major was cordial and offered to send his jeep round to pick

Bill and me up. Remembering security regulations, I hastened to explain that the place would be too hard to find.

"If you mean that white elephant of a house OSS took over," the major chided, "you can see that on a clear day from Meerut!"

We had just started out in our own jeep when a hysterical yell came from the third floor of R House and we saw guards pointing to a white object.

"Angel Puss has hanged himself," Winifred Jub screamed.

He was quite limp when they pulled him up on the flat roof where I'd tied him out of harm's way. Slowly his sly pink eyes opened, he coughed and revived with a spasm of yips! Even Bill relented, and Angel Puss accompanied us on our trip, to everyone's eventual regret.

To reach the major's office, we drove through a quiet residential district, past large estates bounded by high walls over which I could see gay swatches of bougainvillaea, coquettish, ragged hibiscus, and purple jacaranda bobbing and hinting at well kept gardens and stretches of lawns.

British headquarters appeared to be a private home, but at the gate an armed sentry stepped forward, demanding credentials. The offices were located in a large building where every inch of space was utilized. The porch overflowed with newsprint and leaflets in gunny sacks ready for the next drop. A large reception hall was lined with cots, and the second story a beehive of small, busy offices. Major Glemser's room overlooked a cluttered courtyard where a trailer truck had been backed against a lean-to. From it came the clatter of a press.

When the orderly had marched off glumly with Angel Puss, Peter Glemser explained something of his work to us. On the two small offset presses in the trailers, they ran off as many as 300,000 leaflets, or "nickels" as the British called them, a month. The *Gunjin Shimbun,* a paper for Jap troops, was printed in town at a larger shop which had been quietly taken over from a bankrupt Indian concern.

In spite of the efficiency and purpose of the place, the British had their problems, too, demonstrated by a series of interruptions. The first was by a perspiring, florid-faced British sergeant who saluted briskly and explained:

"They've made off with them again, sir!"

Major Glemser shrugged and asked how many.

"The lot, sir!"

"We'll just have to use the bathtub in my flat after this, Farnsworth."

After the sergeant dashed out, the major explained that he had been floating about six dozen bamboo containers in a pond in the rear, to waterproof them. The containers were designed with plexiglass windows and were decorated with British and Burmese flags. Fitted into the bamboo cylinders were sewing thread, needles, salt—items desperately needed by the Burmese. As soon as the containers were conditioned, they were to be floated down the Irrawaddy.

"But the Indians around here keep stealing them before we condition them—because they need the stuff as much as the Burmese, I suppose."

The major's aide entered shortly afterwards, holding a gray blanket at arm's length.

"Lice, Peter, all over the filthy thing, and it was clean when we gave it to them."

Major Glemser shied away from the blanket and told his aide to have both blanket and prisoners fumigated.

"I—rerouted a couple of Jap prisoners of war who were being transshipped from Calcutta to Delhi," he confided, a trifle embarrassed about the whole episode. "Had absolutely no right to, of course; but we need help badly, and it would take forever to go through channels. We were in luck the night my translator and I went down to the ship that just got in from Burma. Found one college graduate—buck teeth, horn-rimmed goggles, and all—and one very good calligrapher. They were more than willing to work for us, so I pulled my rank on the guard, signed up for them, and now I've got them out in the garage and don't exactly know how to explain them away—or what we'll do with them once the war's over. We call them Tweedledum and Tweedledee. They think I'm their special Mikado, and every time I go out to see them they bow!"

A clamor from the courtyard interrupted the major's confession, and we all reached the balcony in time to see Angel Puss at the throat of a fat rooster. Farnsworth arrived seconds too late. He retrieved the lifeless bird from Angel Puss and held it up to Major Glemser with a tremor in his voice:

" 'E's done in our Sunday curry, sir!"

It wasn't a propitious moment to request the use of the major's agent network in the Arakan for disseminating MO material which he would print, but Bill must have decided to plunge in before another catastrophe could occur. The major listened carefully and seemed agreeable. Approval for a merger of black and white must come from headquarters in Ceylon, known as P Division. Now we could be certain that MO would be in the field within forty-eight hours after it had been produced.

The British agent network in the Arakan was operated by a secret group known as Force 136. This organization was an arm of British intelligence which theoretically combined guerrilla activities, intelligence, and black morale operations. It was commanded by Colin McKenzie in Ceylon, and its men trained at Meerut. The personnel included young British colonials and a few leftists with a taste for dangerous living who had penetrated the Arakan and joined forces with the anti-fascist Burmese League. The two groups operated together with Rangoon as their eventual target. They organized the Arakan and planted agents in all important Burmese villages where they obtained intelligence, arranged air drops, and distributed much-needed supplies in village markets.

Force 136 supplied Major Glemser's office with intelligence on local Burmese problems and Japanese morale which he incorporated into white psychological warfare campaigns. Because the British black was not too strong in the Arakan, he held out hope that P Division would agree to our proposal for joining forces against the Japs.

"I'll tell them that our Mr. Freud of 136 likes your work," he grinned. "He's a descendant of Sigmund Freud. Whenever he says something's psychologically sound, we never have any comebacks from the higher echelon. He's our last line of defense. His name works like a talisman."

After the interview, the major invited Bill and me to lunch at the last all-British stronghold in Calcutta, the very select Saturday Club. It was a charming establishment with circular swimming pools, clay tennis courts and formal gardens ablaze with larkspur and rhododendrons and hollyhock. Meals were served by white-uniformed bearers in blue satin turbans, and the club lounge was a bumble of polite, low voices punctuated only with the swish of soda being ploshed into iceless whisky.

In the club's powder room I had my first brush with the Anglo-Australian social situation when two attractive women in British uniforms of some auxiliary group entered. One of them, with an array of service ribbons across her well tailored white suit, announced to her companion:

"My dear, you know she *is* nice, even if she is Australian!"

Later Major Glemser pointed to a group of women at a large luncheon. At the head of the table sat the lady in the ribboned uniform whom he pointed out as the wife of Lord Louis Mountbatten. At her right sat a woman in civilian dress—Mrs. Richard Casey, wife of the Australian Governor of Bengal!

Relations between British and Americans in Ceylon were far too complicated to result in immediate action on our request to merge black and white operations in the Arakan.

The situation was further complicated by the sudden appearance upon the scene of a five-kilowatt radio station which reared its antennae up from the Burma bush in a place called Chittagong, ten miles outside an RAF base in the jungles. The station had been erected for British use, but most of the radio technicians for the project had been rerouted to the powerful All-India radio station in New Delhi with which the British blanketed SEAC in seven languages. The Chittagong station had been offered to MO-SEAC for black radio warfare, once a covering P Division directive was written in Ceylon outlining the scope of the broadcasts.

Major Glemser was deluged with "signals" from Kandy. Did OSS want to work with native populations and puppets? If so, where would proper coordination be maintained? What work would be duplicated by the MO branch in Ceylon?

During the two months we spent waiting for high-level policy decisions, the Calcutta unit limped along on a patched-up multilith, a varitypewriter with changeable belts of English, Thai, and Malay type, and an air-conditioned darkroom which depended upon erratic Indian current for power. There was no way of telling when the electricity would fail in the middle of a sultry Calcutta night and the chemicals spoil before the engravers arrived in the morning.

Quite regularly from Washington came those cheerful cables that the Japanese typesetters had nearly won their passports from the vigilant Mrs. Shipley of State; that more equipment was en route; and that the new head of MO for India, Burma, and SEAC was being selected and could be expected momentarily. A great shipment of crayons for the art department arrived while I was there, to melt in glorious technicolor in the R House storeroom; but that was all.

Washington also sent us two MO projects. One was probably technically the best Jap forgery ever printed on an American press, and the other was probably the greatest fiasco ever sent abroad under top-secret cover.

The forgery was of a Japanese news magazine for troops published by the Ministry of Information in Tokyo. Bill and I had dummied it in Calcutta and sent it back for reproduction to Captain Kleiman in New York. One picture story gave a complete account of the striking power of the B–29, an American plane which had been given little publicity by the Jap government. In "captured" pictures of the giant bomber we illustrated how it dwarfed the largest Jap bomber. We ran a similar story on "captured" American equipment from the Southwest Pacific, showing how superior it was to Jap matériel. The reason: America still had factories which were producing supplies for her soldiers. A third story decried the use of American Indians in the jungles, placing them on a par with germ warfare. (Bill divulged that the Japs had a great fear of American Indians and Chicago gangsters.) In a "home-front" story we described the American prisoners of war in Japan, pointing out that they were physically below standard and could not compare with the average Jap workingman. We added an MO twist that whenever the tall Americans marched through the streets on their way to work on the docks, "foolish" Japanese maidens followed them asking for their autographs.

When we received the first hundred copies from Captain Kleiman, Bill said it was impossible to detect a technical or psychological flaw in the material. The magazine was distributed throughout occupied territories, and copies were found months later after VJ Day in Jap mess halls and barracks.

The fiasco, on the other hand, was basically sound but carelessly executed. It involved some fifty pounds of Japanese railroad tickets printed in the States from an original which had been smuggled out through China. Under separate cover came another fifty pounds of messages, to be attached to the railroad tickets. These messages were official notices from the Japanese Bureau of Transportation urging all city dwellers to evacuate to the country, using the attached pass to travel on the railroads. The object was to create panic in the city, and congest the lines of communication in Japan. Dissemination was to be under cover of the last B–29 raid on Tokyo from the Barrackpore base outside Calcutta. It would be presumed that Jap attack planes had dropped the tickets during the air raid. The purpose, instructions and method of stitching the material were carefully explained. The only thing Washington forgot was that Calcutta did not possess a mechanical stitcher!

Bill set up an assembly line in his office at R House. We divided into teams. Grace and I stapled with a crotchety Indian stapler. Al and Bill pasted with evil-smelling Indian paste and, whenever possible, Angel Puss quietly devoured the tickets with the paste on them. Winifred Jub stuffed. After three days Major Glemser's office joined forces as the B–29 dead line drew near. He reported an occupational twitch developing among the Indian help, who were working day and night shifts at the stitcher. At the end of five days, when slightly over fifteen pounds had been done, Bill decided that the Japs could match up their own tickets and messages. We divided the remainder roughly in two, poured the project into gunny-sack containers, and Bill drove off at dawn one day with a weapons carrier full of a top-secret cargo.

He was still on his way out to Barrackpore when Winny Jub, tidying up the office, discovered the terrible error. She had picked up one of the messages from the Japanese Bureau of Transportation and held it to the light.

"Look at the pretty bird," she exclaimed.

It was certainly a very pretty bird indeed! It was a watermark of an American eagle, printed on good American bond paper!

Luckily, the passes were never dropped, because the B–29 raid was called off and the planes flew back to America instead, en route to their new Saipan base. As far as I know, the passes are still at Barrackpore, but I think the date has expired.

Most of our work still depended upon assistance from Major Glemser, who had long ago given up any illusions he may have had about the OSS bonanza I'd promised to share with him, after one quick inspection of our crippled presses. He was charming about it all, and allowed us to sandwich one MO project a week into his busy press schedule. I always felt that his aide was secretly scoffing as he chalked up MO titles on the master scoreboard in the print shop. British projects were always primly coded, listed numerically with the first initial of the target as a guide, such as J for Jap, B for Burmese.

"J–675 goes down at 1300 hours, sir," the aide would chant like a train announcer, "followed by 'The Hong Kong Soothsayer' and 'Goodbye, Shanghai!' "

The Soothsayer was a series of evil prophecies by a famous Hindu sage who foresaw Japanese military defeats by the simple expedient of juggled dates. When our fleet steamed into Leyte Bay on October 20, the Soothsayer promptly produced a brochure, dated the previous month, announcing the event. His prophecies were even quoted in Major Glemser's *Gunjin Shimbun* to give the sage a wider following!

"Goodbye, Shanghai" was a nostalgic poem I had written to give credence to rumors that Jap civilians were being evacuated from Shanghai in preparation for possible Allied landings there. The poem,

which I blatantly announced had won first prize in a contest held by
the women's magazine, *Fujin Kurabu*, was supposedly written by a
Japanese civil servant who had been sènt to Shanghai with the army
of occupation.and had spent four years there. Now he was returning
to Naichi, the homeland, with tears in his eyes. He had grown to love
Shanghai. The editor's note mentioned that the poet was one of
thousands of Japanese who had been ordered home by the government.

In the middle of January it was decided that somebody should go
down to Ceylon and find out how the other half of MO lived, and
what progress was being made on higher echelon levels in the Arakan
merger. It was Bill's idea to have everything shipshape before the
new MO head, Lieutenant James G. Withrow, arrived in the theater.
We drew straws—and I won!

Bill said it would be a simple, office-boy errand: find out how we
could coordinate in producing black material for the Chittagong
radio station; determine what progress had been made with P Division
in using the British intelligence net in the Arakan; discover what type
of MO was being sent into Sumatra, Java, and Thailand; bring sam-
ples back; and cut it down to a week-end trip!

My plans for departure were delayed a few days by news of the
imminent arrival of General Donovan and what was loosely referred
to around the shop as the "flying circus"—a collection of branch
chiefs from Washington, aides, and Far Eastern theater officers who
had just made a swing around China. From the Great White Maharaja's office came word to tidy up the building and have some sort
of production on hand to show the general.

Bill checked with the pressroom, and again his grimmest fears were
confirmed. Not a press in the building would work! How to dramatize our endeavors and create the illusion of a busy production unit
at work? When I mentioned the tense situation to Major Glemser he
nodded.

"We have the same trouble with our big fellows, too. Always have
to dress up the old shop. We lose all sorts of valuable time that way."

He had a suggestion which Bill approved. Sergeant Farnsworth
could bring a hand-operated proof press to R House, and while one
person inked the rollers another could pull off supposedly operational
leaflets. Since they would be in Japanese, no one would know the
difference.

On the day of the general's visit we planned to smuggle Sergeant
Farnsworth out of the secret pressroom before the official party ar-

rived; but through a hitch in schedules the Flying Circus came in half an hour early. Most of the MO staff was on the second floor arranging material in strategic places to catch the general's eye. Bill, the sergeant, and I were in the pressroom aligning the press stand with the uneven cement floor. The sergeant was under the press calling for blocks of wood, which I was supplying. Bill was inking the rollers, and we were all pretty greasy.

Suddenly Prasenjak's voice rang through the room:

" 'Ten-n-ntion!"

Almost immediately the place was lighted by the glitter of polished brass, and officers in impressive dress uniforms gay with theater ribbons. I saw by the bleak look on Bill's face that it was too late to hide Sergeant Farnsworth. He had crawled out from under the press and automatically snapped in to the unmistakable salute of the British soldier, with concave back and rigid hand twanging at his forehead like a broken spring. The general didn't seem to mind his British stripes, and shook hands pleasantly with all of us; but I was uncomfortably aware of icy stares from some of our Far Eastern colonels.

The sergeant was the first to recover. He inked the block of type on the press and rolled off neat, clean leaflets in Japanese. Bill handed them around, explaining glibly that they were crude messages supposedly printed by a group of dissatisfied front-line Jap soldiers. They all nodded politely and took the souvenir leaflets. Just as the first of the Circus reached the door on the way out, Bill moved swiftly toward them, requesting that they leave the leaflets behind for security reasons.

When they had departed Bill came back to us, crumpling the still-wet copy.

"Lucky no one could read Japanese," he muttered. "Listen to this: 'Greetings to General Donovan. This leaflet comes to you through the courtesy of the British Psychological Warfare Branch. It is printed on Lend-Lease equipment. Welcome to our theater!' "

CHAPTER NINE

LAND OF THE LOTUS EATERS

The smooth, pleasurable voyage along the coast of India from Calcutta to Ceylon which I anticipated turned out to be one of the roughest flights I had yet made with the ATC. We hit a glowering storm front just before we left the mainland and were buffeted for over an hour in a gray world of turbulent air that occasionally parted to expose, far below, a glittering blue Indian Ocean mottled with sunlight. The only thing that kept me from getting airsick was the vast quantity of K ration cheese which a solicitous flight clerk fed me, while he munched on creamy-rich chocolate bars. The storm cleared about a hundred miles from the island, which I fancied from the air looked like a great teardrop off the nose of India.

Jane once wrote me that Ceylon was an Elysium far removed from reality where everyone had an academic interest in the war but found life far too pleasant to do anything too drastic about it.

"To those red-blooded Americans who signed up to fight somebody and arrived in Ceylon to find themselves pinioned beneath P Division directives, the SEAC situation was just another form of British tyranny—frustration without representation," she informed me.

"But to the Americans with a planning-staff mind-set and a penchant for major and minor intrigue, Ceylon was the palm-fringed haven of the bureaucrat, the isle of panel discussions and deferred decisions."

We swept in over white beaches and glossy palm tops and landed at a busy little airport outside Colombo. I spotted Jane immediately at the terminal—the same freckled, friendly face, the same broad grin. She was wearing a comfortable gingham dress and sandals. Almost the minute I stepped out of the plane she was accusing me of being a Calcutta security office spy "on a boondoggling hejira to the Land of the Lotus Eaters" to expose the MO people for the charlatans they were—taking their ease in thatched bungalows by the sea and sleeping the war away under the influence of siren songs.

It took a bit of glib talking to convince her I had come to get the over-all picture of the over-all picture—that handy government portmanteau word we were both fond of bandying about.

"Just so you aren't here to coordinate," she warned. "We like it the way we are now—uncoordinated."

Jane explained that it was difficult to discover where things began and ended in Ceylon because the island was divided, like Gaul, into three parts. The most important of these divisions was Kandy, high in the mountains where Lord Louis Mountbatten could occasionally be seen on a clear day on his way to work in the Botanical Gardens, and where OSS headquarters were sequestered in a tea plantation.

On the other side of the island was Trincomalee, the British naval base and location of the OSS top-secret Camp Y where we briefed native agents for infiltration and long-distance American swimmers for underwater sorties off submarines against Jap shipping, which they sabotaged with magnetic time limpets.

Colombo was the port town where several handsome resort hotels and night clubs did a booming wartime trade, where operational supplies were landed, and where our printing unit was established thirty miles from Kandy to keep MO types out of the sight and mind of the higher echelon, Jane informed me.

We were driven from the airfield by Captain Howard Palmer, the son of a Thai missionary family, who was in charge of MO for Thailand. Skirting the main part of the city, which was so clean that it had a freshly washed feel to it, we went down a palm-lined road, entered a stockade, and threaded our way across hard-packed sand to the main building of the "MOtel," which faced a sparkling white beach and the Indian Ocean, and was camouflaged beneath a green canopy of ancient palms. The print shop was set back as far from the spray as possible, to save what machinery was left after a rough voyage across three oceans from further disintegration by corrosion. Workshops of plywood and thatch were scattered through the grove, connected by small, irregular flagstones, a Morse-code path of dots and dashes tapped out in the rilled, raked white sand. It was delightfully cool, and the only suggestion of an Army establishment was a barbed-wire fence and doll-like Gurkha guards at the entrance.

More of these dreamy-eyed lads, and a few of the Singhalese in orange and green plaid sarongs, were serving tea in the main MO lounge.

"Don't be too impressed with their tidiness," Jane cautioned. "This shop and the boys' sarongs were washed for the first time last week for General Donovan's visit. He was here, too, you know—like Kilroy."

Jane told me that I could find out all I wanted to know about MO the following day when we drove up to Kandy, where our acting chief for SEAC, Dr. Carleton Scofield, was in charge.

"I have to drive up anyway," she explained. "One of our Thai agents—Chop—says he has worms again. He's something of a hypochondriac. Doc Murphy slips him an aspirin, and he's fine for weeks."

And over our afternoon teacups I heard from Jane and Howard something of the grave responsibilities which they shared in the care and training of native agents. Up to now, I had imagined our agents following the approved Hollywood pattern: slinking silently through jungles, leering through open windows at intended victims with knives in their mouths, and thinking nothing of slitting anybody's throat from ear to ear. Fainting Frieda and the assorted Batak, Malay, Thai, and Karens whom Jane and Howard shielded from the cruel white light of reality, shattered these illusions. I soon learned that most of the MO agents were afraid of knives, they never slunk when they could ride in a jeep, and they had to be constantly guided.

Howard's wisp of a Thai agent is probably the only person I shall ever know who jumped out of an airplane twice without touching the ground. The first time his static line became snarled and he dangled and banged against the underbelly of the plane until someone opened the door and pulled him back in. The second time he left the plane and landed in a tree. Fainting Frieda was carried on the records as "Myaung, 18, native of Ramree Island; woman agent now believed operating in and around Rangoon." This was her story, as Howard related it:

When the British and Americans first landed on the twenty-five-mile-long Japanese-held island of Ramree off the Burma coast, we occupied the northern end of the island and Jap troops fought on at the southern tip, communicating with headquarters on the mainland at Taungup through native runners. As part of OSS intelligence gathering, we decided to infiltrate Jap lines to the south and steal their mail sacks. Perpetrators of this scheme were two OSS captains, Manley Fleischmann and Robert Koke, and a civilian, Lucien Hanks. They discovered a Burmese postman in the town of Kyaukpu, five miles from the Jap lines, who said he would attempt the Great Mail Robbery. While the boys were interviewing the postmaster, they also met his beautiful daughter, Myaung, who had been educated at a Catholic mission at Sandoway on the Arakan coast and had returned to Ramree during Jap occupation. While her father was off rifling the Jap mail, the three operators enticed Myaung—later known as Fainting Frieda —into becoming a runner for the Japs between Ramree and Sandoway, a rather tricky double-agent job which Myaung agreed to attempt. She was to spy out the disposition of Jap troops, posing as their own runner, and then send back information to the OSS men in a hollow bamboo stick. Myaung was well acquainted with Ramree and Sandoway and, according to reports, made an excellent agent for a few weeks, until the OSS boys decided to launch her into a more important area—Rangoon—to pass on the same type of information. Myaung, a bit timid about her new assignment, disappeared into Burma and was never heard from until the fall of Rangoon, when Captain Koke spotted her one day in the Rangoon Public Library. She confessed then that she had been so frightened by the Japs that every time she tried to get information from them she fainted and had to be returned to the home of relatives in a coma.

"In general"—Jane assumed her Herr Doktor pose—"our native agents for Southeast Asia haven't a subversive bone in their bodies. In fact, they favor the direct approach to propagandizing their own people. They can't understand why we just don't drop leaflets into occupied zones telling the natives how bad the Japs are."

Then she told me about Danny and Nick, Sam, Haji and Chop, as odd a lot of secret operatives as ever had their names recorded in the most secret files of OSS in double-doored safes.

Danny, the Karen, was seventeen years old and had been captured in Burma after he had fallen on his head in a flight from the British, and sustained a concussion. Ever since his accident he had suffered from the delusion that he was going crazy although the OSS psychiatrist in charge of Camp Y ruled him perfectly sane. Howard had plans to use Danny as a radio announcer at Chittagong after he recovered, but Danny never advanced to that level. He was unaccustomed to clothes and was always removing his shirt, tie, and cap if not carefully supervised. Once, Jane told me, Danny appeared at the openair movies in Kandy, stood up in front of the audience, and began to remove his pants. Howard returned him to Camp Y after that, where the psychologist thought Danny might possibly be lonesome for another Karen. He was the only one of his kind in Ceylon.

Howard also had two Thai agents, Chop, who weighed in at eighty-five pounds and was smuggled into Bangkok in a rice basket, and Sam, who held a high position in the Thai government in exile. Sam was hired to give advice on propaganda material slanted for Thailand, but he had the sweet habit of agreeing with any proposed program, which made it difficult to know just how good or bad an idea really was. The boys who taught Sam to play poker lived to regret it, because they never knew when he was bluffing. With every hand he drew he smiled and muttered: "Good—good—good!"

Early in Jane's life in Ceylon she was called in by Dr. Scofield and told she had inherited a Malay named Haji Mukdar who had just come from Mecca and was consequently fairly high up in Malayan society. He had attended a Moslem university in India and spoke only Malay. Shortly after Haji, a Batak named Chabudeen was presented to Jane who confided to her in Malay that he had been captured by a British submarine off Sumatra while en route to teach school. The British turned him over to the Americans after they interrogated him at Trincomalee. He wilted whenever anyone spoke sharply to him, and they couldn't imagine sending him back to enemy-held territory with a radio set that would not only confuse but terrify him.

Both Haji and Chabudeen, whose agent name was Nick, imagined all manner of slights and prejudices until they were accorded officer privileges. Then, when no one else in OSS would eat with the MO agents, Jane and Howard were forced to move to a special table at mealtimes so that no one's feelings would be hurt. Jane was the official taster for the Moslems because their religion forbade them to eat anything that had been cooked in animal fat.

Haji had a great dread of his body being cut, going back somewhere to an ancient Malayan fear of the knife. Once, suffering from an infected wisdom tooth, he quivered at the thought of a dentist.

"No, don't pull," he moaned, "they'll cut me."

Jane assured him that American dentists were different. They only filled teeth. She finally lured him off to the clinic. That night Haji ran screaming into the mess hall, holding his face.

"I am now an old man. I am going to die. Had I been a white man they would not have pulled my tooth!"

He was in such a fever pitch of indignation that Jane drove him thirty miles up to Kandy, where Dr. Murphy calmed his hysterics with an aspirin tablet.

Later, when Haji went to Chittagong, Jane received a strange note from him in faltering English:

"I will never forget you. Every time I put my tongue up where my tooth was I am remembering your love present to me."

Nick, too, developed strange ailments, mostly mental, which kept Jane running to and from dispensaries because she was the only lingual link between doctor and patient. Once Nick wilted, and she rushed him to Dr. Murphy.

"He says he's emptying out blood," Jane translated.

"Which end?"

Further questioning revealed the doubtful presence of ulcers, and it was decided to put Nick into the British hospital for observation. Jane registered him as an American sergeant and, to maintain this impression, she told him not to speak to anyone. Instead of being delighted with a bed in a hospital, Nick developed hysterics. The hospital roused Jane out of bed in the middle of the night. The mute "sergeant" had written her name on a piece of paper and must see her at once. Jane jeeped seventeen miles out to see Nick.

"They don't like me here," he insisted. "They want me to die. They are starving me to death. They are feeding me only milk."

Jane explained about the conventional treatment for ulcers and arranged for a nice British nurse to pat Nick's head every so often. Within the next three days his "ulcers" had cleared up nicely, and he begged to return to Colombo by Friday, when he and Haji went to the mosque to pray in an OSS jeep which Jane had to requisition for them.

Nick was quite a hero in the little group when word went round that General Donovan, on his trip to Colombo, had paused to take notice of Nick as he was performing a lowly MO task.

"I suppose anyone would have stared at Nick that afternoon," Jane told me. "We weren't prepared, of course, for the visit, which was ahead of schedule. Our wilting Batak was the only one at work. We were preparing to float some MO material and quinine pills ashore off Java by submarine. The only waterproof containers we could find were those convenient little gadgets in agent prophylaxis kits. Chop was systematically blowing them up, inserting our messages and pills, and tying them up like little balloons. The task delighted his artistic soul. He'd arranged his display nicely on one of the desks. When the inspection party whisked in on us we were all off guard, including my pet chipmunk, Christopher, who fell squeaking like the dormouse into the cream pitcher on the table, escaped from that and knocked over Nick's odd display so the little balloons went floating all over the room, and Nick went crawling in and out among higher echelon legs to retrieve them. No wonder the general stared!"

Unfortunately my arrival coincided with the beginning of a Colombo week end. All transient billets in the OSS compounds were crowded, and Jane's own small room was occupied by four guests down from Kandy for a seashore visit.

"But don't worry," my fine Irish friend explained. "Howard has the key to Area V, which he hasn't given back to the security officer yet. That's an agent house in town where we hide native agents until it's time to send them behind the lines. If we didn't hide them, they'd be blabbing all over Colombo about going back home and offering to take letters for friends of friends."

Area V had been the rendezvous for a gay band of four Malay pirates, I learned, who had just been shipped out three days ago. The place had electricity, beds, a bath, and kitchen facilities. As far as Jane knew, there weren't any trapdoors or secret entrances, and the house was in a middle-class Singhalese community at the center of town.

"If you get scared, just yell, and you'll have all the neighborhood at your door," Howard reassured me, although I didn't fancy the idea of calling on strange Singhalese for help.

After dinner and dancing at a fabulous pink and white night club called the Silver Fawn, we drove out to Area V in a mood of gay abandon, sparked by champagne for dinner. The house at first seemed quite charming, set off from other houses in a graceful cluster of palms and bamboo. As soon as Howard and Jane drove away, my champagne-inspired bravado gave way to a vague apprehensiveness. The European-type frame house was strangely silent—and dark. It was a two-story affair, and in order to reach the front door I climbed an outside flight of stairs. In the bright moonlight I walked along a narrow deck to the door which was fastened with a ponderous American lock. Inside, the blinds were drawn. I played my flashlight along bare, whitewashed walls until I found the switch. When I ticked on the lights, I was standing in a low-ceilinged, partially furnished room which smelled of disinfectant.

In the center of the room was a round bamboo table, primly surrounded by four stiff, straight-backed chairs. I could imagine the four pirates sitting around the table, staring at one another, waiting for the Word! I could even visualize their gleaming cutlasses swinging at their sides, their red bandannas and gold ear loops. I hoped, suddenly, that they all had gone away on schedule.

I walked into the kitchen and turned on the light. There were a stove, an ice chest, a sink, all smelling slightly sour, like a beach-cottage kitchen that has been closed for the season. The only sign of pirate activity was a large dishpan in the center of the floor, containing the remains of a fire. Probably the pirates hadn't understood the electric stove and preferred to cook their simple meals over an open fire. I suddenly froze in my tour of inspection. There, hanging from the dishtowel rack over the sink, were the shriveled remains of a dried squid! Perhaps it was meant only in hospitality—an invitation to the next occupant to partake of this rare delicacy!

The house was peopled with pirates by the time I reached the bathroom. Here again I was startled—by four distinct rings around the bathtub which led to all sorts of conjectures as to the relative size and weight of the former tenants.

Approaching the bedroom I felt a little like Goldilocks, expecting to find them all in their beds, Mama, Papa and the two baby pirates! When I turned on a garish pink bedside lamp I was vastly relieved to find that the room was empty except for a cot, a blanket roll, and a night stand. Here, I determined, I would set up my defense of depth. This would be my redoubt. I obtained a knife from the kitchen —a dull butter knife, but still a weapon—and I barred the door leading to the bath. I unrolled the blanket, stretched it over a lumpy mattress, and timidly undressed. The air outside was soft and warm, but the house itself was musty. It had by now begun to assume the texture and atmosphere of a Charles Addams drawing, and I expected Boris Karloff to walk in, any minute, with a nice hot cup of chocolate-flavored strychnine.

I stretched out wearily, arranging myself over and around the lumps. I wondered if all four pirates had slept in this bed. Perhaps it contained bugs, hardy bugs who didn't mind the lumps.

There was a small drawer in the night stand, and I couldn't resist the impulse to open it. Perhaps the pirates had left incriminating papers around, a clue to their operations. I pulled it open cautiously, and a large, glossy cockroach leapt out, quite as startled as I was, and scurried across the floor, its legs rasping against the wood. I found a grimy piece of paper covered with figures which proved to be bridge scores of four people clandestinely noted as A, B, C, and D. There was nothing else, but surely now was the time to find that old copy of the *Reader's Digest* that always pops up under such circumstances with just the right message—something by Bruce Barton, perhaps, on "Life Can Be Beautiful"!

By now the pink light had attracted a swarm of night insects which spent themselves against the heat of the globe and fell dead on my exposed neck and shoulders. I turned off the light and lay grimly silent on the lumps. For some reason, I began to brood about my past, like a prisoner in the condemned cell. I was always getting myself into seemingly inextricable situations just because I didn't have the sense to finesse in the first place.

There had been that mercy mission on a sampan I made around Hawaii just after Pearl Harbor with the girl navigator, Judy Hall, delivering supplies to stranded islanders and running the risk of being blasted out of the water either by our own shore batteries or by a Japanese submarine.

And covering the eruption of Mauna Loa, walking miles across brittle lava in a pair of tennis shoes that were cut to ribbons, just to write a gag story about the volcano that violated a territory-wide blackout.

Or telephoning home that lovely May Day in 1941 to say I was sailing as a stewardess at four o'clock on an Army transport, to evacuate women and children from the Philippines. It was a fine idea, except I didn't know anything about the care and feeding of children, any more than some of the Army wives did: they couldn't even change diapers, they had been so dependent on native help. My brood on third deck center lived on baked potatoes and split-pea soup from Manila to the States.

I had just started to relax when something crashed against the bedroom screen. I heard a clawing noise, and stared into two luminous yellow eyes! I felt for the knife. As is always the case with perverse inanimate objects, it clattered to the floor and I touched the cold, reassuring metal of the flashlight instead. At least here was a blunt instrument, I reasoned. After an interminably long period of indecision, I risked all and flashed the light toward the eyes. There, silhouetted against the screen was a blob of white feathers and the solemn face of one of those small Ceylon owls which Jane had once told me about!

"Oooh!" the feathers said in a peevish voice.

He clung to the screen for quite a long time, probably waiting for an answer to his query. Finally, after a second "Oooh!" he scuttled away, and I felt quite alone again, and very sleepy and relieved.

The next morning the House suddenly became nothing more than a house again. The pirates were gone, the men with knives gave way to sweet-faced natives walking in barefoot unconcern outside the house. A light rain was slicking the palms when I walked stiffly into the living room and slit open a box of K rations, stenciled "Breakfast."

By the time I had finished the asbestos biscuits and a clammy mass of proteins which the Army said was pork and eggs, Howard and Jane were tooting outside in the MO jeep, the Black Tulip. Also in the jeep were Chop and his assorted worms, and a pretty girl named Patty Norbury who worked for the OSS Registry in Kandy.

The road to the high echelon headquarters wound through a lush jungle of palms, acacia, and matted liana and climbed heavily forested mountain slopes where giant tree ferns and ground orchids began to remind me of Hawaii. At one bend Jane pointed out a tribe of flying foxes, hanging from the limbs of a great monkeypod tree where they slept during the day. Once we detoured around a plodding elephant with a little Singhalese lad sprawled on his back.

Howard said there were all sorts of wild life in the forests: bandicoots with long hooked red noses, cobras, iguanas, swifts that furnished the Chinese with their bird's-nest soup, anteaters, panthers, even leeches—nasty things that were a special torment to pet dogs in Kandy because they attached themselves to the animals' eyes.

"And there's a famous footprint at a pilgrim station near here," Jane informed me. "The Brahmins say it's the footstep of Siva. The Buddhists say it was made by Buddha; the Mohammedans, Adam. And now that the Americans are here in Ceylon, the gag, is of course, that George Washington stepped here!"

On the long ride, Patty told me something about the reason she was in Ceylon. Her fiancé, Lieutenant Roy Wenz, Jr., had been reported missing in action over Rangoon on a bombing mission with the 10th Air Force in December, 1943. Everyone but Patty had given him up for dead.

"I took this job with OSS just to be as close to Burma as I could," she said. "I watch every report that comes over my desk from our men in the field. One of their jobs is to report on Allied prisoners of war. Some day, someone will pick up Roy's trail. You see, no one ever saw his plane go down. No trace has ever been found of the crew . . ."

(Months afterward I heard that Patty had finally discovered the first clue to the fate of Roy Wenz in an OSS agent report about a sergeant who had been on the same plane. Later, Roy himself was discovered, alive but wasted to ninety-five pounds, in a prison camp. Patty joined him in Calcutta in May, 1945, and they were married the following October.)

It was drizzly when we reached the OSS tea plantation head-

quarters—a series of long thatched bashas which seemed to be anchored precariously to the steep slopes of a hill and held in place by
neat rope hedges of bobbing, clipped tea plants.

Dr. Carleton Scofield greeted us in an office that was a fair imitation
of the lair of a Washington desk head, complete with wall maps, a
polished desk, a name plate, and a rug on the floor which in my mind
always tacitly implied that an executive worked here. The doctor
himself was most enthusiastic in his greeting. I had heard that he was
a bit hesitant in making commitments but was a loyal advocate of
MO, who gave the branch a certain dignity when he represented it
at P Division conferences. In peacetime, he was a psychology professor at the University of Buffalo.

With him was Dr. Cora Du Bois, head of the Research and Analysis
branch for OSS, formerly on the faculty of Sarah Lawrence College,
who had made several trips to the Netherlands East Indies with
anthropology field teams. Cora was a handsome woman, willowy,
with a deep voice and an odd way of peering over her glasses and asking questions as if you were in the front row of Anthropology I at
Sarah Lawrence and hadn't prepared your lesson.

Cora had arrived in SEAC in May of 1944 to set up a Research and
Analysis branch which had grown from a staff of two into some
sixty-five researchers scattered from New Delhi to Assam. She came
to Kandy after setting up the Netherlands East Indies section for the
Washington Research and Analysis branch.

"Escape was necessary after that," said Dr. Du Bois.

Like Marj and me at New Delhi, Cora arrived at Kandy with no
material, no reference books, no staff. She had been promised the aid
of a wispy lad who somehow was lost on the way out and later turned
up with Merrill's Marauders through an error in orders. She scarcely
recognized him when he swaggered into her office in Kandy after six
months, bronzed from his jungle adventures and not at all inclined
to desk work.

Cora had participated in the Arakan planning for Research and
Analysis and had organized document collecting teams which later
entered Rangoon ahead of the Allied armies to obtain some five
thousand important documents including the minutes of the meetings
of the Burmese Committee on Cooperation with the Quisling Ba Maw
which showed the degree to which the Burmese interim government
stalled off the Japs.

Under her guidance, Research and Analysis developed intelligence
kits in waterproof bags which included fifteen target maps, dic-

tionaries and descriptions of all important areas in the Malay Peninsula to be used in the campaigns planned for early September. When the invasion was called off at the end of the war, the kits were used by early reoccupation teams.

"Fighting the Japs isn't an R. and A. problem," Cora pointed out; "but what goes on in Southeast Asia is our problem. We've been able to trace a gradual trend in this area through intelligence reports that may be of value to someone some day. The Japs, by breaking up the European colonial system, seem to be advancing the cause of liberalism in Southeast Asia. They've injected a new self-confidence in the natives. It'll be next to impossible for them to go back to the old way of life after the war. The British, Dutch, and French have no positive program to offer these people. The United States has a backlog of prestige over here now; but the generalities in our foreign policy must be made specific, or we will soon use up that prestige out here."

As we were talking, Howard came in with some MO reports, and Jane arrived with Chop presumably dewormed by that great Far Eastern panacea, the aspirin tablet. The meeting was beginning to assume all the grim aspects of a Washington round-table conference, particularly when Dr. Scofield's secretary entered, seated herself, crossed her legs, and poised pencil and shorthand pad. She was about to take notes which would go back to Washington in the form of minutes. Unedited, they should have read something like this:

SCOFIELD: The idea of this meeting, as I gather, is to coordinate MO in Ceylon and Calcutta.
FOSTER: Howard, the ash tray, please.
MACDONALD (*aside*): Jane, have you ever seen Lord Louis?
DUBOIS: Is it all right for Chop to hear about Chittagong?
CHOP: Pome roo lao!
HOWARD: He says he already knows about it.

Actually, I learned quite a bit at the meeting. MO-SEAC was more or less uncoordinated through no fault of its own. Targets set up by Washington planners included Japs, collaborators, and native populations of Thailand, Burma, southern French Indo-China, and most of the Netherlands East Indies. But the psychological warfare policy of both British and Dutch in Kandy had been hands off—or, at best, a negative approach asking the natives to protect the property of their white masters who had fled the Japs. They agreed that we could undermine the morale of the Jap soldier, but at present we had no MO agent net and very little equipment.

"Of course we get a few things done," Jane pointed out. "We send handwritten, chin-up material, and sometimes medical supplies, in with submarines that the British use for their snatch sorties. Snatching is a method of collecting intelligence. The subs go over to the mainland, wait around for a native fishing junk to appear. It's a case of sighting ship, sinking same and snatching survivors. The British bring them back to Trincomalee for questioning. If they are of any value, they train them as agents. Otherwise they are placed in internee camps, or employed whenever possible."

Like the Calcutta unit, the people in SEAC were excited about the possibilities of the black radio station at Chittagong. Dr. Scofield had already dispatched a Lieutenant Commander Alexander MacDonald to the site to study the possibilities. The commander had submitted an operational plan which was now before P Division for implementation. The station would operate under cover of language broadcasts supposedly coming from Radio JOAK and slipped in so close to the Tokyo frequency that monitors in occupied countries would have difficulty distinguishing black from Jap. Commander MacDonald had already done a trial broadcast that had duped British direction-finding units in Burma, who reported an enemy station operating in the jungles. A test program beamed to Siam, describing damage done to Japan by Allied bombing raids and the resultant instability of Japanese markets, was reprinted in Bangkok papers as a bona fide news story; and they credited it to the Siamese hour over JOAK in Tokyo.

"We'll need cooperation from Calcutta in producing radio scripts for the station," Dr. Scofield told me. "When the station starts operating we'll broadcast all hours of day and night."

Most of the other MO discussion was of a routine nature, except the story about Gregory Bateson, a British anthropologist on the staff, who won P Division permission to paint the Irrawaddy yellow! During his Ceylon sojourn, Dr. Bateson discovered a Burmese legend which revealed that when the waters of the Irrawaddy turned as yellow as the pongys' robes, the foreign enemy would leave Burma forever! While the Burmese were probably referring to the British, Dr. Bateson decided that the slogan could also be applied to the Japs. He procured, at vast amount of trouble and high echelon conniving, several dozen cans of yellow oil, used by downed planes as slick smears to attract rescue parties. Just before the doctor launched his MO whisper campaign in conjunction with floating yellow oil slicks down the Irrawaddy, he poured a sample slick into his own bathtub.

It sank immediately. The instructions read: "For use in salt water only."

I suppose we should have talked ourselves through the stenographer's notebook, up one side and down the other, if I hadn't looked at my ankle at a sudden, large, fat, sausage-shaped growth. It expanded under my gaze like a fountain pen plunger—filling up on very bright, red blood!

Dr. Scofield said it was the first leech he had seen in Kandy, an academic statement which failed to interest me at the moment. Jane led me off limping (although it didn't hurt a bit) to Dr. Murphy, who lighted a cigarette and touched the end to the leech. The Thing dropped off my ankle, reared up on its haunches, and weaved back and forth in what appeared to be a consuming rage.

"He's still hungry," said Dr. Murphy, finishing the cigarette.

The last time I saw Jane and Howard in the Far East was through the plexiglass window of a C-47. They were making farcical farewell gestures, mouthing words that I could not hear, and we were all grinning back and forth like three foolish people while my plane lingered too long at Colombo.

Not long after my departure, Howard was ordered to Bangkok to a plush, behind-the-lines existence in a Thai palace surrounded by servants who stole special food and drink for him from the Japanese commanding general. Howard's arrival in Bangkok was one of those OSS sagas repeated whenever CBI veterans meet. He was sent to Thailand by a Flying Boat, and taken to the capital in broad daylight aboard a motor launch. Wearing full American uniform, Howard was whisked through the streets of the occupied city in the rear of a crotchety taxi whose horn stuck, directly in front of a detachment of Jap soldiers. Howard crouched on the floor of the cab, and the Japs marked time behind him while the driver got out and fixed the horn!

Jane's last confidential plan which she divulged only to me was to infiltrate the island of Bali by submarine, plunge into the jungles, and emerge long after World War II as the Great White Queen of Bali. However, she was destined for more important things and, immediately after cessation of hostilities, became the first link between the Allies and the Indonesian Republic in Batavia.

Calcutta seemed even more dirty, dismal, and sultry after the tropical beauty of Ceylon, and within a few brief weeks we again went through a complete reshuffle in organization with the arrival of the new MO chief, Lieutenant Withrow.

Bill Magistretti, severely ill with dysentery, was sent home to San Francisco, where he eventually took part in the black radio project, Operation Blossom, which was beamed to Japan. Lieutenant Gilmore was sent off to the Arakan, and Al Pindar became "city editor" at R House. In the last week in February I was told that I had been requested for Künming! Could I be ready within the week?

Shortly before I left I was to sit in on the uncomfortable meeting between psychological warfare representatives from P Division, Major Glemser and his chief, and MO-Calcutta personnel. Plans were made to disseminate MO material against Japanese troops through British channels. Propaganda lines against native peoples were drawn up, following a fairly general thesis of Japanese defeat.

The meeting, in a way, meant that most of our dealings with the British had finally been vindicated. The rapprochement eventually proved that Anglo-American cooperation was not entirely impossible. At the end of the war I was informed that 98,625 pieces of black material had been disseminated for us by our British allies.

CHAPTER TEN

APO 627

THE symbols involved in military orders have always been as unintelligible to me as the cryptic cadence of a drill sergeant's commands on a parade ground.

Orders assigning me to China read:

Pursuant to co SSO IBT the fol named civ emp WP o/a 14 Mar 45 fr APO 465 to APO 627 RUAT to CO OSS SU Det 202 for dy: E MacDonald.

"That just means you're officially transferred," the transportation officer told me with the resigned patience Army men reserve for the handling of civ. emp.

"Be at the ATC terminal at the Hindustani Building at 0615 hours. You get 172 pounds baggage allowance, and that doesn't include your half-wit dog! Your plane leaves from Barrackpore—about half an hour's ride out of Calcutta."

Since the world-publicized incident of Elliott Roosevelt's dog usurping a GI's seat aboard the ATC, canine travel over the Hump had been at a virtual standstill, every ounce of cargo being jealously weighed in ratio to American soldiers to feed in China. Therefore I had to select a new master for Angel Puss, and found him in a young, uninhibited pilot named Dabney who said he was looking for a mascot to keep him company on his dreary bombing sorties over the jungles of Burma. My last sight of the Puss Sahib was that of recalcitrant disobedience as Dabney dragged him along the marble foyer of Harrington Mansions. Months later, word reached me in China that Angel had fallen out of Dabney's bomb bay on a routine mission over Burma, part of the bomb stick that wiped out a small Jap supply depot on the Irrawaddy.

Preparations for China included not only an exchange of rupees for Chinese National Bank currency (CN), visas, a wardrobe of warm clothing and a series of plague shots, but a reorientation course (reading time, twenty minutes) in a GI handbook entitled "Pocket Guide to China." In this brochure, the Special Services

Division broke the news gently that the Chinese "think we look queer because they are accustomed to everyone having black hair and eyes." We were also warned about "surprises" in store for us in a land where mothers nurse babies in public, men relieve themselves whenever and wherever nature demands and children run about with nothing on in the summer.

"Take it all as a matter of course—don't offend them by seeming to notice it," was the Emily Postscript.

A trip over the Hump was still something to contemplate seriously. Just two months before, storms had claimed twenty-six planes within a ten-hour period on New Year's Eve. Veteran airmen regarded our present course, over the newly acquired Burma territory, as a milk run; but, even so, a recent intelligence intercept reported Jap raiders opening fire on an ATC cargo plane. I derived some small comfort from a farewell gift presented by Lieutenant Edward Mitsukada—a captured Japanese thousand-stitch belt designed to protect the owner against any eventuality. The stitches represented prayers by as many Japanese girls for the return of the wearer, who had evidently been safe until he met Eddy. The bulky red and white belt was now tucked into the pocket of my flight jacket along with other talismans for riding in airplanes, such as a St. Christopher's medal and a five-leaf clover.

While we were being fitted for parachutes at Barrackpore, I covertly studied the crew of the plane, hoping to reassure myself that the pilot, at least, was head and shoulders above his fellow men. I was discouraged to find that he was pudgy, his beaver collar was flecked with dandruff, and he had the irresolute air of a shoe clerk who might hesitate to cross the street on an amber light. It would certainly pay ATC in the long run, I decided, to hire Tyrone Power models as stand-ins for such milk-toast types, even if it was just to dash through the plane, chin up, eyes clear, step firm, adjusting a soft white silk muffler and whistling "Off We Go, into the Wild Blue Yonder." When he got forward and slammed the door behind him he could crawl out at the plexiglass window and go on with his act for the next take-off, for all I cared.

While the crew was making a last-minute weather check, I renewed acquaintance with Julia McWilliams, bound from Kandy to Künming as head of the registry office, and Louis Hector, a civilian lawyer on the OSS Secretariat. Louis was said to be one of the best boogie pianists on the Atlantic seaboard-keyboard and was the author of such librettos as the Chinese Money Lender's Song, "I'll Be CN

You," and "Meet Me in the Paddy, Laddy"—all included in his port-folio, "Swing Low, Sweet Secretariat." He complained of being bumped off flights for the past two days because of his low priority and of having had to slink back to work after farewells had been said, gifts distributed, money changed. The experience had inspired him to write a new burlesque ditty titled: "Bumped Again, and Back to the Same Old Grind."

Louis offered pleasant conversational escape from the immediate *bête noire*—the Hump—but as take-off time approached we began to swap stories of the Himalayan run. Julia recollected that an OSS officer, Lieutenant Colonel Duncan Lee, had gone down over the Hump a few months before in the same plane with Eric Sevareid and had rescued only one item in the split second aboard the disabled plane before he jumped. The item—a quart of gin he had promised a friend in Chungking.

"He was terribly conscientious about it—delivered it intact! Didn't touch a drop during the two days he was walking through the jungles!" Julia confided.

Louis informed us that the real reason for building the Burma Road was that a couple of generals had made such a rough flight to China over the Hump that they swore they'd return by land.

Once air-borne, we had a smooth flight over India and Burma. After several hours we could see the Burma Road like a thin red artery, a one-track line to China, convoluting through the jungle far beneath. Then we began to climb toward snowy peaks where some three thousand Chinese, American, and British planes were said to have been lost between 1942 and 1945 and where the Hump had exacted 100 per cent replacements in three years. Here great cross-currents of air had been known to suck airplanes down from an altitude of 8,500 feet to 2,500 in ten seconds. One pilot told me that during a storm the black paint on his flashlight had been completely skinned off by some electrical effect in a dive.

There were thirty passengers aboard our bucket-seater, which had been named, in large scrawled script across the nose: "Is This Trip Necessary?" A staff car was lashed to the center of the ship, and supplies of food and ammunition were piled against the crated car. A sergeant had already stretched himself out on top of the cargo, sleeping with his head on his parachute. Next to me, on the floor, a soldier was playing a harmonica, accompanied by his buddy on a guitar. Everything was drab khaki—clothes, cargo, fuselage, K-ration containers.

As we began to climb to 18,000, the flight clerk came around and told us to put on our oxygen masks, and the boy with the harmonica stopped playing. We were flying above clouds which occasionally parted like thin chiffon to reveal unending stretches of snow and jagged aiguilles. Willie Clarke, a mountain climber of some note in India, had once told me that the Indians thought of the Himalayas as the roof of the world. Perhaps it was from these vast reaches of silence that Indian mysticism flowed—embodied in the sacred rivers which were born in these snowlands. Only lichen and scrub pine lived at such heights over which we flew, sucking nourishment from volcanic rocks. Airmen forced to abandon their planes had been frozen to death before their parachutes folded around them like shrouds in the domain of ice and snow. There was a strange aloofness in this land, and our noisy, throbbing plane with its assortment of human passengers, was a transgressor speeding unwelcome through the Himalayan quiet. Mists, sent up like couriers from below, began to envelop us with silent, possessive, curious fingers, passing over the windows, clinging to the wings. Suddenly we were encased in mist, suspended over a continent of frozen things, over glaciers sawing new patterns on the earth's surface, over the white, unmarked graves of other planes. The white mists turned gray, then black, concealing what was below us, and directing my thoughts back to the ship, to small details like the spot on the fender of the staff car where the cables had rubbed off the olive-drab Army paint and a robin's-egg-blue civilian color peeped through.

The flight clerk swayed through the debris of passengers' gear and cargo, instructing us to adjust our flight belts and prepare for rough weather. One of the lads on the floor—his arm-patch insignia read "14th Air Force"—took off his oxygen mask, leaned closer to his friend, whispered, and then pointed toward our Number Two engine. The friend put his guitar aside and listened intently, head cocked. I exchanged looks with the artillery captain beside me. A few minutes later he turned to the man on his right, and whispered. Uneasiness swept the plane. Suddenly the ship plummeted, and we were spiraling earthward like a winged duck. The lights in the plane went out. We were in murky darkness. The C–54 shuddered, leveled off with a roar. Above the noise, there was the tick of ice against the windows, the whoosh of deceptive, billowy cloud masses which we sometimes outflanked but usually bucked, like a football line. Lightning laced the darkness. The flight clerk emerged again from the pilot's compartment, like a nurse from an operating room, and we all turned expectantly.

"Künming is closed in. May have to make an emergency landing at Yunnanee. Keep your masks on. Tighten safety belts. We're over the worst of the Hump, but there's turbulent air ahead . . ."

Our plane was storm-tossed for over an hour. Number two engine choked, and when they feathered its propeller there was a quietness, an unsymmetrical roar which all ears caught. After one violent updraft the man next to me got quietly sick in his handkerchief.

I suppose the thought crossed everyone's mind that we might crash. I finally worked up enough courage to look at my parachute, and wondered what cord I should pull. If we crashed suddenly, and there was no time to jump, would we be conscious long enough to hear the rock and ice crunch through the fuselage? How would the newspapers say it? Charred bodies. Frozen bodies. Fragments. Rescue parties searching. Investigation (always there must be an investigation).

In the midst of these fumbling fears, half-formulated promises to be a kind, dutiful daughter if we only reached Künming safely, partial resignation to the man at the controls, a wonderful blue flash of sky lighted up the interior of the plane. We dived sharply, then we were leveling off toward a red-dirt air strip where a rabble army of blue-jacketed coolies was painstakingly grading a portion of the field, towing great sledges of dirt and rock through the thin drizzle of rain. Above us, the storm had closed over that patch of blue, the hole our pilot had miraculously found directly over the Künming airport.

The boys began to play "Coming In on a Wing and a Prayer" as we landed and trundled up to a terminal flanked with long lines of the famous shark-faced planes of the Flying Tigers.

Julia, climbing down first, looked over the low, red hills and the curling rooftop of a small temple near the field, received a cheerful "Ting hao" greeting from some red-cheeked children, and turned back to her fellow passengers:

"It looks *just* like China," she told us.

China was a bright, hard impact after India. The peasants at the airport, with polished apple-red faces and threadbare homespun clothes, were just as bound to the soil as the Indian peasants; but to me they were a free people, holding their heads high, unsubservient. And the Chinese children played boisterously. I could not remember seeing an Indian child romp.

At the airport I felt for the first time since the early Pearl Harbor days in Hawaii that a war was being fought not too many mountain bends away from Künming. I understood that plans had already been drawn up for evacuating every American installation in the city in case of a Jap attack. There was an urgency and purpose, too, at the airport, where the Tigers had drawn first blood against the Jap in China. We were at the end of the supply line that stretched all the way from America. Planes landed every two minutes at this busiest airport in the world, and American equipment was convoyed from this field to China's armies in training, to pockets of Chinese resistance within Japanese lines, to our own OSS people at weather posts, airstrips, guerrilla outposts. The barracks and buildings at Roger Queen Airport—Künming's code designation—were constructed of Chinese mud and tile. The personnel who worked there wore heavy flying jackets, flight suits tucked into mosquito boots, for the air was brisk and invigorating at this Allied stronghold in the Himalayas, some six thousand feet above sea level.

An OSS jeep drove us into town along a rough mud road lined with slim, straight-shafted cedars whose dead leaves still rustled like a first-night audience. There were great flowing fields of millet, cultivated along the tidy, opera-seat tiers of the rice paddies. We passed roadside markets offering handsome, polished vegetables for sale. These, the jeep driver warned us, were full of dysentery germs, because the Chinese used "night soil" (human feces) for fertilizer and also waterlogged their vegetables in foul canal water to add a few liang to the weight. Here and there we saw Chinese in bright blue coolie suits driving sway-backed, long-eared pigs which stepped daintily along the rough road on hooved feet. Once Julie spotted a flotilla of baby ducks, followed through a knee-deep pond by a young duck-herd who kept his fluffy charges in formation with an expert flick of a long willow wand.

To enter the walled city of Künming, we drove through an ancient gate which coquettishly tossed its four curling corners to the winds. Chinese guards saluted as we passed. They wore padded brown uniforms hitched with Sam Browne belts, straw sandals, and snug little caps with the blue and white Kuomintang star over the visor.

We drove along a canal where the clear water rippled with the patterns of duck maneuvers, turned up a well paved street in a newly opened subdivision where the driver said American generals, Chinese bankers, and the OSS girls lived. My home for the next eight months was concealed behind massive wooden gates—a modernistic stone house with tiled roof and encircling balconies overlooking formal Chinese gardens.

"The girls call it Mei Yüan—means Beautiful Garden, I think," the driver told us. "That's about all you got though. Just the other day the cook asphyxiated himself with one of those open, potbellied charcoal braziers you have for heating the place. Your johns are always on the blink—the Slopies don't know much about American plumbing yet. The roof leaks and there aren't enough rooms. For the million C.N. rent you have to pay a month you should be taking over the governor's summer palace."

Leaving us before the whited sepulcher of Mei Yüan, the driver spun out of the compound. Julie and I lugged our bags up the steps and into a large room which somehow gave the impression of a plush airplane terminal lounge with chairs ranged stiffly against the walls, curtains of white parachute silk ballooning from large, full-length windows. As we entered, a Chinese lad approached in blue uniform, with large GI boots on his pigeon-toed feet.

"I am Lee Ming," he told us in perfect English.

We introduced ourselves and asked him to help us with our bags, but we suddenly realized that the exchange of amenities had meant nothing to him.

"I learn English at the Y.M.C.A. in Canton. What is your name?" He continued with a smile on his face.

By this time a neat little girl in the uniform of a technical representative had come downstairs and introduced herself—Mary Hutchison of Research and Analysis. She then turned to Lee Ming and rattled off something in Chinese which sent him diving for our luggage. She told us we should be billeted in a large dormitory room until we chose up roommates.

Mary, with whom I later roomed, had been a prisoner of war at Weihsien together with Dr. Leighton Stuart, whose secretary she had been in Yenching. She was motivated by a desire to help end the war as soon as possible because she was one of the few to be sent home from the prison camp over her own protests, while older and more helpless people remained behind to face the Japs for three years. Mary's job with OSS was to implement target studies for the Fourteenth and Tenth air forces.

I met most of the other girls that night at a singularly tasteless dinner that seemed to mark all American-style meals in China. I soon learned to my regret that the real piquancy of Chinese cooking was found in the out-of-bounds restaurants, where fine flavor and dysentery went hand in hand.

We were a conglomerate American group, all of us a little bit pampered, I think, by the woman shortage. But Künming, I discovered, had nothing to offer like the fleshpots of Calcutta, and there was little entertainment except what we made for ourselves—picnics, boating parties on the lake, occasionally a movie at the compound. One of the few accepted night clubs was the gaudy, expensive Tennis Club, over the doors of which was affectionately inscribed the friendly typographical error:

"Welcome to soldiers of the Untied States."

The girls were crowded, as many as four or five in a room, for several months until we expanded into the servant quarters; but hard work, a plethora of male visitors, and a sharing of responsibilities at Mei Yüan somehow did away with the usual feminine bickering present in most women's barracks.

There was a Chinese WAC from New York, Captain Emily Shek, an intelligence officer who lived for the day when the war would end and she could go to Canton to determine whether her husband, son, and mother were still alive. She had not heard from them since the Japanese occupation.

Another intelligence operative, Marjorie Kennedy, had just arrived from Washington, where she had trained in Jap order of battle at the Pentagon.

From Kandy had come Jean Taylor, an artist with the presentation board credited with the discovery, in captured Jap blueprints sent her division in Ceylon, of the specifications for the Jap "splinter" fleet of wooden transports they were building in the Indies as fast as we sank their steel ships in the Pacific.

There were government girls from the Alcan Highway, Cairo, London; missionary daughters from China and Japan; artists, architects, writers, analysts, secretaries, dietitians.

There were about twenty of us, and a beautiful Chinese-language teacher named Margaret Leong who everyone said was a Mongolian princess and, according to a few, was a Tai Li spy because she briefed all our saboteurs before they went out to the field in the dialect they would have to use in their areas. I think we were all disappointed when she turned out to be a schoolteacher from Peiping who was sending her brother through Harvard!

That night I slept under two Army blankets and a brown Army

mosquito net in a room with seven of the girls and two small Chinese-type underslung puppies, fat and bowlegged and cold, who made a nest in my pile-lined flying jacket.

When the truckload of OSS girls drove into the detachment compound the next morning, through the heavily guarded gates set in mud-brick walls, the flag was just being raised in the center of a quadrangle of low buildings. A company of OSS men stood at attention in heavy winter uniforms, and you could pick out the field soldiers from the nonmilitary Research and Analysis boys by the confident way they handled their rifles, and the clipped military precision of their marching. The saboteur groups were lean and tough, and I noticed among their ranks the supersecret, OSS-trained Chinese paratroops in American uniforms with gold wings on their tunics.

Julia, Louis, and I were to meet again in the offices of the head of OSS in the China theater, Colonel Richard P. Heppner, reportedly one of the smartest strategic services commanders in OSS. Colonel Heppner, former special assistant attorney general in New York State, was a practicing lawyer when he was called to active duty in June of 1941 as a first lieutenant. After being transferred from the 35th Field Artillery to OSS, he was graduated with highest honors from the British intelligence school in Canada. He had directed sabotage efforts for OSS in London and had participated in the North African invasion. He was later loaned by OSS to the William Phillips mission in India as personal assistant to Mr. Phillips. He was commanding officer of OSS in Ceylon before assuming duties in China. Julia, who had known the colonel in SEAC, said he wore a rainbow of ribbons including the Legion of Merit, campaign bars and battle stars for the European, African, Pacific, and Middle East theaters, and the golden wings of the first Chinese parachute regiment. For his work in China, he was later to receive the Distinguished Service Medal.

The colonel, like most of our officers in China, was a young man of about thirty-five years. He was the type Chennault said we needed for coping with the exigencies of one of the toughest theaters of war. In China, imagination, resilience, cool reserve were essential for working with our strange and sometimes reluctant ally, and for fighting in territory which was not far different from American frontier country in the days of Daniel Boone.

Colonel Heppner explained our jobs briefly, and then told me that the MO chief was Mr. Roland Dulin, just in from the Middle Eastern theater of operations.

"We haven't much of an MO production staff here yet—matter of fact we have a chap out now trying to buy a Chinese stone press—Frank Halling. Then there's Dulin and his assistant, Major Faxon, a couple of Chinese boys we hired yesterday, and yourself," the colonel pointed out as I rose to leave. "But we'll have more as soon as we have billets, office space—and food. Every mouth that comes over the Hump has to be fed, and the food doesn't grow in China!"

I found Mr. Dulin alone, leaning against a charcoal stove in a damp room which was furnished with two crude desks, two chairs, and two ornate Washington name plates upon the mahogany surfaces of which were etched the names of Roland Dulin and Major Harold Faxon, A.U.S. The major, whom I had met in Washington, was a genial, old China hand on loan from the A.M.G. Mr. Dulin was a completely new experience. When I reported for work he looked quietly out into space for several seconds, sighed, drew a long breath, and said:

"There's nothing to do, yet, really . . ."

Mr. Dulin might have stepped right out of the fifth dimension. He was a slim, tall, blue-eyed pixy across whose solemn face occasionally flickered a crooked smile of some deep inner satisfaction and joy which he never shared with the outside world. He had a detached way of talking. His words floated down, tinkling, unsteady, bearing fragments of thoughts, never welded together into complete sentences but made the more melodious by a mixture of Irish and southern accents. He was originally, vaguely from Virginia, had played football and baseball at Columbia, worked for magazines and newspapers in Europe.

I could see that my apparent eagerness for work bothered him. Roland Dulin was never one to dash hastily into a project, and his thoughtful planning of MO programs in China eventually proved to be the best example of coordinated field work MO demonstrated during the entire war.

"Before we do anything rash"—he offered me one of the chairs, and perched himself on the desk—"I'll have to brief you on this country. Part of your indoctrination. Now, what don't you know about China, hm-m-m?"

Before I could think of an answer, he hastened to preface his remarks:

"There's no unity—nothing holds together logically in China. The trouble probably is that there are too many Chinese—too damned many. *Autant d'hommes, autant d'avis.* My own theory, of course. None of the Chinese agree for a minute."

And then Mr. Dulin launched into the story of what the Americans found when they started work in the newly formed China theater in October, 1944. I began to understand better, then, the diplomacy which General Wedemeyer needed at the conference tables in Chungking when he assumed command.

Although the Joint Chiefs of Staff directive stated simply that General Wedemeyer's primary mission was to assist the Generalissimo in military operations against the Japanese, the general entered a theater which was spinning in a vortex of distrust, resentment, war weariness, political intrigue, and military near-collapse.

China faced the most critical period in her thirteen years of war. The Japs, advancing on Kweilin and Kweiyang, were threatening Künming and Chungking in an attempt to establish an unbroken line of communications from Tokyo to Singapore. The situation at this time was so desperate that Chungking embassies were advising civilian women, children, and unessential men to leave China when the enemy's advance on Kweichow Province seemed imminent. Against seasoned Jap troops Chiang claimed he could raise some 450 divisions; but his soldiers were badly equipped, underfed, and poorly trained. In many cases, so-called divisions were only paper armies. Chinese officers in the field, in order to draw the full amount of monthly rations to sell on the black market, failed to report a depletion in ranks. One division, which had suffered severely in battle, was still carried in the Chungking records although it had a total complement of ten men. As the war progressed, our basic strategy toward Japan was changing. In 1942 General Stilwell's plan for the opening of a road into China had been accepted by the Joint Chiefs of Staff. However, when we were at last able to truck supplies over the Burma Road, the Pacific War had speeded up. The Jap navy was no longer formidable. The shift of emphasis was to the Pacific and, until the European war was written off, China would continue to be a secondary theater although the situation did not reduce her importance as an intelligence base or a country excellently adapted to guerrilla warfare.

This shift of emphasis had a bad psychological effect upon already strained Sino-American relations. The Chinese accused us of failure to provide adequate matériel for China's military machine, which could not be supported by her own inadequate war production. Actual tonnage in supplies earmarked for Chinese armies in east

China since Pearl Harbor was not sufficient to sustain a single American or British division in combat for a week, the Chinese press pointed out bitterly.

Chiang Kai-shek himself had criticized the "Europe first" attitude of the Allies in a New Year's Day speech, indicating great disappointment that the all-front offensive promised at Cairo had not materialized.

Internally, China was shaky, and the Generalissimo's control over his subordinates wavered with threatened insurrection in southeast China. Among the dissatisfied minorities were the small shopkeepers, manufacturers, petit bourgeois who were irritated by inflation, extreme corruption, and increasing monopoly of all business by the Kuomintang. There were the free-enterprise groups, too, who saw no opportunity to emerge from their present bankruptcy under a set-up where they were offered only managerial jobs with the central government. These two elements were partially strengthened by war lords such as Lung Yün, governor of Yünnan, and Marshal Liu En-hui of Sikang who felt they might be able to make better bargains with the popular front.

To counteract this pressure group which was allegedly planning to coalesce if the Japs threatened Yünnan Province, the Kuomintang was forced to stall for time. Tai Li's secret police was increased with attendant terrorism and regimentation. At that time, it was estimated that not less than 60 per cent of the Chungking military effort was directed at suppressing internal forces that threatened Kuomintang monopoly, and that less than 40 per cent of the military effort was capable of being used against the Japs.

In addition to the pressure from the southeast was the increasing clamor of Communists under Mao Tse-tung who demanded a coalition government, cooperation against a common enemy, and lifting of the Kuomintang blockade of half a million central government troops who were opposing Communist expansion.

Chiang's seeming reluctance to mobilize actively an all-out offensive against the Japs gave rise to much conjecturing. Some Kuomintang critics believed that while Chiang outwardly resisted the Japs, his government was fundamentally sympathetic to the general economic and political objectives of both puppet and Greater East Asia philosophers.

According to many current Chungking rumors the Kuomintang had actually entered into direct negotiations for bargaining purposes with both Japs and puppets. One of the stories most often repeated

over the teacups was that of an intercepted letter from the puppet
governor of Hunan, General Tung Szu-min, to the Generalissimo.
The letter purported to state that it had been agreed that the Japanese
would not attack Chungking and would permit Chiang to concentrate his strength in west China for postwar purposes. To obtain this
concession, Chiang was alleged to have agreed to withhold his military
forces and allow the Japanese and Americans to indulge in an ex-
clusive war. This same agreement was also reportedly made with
Wu K'ai-hsien, member of the CC Clique, who had flown from
Nanking twice in the past year, according to gossips, to arrange to
withhold Chinese help from the Japanese-American war, to col-
laborate with the puppets in a vigorous anti-Communist campaign
and to suppress the growing democratic forces in China after the
war.

"Of course," Mr. Dulin hastened to point out, "this may all be
Communist-inspired MO—but you can see how complicated things
can get in this country."

In addition to all the other worries, the Generalissimo faced the
needling of American public opinion, Mr. Dulin continued. We were
interested in seeing such reforms in China's administration as were
required to make her share in the war effort effective. To meet this
situation, Chiang's government talked loudly of reform, yet actually
gave no real control of government to the Chinese people, as her own
press revealed in reporting the mummery which went on in the name
of democracy at the People's Political Council meetings, packed by
the central government.

To resolve these difficulties, General Wedemeyer advised the
Generalissimo to streamline his armies and speed up war production
on the lines suggested by the Donald Nelson mission. General Wedemeyer next obtained permission to train and equip thirty-six Chinese
divisions, using American liaison teams for the job.

Gathering his American command more closely about him, the
general set up headquarters in Chungking and brought the 10th and
14th air forces, China Air Service Command, OSS, and the Services
of Supply as separate commands directly under his jurisdiction.

"That just means we have an American boss—not Chinese, or
British," Mr. Dulin explained. "And he's the kind of an enlightened
boss who even believes MO will work! Now, if you've never seen
a top-secret order—and there's no reason why you shouldn't if you
button your lip—take a peep at Operational Directive Number 4."

He rummaged in his desk drawer, which contained a mass of uncorrelated papers and noisy Chinese cockroaches, to judge from the scurrying sounds of activity that came from the desk when he disturbed the papers. He held out a paper marked "Secret."

"This is what we can do in China." he said, and read out loud to me:

"OSS will be charged with:

"(1) The organization, supervision and direction of guerrilla activities, support of resistance groups both underground and open.

"(2) Delay and harassment of the enemy, and the denial to him of the use of lines of supply and communications and strategic facilities.

"(3) Collection of secret intelligence, evaluation of same and dissemination.

"(4) Lowering of morale of enemy and puppet troops and enemy civilian personnel wherever found.

"(5) Accumulation, evaluation and analysis of economic, political, topographical, psychological and military information concerning enemy territories.

"(6) Expansion of present OSS communications network in China.

"(7) Training of twenty Chinese commando units.

"Now—let's see," Mr. Dulin mused, after I had reverently inspected the paper. He seemed to be fumbling for time and a way of temporarily disposing of me. Suddenly his face brightened.

"You should get acquainted with Ma and Ting—they're two refugees from the Shanghai literary set we just hired for MO. Go on down, all of you, and have lunch at the Peiping Café. Relax. Absorb atmosphere. Let China come to you. Don't be eager beavers. There'll be plenty to do later on."

Some eight hours later, after establishing a cornerstone of fine friendship with two Chinese artists, and having been introduced to real Chinese cooking, I took my first paregoric tablet from Mary Hutchison, who told me not to worry.

"Everybody gets a touch of dysentery after the first meal in an out-of-bounds restaurant," she explained calmly.

China had come to me, indeed! Right down my alimentary canal with fried wun-tun and frog legs. A sly one, a beguiling MO type, our Mr. Dulin!

CHAPTER ELEVEN

CHINKS IN THE JAP ARMOR

THE map of China, even under Mr. Ma's patient tutelage, was just an amorphous land mass with at least two names for every city, river, or lake of any importance. Because the operational maps we studied were never colored like the ones in my old geography books, all the provinces seemed to run together, identically the same in my mind, although Mr. Ma assured me that they were as different as New York and Florida and the people from Shantung were as different from the people of Kwangtung as a Bostonian was from a Texan. (Mr. Ma, I noted, pronounced it "Goo-ang-doong" while Mr. Ting, to confuse the issue of pronunciation further, said "Kwang-tongue.")

It was a relief to discover that on all OSS maps of China the country had arbitrarily been divided by Colonel Heppner into three parts as if he, too, were in search of simplification.

All the territory north of the Yangtze River including Korea was assigned to the OSS Field Command at Hsian, Shensi Province (not to be confused with Shansi Province).

Operations south of the Yangtze (including Formosa by special permission from Washington) were mounted from Chihchiang, our advance base in Hunan Province (not to be confused with Honan Province).

The third zone was easy to remember because Mr. Dulin said never to mention it upon pain of torture. It was the Communist headquarters in Yenan, where OSS and the Army maintained a joint observer unit working warily with Mao Tse-tung with lukewarm approval from the Generalissimo.

That fat land appendage to the south, French Indo-China, was shared more or less grudgingly by OSS-China and Mountbatten's Force 136 in SEAC; but it was from OSS bases at Pakhoi on the China coast and Szemao on the border that the most effective operations were eventually mounted.

Since Künming and Chungking were two of the few important cities left in central government hands, it was relatively simple to remember that Künming was the base from which most field projects were organized, where Chinese troops were trained, and where most of the ATC freight was unloaded. Chungking was high echelon headquarters where Chiang and Wedemeyer plotted the war over glasses of ice water in the Generalissimo's high-ceilinged living room and where OSS's liaison with the Chinese government was maintained by our carefully selected man with the popular name among Chinese, Colonel Quentin Roosevelt (pronounced Lo Ssu-fu).

Although I finally mastered the map of OSS's China so that it came to me as a badly dissected piece of pie, it was another thing to chart the factional jealousies, political upheavals, wars-within-wars which fomented in China's pockets of resistance, those little islands of chaos between the relatively peaceful Jap-held coastal areas and so-called Free China. Chinese fought Chinese. Japs curried favor with puppets. Korean opportunists used their Japanese, Chinese, or Korean names as befitted the occasion. Itinerant merchants, passing from Jap to Chinese territory after paying the fixed tariff to both sides, knitted all factions together in common trade and exchange of necessary commodities, and only the Americans seemed to disturb this odd *status quo* when they became too inquisitive observers, too energetic saboteurs.

But it was generally conceded, after the first few months of Chungking conferences, that the China war effort was gradually stiffening under the steady, thoughtful pressure exerted by General Wedemeyer. The effect was felt in all his commands including OSS's three main operational units—guerrilla-saboteurs, intelligence collectors, and MO missions.

The work of the guerrilla organizers and saboteurs followed the General Donovan "sting and run" pattern of irregular warfare along the strategic land corridor the Japs held from Nanking to Singapore which, I was informed, was not only their back-door retreat from Southeast Asia but also a line of communications that enabled them to rush troops to pressure points anywhere along that continental railroad line.

The general succinctly summed it up in one of his memoranda to the men at the front:

To me the problem of the OSS guerrilla in China is much like that which Lawrence faced in Arabia. Like the Turk, the Jap has a long railroad line. It is his weakest resistance link. Pressure on that link by disposition of your groups assigned a particular segment will give you at once dispersal along the line of track, and concentration at selected points. By attacking railroad stations, telephone and telegraph lines, destroying culverts, bridges, track, you will impose upon the enemy a passive defense confined to that railway. This will give him flank but no front. Our resources lie in the young men who have mobility, physical hardness, knowledge of the country, in American leaders with experience in irregular warfare and in special weapons unknown to the enemy.

Each sabotage team that went into the field became an isolated American unit somewhere on the map of China, designated by a red pin in the war room, and an animal code name—Elephant, Spaniel, Goat, Mink. Somehow, during the course of the months, they seemed to assume the qualities of their code designations. Elephant trumpeted through the corridor near Kiyang and did away with 633 Japs at the end of its first thirty days. Jackal, lurking beneath the huge arches of the Yellow River bridge, employed river coolies to dynamite two spans of this largest bridge in China and wreck a Jap troop train that was crossing at the time. Dormouse spent the first month of its time behind the lines hiding from Jap patrols, later emerged with one of the best combat records on the books.

Guerrilla life in China was vastly different from the more civilized existence some of our men enjoyed with the French Maquis in the European theater, and before they went into the field, any illusions they might have held about the exotic East were dispelled in a pamphlet printed on our MO multilith press which explained:

Your team will be alone in hiding, surrounded by millions of Chinese. Since you deal with them constantly, you must be correct. Patience and tact will be your most important assets in meeting your interpreter, your guerrillas, your coolies, your village magistrate and the local governor and generals. Chinese like long negotiations. You can't hurry them. Above all, don't lose your temper or you'll lose face.

Water must be boiled and chlorinated before drinking, or brushing your teeth in it. Halazone tablets will not kill amoebic cysts. Eat no raw vegetables unless they have been chemically treated. Only bananas, tangerines and oranges are O.K. In the field use louse powder when you sleep in Chinese beds.

The Japs have all the advantage of infiltration of agents. Be careful in front of servants and when using the phone. Burn any classified scraps of paper.

The sabotage teams left the cloak-and-dagger glamour world behind once they stood up, hooked up and parachuted out of their plane toward the green rice paddies and the low dirt hills of occupied China.

Even some of their jumps ended in ignominy. One medic dropped into a well on his way to perform an appendectomy. Another lad landed astride a Chinese pony. Members of Team Spaniel reconnoitered after a jump near Peiping to find themselves surrounded by hostile Communists who promptly jailed the lot on the ground that they had not been cleared through Yenan. Only a stern note from General Wedemeyer to Mao Tse-tung, threatening to use armed force, had any effect.

Most teams reported a baffling inertia on the part of the Chinese. They were often supplied with the worst guerrilla material possible, described by Team Lion as "conscripts from Tobacco Road." (However, once these ragged guerrilla bands were trained, fed, and equipped with American supplies, the enlisted men proved willing, if perhaps inept, fighters.)

Even the "help" situation in China was critical, and our boys frequently "ambushed" coolies to help transport supplies. The Chinese coolie was tracked to his lair—usually a pitiful mud hut in the midst of his small paddy—surrounded and lured out with promises of great wealth and eventual recognition from the grateful people of America. (Often the lads from OSS were the first American emissaries these coolies had ever seen.)

A typical message from the field from Team Leopard reported that the boys had managed to crater a road at a defile over strong opposition from their Chinese allies and had then been forced to flee to avoid Communist reprisals!

Team Goat wired in that they had rescued an American flyer from "unidentified Chinese elements—possibly real bandits" who had planned to turn him over to the Japs as a part of the spoils of war. Top rewards were offered by Japs for American pilots; lowest prices were paid for "official observers."

Even after our men had trained them, the Chinese in the field seemed to have no real grasp of the basic principles of organized guerrilla operations. They were particularly oblivious to security and often exposed the presence of OSS teams by detonating explosives for the sheer pleasure of hearing them go *Boom!*

One exasperated team captain complained that his Chinese brothers-in-arms did not have the slightest concept of ambush discipline.

"Just when a Jap column came marching around the bend and silence was something you'd think any human being hiding in a ditch directly below them would crave, a Chinese guerrilla lights a cigarette, or coughs, or starts to talk in an ordinary voice to the man next to him, or even shoots his rifle in the air by mistake!"

I always had the feeling that our boys behind the lines were so frustrated by their allies that they took out their spite, whenever possible, on the one target they knew was legitimate—the Jap. At the end of the war they had killed off 12,348 of them, had inflicted 912 casualties, destroyed one hundred Jap vessels, vast quantities of ordnance, rolling stock, pack animals.

"But we did it," one fine specimen of frustrated American manhood once told me when he returned to Künming, "over the dead bodies of our allies."

(Chinese casualties, evidently, were not reported.)

Our intelligence teams found their tasks a little easier. It was one thing to walk into the interior of China and blow up bridges and roads used by both Jap and Chinese in going about their daily tasks. It was another thing to sit quietly over a steaming glass of *lung ching cha* and discuss the movements of the Japs and their plans, particularly when the Chinese informer had been prodded liberally with what OSS operators referred to as "operational supplies."

As the booklet said: "Lack of patriotism on the part of many Chinese may discourage you. Remember that their social system has been built on a strict loyalty to family rather than state."

One of the theater's most important intelligence operations, in preparation for a possible Navy amphibious landing in south China, was accomplished by OSS Team Akron which parachuted into the Kwangtung Peninsula in late February, 1945, under Major Charles M. Parkin, with top-secret instructions to make a reconnaissance of the entire coast between the Liuchow Peninsula and Hongkong.

They divided the 250-mile area into four sections, and by mid-March they had mapped most of the territory in much the methodical manner of a group of engineers surveying a building site.

Guided by guerrillas who stood by with schoolboy curiosity, Akron collected sketches of beaches, airfields, and harbors and took over seven hundred photographs. The guerrillas took them down the Nagemoon River within a mile of an enemy-held leper asylum where they photographed Jap sentries walking within carbine range on the far side of the bank. They later drew Jap fire when they crossed the river and were whisked promptly out of danger by chary guerrillas, all too anxious to keep both Jap and *Mei Kuo ping* happy.

When the mission was accomplished the group kept rendezvous with a PBY flying boat off Huiling San Island in a thirty-five-foot open junk. Ironically, they were almost killed through the pilot's miscalculation when he cut his starboard motor a fraction too soon, approaching the junk head on. The boys in the open boat were directly under the still-moving propeller blades. Only a chance concave swell in the ocean gave them a two-foot clearance.

By the end of the war, OSS's initial contribution of 10 per cent of theater intelligence had increased to 67 per cent, including a direct line into Japan through Korea. Agent radio sets, smuggled through Jap lines in rice baskets, hulls of junks, under loads of night soil, tapped out daily intelligence from all important zones held by the Japanese.

"The only difficulty we have," wrote one of our intelligence operators, "is to keep the Slopies from selling the tubes!"

The China theater planners wanted a variety of information from their "eyes." Sometimes they got it, sometimes we slipped up on intelligence that might have been of great consequence in Allied strategy.

We faithfully charted Jap order of battle in all zones we covered in occupied China. But what a different trend the Yalta Conference might have taken if our intelligence could have reported that the much vaunted Kwantung Army on the Manchurian border was padded with raw recruits from Japan—shoe clerks, students, taxi drivers—and that seasoned troops had long since been withdrawn to Okinawa and the Philippines! In spite of Colonel Heppner's constant requests to send OSS teams to Manchuria, our government stalled, afraid of "political repercussions," since most approaches to the north led through Communist territory. At Yalta, we exchanged the Kuriles for Russia's entry into the war when we believed she faced the flower of the Jap Imperial Army across the Manchurian border!

But the Navy and air forces in the Pacific received full benefit of OSS weather reports relayed from eastern China and Korea, which could be depended upon to indicate conditions in Japan a few days later.

Chinese coast watchers, supplied with silhouettes of all important Japanese vessels and corresponding code numbers, were finally able to flash word to OSS that they had spotted a Nip battleship of the Kongo class off Formosa—and not just a "large junk with guns."

In this country of divided loyalties MO was the American weapon most easily comprehended by the Chinese. Naturally they never became fond of the Jap conquerors, and feared organized opposition. Consequently anything ridiculing the "dwarf men" appealed to the Celestial sense of humor. Children were delighted to learn MO adaptations of familiar nursery rhymes, such as the ditty about "the old black crow, Mr. Jap" who was shot dead by a farmer for stealing rice. Mind-over-matter MO campaigns were far more popular among our civilian agents than the louder explosions caused by our saboteurs, which only meant that some day, after Jap and American had gone, Chinese would have to rebuild patiently what had just been blown up.

MO developed slowly at first. Mr. Dulin insisted on a careful selection of targets and concomitant development of distribution channels. Künming, the frontier town where I was stationed for most of the war, was the center of long-range MO editorial production. Our field missions, dropped in roughly the same areas as guerrilla and intelligence teams, waged "spot" psychological warfare using crude presses of the country, or sometimes the three-pound aluminum offset agent presses developed by Washington for MO. At one time it was planned to use a mobile trailer-press which loving 101 hands had driven over the Burma Road into China. But when the huge truck and trailer unit trundled northward to Hsian along the winding Chinese roads, the project was abandoned at the first walled town the convoy reached. The truck could not clear the ancient Chinese gate with its guardian dragons carved in the low overhang, especially designed to prevent such things as mechanized presses from reaching the interior of China.

Our first MO production office was a large tent pitched next to a crude mud-brick print shop abutting the OSS compound wall. The nuclear China staff included Ma Kuo-liang, a young liberal magazine editor from Shanghai; his partner, Shao Ting, an enthusiastically explosive cartoonist with froglike face and a prickly sense of caricature, and myself. We were soon joined by Sergeant William Arthur Smith, an artist and gourmet from New York whose stomach was as sensitive to the flies which hovered over his food in the GI mess as his soul was in harmony with the rich colors in the Chinese landscape. Attached to our little band like some fluffy, feathered milkweed seed was Colonel Heppner's golden cocker spaniel puppy, Sammy, who seemed to prefer the informality of the MO tent to the discipline of the colonel's offices. Sammy was also nearer, we learned, to the war dogs, several tents beyond us, whom he worshiped.

Through Ting and Ma we were able to peek through the moon

gates and over the tall walls that hid the real Künming behind the brash front it put on for the American Army. We dined on teak-carved balconies and sampled the famous *maotai* wine of the district, which tasted like liquid Roquefort. We spent one night on the stone floor of a Taoist monastery, encased in sleeping bags, high above Künming Lake in a cloudy Camelot of temples carved in the rocks of West Mountain. We crawled through underground passages in a towering wooden statue of Buddha to a smoke-filled room where priests once hid from Yünnan bandits. We took moonlight rides in creaking sampans on the lake while Ma sang Chinese folk songs in a curious falsetto and Ting played the butterfly harp, which he said should be heard only in the moonlight where all color was one color, and the pure distilled harp notes were all sounds merged into four.

Künming, in the eyes of the Army, was a wide-open boom town at the end of the Burma Road and the pipe line from India. Day and night, convoys caked red with Burma dust rumbled through the streets. And at the last bend of the road leading into town trucks and jeeps and armament, the precision instruments which careful American hands had prepared for war, were passed to the Chinese army, who received them greedily and then treated them with the characteristic Oriental disdain for things mechanical which they could not under-stand. This backwoods part of China was not yet ready for the Ma-chine Age, a fact proved every day in the streets of Künming when Chinese walked blindly out in front of our jeeps, looking up with surprise or anger as we stopped with a screech of brakes. As Bill pointed out, traffic sense is an acquired Western reflex. The Chinese were never taught to look up and down the street before crossing.

Shops that lined the back lanes of town had little to offer but tawdry black-market parachute-silk pillowcases and scarfs with crudely embroidered phrases such as "God Bless President Roose-velt," or "Mother," or "Künming, China."

Künming was not a dress town, and the American GI was at his sloppiest in fatigues, mosquito boots, and jackets with the usual Chinese-American rescue flags sewn inside the flap. Below the flags was a message in Chinese characters, to whom it might concern, that the wearer of the jacket was an American aviator, forced down over enemy territory, who must be returned to where he came from in great haste. The soldiers usually queued up at the Red Cross hostel—an entire building that had been converted into something resembling the carefully tended cheerfulness of a Y.W.C.A., complete with a piano for song fests, a writing room, and a cafeteria that specialized

in baked beans every Friday. Most of the boys who came to Künming went immediately to the hostel because everyone said it was
just like stateside.

Künming's winding alleys followed no set pattern. They twisted
through lanes lined with acrid-smelling opium parlors where smokers
sprawled on wooden tiered beds, through Thieves' Row where all the
things stolen from Americans were resold, through walled-off por-
tions where the wealthy lived apart from the noise and odors in their
tiled homes and gardens of plum trees and jasmine.

The hub of town was the Flower Circle, where venders sold car-
nations, shaggy asters, chrysanthemums, and tuberoses. From it we
often climbed to the top of the near-by West Gate, to look out on an
ocean of rolling, pitching rooftops with a toy dragon, perhaps, or a
household god perched precariously at the crest of an unmoving
tile wave.

Beyond the city was blue Künming Lake, where pagodas reared up
above the weeping willows and dumpling children in quilted red
robes and caps fashioned like ferocious tiger faces played a Chinese
version of hopscotch.

Outside the city, too, far beyond the fetid flats where the garbage
men dumped their reeking "honey pots," there were expanses where
the steady marching lines of symmetrical rice paddies seemed to stop
reverently for the bald hills, humped with mounds where the Chinese
dead were buried and where no crops would ever be planted.

The four of us and Sammy often walked along the grave mounds
after work, through the brown grass and crumbling monuments.
From the top of the ancient cemetery we could see the Burma Road,
and sometimes the thundering convoys, and thin strings of people
coming to the city.

"Why," I once asked Mr. Ting, "can't Japs send hundreds of spies
into Künming over the road? The Japs look just like the Lolo beg-
gars we see all over town. Who would know?"

Mr. Ting replied at once: "You may not know the difference, but
the Lolo does!"

Mr. Ma, the philosopher of the two, could always checkmate his
friend. "True, Mr. Ting, the Lolo may know—but he's in such a de-
pressed state in Yünnan today it's altogether possible that he doesn't
care!"

Our first few weeks in the MO office were spent under Mr. Ma's
wing, learning that everything Washington had taught us about

"emotional appeals" and "patriotic stimuli" would have virtually no effect on the Chinese.

"You tell a ferry operator in Kowloon to sabotage his boat for the glory of China, and he'll laugh at you. After all, it's his whole livelihood in a land where livelihood comes hard," Mr. Ma instructed us. "But offer him a certain amount of money to pour salt water into the machinery, and he may listen."

We learned that not all of the people in occupied China were fond of Generalissimo Chiang Kai-shek and appeals from the Kuomintang were sometimes like "whispers in the willow trees."

One of our best approaches was through the marvelous Chinese sense of humor, geared to our custard-pie-throwing level of levity. They would take sabotage suggestions much more readily if we hinted it would be a great joke to throw a lighted cigarette into a Jap fuel dump.

Americans were generally regarded as immensely wealthy tourists, easily hoodwinked. The ordinary merchant wasn't particularly interested in the democracy which the Americans were killing themselves over, but he brightened visibly at the suggestion that our liberating armies would bring a lot of ready cash with them.

It brought everything down to the practical level, including our purchase of a stone press for what Ma said was three times its value. With the press came odd attachments such as three coolies and a type cutter—a thoroughly recalcitrant, shrewd little man who made up for any deficiencies in the font by carving characters on the spot, in either wood or metal. Our type cutter was a portal-to-portal man on a six-day week, but he eventually built up our stock to a point where we were able to print a two-page guerrilla newspaper. In his spare moments he carved exquisite MO wood blocks which printed sometimes in as many as four colors.

Early in the year our foursome did little but generate plans and electric impulses. It was weeks before we found our first conduit—frail, wispy Henry Lacy, one of our Delhi-trained missionaries, who walked into the tent one day, cocked his feet jauntily on Bill's desk in a position I was certain he had never learned at the mission, and announced that he was going home to his father's old parish, to do MO work.

"I've got a lot of friends there," he told us. "Be good to see them again."

When Ting asked where Henry's old friends lived, the answer came back in a well couched security whisper:

"Meihsien."

Both Ting and Ma whistled.

"You will be close to the Japanese—quite close." Mr. Ma reminded him.

Henry nodded. "I've got a place all picked out in the basement of a convent. It'll be a big surprise to the sisters, though."

He talked with us for quite a time, about getting material and setting up shop. He listened to what Ting and Ma could tell him of the Canton area, which they had fled only a few months before to join guerrilla bands outside the city. They talked as if Henry Lacy were catching the five-thirty commuters' special to Long Island, instead of parachuting into the center of one of the most highly fortified bastions of Japan's line of coastal defenses.

"And don't forget to forward my mail—my wife's expecting a baby," he reminded us, again as if it were a simple thing to drop him a note, instead of an operation that called for a convoy to Chih-chiang, a special plane to Lacy's drop area, and innumerable radio checks.

Several weeks later Henry made his first contact with Künming under the code name Turtle. His message, like Henry, was a masterpiece of understatement. He had obtained the use of a small press and had set it up in the convent basement. He was presently dispatching an agent, a Mac Wong, to pick up more MO material in Künming. His father's parishioners had welcomed him with celebrations and several official functions. They had expressed a willingness to carry MO into Hongkong, Kowloon, and Canton. They would also contact friends in Haifong, Lukfong, Kityang, Chaon, and Swatow— names that sent me reeling off to the atlas to learn that they formed a two-hundred-mile circuit and covered practically all the Kwang-tung coast! Henry was still waiting, impatiently, for his mail.

From then on we concentrated on producing material for Henry's agent, whom I imagined to be an elderly gentleman with the acumen of Charlie Chan and the guile of a Sax Rohmer character. He had been, perhaps, an early convert and was devoted to the Lacy family. I was hardly prepared when Mac Wong actually walked into our office, but after making his acquaintance I realized that the popular concept of an espionage agent definitely dates the American public as of the early 1900's.

If OSS regulations hadn't forced Mac into khaki, he would have been wearing a zoot suit and straw hat. A Chinese version of a dead-end kid, he was short, sharp-faced, and looked as if he had just made some fast money on the horses. He was the kind of lad who would whistle at girls from the corner drugstore, in America. In China he probably tripped old ladies as they stumped along on bound feet.

"I'm from Lacy," he said, cigarette dangling with studied arrogance from the side of his mouth. His English was perfect.

I could see that my girlish gush about meeting a real agent didn't set well with Mac Wong. He came to the point immediately:

"Dulin told me to see you. Says you have a list of everything you want out of Hongkong, Canton, Macao—stuff like posters, newspapers, and Jap orders you can fake back here. I'm to take whatever material you have ready."

I turned over our requests to him, and he took the paper casually as if it were a list of groceries he was to pick up at the corner store.

I began to apologize for the length, but he shrugged.

"Don't worry, sister. I have my contacts. I'll get your stuff—telephone books, military orders, hotel menus, ration books, puppet addresses, censor stamps, postage stamps." He read the list off, then snidely asked: "You haven't forgotten anything?"

"Sure—a pair of silk stockings." As soon as I said it, I was sorry I'd shown my irritation.

Just then Bill came to my rescue with a small packet of the material we had produced: a few posters showing a gaunt pair of hands holding out an empty rice bowl, with space left for the agent to write his own message; an engraved wooden seal to be used on all material issued by an Anti-War League, a cover organization we planned to use in Henry's area; and the first copy of our single-page Cantonese guerrilla newspaper, *Jih Pao*, in which we announced our program— anti-Jap, pro-Chinese in line with Sun Yat-sen's principles. We hoped to add further authenticity to the second issue with bona fide "live" material sent by Mac—names of night clubs frequented by Japs, hotel menus to show what the wealthy puppets were eating, addresses of Jap civilian authorities.

Bill had a little better luck in talking with our agent. He learned that Mac had been graduated from St. John's in Shanghai; that he had started out to make a million dollars but the war came along, and he had then joined the refugee bands to Free China and American gold.

"After all, I am an American, so why not cash in?" he said evenly, as if his citizenship were a sudden, war-born convenience. "I was born in Hawaii. My father worked on a plantation. That wasn't for me. I'm going to make my fortune in China, but it will take more than this lousy hundred dollars a month gold I make with you."

He stood defiant, and for a sentimental second I imagined he was just a young, lonesome kid. On an impulse, I pulled out a clipping from my desk I had received from home about some of the Hawaii boys who had been killed in the Pacific and Italy, a polyglot mixture of Hawaiian, Chinese, Japanese, American names. It described memorial services at Kawaiahao Church, when the whole town turned out to honor them.

I handed Mac the clipping and asked if he remembered any of the boys. His crafty eyes seemed even more alert as he read the story rapidly through, twice.

"They were older," he said.

He put the clipping down, picked up the MO material, and for a minute I thought he might soften. After all, he was doing something as important as those lads. Maybe he wouldn't come back either. Maybe the names really meant something to him; but he wouldn't admit it. Maybe it would help for him to know the people back home cared about Americans, wherever they died, no matter the color, the creed. I'll never really know about Mac because all he said was:

"So long. I'll be in Canton next week."

I saw him again the next morning when he was climbing into the back of an OSS truck bound for the airport. He was wearing a long blue student uniform and he carried the MO packet under his arm.

Through intelligence reports we followed his trail to Canton where he purchased information that a Japanese "hospital ship" was leaving Hongkong at a given date carrying troops—no casualties—aboard.

He entrained with false credentials for Hongkong where he purchased several types of ration books and a Japanese naval code book. In Victoria City an irate storekeeper caught him filing the chain which held the telephone directory to the counter and told him testily to obtain his own book through the telephone company—which he did.

As a final arrogant gesture before leaving the island Mac pasted one of our empty-rice-bowl posters on a Domei bulletin board, chalking in large characters at the top, "Greater East Asia Co-Prosperity Sphere!" It was several days before someone pointed out the "mistake" to Japanese Thought Police.

In Kowloon Mac picked up the remaining items on our list, after distributing our guerrilla papers on the ferry trip across. The material arrived by courier-coolie, packed in tea leaves which kept it dry on the humid trip north from occupied China. Also intact was a pair of silk stockings, the first I had seen in three years. Unfortunately they were designed for dainty Chinese feet! Size tens had not been included in the Japanese program for economic expansion in Greater East Asia.

Like some sly, quiet octopus, MO was reaching its tentacles across China; and by May the secret map which Mr. Dulin kept in his field safe was a maze of contiguous circles which the chief referred to solemnly as his "Spheres of Influence."

MO teams from the States and from other theaters remained in Künming only long enough for supplies and briefings, and I came to know them better by their reptile code names when they started to send in reports, first from the southern command, later from Hsian.

Mission Gila's team leader, Captain Bob North, fought off a band of armed bandits who stole his trousers, worked his way to an area near Shanghai, and finally reported that an underground MO news sheet, *Dawning*, was being distributed in the streets of Shanghai.

From Hengyang, north of Lacy, Lieutenant Stanley Sheehan's Team Bushmaster brought about the surrender of puppet and Korean troops by a series of persuasive letters from Korean deserters to their friends in the Japanese army.

Lieutenant James Carr and Team Crocodile started a campaign in Amoy to disrupt puppet currency by writing anti-Jap slogans across the money. On two occasions the Japs declared martial law in the city in an effort to track down the Crocodile.

Lieutenant Roy Squires' Team Diamond set up printing facilities in the plant of a Jap-controlled Foochow newspaper and poured MO vitriol steadily into the area, fomenting a large ricksha strike that impeded Jap movement within the city just before it fell to the Chinese.

Our Künming staff was augmented by the arrival of Marj Severyns from Delhi, and Burton Crane, *New York Times* correspondent, who set up an intelligence office for us, and by Lieutenant Roger Starr, just out of the Burma jungles where he had been doing front-line MO with Detachment 101. He was followed shortly by the entire detachment, a tough, bronzed, shirtless crew of gypsies who marched up the Road at the close of the Burma campaigns, singing and swaggering with their wide Gurkha hats pushed back on their heads. They almost disrupted the China morale until our cunning secretariat issued an order banning their symbol of superiority, the Gurkha hat. Eventually 101 lost its swagger and its tan and merged with the rest of the unit.

Meanwhile, Bill, Ting, Ma, and I continued to channel most of our thinking toward Turtle Mission and activities in the south of China. At the time it was just a convenient, functioning circuit. Mac Wong supplied us with intelligence; we "packaged" it and shipped it to Lacy, and the Voice of the Turtle was heard as far south as Hongkong in hotels, Japanese military clubs, stores, theaters, barber shops, and on public wall boards.

If I had been at all discerning as an intelligence agent I should have known that something was actually about to happen in the Canton area. Right under my unsuspecting nose was an imperceptible focusing of plans toward the south.

My roommate, Mary Hutchison, spent months on a top-secret economic study of the Canton area. It was "for some 14th Air Force colonel who wants it as of yesterday," she complained, poring over maps, intercepts, and reports which told her of the basic economy of the place, how it might sustain an invading army, the port facilities, communications system, morale of the people.

In the order-of-battle section I once found Marj Kennedy puzzling over the strength of Jap troops in French Indo-China, where a large holding area had been reported by our intelligence. How quickly could these reserves be rushed to Canton? What was their strength? their disposition?

Our guerrilla activities to the south seemed to increase with every report. Teams Ermine, Goat, and Bear had augmented our other sabotage groups near Hengyang, harassing Japanese lines of communication, blowing supply dumps, wrecking rolling stock. A concentrated drive seemed to be on to cut all important rail lines to Canton, particularly the spur from Hanoi into China.

Intelligence teams reported increased agent activity in the Fort Bayard region on the Shantung Peninsula and by June six agent nets covered the Canton area, far the heaviest dispersal of personnel in all of China.

Once, when I was returning Sammy to Colonel Heppner's office after his day in the tent, the colonel asked what area I was working on.

"Canton—we're trying to get the Chinese to hate the Japs, love the Americans, and sabotage the city."

The colonel nodded. "Canton is a good area—a very good area. But tell them to go easy on the port facilities. We might want to use them some day."

A bell should have rung, a light flashed, but the only solace I found for my own stupidity in later months was that nobody else suspected the Plan even though it involved close to half a million Chinese and Americans. Instead I rushed blithely back to the tent and told everyone that Colonel Heppner thought Canton was a good area!

We developed a fairly comprehensive campaign for Japs, civilian Chinese, and puppet troops in the Lacy orbit, which began to bear fruit when Turtle reported back that the Japs had offered three catties of rice to any person bringing in an MO leaflet or copies of *Jih Pao*, the guerrilla paper which Mr. Ma had spiced up with a salacious serial that seemed to have all Canton panting for the next issue.

Against the civilians we built up the fictitious Anti-War League, founded on the platform that the Japs were losing the war, the Chinese under their control were backing the wrong horse, and war was economically unprofitable for the average Chinese.

For our conquest of the Philippines, home of many of the overseas Cantonese, the League produced a memorial leaflet to a popular Cantonese consular official in Manila who had been tortured and shot by the Japs early in the war. The tribute was written by the man's widow who described how her husband had been bayoneted on his way to the torture chambers in the walled city.

"Beware of these pretenders who preach Sino-Japanese brotherhood. They build for a greater Japan, not for a Greater East Asia," the leaflet warned.

Jih Pao printed an intercepted radio speech by President Sergio Osmeña, himself part-Cantonese, in which he allegedly described the wholesale slaughter of Chinese nationals in Manila by Japs who "pretended to be brothers to the Chinese in Canton, and several hundred miles away repudiated their own words by such actions!" As a practical touch which Mr. Ma said meant even more to the Chinese, Osmeña told how the Jap conquerors forcibly extorted money from the Manila Chinese to carry on the war, repaying them in worthless bonds.

The Anti-War League also supported a simple sabotage movement initiated by a comic cartoon booklet entitled, "Mr. Wong's Secret War with Japan."

"Make simple sabotage your hobby," Mr. Wong slyly instructed in a series of drawings. "I've been doing it for months now and the Japs can't prove a thing. I make everything look like an accident. When there's a chance, I slit Jap rice bags on the docks, along the seams, so it looks as if the containers were faulty. At the office I once inserted a copper coin into the light socket and when my Jap boss turned on the switch, he blew the circuit. You can do it, too. Be late to work, and blame the civil government for bad transportation. Take up your boss's time with unnecessary questions, but always be polite. Urinate sometime in the gas tank of a Jap vehicle and see what happens!"

Over ten thousand Mr. Wongs rolled off our press for Lacy. In two enemy-controlled newspapers in Swatow, stories appeared denouncing the League as an existing organization "which must be stamped· out." The Japs instituted searches of all publishing houses and printing supply stores in an attempt to match the paper stock and ink and even went to the trouble of planting "counter agents" in stores to watch for our agents. One of Lacy's best operators, a pretty Chinese girl who ran a lending library in Hongkong, complained bitterly to the Jap officers who patronized her shop that "subversive agents were using her books to disseminate their propaganda." To prove it, she showed them some of the League leaflets she had found in one of her volumes.

For the Jap soldiers stationed in the area we tried other methods of heckling. We issued protesting leaflets from Chinese puppets asking the Japs in Canton why their brothers in Shanghai were sponsoring a peace move, with the Emperor's brother, Prince Chichibu, as their figurehead. Chichibu, long a proponent of peace, had been held by militarists as a virtual prisoner in Shanghai, we learned through intelligence reports. We now set him up as the Prince of Peace, who desired "peace for Asia through negotiation, not bloodshed."

We produced a booklet, ascribed to the "XXth Century Press" in Shanghai (a Nazi publishing concern run by an agent named Klaus Mehnert), in tribute to the passing power of Germany. The brochure was illustrated with photographs of bombed German cities, dead civilians, blasted factories, and the captions were·in German, Chinese, and Japanese. The editor exhorted the people of Asia to make a final, last-ditch stand, as Germany was doing, against a ruthless aggressor who surpassed the Axis in arms, but not spirit!

At one period I became known around the tent as a combination Dorothy Dix and Mr. Hyde because of a series of "bomb loneliness" pamphlets I wrote for the Jap soldiers describing the psychological reaction Japanese women had to bombings. Ghosting for a well known Tokyo physician with approval from the Medical Department of the Japanese Army, my treatises explained: "The girl you left behind you may never bear children again because of the shock to her nervous system, and she may also suffer from bombing neurosis which often expresses itself in maniacal desires to murder those dearest to her." Knowledge was better than ignorance in cases like these, I pointed out, and it was well for returning soldiers to be on their guard in order to cope with the little woman who might take to sleeping with a hara-kiri knife under her wooden pillow.

We also tried to upset the little Jap soldier away from home and *okasan* by forging Chinese newspaper clippings in which we announced a new Japanese "production" program (based on Nazi techniques) of encouraging Japanese women to produce as many children as possible for Dai Nippon, with or without benefit of marriage.

One of our most intensive puppet soldier campaigns developed during a chance conversation with Ting after we had read about the fanatic Jap suicide squads in the Okinawa battles.

"Would the Chinese soldiers ever go in for this Kamikaze nonsense?" I asked the little cartoonist, just as a matter of academic interest at first. But Ting's reply gave birth to our Kamikaze Campaign, which was eventually implemented by our teams all over China:

"The Chinese think the Japs are crazy! Why die before your time?"

It started with headlines in our guerrilla paper: "Japanese Organize Chinese Suicide Squads to Fight Foreign Devils!"

On the walls of occupied cities recruiting posters began to appear— a Jap and a puppet soldier walking arm in arm, chins up, eyes straight ahead, toward a Kamikaze Induction Center.

Leaflets announced the establishment of training centers for Chinese Suicide Squadrons called the Purple Dragons, in lonely districts too far from our target area to allow a verification of the story. Training details were announced, instructing soldiers in methods of detonating bombs hidden under their clothes. Bill drew up a dramatic poster of a Chinese soldier swimming under the hull of an American ship, entitled "You, Too, Can Become a Human Limpet!"

Official-looking lists of compensations to be paid families of Chinese Kamikaze heroes were issued by the Japanese government.

The Japs' own glowing propaganda about the exploits of their Wild Eagles who crashed into American carriers played nicely into our hands, until the Chinese around Swatow were muttering that the Japs kept their eagles under the influence of sake and dope and the Anti-War League developed a series of wall stencils which said: "The Chinese shall live to build a greater China over the bones of dead Japs."

With the launching of the Kamikaze Campaign the Japs in Hong-